THE LAST CHANCE

WALTER ROWLAND

CONTENTS

CHAPTER 1 NEW HOUSE

Change! Everyone has at least one life moment that completely alters their course. It alters the course. It alters the tempo. It alters the direction. It modifies lives.

One's fate, purpose, and lifetime value are all determined in that one instant. One has been living their worth for others, but the moment of transformation forces them to live it for themselves. That is how one small event may alter the course of your entire life. The world around you is replaced with a straightforward choice. occasionally, humans too. An instant of clarity can completely alter the situation.

Currently, Dev is going through that transformation in his life. His entire environment will change as a result of this choice. He is not aware of that one. Despite the fact that someone else forced him to take this stand. He still will remember this day as the most significant day of his life since it was meant to be. However, it won't be remembered for the same purpose it was meant to be; instead, it will be remembered for something else. The day Dev anticipated making his life-changing decision for the rest of his days. But he didn't anticipate things to play out this way. He had just been married. His girlfriend and he were about to be married. the person he had been dating for the last six years.

They were finally here to tie the wedding that was intended to last after much drama and convincing their family for this union. However, something altered before doing so, specifically the bride, even before stepping up upon the podium.

Dev marries Mahi rather than getting married to his longtime girlfriend. Since Mahi's parents relocated to the same city or when they were children, Dev and Mahi have known one another. Since their days in school, Savitri, the mother of Dev, and Shree, the mother of Mahi, have been close friends. In fact, they were more like family than friends after they moved. When Dev first encountered Mahi at his home when she was nine years old, he was fourteen.

Mahi has never been anything more to Dev than Shree Aunty's or his mother's goddaughter. So it was for Mahi Dev. He is now her husband.

Mahi's choice to wed Dev at this time was solely a matter of chance. a chance to give her Saavi Maa and her family a small token of appreciation in return. Simply put, Saavi Maa wasn't her godmother. But a lady who, a long time ago, was in charge of saving her life. She had no problem sacrificing herself for Saavi Maa's family. When they most need it, Mahi has the chance to free herself from the burden of the same respect Saavi Maa demonstrated at her time of need. As a result, she found it rather simple to decide to wed a man she is not in love with. Saavi Maa and her father, however, found it challenging to accept this choice. And they both fiercely opposed it. Mahi nevertheless made it through it despite her father's opposition. While Mahi's decision was difficult for her mother to comprehend, it was not impossible. Yet she could sort of live with this. Even before they were born, she had always wanted Dev and Mahi to be together. Getting her beloved daughter married to the son of her best friend was like realising a lifelong dream for her. Friends become actual family as a result. Naturally, how it actually happened was never what she had in mind. Still, it did.

In all of this, Dev remained silent. For hours, he felt numb. It didn't really matter at this point whether Mahi agreed to the wedding or not; what mattered more was how this fateful day would finish. It finally happened, however it was the start of a new chapter in his life with Mahi.

As they arrive at Dev's Pune home, he says, "I have already asked them to get one of the rooms ready for you."

Mahi nods and says, "Ok!" while glancing around. She has never been to Dev's Pune residence before. She is familiar with the history of the home because Dev built it himself when he first began collaborating with his father on their hotel network venture.

Since her recent assignment as a DO (Development Officer), Mahi has resided in Pune. But she had never been to this area of the city before, let alone to Dev's home. It is a sizable home with two entry gates on either side of the front grounds, a sizable front lawn, and a porch. The large doors that provide entry into the house are where the car stops on the front porch. The young pair rushes to welcome the owner and the newlywed as they enter the living area.

Dev replies, "This is Karim and Salma, who looks after the house, er, property." The word "house" makes him flinch, which Mahi is forced to observe.

Anything you want, just tell them, he continues. They will escort you to your room as well.

He exits the living area and makes his way to the right staircase leading to his room. Mahi is now awkwardly positioned in front of his housekeeper. She is warmly greeted by the couple. They bring her up the same stairs Dev did only a moment before to get to the room. However, her room is adjacent to Dev's and farthest from the house on the right.

As she walks into a large area with windows on both sides. which has a side that leads out to a balcony. She found herself facing the front gates and lawns when she slid open the balcony door.

She stood there contemplating the fact that she wouldn't mind living there for the ensuing two years. Dev stated two years when they were travelling to this location.

Dev remarked, averting Mahi's eyes, "I think two years would be enough, keeping this marriage for the sake of our families and others." He felt anxious at the notion of disappointing them for some reason, and he quickly adjusted himself in the backseat of the automobile.

Mahi responded, "I am good with two years," acknowledging the predicament and the circumstances surrounding their marriage. Dev stated this without looking at her, and she attempted to understand his unease as he spoke. Mahi would have taken objection if it had happened somewhere else and someone else had dared to act similarly. She also would have taught a valuable lesson. However, it wasn't someone or a typical circumstance. She thus attempted to ignore it and grab hold of this.

Dev found himself responding, "Since we are already married for the world, we'll have to live under one roof even when we are not in the same city," after being taken aback by her polite reaction.

Living together doesn't necessarily imply that we are husband and wife. Mahi agreed with Dev, "but it does mean we are for others. This was a tip with a warning for Dev. They are not allowed to go too far with one another. When the time comes for them to cohabitate as husband and wife, "Bhabhi... Bhabhi aapke liye chai ya coffee le aao?Should I fetch you some tea or coffee? Salma, who is standing a little distance away from Mahi, says in a quiet voice. She is returned to the present in her new room as a result.

Mahi quietly responded, smiling back, "Nahi, chai ya coffee main peeti nahi (No, I don't drink tea or coffee)." Salma was kind of in an odd position as a result of the new lady of the house's response. She believed she could open up to her by making her tea or coffee. and help Mahi feel a little at home in the new home. From the watchmen to the housekeepers, everyone in the room was aware of what had happened at the wedding. In addition, it was made plain why Mahi had to be welcomed instead of the woman who was meant to be present. Since they greeted the return of their original homeowner with the new wife, a new person, they have all been alert.

Mahi notices Salma struggling to speak as she stands awkwardly in the middle of the room and asks, "Salma, kya aapko naam se bula sakti hoon?" (Salma, might I use your name?)Yes, yes. Haan haan, bilkul. Without a doubt)," Salma responds, And don't call me in a formal manner because I am much younger than you, she said, smiling shyly, "aur "aap" mat boliye kyuki main aapse umar mein shayad bhahut chotu hoon."

"Ok Salma, toh aaj se aapko, sorry, tumhe Tum hi bulaungi (Ok, so from today I'll call you[formal], sorry you[informal] by name)," Mahi giggles at her reaction.' Finding the new lady of the home to be such a lovely talker gives the girl an instant sense of relaxation.

The question is, "Acha humare paas chai ya coffee ke alawa kuch aur hoga peene ke liye?" (Alright. Do you have any beverages besides tea or coffee?" Mahi queries her.

"Whatever you'll say. Ap jo bolo, juice, milkshake, umm, green tea, soft drink aur ap bolo toh hard drink bhi milega." Juice, milkshakes, green tea, soft drinks, and even hard drinks, if you like.

That is also an option)," Salma responds. She responded innocently, and Mahi couldn't help but laugh a little at her.

I suppose abhi ke liye green tea hi kaafi hogi mere liye, bina shahad ke na please (I think for now green tea would be enough for me, without honey please), Mahi says, quickly changing her laugh into a pleasant and welcoming smile.

The girl is already on her way and cheerfully says, "I'll get that, right away," as she finishes her sentence.

Mahi takes a seat at the end of the king-size bed in the middle of the room, facing the balcony, holding a warm mug of green tea. While taking a sip of her tea, she casts a gaze over the house's exterior wall. She then glances briefly at her luggage near the room's door. Next to where her suitcases are situated, there was a gap. It leads to a bathroom and a compact wardrobe area. She would watch the outer sky as it changed colour with each sip. As the day progresses, nightfall will ultimately arrive.

Mahi and Dev didn't come downstairs to eat dinner, so the home was quiet the entire night. Instead, they each ate in their individual rooms. The next morning, both left for their respective workplaces one after the other, going about their business like machines that only knew how to function. Or maybe it's just two people who wanted to lose themselves in their work and their realities. There was a defined pattern. Breakfast at home, followed by a trip to work and a return for dinner, with plans to repeat the process every day. Both of them thought it to be cosy. They were working extremely hard to allow each other and themselves some time to adjust to their situations. The following few weeks were spent in this mode of coping and space management. With the exception of "good morning" and "hi," there was no interaction or conversation during this time.

It is the weekend. Although it is a bad day for any government employee. However, Mahi's employment only offers this off sometimes during the year. Mahi would seek out a nice book and lose herself in it whenever this happened. Until dinnertime, that is. One of those days is right now. The majority of her belongings came from her previous government-allocated home, although they were packed in large boxes. She didn't even want to consider the additional task of locating a book among those cardboard boxes at this time. Since engaging in her favourite pastime would ruin the fun, she keeps herself occupied with a few calls from work. She even manages to escape those, though. From her window, she can see that the day is getting darker outside as the sun sets. She makes the decision to go downstairs in order to disguise the atmosphere of early evening.

Mahi discovers herself ambling around the home. She is praising the architecture and the meticulous upkeep of the property. She starts her tour in the kitchen because she liked its size and the people who worked there. She proceeds to the back, where a tiny entrance leads to a substantial ancient home that resembles Verandah. A huge, open garden with brown breakfast or evening tea chairs in the middle and a little, white swing hanging from the left corner follows. Mahi muses to herself, "Even for a high ranking government officer living in a businessman's house that is not less than a mansion, the scenery is quite aesthetic." Mahi sees a little closer yet doorlike aperture as she searches the green hedges to the right of the lawns. She pushes through that gap and notices a brand-new hue. She had previously believed that it was absent from this mansion. an outdoor pool. She moves in the direction of the pool's edge. She is in awe of its beauty and the water's immaculate clarity. She dips her hand into the pool while sitting on her feet, feeling the impulse to contact the water.

But she is unaware that someone is subtly observing her. watching her every move ever since she arrived at the pool area. Dev was immobile as he stared at her with increasing curiosity. But gradually he exits the shower room and moves in her direction. Mahi was so lost in her thoughts and the sensation of the water that she was completely unaware that Dev was standing just behind her.

A deep voice asks, "Do you swim?" startling her. She jerks herself to stand and make a shift in its direction. As a result, she stumbles and falls. She falls into the pool as Dev tries to reach out to catch her but misses her.

Chapter 2 New Housemate

The Jamwal Hotels & Resorts staff did not anticipate a swarm of income tax officers at their headquarters. Furthermore, they never expected it to occur on the wedding day itself. The staff at this office were chatting amongst themselves about Devrath Jamwal's long-distance wedding. The attention was now distracted from the wedding to this commotion as the tax agents turned the entire office upside down. Even the media was more interested in the tax heist than in the wedding. Devrath Jamwal was watching all of this from a desk in the office's corner. He was quietly observing the entire scene as it developed.

Everything that happened was pointless. At the lowest level, the officers pointed out certain document errors. As they were leaving the building, they expressed regret for the trouble. Dev additionally made no unnecessary effort to solve the problem. And ascertain the actual cause of the alleged document error made by the bureaucracy. He had already been thinking about what had happened yesterday. One name he knew was his past, present, and future until yesterday. However, as of last night, this person's name has been changed to Mrs. Maherishi Jamwal or Maherishi Solanki.

And for the following two years, this moniker would continue to play a role in his life. At least, it is the course of action that Mahi and Dev have chosen.

Being back in his own home gave Dev a strange mix of comfort and unease. Being removed from the commotion that had occurred over the previous couple of days—the wedding and the tax raid—gave him comfort. He noticed a sense of unease when he went into his own home with a stranger at the same time. He noticed when he could no longer use the word "house" to describe his own house.

While he didn't exactly dream about this day, he had a quite different perception of it. He never expected something like this when he and his wife initially entered this mansion. However, something that is more colourful. having a larger crowd, more family members, and fewer festive decorations. His return to reality was aided by Mahi's pleasantries and the notion that gave him a light cold.

Dev walked a flight of stairs that brought him to the confines of his chamber to escape this stifling reality, leaving his new wife in the care of the housekeepers.

Dev made a concerted effort to overlook the presence of someone new and someone other living in the same house during the course of the following two weeks while remaining silent and immersed in his job. Dev reasoned that it wouldn't be too difficult to live in a similar manner for the following two years after observing how the previous few days had passed without interfering with the serenity and quiet of the home. the predetermined schedule of going to work and returning home just to eat and rest.

Dev's thoughts quickly return to the paper in the study's right drawer as soon as he feels at ease with them. He learned about it that evening, and the circumstances that followed led him to marry Mahi. He was helpless to stop that. The reasons behind his new life are explained throughout the letter, not simply in the text on the letter. He is living somewhere voluntarily but with some force.

Dev spends his one day alone each week on Saturday, free from distractions like his job, daily activities, and outside noise. But he has been avoiding it for the last few Saturdays. The time and space he has to himself are being resisted, especially by him. The only way he feels he can maintain his sanity and avoid thinking about being left with only a letter is to keep his mind occupied with work. Despite the fact that he is required to come home every Saturday, he spends the day buried in work.

Even now, he continues to do so. He becomes too exhausted from doing the routine. He exits his room via the balcony. He decides to take a few laps in the pool directly below to reenergize himself before returning to the exercise.

He was getting into a new set of clothes after refilling through a shower and a fair number of laps. The T-shirt is the last item of clothes he puts on. He lifts his eyes to the left, where the rear lawns are, behind the hedges, where he hears the sound of footfall. A slim figure dressed in black tracks and a loose-fitting pastel pink shirt emerges a little while later. Dev observes her right hand as it moves from her side to her loose, midlength hair. Mahi tucks her hair behind her ear as she marvels at the pool. Dev couldn't help but watch her every move in anticipation of what she would do next. When she sits down on her feet to touch the water, he keeps staring at her even though he sees her approaching the pool. The following few minutes pass without her moving. Dev awakens from his state of passive observation of her. He exits the shower through the curtain. As he approached her, he was waiting for a reaction. Dev remained motionless a few feet away from her with her back to him for a few seconds while he observed her not moving other than to feel the water at the tip of her palm.

Having trouble keeping his curiosity in check, he asks, "Do you swim?"'. Mahi is startled by his voice and turns to face him. She consequently loses equilibrium as a result. Dev reaches out to catch her before she falls after observing her act in this manner. But every time, she makes a splashy dive into the water.

Dev dives into the water right away and holds her to the level after observing her fighting to stay afloat and recognising that she cannot swim. She clings to Dev like a baby as soon as she feels his hands around her. In reaction, Dev tightly holds her while noticing her trembling and leads her to the pool's shallow areas.

Dev stayed motionless beside her in the shallows, giving her time to collect herself. Mahi quickly notices that Dev isn't moving. But he is still firmly holding her. She won't let go of his hand, clinging to him like a newborn refusing to leave its mother.

She quickly inhales deeply before breaking the embrace and coming face to face with him. Dev pulls up the damp hair from her face and gently places it back so he can view her face while keeping his one arm steady around her. He does this automatically. He appeared to be stroking her face and hair for the second time. And even when he touches her, she doesn't flinch. she is aware of it. She is undoubtedly feeling a little uneasy about it. Both were compelled to exchange curious glances with one another. Mahi could see the man's features clearly because their faces were only a few inches apart. In addition to the anxiety she was already experiencing from the fall, it makes her even more tense. His sharply razored edges and flawless jawline. His deep breathing was noticeable to her, and she could tell that he was asking the same questions she was. Her eyes caught Dev's attention, however. They were shaky and roving. He is intrigued and worried about her because of them. He has only recently realised how stunning they are. They are large and have kajal traces all around them. He's heard his mother and sisters complimenting them over and over. Now he is aware of their praise's origin. Most likely, he had never before seen them up close.

'No! After regaining some composure, raising her voice somewhat, and staring at the other person for a minute, Mahi declares, "I don't know how to swim."

Mahi responds to Dev's perplexed gaze with, "You asked me...before I fell," after taking another big breath.

Dev responds amusingly to her statement while simultaneously feeling bad for feeling like he was to blame for her fall. "Yeah, I figured," he adds. He apologises, saying, "I'm sorry, I shouldn't have jumped you like that."

Mahi shakes her head and says, "I should have been more cognizant," to which.

We are in shallow waters, by the way. Dev stands holding her firmly and says, "If you'd like, you can feel the floors yourself.

Oh, yes, Mahi responds as she tries to stand on the pool decks as she realises how long he has been holding her. She is startled and uneasy, but her legs instantly betray her. She discovers herself grabbing Dev once more. He holds her in his grasp and won't let go. even when she makes an effort to escape his grasp and stand on her own. even when she doesn't succeed.

He comforts her while maintaining one arm over her and says, "It's okay. Let me help you." He then carries her up and forces her to sit on the edge of the pool.

'Better?Dev inquires after setting her up at the pool's edge. Mahi merely nods, saturated in water from her own wickedness like a small child.

Unknowingly grinning at her brief, innocent nod, Dev jumps up to leave the pool. He swiftly walks over to the shower section and vanishes behind the curtain that separates the pool area from the shower area.

He reappears shortly after with a towel in his hand and one draped over his shoulders. Mahi just keeps observing Dev's motions as he appears and vanishes while still experiencing the shivers from the water and nervousness from the embarrassing fall. He swiftly unfolds the towel in his hand and covers Mahi in it. He then takes a seat next to her at the pool's edge.

Feeling good?', Dev wonders with troubled and perplexed gaze. He is unable to remove them from the woman seated next to him, who is covered in water and, based on appearances, also embarrassed.

She nods more calmly now, "Yes, thank you," using the towel ends to wipe her face and wet mid-length hair.

Mahi replies as she dries her hair, "I didn't know you were home.

"Today is Saturday! I'm always here, Dev responds, briefly averting his eyes before bringing them back to her.

Mahi notices that he is looking at her, which causes her to feel uneasy and aware at the same time. Dev detects her anxiety and humiliation. He asks, "Where else do you think I would be if I weren't here?" to divert her attention from that..'

'Haan! Nowhere. She responds, giving him a short glance, "It's just...I thought corporate people didn't stay home on Saturdays."

When they own that corporate establishment, they do, adds Dev while grinning at her remark.

In the instant after nodding and grinning slightly, Mahi sneezes and says, "Excuse me."

Thank you!Dev says. As someone goes to buy her something warm to drink, he wants her to change right away. Dev assists her in standing up, and the two of them return home together. Dev stays behind to educate Karim in the kitchen as Mahi departs for her room. He requests that he deliver Mahi some masala tea or whatever else she usually drinks.

Dev continues to glance towards her chamber as he descends the stairs to his room. As he approaches his own door, he sees that this has been their least amount of interaction since they have known one another. Not really that horrible. Nevertheless, it took place after he forced her to fall into the pool.

Dev leaves his room the following morning to head to the office. He hears the kitchen's little, recognisable sneezes as he makes his way down the stairs. When he gets to the kitchen door, he notices Mahi's back leaning awkwardly against the wall at the entrance. She is covered in a brown shawl, and she is holding a tissue to her mouth. She was occupied observing the household staff as they made breakfast.

That awful, huh!Dev, who is standing just behind her, leans down to her height and speaks inches from her ears.

She is little startled by the voice, but she restrains herself from yelling. When she hears a voice, she turns around to discover Dev dressed in formal wear, holding a tiny notebook bag in his hand while holding a pair of black slacks, a light blue collared shirt with the top button undone, and a black blazer.

Noticing her bewildered expression, Dev continues, "Cold, you've got it." He notices her heavy eyes and her nose's redness. Dev mutters to himself, "Cute."

'Yeah. Mahi responds, adopting a tiny sorry expression as she sneezes one again, "I am kind of prone.

"Pardon me."

Thank you.

Dev apologises, "I'm sorry, it's my fault," feeling bad for making her endure yet another sneeze.

Oh, don't be, I beg you. It wasn't done yesterday. I'm still getting used to the weather here, Mahi says, feeling a little self-conscious after last night.

He replies jestingly, "Hmm, I remember it being quite sunny yesterday."

Simply unable to respond, Mahi gives up with a smile and says, "And as I remember, today is Sunday." It's a free for all, whether it's the government or business.

Yes, but not for those employed in the hotel industry. With an easy, witty smile, Dev responds, "It's their busiest day.

Mahi once more slightly leans against the wall and nods with a smile of submission.

Dev had never experienced this comfort with Mahi before. When he realises this right away, he pushes back and says, "I have to leave. You are cautious. And let them know if you need anything," he adds, motioning to the home helpers who are quietly working behind Mahi.

Dev turns to face the pair while gazing over at Mahi and says, "Salma Karim, take care and see if she needs anything," before bidding Mahi farewell.

Dev arrives at the hotel a little while later. He goes into his office and finds a well-known person waiting for him.

"Khan yaar?" The man on the couch asks, "Where buddy? I have been waiting here for an hour," as Dev opens the door and enters the room.

'Great! You have arrived already. Dev approaches his table, blazer on the chair, and bag on the side table, saying, "We need to chat. He seemed tense.

'Yes. We do. I am here for that reason. What do you need to discuss?", wonders the perplexed man. presently across the table from Dev.

About the property for the new project," Dev says, his jaws set tightly and his rage under control.

The man responds by softening his look, "That's why I'm here. How did you know?"

"I just left there," I said. The border wall was breached, and the billboard was demolished. Again!!Dev declares, nearly raising his voice.

"We have reported this to the police." However, it appears that no effective answer has been given,' the man continues, his expression showing dissatisfaction. I think leaving this to the police has been a waste of our time, he continues.

"Rohit, you are my attorney. Dev asks gravely, little shocked by his friend's intentions, "You seriously can't be suggesting I use illegal means."

Of course. No, I'm not requesting that you employ goons to deal with goons. In response to his companions' accusing looks, Rohit adds, "I'm only suggesting we take this matter to someone else rather than the cops. I can look into it because I have some contacts. Only if you say so," he said, lifting both of his palms.

'No. not right now. We'll continue engaging with the local police for the time being," Dev responds after giving it some thought.

Rohit sits down in a chair behind him and says, "You know we really don't have to look far," taking Dev's attention away.

Why do you ask?"Do you stand straight?" Dev queries while placing one hand in his pants pocket and the other on the table in front of him.

I refer to your wife. She is not your typical government employee. She is a DO,' adds Rohit, anticipating a reaction from his friend who is aware of the area of his life he is attempting to push.

Dev merely ignores his friend's attempt to elicit a response and responds, "We are sticking to local police," while simultaneously picking up the phone in front of him.

Dev asks into the phone, "Can you tell Shankar to go home and bring some cold medicines with him," before continuing to change his mind, "Wait, send him in here instead."

When Rohit returns the cordless phone, he says, "Cold medicine? who for?'

To Mahi. Dev responds in the most casual way he can, "She developed a cold.

Rohit notices his friend's guilty and worried appearance and says jokingly, "What did you do?" while attempting to maintain his composure.'

You don't have to answer it, Rohit teases Dev once again as he notices a scowl on his face. Rohit then abruptly becomes serious, saying, "Arre, call Ekta." She'll bring the medications to the patient.

Why would Ekta give her medication?Dev, who was truly perplexed by Rohit's offer, asks.

Rohit responds, glancing at his watch, "She must be on her way to your house."

'What? Why?Dev, who is astonished by this new revelation, asks.

When Rohit sees Dev's perplexed expressions, he replies, "Don't tell me you didn't expect this." Dev continues to express surprise when he narrows his eyes, admitting the charge that he did not anticipate this.

"What happened at the wedding happened weeks ago, and you returned weeks ago. In response to Dev's accusing eyes, Rohit says, "Ekta knows that you are avoiding her.

When Shankar walks into the room, everyone immediately turns to face him. When Dev first sees Shankar, he makes up his mind. Then he says, "Shankar gaadi nikalna," while picking up his blazer. In ghar chalna. Abhi!! (Shankar, get the car out; we must leave immediately for home!)

Dev notices his friend enjoying his stressful position while sitting down, to which the guy replies, "Tu saath chal raha hain." (You are accompanying me)

'Yaaar! When his friend orders him to go with him, Rohit exclaims, "Buddy! What could I do there?," quickly losing his smile.

Bahut kuch!" (A lot)," Dev responds.

Chapter 3 Old and New Friends

Mahi settled herself on a sofa in the living room. After she had lunch, she sat down with a cup of masala tea. Her sneezing hasn't stopped yet but has just gone down a little. She was still feeling the chills so, she wrapped herself in her mother's old shawl. She loves the way it smells. Another sneeze made her almost curse the pool. With that, her thoughts go back to yesterday evening's events followed by morning's conversation. That would be the first time she had a proper chat with Dev. In all these years of knowing each other, they were nothing more than just acquaintances. Even though their mothers were besties. As Saavi Maa's son Dev was often part of their conversations but never conversed personally. After all these years, this was the first time she ever spoke to him for that long. She felt nervous and at ease while talking to him.

Mahi takes another sip from her tea. As she puts down the mug, she sneezes again.

'God bless you, dear,' said the lady standing at the entrance.

'Thank you,' Mahi says reflexively and turns towards the voice. She sees a woman probably in her late 20s or early 30s. She is wearing a loose fitted full-length shirt that looked like a maternity gown. It is a maternity gown after looking longer and a belly sneaking out.

'Hi!' said the lady on the door. She starts walking towards Mahi and continues,' You must be Maherishi if I am not wrong.'

'Hi!' says Mahi getting up from her cosy chair and ask the lady,' Do we know each other?'

'Well, I was hoping you would. But again, I really can't trust an asshole like Dev to tell you about me,' says the woman as she comes in closer and continues,' Sorry for my language'.

'Umm, I still don't know who you are,' says Mahi. She guesses her to be really close to Dev, seeing her curse at him like that.

'Sorry! I am Ekta. Dev's old friend, plus his other old friend's wife, also happens to be his legal advisor.' Finally, the woman introduces herself.

'Ohkay! I am sorry but, he is not home at the moment,' Mahi replies.

'Oh, that I know. I didn't come for Dev. I am here for you. We were not able to meet during your wedding,' says Ekta smiling. She looks at her pregnant belly as she rubs her hand over it. She continues,' You see, I am not really alone so, I was forced not to travel.'

'Please sit. I am so sorry to keep you standing like this,' Mahi says, immediately realising for how long she kept the woman standing.

'That's alright,' says Ekta taking a seat and looking at Mahi's red nose,' So you caught a cold, huh?'

'Yeah. Kind of,' replies Mahi sitting back in her chair.

'I know. The weather here is like that,' says Ekta.

'Yes,' says Mahi keeping the face as straight as she could.

'If you don't mind, I make a really amazing desi remedy for cold,' replies Ekta watching Mahi go through another sneeze.

'Wow! I wouldn't mind anything at this moment,' Mahi says while sniffing and continues saying,' please do let me know the recipe. I'll ask Salma to make it for me.'

'Oh no, I can't! It's a family secret,' says Ekta and continues,' It has to be me who makes it,' smiling widely.

'I really can't ask you to do that for me,' says Mahi glancing quickly to her belly and back to her.

'I am pregnant, not disabled. Don't worry. My doctor said to keep working normally,' replies Ekta winking.

Mahi smiles as she gives up on her adorable response.

'Come on, lead the way to the kitchen, since you are the lady of the house,' says Ekta teasingly as she gets up from her seat.

'Oh, I am sure you know the house much better than I do,' says Mahi getting up as she continues, 'I discover something new every day.'

'Haina!! Finally, someone noticed this,' says Ekta with an excited voice as she found someone who shares the same mind as her.

Both women started walking towards the kitchen as they talked their way throughout and continued to do so.

Ekta and Mahi gelled like old friends who met after years. Mahi could feel her vibe familiar to another friend of hers. She missed her friend while she talked to Ekta. She thinks to herself that it would definitely be a blast if the two could meet each other.

Mahi sensed Ekta's closeness with Dev and realised that she is one of those friends who pretty much know everything and everyone in his life. As they continued talking, she realised that she even knows the arrangement between Dev and hers. Because Ekta responded quite casually when Mahi mentioned something about her room upstairs.

While ladies were busy having their little bonding, along with fun in the kitchen, they were unaware of men outside the gates who just arrived. One of them was almost panicked to reach home.

Dev and Rohit enter the house. Dev hears the sound of soft giggling and someone speaking continuous next to it. The sound is coming from the kitchen. The giggling is followed by a burst of laughter. Loud, yet soft and cheerful. Rohit recognises the voice of one talking as Ekta. He enters the kitchen and sees that laughter is coming from Mahi. As Mahi sees Dev, she loses her laugh and brings her face to a small smile. She was sitting on the slab. She dangles her legs at one corner of the kitchen, whereas Ekta was seated in one of the stool chairs next to the work station opposite Mahi.

'Hi! Remember me?' says Ekta to Dev, hinting sarcastic smile at the end of it.

'Ha, very funny. What are you doing here?' Dev says, responding to his friend.

'What do you mean?' says Ekta raising a brow at her friends irritating questioning.

'You didn't call me,' says Dev.

'Oh, buddy! I called you many times. Take a look at your phone log. You are the one who is running away,' says Ekta.

'I meant before coming here,' says Dev.

'Like you would have picked up,' says Ekta, sarcastically scoffing and continues,' Anyways, do I always call before coming? I didn't come here for you,' says Ekta, hinting at Mahi.

'I am sorry for this,' says Dev realising Mahi listening to this conversation. He continues,' My friend here has a habit of bombarding people unannounced.'

'No! No! In fact, I am glad she came,' replies Mahi smiling softly and trying to keep the calm between the two.

'You see. There is someone who appreciates my company, unlike some,' says Ekta narrowing her eyes at Dev. She further says,' you seem like quite a protective husband.'

'Speaking of husband, Hi! I am Rohit,' says Rohit reaching out a hand to shake with Mahi's. He continues,' The husband of that wife,' says Rohit while pointing towards Ekta.

'Hi! Mahi,' says Mahi shaking the friendly hand.

'Guys, behave! Let's not spoil our impressions for Mahi,' says Rohit putting a hand on Dev's shoulder and looking at his wife seated across the room.

'How are you feeling now? Any better?' asks Dev to Mahi. He seemed genuinely worried. Ekta notices this.

'I am feeling much better. Thanks to Ekta's amazing Desi remedy,' Mahi says, glancing back and forth to Ekta and Dev while saying this.

'Yeah. One thing Ekta is really good at,' says Dev, teasing his friend who is still giving him looks.

'Ha,' Ekta grunts loudly.

'Here! I was on my way here. So I got these,' says Dev handing out the cold medicines to Mahi. Rohit scoffs a little in the back.

'Thanks, you really didn't need to,' replies Mahi, taking the medicines from him. She doesn't know how to respond when someone like Dev shows care.

'I think I had to,' says Dev, hinting how bad he feels about her catching a cold.

'You need to stop blaming yourself for this,' replies Mahi, noticing his guilty expression.

'I will until you get absolutely better,' says Dev, smiling as he notices Mahi's concern and embarrassment.

Looking at these two lost in their own conversation, Ekta and Rohit exchange some looks as they were unable to follow. Moreover, they were amazed at how Dev was concerned for her health. He was smiling genuinely at her response with a weird sense of comfort. They never saw their friend at such ease while he was speaking to Mahi. Such comfort was definitely absent even with his ex, the one he was supposed to get married to. That's what amazed them at this moment.

'How her cold is you to blame?' asks confused Ekta breaking Mahi and Dev's little bonding moment.

Both Dev and Mahi look at each other before saying anything.

'Aaahmm, I kind of pushed her into the pool. Indirectly,' says Dev scratching one of his brows quickly.

'No, I slipped. It wasn't your fault,' says Mahi, immediately saving Dev from taking all the blame.

'I startled you without making myself present enough,' says Dev defending Mahi while looking at her.

'I lost control because I was too absent to feel your presence,' replies Mahi immediately to Dev.

'And I should have figured that out,' replies back Dev.

'And I should not blame you for this. So shouldn't you,' says Mahi.

'Only if you could have blamed me a little,' says Dev replying back instantly, not backing out and teasing her.

'Alright! I blame you. But then you saved me from drowning. I guess we are even now,' Mahi says, hoping to win this one.

Dev finally gives up, letting out a little chuckle at the end as he smiles widely with a full nod looking at Mahi.

Mahi smiles back, widely attaining the victory.

'Baby, have you ever felt like being invisible?' says Ekta sarcastically to Rohit.

'Not before today Babe,' replies Rohit, in a mood to tease the duo standing between them.

Listening to his two friends back to their favourite hobby of pulling his leg, Dev just rolls his eyes at their jokes. He replies to Mahi's silent, confused looks with an assuring shake of his head with a smile.

'Right! It's a first time for me too, Baby,' replies Ekta.

'Maybe we are in their house and disturbed their privacy,' says Rohit teasing outrightly.

'Maybe someone came here uninvited,' injects Dev in between.

In all of this, Mahi just looks at everyone's faces. She didn't know how to respond to this.

'Haww!! People change once they get married. I am witnessing it now,' says Ekta taking another jab at her friend.

'I guess I should leave,' Mahi says, getting down from slab after thinking how she must leave this confusing situation without offending anyone.

'No! No! No!! We are just pulling his leg. Don't take it seriously,' says Ekta, immediately realising how their friendly banter must have made her uncomfortable. She continues,' my friend here likes to keep it to himself, so I just have to do my part as a friend,' commenting sarcastically towards Dev.

Dev just smiles at this. Looking at him, Mahi simply becomes more relaxed.

'You'll get used to it,' says Rohit adding to his wife's comment.

'Speaking of getting used to it, Mahi, you should come to our house this Saturday. Rohit and I are throwing a little get together dinner at our place. It will be a small crowd consisting of our friends from school and college. We do this very often. This time it's our turn,' says Ekta.

'I don't know if I can. My weekends are not usually free,' says Mahi trying to avoid getting too mixed up with Dev's life.

'I know you work for the government. And I also know that if you want you can make the weekends free. Anyways our party starts after 8. So you don't have any legit excuse to miss,' replies Ekta outsmarting Mahi.

Mahi simply smiles back guiltily and looks at Dev, if he'll be alright with it. Dev smiles softly, blinking, assures her that he won't mind if she doesn't. Reading this much saying nothing, Mahi looks back to Ekta and says,' Ok! Why not.'

'Great! You know since you'll be part of our gang now, coming days you'll two have to throw one of these,' says Ekta.

'I guess I have to,' replies Mahi smiling awkwardly.

Seeing Mahi smile unwillingly at Ekta's instructions, Dev chuckles softly and says,' You don't have to if you don't want to.'

Mahi becomes relaxed again after listening to Dev and looks back at Ekta for confirmation.

Ekta notices his friend's detailed attention towards Mahi and sees a totally different version of Dev. She simply nods, smiling and says,' Whatever he said.'

Mahi smiles, now more relaxed.

Salma enters the kitchen breaking the light mood,' Bhaiya bahar police aayi hai.'

Everyone moves out of the kitchen towards the living room, where a young police officer stands next to Karim at the entrance.

As soon as he spots Mahi in the group of four people coming out of the kitchen, he salutes her immediately.

'Jai Hind Ma'am,' says the officer saluting Mahi.

'Yadav! Kya hua? (What happened?)' Mahi replies as she recognises the officer and moves towards him.

'Ma'am, ACP sir kaafi der se aapko call kar rahe the. Aapse phone pe baat nahi ho paa rahi toh unhone mujhe bheja (Ma'am ACP Sir has been trying your number. He wasn't able to get in touch with you so he sent me),' replies the officer, with a hesitation in his tone.

As he mentioned the phone, Mahi instantly moves towards the sofa she was sitting on. She shuffles through the cushions on it to find her phone. She grabs it as it was still ringing on vibration mode.

She picks up the call and says,' Haan phone silent pe tha (Yeah. Phone was on silent mode). What's wrong?'

She listens to the call and tightens her jaws controlling her anger as she rubs her forehead with her other hand. As she moves her hand back in her hair, she looks at the officer with a look filled with disappointment and anger. That makes the man standing in uniform terrified.

After few seconds of listening to the call, Mahi speaks into the phone,' I am on my way. Make sure they don't leave before I reach. I like to see their faces.' Then she hangs up the call and looks at the officer standing there.

He starts speaking frantically,' Ma'am, woh main team ke saath lunch pe nikal gaya tha aur fir Sunday tha isliye maine socha..... (Ma'am what happened that I went ahead with team for lunch. And then it was Sunday so I thought...)'

'Yadav! Gaadi laaye ho apne saath? (Did you bring the car with you?)' Mahi cuts him and asks, keeping the straight yet pissed off face.

'Yes, Ma'am,' replies the officer standing anxiously in attention.

'Bahar wait karo main 2 minute mein aa rahi hu (Wait for me outside. I am coming in 2 minutes),' replies Mahi, without giving out any hint to the man what will happen next.

The man salutes and leaves the house to wait outside.

Mahi turns around to go to her room to change and finds Dev, Rohit and Ekta standing there witnessing everything silently.

'I'll have to leave. Duty calls. I'll catch you later,' says Mahi looking at Ekta at the last sentence.

'Yeah! Definitely. We'll see you on Weekend then,' replies Ekta smiling.

'Great! See you then,' says Mahi to Ekta and Rohit simultaneously and starts to move towards stairs as Dev blocks her way.

'Do you have to leave? I mean, you haven't completely recovered,' says Dev, genuinely worried.

Mahi looks at him getting concerned. She simply replies without reading too much into it,' it's just a cold. I can manage.'

Dev nods, taking a step back as he realises that he might be crossing a line here, showing his concern.

'I feel much better anyways,' says Mahi smiling and sensing his concern. She says this not to offend him by sounding too rude.

'Hmm,' responds Dev smiling politely.

Mahi leaves the living area taking the stairs. While Rohit says, 'even I'll leave. I have a few things to take care of.'

'See you at home then,' says Ekta hugging her husband.

'Don't exert yourself and try to be soft,' says Rohit pointing towards Dev.

'Okie,' replies Ekta cutely to her husband.

With this, Rohit leaves the house too.

'Let's sit in Verandah,' says Ekta to Dev.

Dev nods and calls Karim to send coffee for them.

Dev and Ekta settle themselves in Verandah with their coffees.

'So how is my godson slash daughter?' says Dev looking at Ekta and glancing at her belly.

'They are absolutely healthy. However, we are wondering where our godfather was for the past few weeks,' replies Ekta keeping a hand on her belly.

'I was busy with office work. You know that before the wedding, I have been postponing a lot of work so, it got piled up,' says Dev.

'Is that the reason you have been avoiding me?' asks Ekta genuinely.

'I was not avoiding you yaar,' says Dev and continues taking a pause,' it's just... I wanted to sort a few things in my head.'

'So did you?' asks Ekta knowing him too well.

Dev sighs and says,' I don't know how to.'

'What do you think about the letter?' asks Ekta in an attempt to help Dev with his pain and sort his thoughts. Ekta and Rohit have always been friends for way too long. They have been there for Dev in his happiness and his doom days since their boarding school days. And so was Dev for them.

Dev, at Ekta's questions, takes a deep breath as he closes his eyes. He takes some time before saying anything.

'That piece of paper states the reason why she couldn't marry me. But, it also shows that she didn't have enough courage to say that to my face,' says Dev.

He continues,' You know what. Yashika is not to be blamed solely. The reason in that letter is very much equally responsible for her leaving me.'

'You mean your mom,' says Ekta as if stating something obvious which she clearly disagrees with.

'You know she never really approved of Yashika. She never accepted her in her heart,' says Dev after thinking through past events.

'My mother is the reason today three lives are destroyed,' says Dev.

'Three?' asks Ekta.

'She made Mahi involved in this,' says Dev.

'How is she responsible for destroying Mahi's life?' asks Ekta trying to get her friend's perspective.

'By asking her to marry me. It was in lieu of so-called gratitude for saving her life many years ago,' replies Dev.

'I think you underestimate Mahi. If I am a good judge of character. She doesn't seem to be anyone who would do anything under duress,' says Ekta after listening carefully to Dev's accusation towards his mother.

'I just know one thing. Mahi did it for my mother,' says Dev looking ahead.

'Speaking of Mahi, I like her,' says Ekta, simply smiling to herself.

Dev looks at her with surprise and says,' Wow, that's a first.'

'What do you mean? I don't like people in general?' asks Ekta taking offence from her friend.

'I meant how you approve of her. You just met her. You didn't approve the woman I dated for 6 years, even when I almost married her,' says Dev chuckling at the end.

'Just so you know, I still don't approve of her,' replies Ekta simply and continues,' No offence, I am glad you didn't get married to her.'

Dev raises his brow in response to Ekta's confession. Though he wasn't surprised. Ekta never liked Yashika, and Dev always knew this. For Dev, Ekta is one who always ok'd people and things around Dev, only if they'll do good for him. However, Yashika was never one of those but, she accepted it because Dev wanted her to.

'Yeah. Instead, I got married to the one you happen to like,' Dev replies sarcastically.

'It doesn't look like I am the only one who likes her,' Ekta says as she slyly points out something.

'Of course! Since you like her, Rohit doesn't have any option but to do the same,' replies Dev, oblivious to Ekta's intentions.

'I wasn't talking about Rohit,' says Ekta while smirking a little.

Dev becomes confused at her reply and suddenly realises what she meant.

'Oh, God! No! I don't like her,' Dev says, denying Ekta's unsaid claim and continues,' Weren't we just discussing the tragedy of my life. How can you jump from that to this?'

'Please! I am not accusing you of something indecent. And I didn't mean like LIKE,' says Ekta immediately and continues,' It's just I noticed something.'

'What?'

'How comfortable you were while you were speaking to her,' says Ekta and takes a pause before continuing,' I have never seen you like this. Not even when you were with Yashika.'

Dev couldn't deny what Ekta said. Even he felt that. Whenever he talked to her in the past 24 hrs, it was there.

Dev leans back and says thoughtfully,' There is a weird sense of comfort when I speak to her.'

Chapter 4 Party is in Session

The next few days till the weekend went by smoothly and differently. They were not the regular days but days filled with more interaction and conversations between Mahi and Dev. Now they were not trying to avoid each other while they had breakfast or dinner. They had them together while talking to each other. They talked about almost everything, from their childhood days to their respective college days. While talking to Dev, Mahi got to know more about his friendship with Ekta and Rohit. This made her more relaxed to attend the upcoming get-together. On the other hand, Dev noticed that Mahi was well guarded when discussing school days. Relatively, she had more to talk about her college years.

Although it was something new what both were experiencing, yet it was refreshing.

It is the weekend. Dev was already home as it was Saturday but, Mahi wasn't. It is already 10 minutes past 8, and Mahi isn't home. Dev got ready before time as he sat down in the living room waiting for Mahi. He was hoping that she didn't forget about today.

'I didn't forget about today. Trust me,' said Mahi as she entered the living room in a rush. She continues,' I am so sorry. I know

I am late. Something urgent came up that I couldn't leave,' while panting.

'It's alright! Breathe!' replies Dev, getting up with a chuckle. Mahi does what he instructs her like an obedient kid.

Seeing Mahi back with relaxed breathing, Dev calmly says,' Now! If you want to change, get going because I am sure you don't want to be late than this.' He continues,' If you want, we can leave like this as well.' Dev said this as he didn't want to sound offensive regarding what she was already wearing.

'No!' said Mahi a little louder in an almost panicked voice. She says,' 20 minutes. Give me 20 minutes. I'll be down in 20,' as she almost runs up to her room.

Dev simply chuckles widely, seeing Mahi care for what she should wear like any other woman. He was glad somewhere that she did not forget about today.

After exactly 20 mins, Mahi comes down, calling out Salma. As she steps down through stairs, Dev couldn't help but get awestruck by her. She was wearing a navy blue saree with soft silver shimmered cut sleeves blouse. She matched it with simple long solitaire earrings that complemented her big beautiful eyes with a soft smoky look. She paired it up with a simple wristwatch in one hand and silver bangles in the other. Dev couldn't move his eyes as she came down while she kept moving around looking for Salma.

Dev pulls himself out of the daze of staring at her and says,' They are not here. Since we'd be having dinner out so, I got them some movie tickets to chill.'

'Oh! Okay!' says Mahi slowly and thinking something up but, she couldn't come up with anything.

Seeing Mahi in some kind of dilemma, Dev asks,' What do you need? Tell me.'

'I need Salma, actually,' replies Mahi, making a little awkward face.

'What is it that only Salma can do? Don't underestimate me,' says Dev teasingly.

'Technically, you could do it too. But, I think Salma would be more appropriate to do it,' says Mahi, tightening her lips in confusion.

'Well, it will take a few hours for Salma to get back. What do you wanna do?' Dev simply asks.

'Ahhh! What the hell!!' exclaims Mahi, finally giving up as she can't afford to be late. She turns around, sliding her hair on one side, giving way for her almost bareback with a couple of laces hanging untied.

'Please tie them for me. I couldn't,' says Mahi hanging her head in embarrassment.

Dev didn't move at first, then he gulped a little. He felt a little uncomfortable to see Mahi like this. As a woman, as an attractive woman. As a beautiful woman. There was no denying that what Dev felt moments ago when Mahi came down from the stairs was the attraction to her. As per Dev, it was the first time in these days he saw her as a woman. As a man would see a woman.

'Yeah! I get it why Salma would be more appropriate,' says Dev, staring blankly at her bareback.

Mahi bites her lower lip nervously as she waits for him to tie them. Dev hesitates for few more seconds and then pulls out his jacket to put it on Mahi.

'Let's do this. When we'll reach there. Call Ekta out for a second. She can help you with that,' says Dev after putting on his jacket on Mahi.

'Not a bad idea,' says Mahi agreeing awkwardly.

'Let's get going then,' replies Dev, awkwardly moving towards the door. Mahi followed him quietly, holding on to his jacket.

Dev and Mahi drove to the party in awkward silence. As soon as they reached, Dev calls up Ekta to come out.

'Acha! Ek toh late aur upar se VIP treatment bhi chahiye tum logo ko (Okay. One, you are late and you need VIP treatment on top of that),' says Ekta as she sees Mahi and Dev standing next to the car side by side quietly.

Dev and Mahi just stand still as Ekta walks towards them.

'What's wrong?' says Ekta as soon as she comes to a halt in front of the two. She continues,' why are you wearing a jacket?'

'I need your little help with little something,' says Mahi softly.

Dev says,' I'll see you guys inside,' leaving them with the needed privacy.

As Dev left, Mahi takes off his jacket and turns around, facing backwards to Ekta. Ekta says,' Oh! You could have asked Dev to do that.'

'I did. Gave me the jacket instead,' says Mahi, amusingly recalling the incident. Ekta laughs softly while saying,' Men!'

Ekta starts tying the laces for Mahi. Mahi sees Dev walking back towards them. He says,' I thought we should go in together.'

Mahi simply nods, looking at him and hands him his jacket saying,' Thank you.'

'Anytime,' replies Dev.

Mahi looks at him, standing quietly next to her as Ekta ties her laces. She finds his awkward yet sturdy posture adoring, and to that, she just smiles to herself.

Ekta finds these two's silent expressions amusing.

'Done!' says Ekta finishing up the laces. She continues,' By the way, you could have warned me if you were planning to look so hot,' complimenting Mahi.

Mahi laughs awkwardly at Ekta's comment. Dev notices that Mahi doesn't know how to take a compliment. Dev finds her awkwardness adorable and smiles to himself.

They move towards the entrance. Entering the house, Mahi sees that the party is in the backyard. Mahi notices a couple of people in the living room. They come and greet Dev. Ekta introduces Mahi as Dev's wife. This made Mahi and Dev look at each other at the same time. This struck them as coming back to reality. As for the past few days, they were simply becoming more like friends forgetting their actual relation.

They all walk towards the back gardens. As Ekta said earlier, there were few people in the gathering. Some were chatting with each other while some were busy refilling their empty glasses. As soon as they stepped out into the garden, everyone was looking at them.

This made Mahi conscious of herself. She whispers, leaning towards Dev,' Am I underdressed?'

Dev leans his head down sideways in response. After Mahi finishes her question, he simply replies as he looks at her,' I don't know about overdressed or underdressed. I know one thing for sure. You look beautiful.'

Mahi doesn't know how to respond to that. But, with that, she suddenly felt relaxed and confident about how she was looking.

The phase of introducing Mahi to everyone starts eventually. Some were their school and college friends with their respective spouses or partners. Mahi couldn't remember each and everyone's name. But, she got acquainted with their faces for now.

As the night progressed, one of the guests was bold enough to mention Yashika in front of Dev as they intentionally tested Mahi. They clearly were interested in creating the new gossip for themselves. However, they were unaware of Mahi's personality of not giving satisfaction to anyone who bores ill intentions for her. She got out of the conversation without giving them the fruits of their poking.

'You stole my spot,' says Dev looking at Mahi. She was standing on the balcony of the kitchen, looking outside. Dev found her after looking for her in the whole house.

Mahi turns around and sees Dev leaning on the kitchen's back door.

'That's my spot whenever I feel like brooding in silence,' says Dev as he walks towards Mahi. He comes close and stands next to her.

'I needed some fresh air,' says Mahi returning to her earlier posture.

'Yeah! The same thing' replies Dev without taking his eyes off her. He continues,' However, brooding in silence sounds more legit since the party is in the open garden.'

Mahi smiles as she accepts the allegations of escaping the crowd. She asks,' what's your reason for running away?'

'I am not a crowd's person,' says Dev as he turns around in the spot and sits on the railing of the balcony to be at the same height as Mahi. Mahi was already leaning forward with the support of her hands. He continues,' Can't entertain people on some pretence. Unless they are really close friends of mine.'

Mahi smirks and replies,' neither can I. Unless I am obligated to do it under my job. The very reason I was late today.'

Dev nods quietly and pauses while he looks at Mahi intently for few seconds. Then he says,' I am sorry.'

Mahi turns her head towards Dev and says,' For what?'

'The very reason that led you to this spot,' replies Dev.

'And that is?'

'They shouldn't have said anything about Yashika to you,' says Dev.

'You were there too. Were just trying to get a reaction from you,' says Mahi as if stating facts.

'And from you too,' replies Dev in the same tone as her.

'But I didn't give them the satisfaction for it,' says Mahi smiling with a smirk.

'Yes. I saw that,' replies Dev grinning as he remembers the moment.

Mahi pauses while gazing in the dark as she says,' They don't know me like they probably knew Yashika. So I could care only less or not at all of what they think of me. They will compare me with her because I am in her place. Legally. I have learnt something from my job that I might have the skill or the power to control what people could think of me. However, that has its limitations,' says Mahi. She continues as she looks at Dev,' So you should not apologise for something like this.'

'But?' says Dev and continues,' that expression always has but in the end.'

Mahi chuckles softly and says, nodding,' But, I appreciate you for even taking notice of something like this.'

'Always,' says Dev smiling as he continues,' And thank you for coming here with me.'

'Always,' replies Mahi smiling back gladly.

Ekta comes and drags them back to the party outside.

'What changed your mind?' asks Ekta to the man who walks towards them with a smirk.

'Well. How could I have missed meeting the great Devrath Jamwal,' says the man scratching his light stubble. He was wearing ripped jeans with a patchy yet not so sophisticated jacket. It seemed like he was pulling off a hippie yet rich kid look. As he says this, he pulls out his hand from the pocket and offers it for a shake in front of Dev.

Mahi sees Dev's unpleasant expression. Dev takes the man's hand and greets him as he let out a detestable smile.

'Too bad. I wasn't expecting the not so great Kabir Jaisingh,' says Dev tightening his jaws.

Kabir laughs at Dev's response and continues,' Of course you wouldn't. Since you failed to get married to my ex-girlfriend.'

Ekta rolls her eyes and says,' Seriously! I was under the impression that women used to hold grudges for years. You men are no less. It's been more than 10 years since we graduated, and you two are still the same.'

'You should have thought this before inviting both of us,' says Dev.

'Yeah! It's my fault. I expected some maturity from teenage boys apparently, who are in their 30s,' replies Ekta with a sarcastic smile.

'Hey! I am mature. I even shook hands with him,' says Kabir smiling at Ekta.

'Aaargh!! I try not to hate that woman. But, you two give me more reason to do so,' says Ekta, now really pissed.

'Alright! Why do I always have to be the one to do this. To remind you guys about the place and people around us,' says Rohit injecting as he holds Ekta simultaneously and rubs her arms to calm her down. He continues,' Also, more importantly, don't you dare forget about the precious cargo here,' hinting towards Ekta and the baby.

'Damn! You are loaded!' says Kabir, instantly realising what Rohit meant.

Mahi couldn't control but chuckles at the Kabir's reaction. Kabir notices Mahi standing next to Ekta. It interests him as he finds her very attractive.

'Yaar Ekta, aren't you suppose to introduce your pretty attractive female guests to your single friends. Rehne de. I'll do it myself,' says Kabir turning his attention towards Mahi. He continues offering his hand to greet Mahi,' Hi! Kabir. These three's college buddy.'

Mahi smirks internally at Kabir's remark and replies,' Hi! Mahi! I am..'

'My wife,' says Dev before Mahi could complete her sentence stating the same.

Mahi looks at Dev standing next to her. She couldn't help but notice Dev interjected himself by introducing her as his wife for the first time. The whole night it was Ekta who was doing the introductions with the word wife. Whereas Dev stood next to her and greeted everyone silently or with little words. And none of those words was 'My wife'. But, this was the first time he said those words. Mahi couldn't help but observe that he did that to mark his territory over her. It became clear to Mahi that there was some displeasing history between the two. That history definitely involved a girl. None other than Yashika.

'Oh! That was quick,' says Kabir poking Dev again while grinning.

Dev looks more pissed off on his comment.

Noticing this, Ekta says, keeping her calm and voice low, at the same time,' I am warning you two. If you spoil my party, I will kill you two with my bare hands. So, BEHAVE!!' She walks off from there after issuing the warning, and Rohit follows her in concern.

'So, what do you do? Mrs Jamwal, except being his wife,' asks Kabir keeping the conversation as casual as Ekta warned.

Dev scoffs, getting irritated at this standing next to Mahi.

'I am a government employee,' replies Mahi keeping a polite smile. And continue to ask,' And what do you do other than spiking people's nerves?'

Dev chuckles loudly at Mahi's comeback.

'I guess I deserve that,' says Kabir scratching his head and smiling. He further says,' I am also guessing you don't read books. If you did, you would have known me. I am kind of a best seller novelist currently.'

'Oh! I do recognise your name now! My apologies! I didn't recognise you earlier. As Indian authors have terribly failed to impress me by their terrible writing,' replies Mahi pulling him on earth from his ride on the ninth cloud.

'I agree. But I argue myself to be different from the other Indian authors,' says Kabir realising Mahi to be someone who could be a valuable critique.

'You are no different. There is a reason your novel is a best seller. Not all things popular tends to be good. Especially writing. Because not everyone can tell what good writing is,' says Mahi with confidence.

Kabir gets amazed at her criticism and her confidence to tell him something this bluntly.

He simply asks Dev,' How do you manage to get the best every single time! ' Dev simply rolls his eyes on his another remark. Kabir continues,' do you mind if I can borrow her for some constructive criticism?'

Dev looks at Mahi and says,' Only if she doesn't.' To this, Mahi simply smiles in agreement. Dev touches Mahi's arm softly and says,' Let me know if he gets too irritating.'

'I will,' replies Mahi smiling and touching the back of his hand where he was keeping his hand on her arm.

'Let me get you the refill,' says Dev taking the wine glass from Mahi as he leaves the two to get back to their conversation.

After some time, Ekta finds Dev seated alone in a corner looking somewhere far. As she approaches him, she follows his gaze and knows where he has been looking without taking any break.

'I know Kabir has his ways of charming women with his way too cool bestseller novelist attitude. But, Mahi doesn't seem like someone to get under his charm. So don't worry. Your wife is quite wise,' says Ekta teasingly, taking a seat next to him.

'Please! Kabir doesn't have any charm. He just knows how to manipulate the attention,' replies Dev without breaking his gaze on Mahi and Kabir seated across the garden, having some serious discussion. Dev continues realising what Ekta just said,' and I am not worried, okay.'

'Hmm! You are surely not about to make a hole in them by staring like that,' replies Ekta pointing out Dev has been looking at them.

Dev breaks his gaze. He looks at Ekta as he lets out a heavy sigh.

'It's just...they just met. What could both have so much to talk about?' says Dev looking at them.

'I am just coming from there. Both were arguing about some British author's biography. Boring stuff. Nothing interesting,' says Ekta reassuring her friend that his wife is not being swayed away by a stranger.

Dev just nods, not relaxing at all.

'So? Did you find out?' asks Ekta after giving little time to Dev to relax a little before questioning.

'What?' asks Dev looking at Ekta with total confusion.

'The thing you were supposed to find out,' says Ekta giving out another hint. Looking at his confused face, Ekta hits him with the back of her hand on his arm and says,' What we talked about that day! Why do you feel how you feel when you are with Mahi! Your weird sense of comfort!'

Dev turns his head in the direction where Mahi was sitting. He just looks at her from far before saying anything.

'No. I thought about this. I won't look for the reason anymore,' says Dev looking at Mahi.

'Why?' asks Ekta.

'I am afraid. Once I found the reason, I might lose the feeling. I don't wanna lose anything anymore. And I don't remember the last time I felt anything like this. I just want to hold onto this little longer. At least till the time Mahi and I agreed to play this facade,' says Dev with a thoughtful expression looking straight ahead.

They were back home. In the middle of the night, Dev sits up as he struggles to sleep. So he goes down to get himself some tea. As he takes the stairs down, he sees the light coming from the kitchen door. He slowly walks towards the kitchen listening to the sounds coming from the kitchen. Who could have been there in the middle of the night? Dev thinks to himself. He simply smiles as he stood still at the kitchen door. He smiles because he finds Mahi in her cute minions' pyjamas. She is cooking something, trying to keep the noise as down as possible.

'It's 2 AM,' says Dev standing on the door frame.

Mahi jumps at the voice and lets out a little shriek. She turns around and says,' you need to stop doing that. Please make some noise before you creep up like that,' in a little aggravated voice.

Dev chuckles loudly at her reaction and says,' Sorry! What are you doing in the middle of the night?'

CHAPTER 5 HER PAST

'I was hungry. I still am,' says Mahi making an innocent face.

'I can see that,' says Dev smiling and continues to ask,' I am curious whether this is a routine?'

'Only when I attend crowded parties,' says turning towards the omelette on the pan.

'You know how to cook?' asks Dev with curiosity.

'You'll be surprised to know I am good at it,' says Mahi unapologetic at her skills.

Dev chuckles softly at her confidence and asks,' And when will I be able to experience that?'

'Well, right now if you are hungry,' says as she tries to flip the omelette on the pan. She does the flipping but the hot butter splashes on her left hand burning it. Mahi winces at the pain. Dev quickly runs towards her. He turns off the stove and takes her hand to the sink. He opens the tap and puts her hand under the running water as she grimaces with pain.

'Just for few more seconds,' says Dev holding her hand underwater.

He slightly moves her hand around so that water doesn't hit the burn directly. As he does that, he sees a scar on her wrist. He looks at it and catches Mahi looking at him noticing it. She quickly pulls her hand and walks to the refrigerator with her back to Dev.

'The wine bottle incident?' says Dev realising where that scar could be from.

Mahi stops in her tracks for a second. Keeping it as casual as she could, she replies,' Hmm mm.'

'I have heard about it. If you don't mind can I ask you something?' says Dev, simply being curious.

Mahi tries to keep her emotions intact. She guesses his question to be about the part of her life she doesn't like to talk about. It is that part that nobody could know how she feels about. So she wears her poker face and takes out the ice tray. She turns around with a polite smile.

'Sure! You are not the first one to be curious about it,' says Mahi keeping the poker face as she takes an ice cube from the tray and puts it over her burn.

Dev smiles as he relaxes at her response. He asks,' I have been curious about how anyone couldn't have known that they are bleeding. Didn't you realise you were hurting?'

The past incident flashes in front of Mahi's eyes. She freezes where she was. She mentally jerks herself out of that day and continues keeping the smile on her face,' It's easy. I was just 17, a teenager high on hormones who dared to open her Dad's favourite wine bottle alone at home. While I was at it, I broke it and hurt myself. Clumsy of me. I was so scared to leave any evidence of my quest as I lost myself in cleaning up the place.' She pauses before she continues,' I didn't realise I was bleeding until I felt dizzy and fainted.'

'Next thing I remember, I opened my eyes in the hospital. Found Saavi Maa in front of me. Ready to scold me to hell,' says Mahi finishing up the story she has been telling to others since then.

Dev notices something off in Mahi's expression as she narrates the incident keeping a straight face. But, he tells himself not to read too much into this. As Mahi mentions his mother, it brings him back to the present reality.

'I wouldn't be alive if it wasn't for Saavi Maa,' says Mahi without faking the emotions she felt.

'Yeah! Also, we wouldn't here if it wasn't for her,' says Dev keeping a serious face. He seemed to Mahi as if he was blaming his mother for their marriage.

'I owe my life to her. If she didn't happen to come to the house that day I would have been dead,' says Mahi with little defence in her voice.

'My mother has a talent of appearing at right places, at the right time,' replies Dev with a clear unpleasant expression. He continues,' like how she was there when Yashika left and how she got you involved.'

'Do you think Saavi Maa asked me to marry you?' asks Mahi with getting a confusion intended to clear.

'Oh! My mother doesn't ask people to do things for her. They owe her. That's how talented she is. It was the same with you,' replies Dev with a conviction.

Mahi doesn't say anything in Saavi Maa's defence because this wouldn't be right as in right now. Seeing Dev indulging in hatred towards his mother looks like a slow and prolonged process. She realises that it wasn't just the wedding or that letter she almost tore are the only reasons for Dev's bitterness. Dev perceived his mother as someone else long before their wedding. And there is nothing Mahi could say to lessen that hatred in Dev. Not at least before she knows the beginning of all of this.

Seeing Mahi saying nothing Dev realises how much he has let it out in front of her.

'I am sorry. I shouldn't have said this to you,' says Dev keeping the calm.

'It's alright!' Mahi replies as she keeps the topic of her Saavi Maa concluded.

'I am guessing, I should leave you to your omelette then. And please put some ointment on that before you sleep,' says Dev taking a step back to leave.

'I thought you were staying to experience my cooking,' says Mahi teasingly.

'Should I?' asks Dev amusingly at Mahi's poke.

'I don't mind,' replies Mahi smiling.

'Okay,' says Dev.

They set out the plates for themselves in the kitchen and continue to indulge themselves in another of their conversations.

In the next few days, Dev often found himself drawn towards Mahi. Be it every day when he goes down to the gym from his room's balcony, where he happens to see Mahi sitting in lawns meditating on the yoga mat. Every morning for Dev this has become part of his routine right before he leaves to workout. He helplessly stops in his tracks and watches her for a few seconds before jerking himself to move. Dev also started indulging in making excuses to spend time with Mahi. Thanks to Ekta, Mahi soon became part of their gang. She started coming to group gatherings almost every other weekend. Even Dev was secretly loving to see Mahi in a Saree in all those events. Informal events became part of Mahi's new social life here. Dev also began to take Mahi to corporate parties in the name of keeping up the appearances for media and his corporate circle. Mahi knew she signed up for this when she decided to tie the knot with Dev. However, all these parties and events were more than bearable only because Dev was next to her. Whenever in those parties she would need some rescuing from unwanted guests. She finds Dev next to her in a blink of an eye. It happened swiftly every time as if Dev didn't lose her from his sight even when they were not next to each other physically.

One of these days, Dev was invited to a brunch with his sports club members. He has to bring his plus one on this brunch. So he asked Mahi to accompany him. So, Mahi agreed. She was anyways not that busy that weekday and needed to avoid few officials. So she didn't mind going along with Dev.

Mahi comes out wearing casual ripped jeans with a long slit yellow kurta accessorising with junk jewellery. Dev couldn't help but noticed that she isn't wearing a saree and still looking stunning as ever.

'What? Something wrong?' asks Mahi seeing Dev standing still and just eyeing her from top to down.

Dev pulls himself out and says,' No! Just that you are not wearing a saree.'

'You only said that it was not a formal event. It is a brunch. And anyway it's daytime. I thought saree would be too much,' says Mahi.

'I did,' says Dev thinking back to the time when he said that. He regretted a little for doing so.

'Is this not okay?' asks Mahi now genuinely worried noticing a hint of disappointment in Dev.

'No. No. You look amazing. Umm, anything looks good on you. I mean..,' Dev says realising he is not in control of the words he is supposed to say. He closes his eyes tightly for a second to gather his focus to say anything appropriate. He says,' you look nice. As usual.'

Mahi finds Dev's fumbling over words amusing. She says teasingly,' I think you secretly liked seeing me in a saree.'

Dev looks at her grinning with a mischief in her eyes. He walks towards her and leans down close to her face as he slides her hair behind her shoulder. Mahi inhales sharply at his closeness, smelling in the musky fragrance coming from him. He touches the neckpiece she is wearing.

Mahi loses the smiles instantly and feels nervous as she feels his breath over her right cheek. He says in a voice as low as a whisper' Even if you are right what you said,' as his fingers brush against her collar bone while he turns the piece of the necklace to its place. He continues,' you'll be the one to blame if I develop any fetishes for sarees.'

Mahi couldn't move but exhales after he left adjusting his necklace and teasing her with his nearness.

'Chalein? (Shall we?)' asks Dev stopping at the door and turning around towards Mahi. Mahi jerks herself out and nods simply and moves towards the door.

Dev smiles to himself seeing Mahi quiet after his teasing.

After concluding the brunch at the club, Mahi was out on reception waiting for Dev as he was seeing off some of the members personally. While she was waiting there, the receptionist asks her to fill their feedback register. As she finished up doing that someone from the office recognised her and came out to confirm her suspicion.

'Maherishi Solanki?' says the woman in formals to Mahi's left.

Mahi turns at her name. She finds the woman familiar but couldn't remember from where.

'It is you. Such a long time huh!' says the woman as she approaches Mahi. Seeing Mahi's confused expressions, she realises that she didn't recognise her yet. So she says,' Varsha Shukla. Golwalker High School!'

It struck to Mahi suddenly as soon as she mentioned the school. Mahi had thought that she had wiped out everything from that part of her life. Her face becomes pale at the mention of the school. She wears a poker smile immediately to greet the person in front of her cordially.

'Hi! Yeah. Long time. How are you?' asks Mahi keeping the fake yet nervous smile on her face.

'I am good. You went AWOL after you left school. Nobody knew where you were since then. What are you doing here?' asks the lady standing in front of Mahi.

Mahi felt an urge to run away from here. She replies,' I was here on brunch. You are the Manager. Nice,' seeing the small-batch on her collar. Mahi makes an excuse for a call and leaves the reception area before the woman starts reminiscing about their school days.

The woman behind the reception asks the Varsha,' It looked like she wasn't that happy to see you, Ma'am.'

'I bet it's just not me. Of course, she could never be happy to see anyone from the school after what happened,' says the Manager to the receptionist turning around.

'What happened to her?' asks the receptionist becoming curious about the new gossip.

'Something tragic that could happen to a girl. Nothing you should be interested in. Get back to work,' says the Manager respecting Mahi's life and leaves from there.

Dev was standing on the other end of the reception witnessing the whole the thing. Initially, he stood there intending to look at Mahi quietly while she was filling the feedback register. However, things turned around immediately, Dev didn't realise when to leave or to intervene.

Dev walks out to look for Mahi. He finds her in the parking next to his car. She was standing there anxiously as if she was trying to hide from someone.

As soon as she saw Dev, she composed herself and wore her poker face. Dev noticed how quickly she changed her expression from being terrified to tranquil in an instant.

They drove in silence. Dev didn't say anything about what he witnessed on reception back there. However, he noticed her hands not being stable. She kept fidgeting her fingers anxiously as she looked out.

'Stop the car,' says Mahi, suddenly with a heavy voice as if controlling herself.

'Why? What's wrong?' asks Dev now worried at sudden instruction.

'Just pull over somewhere on the side. Now,' replies Mahi keeping her calm.

Dev does what he has been asked. Mahi opens the door as soon as Dev pulls the breaks. Mahi almost runs a little far from the car and bends down half to puke. Dev gets the water bottle from side seat and runs to her. He gathers her untied hair from her side. As he held them together in one hand, he rubs the other on her back. She throws up for the next couple of minutes more. As she was done and exhausted from pumping her stomach out, Dev hands her the water bottle. She cleans up with the water and straightens her back as she gulps down a few sips of water. Dev takes out his handkerchief and hands it out to her.

'Feeling better?' asks Dev as she hands him back the bottle and takes the handkerchief from him. She nods back in response and wipes her face roughly with it.

Dev takes the piece of cloth from her hand and takes a corner of it to wipe off the smudged kajal from the side of her eyes. As he cleans off the kajal with one, he sets her tousled strands of hair with the other. And looks at her exhausted face and asks out of concern,' you sure?'

Mahi nods and says softly,' Take me home.'

'Let me take you to see a doctor first,' says Dev.

Mahi shakes her head before she says,' no! I feel much better. Whatever it was. I am sure it's out. Please! Home,' says Mahi in an exhausted voice.

Dev takes her back to the car and drives off to home. The whole way to home, Dev kept glancing at Mahi next to him in concern. He kept holding her hand as they drove back. Even Mahi didn't flinch at it. On the contrary, Mahi felt at ease with his touch.

Dev pulls up the car in the porch and gets down immediately to open the door for Mahi. Mahi already got out before he could reach her.

'I am fine. I am sure its just food poisoning. I'll sleep a little and feel like before,' says Mahi to worried Dev.

'You sure?' asks Dev again not sure of himself as to whether to listen to her.

'This is the 4th time you've asked me this. Yes, I am sure. Go! Do whatever you were supposed to do after this,' says Mahi walking towards a couple of stairs before the entrance.

As she walks past Dev and takes the stairs. She stops in between. Dev looks at her and next thing Dev knew that he was catching her from hitting the ground.

'Mahi! Mahi!' calls out Dev to an unconscious Mahi in his arms.

Chapter 6 His Past or His Confused Feelings

Dev carries unconscious Mahi to her room and asks Karim to call the physician and ask him to be here as soon as possible. As Dev waits for him to arrive, he sits next to Mahi on the bed.

Mahi opens her eyes wide, followed by a strong gasp as if she woke up from a scary nightmare. Her hands tightly clenched in a fist. She sits up quickly, looking dazed, trying to gather herself while panting frantically. Dev calms her down by saying,' It's alright. It's okay. Hey! Hey, look here! It's me. Dev.'

She looks at Dev and around, realising she is in her room. In exhaustion, she leans her head down on Dev's shoulder. She loses her consciousness again in that relaxed manner on his shoulder. Dev slowly cradles her head in his hand and lays her down on the bed. Dev gets worried seeing Mahi in such a state.

He couldn't help but remembers the incident that happened earlier back at the club. It raises questions about whether the sequence of events is somehow related. The Manager lady said 'something tragic', Dev thinks.

Dev just sits there thoughtfully, looking at Mahi. He runs his hand through her hair. He caresses her face softly. His fingers move slowly from her forehead, through her temple and drawing softer strokes on her right cheek with his thumb.

The physician arrives and puts her on an IV drip to treat her dehydration and supposed food poising. He assures Dev that she will be fine in a few hours. He leaves Dev with some specific instructions on what Mahi should be fed once she wakes up.

For the next two days, Dev made sure that Mahi follows up on what the Doctor instructed. He made her work from home for those two days as he remained home to check on Mahi personally.

After a few days, Mahi and Dev are hosting dinner with Dev's friends. As both were welcoming the guests, Dev sees Kabir getting down from his car on the gates.

'Did you invite him?' says Dev to Mahi, questioning Kabir's presence in his house.

'You only approved the guest list before sending out the invites,' replies Mahi keeping the smile for arriving guests. She continues,' Didn't you go through the list?'

Dev closes his eyes on his mistake of not going through it. He says,' Still, why did you put him on the list?'

'I didn't. I sent you the same list Ekta forwarded me,' says Mahi. Dev rolls his eyes on that. Mahi further says,' She was helping me to organise this. Sorry.'

'Don't be. Someone else should be,' says Dev while eying Ekta.

Mahi sees Dev being pissed off, holds his arm softly and says,' We are the hosts. Please remember that,' smiling making an innocent face.

Dev loses the grimace and smiles instantly, looking at her adorable insisting. He says,' Have I mentioned today how nice you look in this saree,' teasingly.

Mahi pushes him lightly with a smile in response as she says,' The joke loses its touch if repeated 5 times.'

'I doubt that,' replies grinning teasingly at Mahi.

Mahi smiles, feeling a little shy at his teasing.

Some time into the party, Dev looks around for Mahi. It has been more than a few minutes since Dev lost sight of Mahi. He walks towards the Verandah and stops as he sees Mahi standing with Kabir. She was laughing as Kabir was speaking. Dev didn't like what he was seeing. Mahi feels Dev's eyes on her as she turns her head in that direction. She sees Dev standing quietly on the door. He meets her eyes and turns to leave. Mahi immediately excuses herself from Kabir and walks quickly to Dev.

'Hey! Were you looking for me?' says Mahi as she comes close to Dev.

Dev stops where he was and faces Mahi as he replies,' Not really. I was just wondering where you disappeared.'

'I am right here,' replies Mahi smiling.

Dev simply nods and turns to leave. But, Mahi holds his arm gently to stop him, says,' Dev. Is everything okay?'

'Yes. Why? Do you think something is not okay?' asks Dev returning the smile with a smile.

'No! I just thought...nothing. Can I ask you something?' asks Mahi looking at Dev intently.

'Anything,' says Dev softly, looking at Mahi.

'Would you mind if I become friends with Kabir?' says Mahi, slowly keeping an observing eye on Dev's expressions. She continues,' I mean, I don't know what your history is with him. And I am not at all intrigued.' She takes a brief pause and says,' What I am saying is I'll be okay if you want me to keep a distance.'

Dev felt an urge to say yes. He would mind a lot. He thinks to himself that he'll be more than glad if Kabir kept his distance from you. But, he doesn't voice these thoughts. He instead says,' It doesn't matter what I want. Because I am no one to tell you who you should be friends with. No one should tell you that. And that's why you never have to ask me. Ever.'

Mahi smiles at his replies and feels glad for Dev for a kind of a person he is. Dev gives her a smile touching her arm as he assures her leaves from there.

Party eventually comes to an end. Dev was just seeing off the last guests before Kabir, Ekta and Rohit.

'Dev, I am so glad to see you moving forward in life. Mahi is really nice,' says the lady friend as Dev sees her off on the door.

Dev smiles and says,' Thanks, Gagan. It's good to see you too.'

'My pleasure yaar,' replies Gagan and continues as she hesitates a little,' I have something for you. I was asked to give it to you. I was hesitating when I arrived. After seeing you and Mahi, I think I can get rid of this responsibility on my head.'

She takes out a small squared red envelope from her sling bag. She hands it to Dev, saying,' Please don't curse me. I am just a messenger.' She doesn't wait for Dev to open it and leaves immediately.

Dev is all confused at her behaviour and the envelope in hand. He takes the white card out of the envelope and reads it. He freezes as he reads what was written on the piece of paper he was holding. It reads YASHIKA Weds ARMAAN. Everything flashes in front of him. Dev's mind goes back to the day when he thought, was the happiest day of his life. He slips back to the moment to his wedding day before he got to know about Yashika leaving him. She left behind the letter with a small tear on the corner of it. Dev becomes numb again, thinking about that day. The day when he faced the biggest betrayal of his life. He thought that was it. But seeing this makes him question his feelings yet again. He raises his head and looks for the only person who could make him forget about this. The only person who was able to comfort him unknowingly for these past months was Mahi. He instinctively looks at her and feels the ease swept over him. He forgets about the card he is holding. He smiles as he watches her smiling brightly. But he soon loses his smile when he sees the reason for her smile. She is sitting next to Kabir.

Mahi gets up from the chair and moves to the kitchen. Kabir doesn't follow her and remains seated. Dev loses all expression from his face moving towards the kitchen as well. He enters and sees Mahi at the other end. Whereas Ekta and Rohit were on Dev's right on the other corner of the kitchen engaged in themselves. They become silent, realising Dev standing there without saying anything.

'Can I speak with you guys,' says Dev with grim expressions, directing at Rohit and Ekta.

'What did we do now?' replies Ekta taking a friendly jab at her friend.

Dev doesn't respond to that. However, Mahi reads Dev's face and asks him out of concern,' Is everything alright?'

'Yes,' replies Dev without looking at her first. But, when his gaze immediately catches her, Dev gives in to his anger. He slowly walks towards her sounding grudgingly rude,' You know what! No! Everything is not okay. Nothing is okay. You. This house. Me. Nothing is okay. But, I am guessing everything is perfect for you. From your perspective, you got everything you want. A mansion instead of a government house. A rich husband. His friends, and for that matter, even his non-friends. What anyone could only dream, you got it all. You know what? That's exactly you should report back to your Saavi Maa. Tell her that you have successfully accomplished her mission here. You got me to forget about my past. You got me dancing as you like. You got my friends to like you. You even got the person I dislike the most to like you. You are amazing. You have even got accustomed to act like my wife in front of my acquaintances.' Without taking another breath, he continues changing his tone,' I think playing my wife for this long has blurred few realities for you. Let me get them clear for you. We might have got married in front of some 500 witnesses or so. My mother might have placed you in my life to attain her objectives. But, don't you ever forget that you are just someone instead of what I couldn't get. And you always will be. You are nothing but a substitute wife.'

'DEV!!!' shouts Ekta stopping Dev from saying anything from where he could never come back. Dev stops in his tracks and breathes heavily, standing inches away from Mahi. Looking at her face with strained expressions.

Mahi stands facing Dev, trying to get her emotion in check, trembles internally. Even though how hard she tries, her eyes well up in a multitude of emotions. She doesn't say a word. Even when Dev stood silently in front of her for a couple of seconds. But, she kept her eyes steady, staring right back into his without giving in to his verbal insult. She kept her stare, even when her vision became unclear with tears.

Dev sees her eyes with nothing but hurt he just caused her. It hits him hard. He turns around to walk out of there to escape this startling reality. He sees Kabir at the entrance of the kitchen, probably witnessing everything. He couldn't take it anymore. So, he walks past Kabir to leave from there. Rohit follows him behind in an attempt to sort out his reason for this outburst.

Ekta walks up to Mahi slowly. She puts her hand on Mahi's shoulder and says nothing. Ekta feels helpless about how should she justify her friend's behaviour. She doesn't know the reason why Dev's frenzied out. Whatever the reason is, she knew one thing that there could be no valid explanation for Dev's affront of Mahi.

'Ekta,' says Mahi after gathering whatever remaining energy she had. She says,' I don't want to be offensive,' with a small voice. She continues keeping her eyes shut,' but I like to be left alone. Please.'

Ekta honours Mahi's wish and leaves the house taking Kabir along with her.

Dev was a no show for the next two days. He didn't turn up to the office or returned home. He drove off after the incident even when Rohit almost ran after him to stop. Ekta tried getting hold of Dev. So that she could school him for his behaviour. However, Dev didn't respond to any calls from her or from Rohit. Ekta couldn't get hold of Dev as of now. So, she couldn't gather enough courage to check on Mahi personally. Still, she drops her a message asking how was she feeling. To which, she receives a very formal response from Mahi, being busy with some work.

Ekta was fuming with anger and was about to burst if she didn't hear from Dev anytime soon. But, she receives the call from Rohit stating that Dev showed up at the office finally.

'Do you have anything to say in your defence before I start beating you up? Literally,' says Ekta, seated in one of the couches in Dev's office.

Dev looked messy and a little out of his mind. He was in the same clothes as he was wearing two days earlier. His face looked hungover and tired. He didn't respond to Ekta's threat. He kept rubbing his temple with closed eyes while seated in his chair behind the desk.

'Dev, say something! What happened? Where have you been for the past two days?' asks Rohit leaning against the drawers on the side.

'I don't have anything to say,' replies Dev keeping the same posture closed eyes.

'Really! Then what the fuck was that? Do you even know how rash you were with your words that night? How hurt was Mahi? She didn't deserve that,' asks Ekta losing her calm for her friend.

Dev opens his eyes on hearing Mahi's name. He sternly looks at Ekta as he tightens his jaws and says,' And you think I don't know that!'

'If you do, then, please care to share why did you do it,' says Ekta keeping her voice in control.

'I don't know,' says Dev looking more frustrated as he kept rubbing his temple.

'What triggered?' asks Ekta seeing Dev's frustrated look.

'What?'

'What triggered your outburst? I know you weren't drunk. What happened before you came in?' asks Ekta directing the question to Dev.

Dev's mind flashes back to the day, he saw Mahi smiling and something changing in him when he saw her with Kabir. Dev pulls the blazer he was wearing from that day. He takes out the red envelope from its side pocket and places it on the table.

Ekta gets up from the couch to take a closer look at the envelope. So does Rohit. She opens it and reads it. She moves her hand through her hair as she exhales out with annoyance.

She slams the card on the desk and says,' So you are telling me that this fucking load of crap is your rationale for pouring out your anger on Mahi.'

'I don't know,' says Dev feeling guilty every time Ekta mentions her name.

Ekta takes in another irritated breath and says,' What did you expect, Dev? No, tell me, what exactly were you expecting? Were you in some kind of a virtual world where you thought that after leaving you like that, she'll come back? And you'll get your happily ever after.'

She continues raising her voice a little,' It's been more than five months. I am amazed she even waited this long to get hitched to someone else.' She further says,' I don't get this. Why are you still torturing yourself for someone who didn't even love you.'

'So six years was nothing,' says Dev in a small voice.

'If those six years meant even one per cent to her, she wouldn't have left you like that. No matter what,' Ekta replies, pulling out Dev from his past.

Mahi's entry breaks the silence in the room. Dev gets up from his chair as he sees Mahi walking in. Ekta and Rohit turn around to see her.

'I heard you were out of your hiding. Since I wasn't sure you would come to the house, I took an effort to show myself here,' says Mahi as she walks in. Ekta and Rohit move to the side, quietly giving way to Mahi.

Before Dev could begin to say anything, Mahi pulls out a small, rectangular piece of paper from her denim's pocket. She places it on Dev's desk and says,' This is the cheque of the amount I owe you.'

Looks at the cheque on his desk in puzzlement and looks up at Mahi.

Mahi says,' It's an estimated rent of a room in a mansion for 6 months. Yes, I included the advance for this month. It just not only the rent but the utilities as well. Like electricity, food and other services. Don't worry. I consulted the expert before I came up with the amount. Anyways you'll find more than the estimate. Still, if you feel it less, don't hesitate to tell me. I can afford it. Beyond your imagination, my government job pays quite well. So expect the cheque every month from now on.'

Realising that Dev has hurt her self esteem badly, he says,' Can we talk about this at home or at least in private?'

'Why? Did you ask me to talk in private before you vent out on me? Oh, wait! You weren't talking then. Trust me. Even I am not here to talk. And I like to keep our odds even,' says Mahi, keeping her straight face.

'As you can see, I am here to clear out a few things. Since how accurately you showed me that they weren't. First. I already did,' says Mahi pointing a finger on the cheque.

'Second. I have asked my lawyer to draw up the contract. Stating our legal relationship to end on completion of 2 years from the date of our marriage. As decided mutually. Without any compensation to pay. You'll receive the documents by tomorrow,' continues Mahi keeping the professional appearance.

'Mahi..,' says Dev in an attempt to reason with Mahi. But Mahi interrupts him.

'You know what,' Mahi scoffs a little and continues,' You not showing up for two days actually gave me time to gather perspective on few things. Unlike you, I am making decisions after thinking it through and rationally. I was bloody, very clear from the start that this was supposed to be a practical and mutual partnership. On every step of it, I looked up to you for confirmation. On every fucking step I took into your life. You let me in. You permitted me to become close to your life, to your friends and even to your non-friends. So you have no right to blame me for this,' says Mahi leaning slightly in as she points her index finger at Dev, keeping a check on her anger at the same time.

'One more thing. I didn't marry you with an ulterior motive of finding a rich husband and a big mansion for a house. Don't live in an illusion that you were some kind of an eligible bachelor. And marrying you changed my life into something I dreamt of. No!

Absolutely not. Trust me when I say this. I had better options, even if I ever dreamt of it. But, you know what, I stopped dreaming of getting a life partner way before yours left you right before your wedding. So don't you dare tell me what kind of perspective is perfect for me. And yes, Saavi Maa is the only reason I got married to you. But, I really don't have the time and energy to waste to explain that reason to you. And I am fucking not obligated to,' says Mahi between her teeth at the last sentence.

Mahi leans back, standing straight, becoming calm and composed again. She continues to say,' I am done here.' With this, she takes the same door to exit as she did to come in.

Dev watches her leave the room. He sits down on his chair with a slight jerk. And looks thoughtfully at the cheque on the table.

'I know what you are thinking,' says Dev breaking the silence. He says this without looking at Rohit or Ekta.

'What?' asks Ekta putting on the straight face.

'That I deserve this,' replies Dev without removing his gaze from the cheque.

'I don't disagree,' says Ekta.

'Neither do I,' agrees Dev.

CHAPTER 7 HER CONFUSED FEELINGS

'I am not here to apologise on his behalf. No. You won't be getting that from me. I can assure you,' said Ekta. She came to meet Mahi when Dev wasn't home.

After Mahi confronted Dev in his office, she didn't see Dev for the next couple of days. She made sure that she doesn't have to face him either. That is why she is used to leaving early and come home early. And the rest of the day, she was spending in the confines of her room or back gardens.

However, Ekta got to her while she tried to avoid her. She didn't have any personal grudge against Ekta. But, the fact that she is part of Dev's life, Mahi tried her best to keep her distance.

Mahi couldn't avoid her because Ekta being Ekta was the best thing about her. Despite that she was upset with her friend, Mahi adored the way Ekta came to meet her. Mahi can never deny how much she liked being friends with her.

'I don't even want to hear any apologies from you. If I deserve an apology. Then you are definitely not the person from whom I should be getting the one,' replies Mahi standing in the middle of the living room.

'You do deserve an apology,' says Ekta. She continues,' Can we still hang out like we used to? I got used to our girl time,' making a small innocent insisting face.

Mahi softens a little and replies,' I am not sure. I am mean I might be biting on my own integrity.'

'No. You won't be,' replies Ekta.

'C'mon! You know it too. We wouldn't have met if I wasn't married to your friend,' replies Mahi.

'Not true. What if you wouldn't have married Dev and I had still come to the wedding. We still would have met. We still would have clicked as we did right here,' says Ekta. She sees a faint smile on Mahi's face and an opening to her. She continues,' Too cheesy, huh?'

Mahi chuckles softly, nodding and replies,' I give up. Can't win this.'

'Good. Because I can't stand any longer and can't come up with great comebacks. C'mon, I am full time. Show some mercy,' says Ekta teasingly as she takes the seat on the chair next to her.

'I am sorry. Please. What you wanna have?' asks Mahi feeling guilty again for keeping her standing.

Both the ladies settled with their choice of beverages in hand in the living room. Talking about something or the other.

'I have a confession to make,' says Ekta taking a small sip from her cup of tea. She says,' I have not come here to apologise on behalf of Dev. But, I was hoping we could talk about it. Particularly about you and Dev.'

Mahi sighs softly and says,' What is there to talk about?'

'A lot,' replies Ekta instantly.

'Like what?' asks Mahi looking intently at Ekta.

'Like what could be the reason he acted out that way?' says Ekta trying to read Mahi from her face.

'I hope you are possibly not trying to justify what he did,' says Mahi expecting a response from Ekta.

'Absolutely not. There is no justification for how Dev behaved. You wouldn't believe this. But, right before you came to his office, I was ready to beat him up. Literally.' replies Ekta assuring her stand on this. Mahi chuckles at her response and replies,' I believe you. Literally.'

Ekta smiles back in response and says,' Though, I am serious. Aren't you a little bit curious about the reason? There is clearly a difference between a justification and a cause.'

'Is there? I don't know anymore when it comes to him,' says Mahi thoughtfully. Even she worked up her mind for days thinking about it. What could have made Dev act like that? Usually, Mahi is always a rational person when it comes to relations. But, in this case, she found herself more affected by Dev's words than anyone else. Mahi stopped getting affected by anyone's rudeness a long time ago. She had closed herself up since the last time she had to give up almost everything in her life, including her life. She had come a long way. It was surprising for her how Dev's words pierced her through. What Dev said was definitely not the worst thing she has to hear in her whole life. Especially in her line of work. Working under uneducated ministers is where Mahi has listened to something worst than what Dev has said. But, somehow, it affected her when it came from Dev. Since that day, she has been questioning herself. Why did it hurt that bad? This even made her go through and analyse the progression of her relation with Dev, looking for answers where she went wrong.

Seeing Mahi lost in her thoughts, Ekta gave her the needed time to search through her heart whether Dev could ever do what he did to her in his right state of mind.

'It might seem to you that I am being biased because he is my friend. But, believe me. This was the first time for me as well to see him like that,' says Ekta after some time.

'I could tell. The way you shouted at him that night,' says Mahi thinking back at the moment. She clearly noticed the tinge of shock in Ekta's voice when she called out his name loud enough to stop Dev in his tracks.

'You know I pressured him to tell me at least what went wrong. Or what triggered him,' says Ekta smiling wryly.

'What did he say?' asks Mahi becoming curious.

Ekta notices the intent in Mahi's voice. She replies,' At first he said he doesn't know but, then he gave me some stupid reason. It was totally unrelated to you.'

'What was that stupid reason?' asks Mahi watching Ekta inquisitively for an answer.

'Yashika sent him her wedding card. Through a guest at the party.'

'Oh!' says Mahi feeling a little disappointed at Ekta's reply. She realises Ekta has been observing her reaction. She changes her expression to indifference and says,' Indeed a stupid reason,' with a scoff.

'Told you so,' replies Ekta smiling inwardly at Mahi's reaction. Ekta saw the disappointment on Mahi's face. Ekta continues,' Anyways, I believe he is lying to himself as well.'

'You think this was not the actual reason? What did you mean when you said it was totally unrelated to me?' asks Mahi becoming confused at Ekta's words.

'Just something crossed my mind. I mean, I expected Dev to give me something related to you since that asshole rained on you. You were not the only one there. Remember?' says Ekta intending to ignite a curiosity in Mahi. Indirectly putting her on the path of inquiring more about Dev's real feelings about her. Ekta knew Dev was lying to them when she asked him about that night. Because she couldn't forget the series of events from that night. He was clearly content whenever Mahi was around. She noticed the genuine concern in her friend's eyes whenever he couldn't find Mahi in his line of sight. And this was the case in every formal or informal party they attended so far. Ekta's mind wanders back to that night in the kitchen right before Dev lost all control. She saw his expression going from all controlled to lose jealous beast in a moment. Ekta was well aware of Dev's dislike of Kabir's proximity with Mahi. She just didn't expect Dev to lie to her regarding the same.

Ekta made a valid point. Her words made Mahi rethink the whole incident with a new set of eyes.

Seeing Mahi's confused and yet thoughtful expression, Ekta decided to leave her with her thoughts alone.

'Oh, I gotta go. I just remembered Rohit told me to receive a package for him. I have to be home,' says Ekta getting up and breaking Mahi's train of thoughts.

'Huh? Alright. Let me walk you to your car,' replies Mahi, gathering herself.

As they start walking to the door, they suddenly halt. Both ladies hear some liquid splashing on the floor. They instinctively look down together.

'My water just broke,' says Ekta keeping her eyes wide looking at Mahi.

'What?'

'I am having the baby,' says Ekta, smiling, looking happy and tensed at the same time. She laughs awkwardly at Mahi.

'OK! OK! Alright! OH MY GOD! You are having the baby. Like right now. Oh God,' Mahi gulps sharply and becomes aware suddenly.

She becomes confused because she doesn't know what to do in such a situation. She frantically continues as she freaks out,' Breathe! You need to breathe. I'll take you to the hospital. That's where I am supposed to take you, right? Of course. Why am I even asking you this? I'll drive you. I need to get my keys. What else do I need to take? A go-bag!! What all goes in a go-bag? Wait. I'll manage it. Don't worry. Just relax! Breathe! I got you.'

Ekta looks at Mahi, getting panicked and losing almost her mind. She calmly says before she sees Mahi literally lose her mind,' Mahi. It's alright! Breathe! You need to relax. There is a go-bag in my car. We'll get that. Now call Rohit. And then we'll leave. I have my car here. You need to drive. Can you?' She asks Mahi getting a little worried.

'Yes. I can. Right, call Rohit. I'll do that,' says Mahi as she takes out the phone from her jeans pocket and dials the number. As she waits for the call to connect, she makes Ekta sit on the settee nearby. She keeps holding her hand.

'It's unreachable,' says Mahi looking at Ekta in a tense voice.

'It's alright. Try Dev. They are together,' says Ekta feeling the first contraction.

Mahi looks at Ekta, grimacing with pain. She immediately calls up Dev. The call rings twice before Dev picks up.

'Hello. Mahi?' says Dev, not expecting the call from her.

'Is Rohit next to you?' asks Mahi as soon as she hears Dev's voice on the call.

'Yes. Rohit is here,' Dev was confused at her query.

'Ekta just broke her water. She is going into labour. I am taking her to the hospital. Reach as soon as possible,' says Mahi without a breath.

'What? Alright! Don't worry, we'll be there ASAP. We are out of town, so it will take an hour or two to get back. Will you be fine to drive her?' asks Dev, getting concerned for both of them.

'Yes. I can. Don't worry. I'll take care of Ekta till Rohit arrives,' replies Mahi. She takes a brief pause and continues more softly and calmly,' Don't rush. Drive safe.'

'You too,' says Dev, smiles at her reply before he hangs up and tells his friend the news.

Mahi takes Ekta to the hospital. Both tell each other to calm down throughout the way. As soon as they reach, Ekta is taken to the maternity ward. Mahi stays back to complete the formality and paperwork of admitting Ekta. Mahi, after some time, joins Ekta in her room. As her contractions become a little more intense, Mahi becomes more concerned until the doctor tells her that it is normal. Mahi relaxes a little, except another contraction takes away her relaxation.

After an hour and a half later, Mahi receives Dev's call asking her the room number and the floor. Dev and Rohit enter the room. Rohit runs to be on the side of his wife's bed, holding her hand. Mahi and Dev quietly see the couple holding onto each other with the expression of concern and excitement together. Soon doctor comes and takes Ekta to the delivery room along with Rohit on her side.

Mahi and Dev wait outside the delivery room. Mahi sees Dev pacing around in the corridor worriedly. She picks up the water bottle next to her and walks up to Dev. She goes and stands, blocking Dev's pacing path. He halts after seeing Mahi in front of him. She offers him the water bottle without saying a word.

Dev takes the water bottle from her and says,' Thanks.' He continues stopping Mahi to turn around and leave,' Thank you. Not just for water. For everything. I mean, Ekta.' Dev says this, hesitating a little.

'You are welcome. For the water. Rest. No need to,' says Mahi pulling up a straight face.

'I know. After everything, you made it clear that you'll have nothing to do with me. Or the people in my life. I was still able to drag you back in here. I am sorry,' says Dev feeling guilty though more glad to see her here.

Mahi looks away for a second and says,' It is true that I met Ekta because of you. But, don't live in any kind of an illusion that I am friends with her because of you.'

Dev nods simply and smiles inwardly. He becomes pleased after listening to Mahi, thinking she is not ready to cut all her ties to him.

Mahi goes back to the bench to sit where she was sitting earlier. She sees Dev when he wasn't looking in her way. She notices how much his looks have changed in these past few days, especially after that night. It looked like he has not stopped beating himself up for what he did or said that night. His eyes looked more exhausted than usual. He has also grown a stubble around his jaws. He seemed rough yet, his best looks escape through his ruggedness. His tall stature doesn't fail to attract the attention around him. It never has. Mahi notices that even standing in the maternity ward, not in the best of his looks, the women here don't fail to steal a look at him. Be it the pregnant ladies or the female staff of the hospital. They all would find themselves ogling him involuntarily. With all that attention towards him, what pulls Mahi towards him is that he is unaware of it. He looks so lost in his own thoughts that he doesn't even reciprocate any of the looks the young nurses in the ward are throwing at him. A smile slips through Mahi's lips as she sees Dev's innocent look and yet on a very handsome face.

WHAT THE HELL!! Mahi thinks to herself as soon as she realises how closely she had been watching Dev's intricate details on his face. That too, with a smile. She mentally yanks herself out of the daze. She suddenly feels the heat releasing from her body. She feels her hand sweaty due to the heat. She instantly wipes them at the side of her jeans and runs her hand through her neck. She keeps that hand on the neck and another clutching the bench beneath her. Mahi becomes shockingly aware of the way she has been eying Dev in the past few minutes. She closes her eyes in embarrassment.

Meanwhile, Dev paces around the hall as he waits for any news of Ekta and the baby. As he does that, he kept stealing glances at Mahi's way every minute or so. He feels her eyes on him. He couldn't stop but become curious about her looks. He sees that she kept looking at him thoughtfully. He tried to keep his thoughts to Ekta and the baby. But, with each second, her eyes on him made him more conscious of himself. At one point, he almost convinced himself that he saw her smiling while she was looking at him. But, he jolts himself mentally not to dream with open eyes. After what he did to her, how can he even imagine something like that? He thinks to himself. He even doesn't deserve any kind of attention, let alone a smile from her. Yet she is here. Her presence here is enough for him. He is grateful for her in his life and always will be, he thinks to himself.

After a couple of hours of waiting, Rohit comes out in a hospital coverall with a big grin on his mouth.

'It's a boy,' says Rohit with a grin and tears at the end of it.

Dev hugs him in response and asks about Ekta. To Dev's query, Rohit tells him that both are healthy. They soon will be transferred to the room. Mahi congrats Rohit hugging him. Rohit thanks Mahi for taking Ekta to the hospital, for being with her when he wasn't there.

Soon Ekta settles in the hospital bed with the baby in her arms. Rohit sits next to her. Dev stands on the end of the bed with a smile pasted on his mouth as he witnesses his best friends' happiest moment. Mahi sees Ekta's exhausted yet content face while she watches the tiny human in her arms. Mahi sniffles softly in an attempt to control her emotions and not to gather any attention towards her. However, Dev turns her head at the sound of her soft sniff. When it comes to Mahi, Dev realises how little sound or movement she makes, always catches his attention. Dev lets out a smile as he watches Mahi seeing his friends and the baby with such adoring eyes along with little water forming at the corner of her eyes.

Ekta looks up to Dev and notices him looking lovingly at Mahi. She elbows Rohit lightly and raises her eyebrows towards Dev. Rohit chuckles as he shakes his head amusingly.

Ekta looks at Mahi and says,' Wanna hold me Mahi Aunty?' in a cute baby voice.

'Can I? You sure?' asks Mahi making a fist of both her hands in front of her mouth in excitement.

Ekta nods in approval. Mahi walks up and softly takes the baby in her hands. As baby coos, Mahi opens her mouth unconsciously and looks awed at the baby.

Ekta laughs softly at her reaction and looks at Dev, grinning at Mahi's response. Dev looks at Ekta, who raises her eyebrows at him. Dev simply chuckles at his friend's teasing and moves his gaze back to Mahi and the baby.

'Mahi. Thank you so much for everything today. If it wasn't for you, I don't know what would I have done,' says Ekta looking up at Mahi.

'Please. Don't remind me how freaked out I was today. You were way better than me. And you did good,' replies Mahi glancing at the baby.

'So If I ask something from you, you wouldn't say no to me. Right?' asks Ekta looking intently at her.

'Anything! As long he is in my hands,' says smiling cutely at the baby.

Ekta and everyone else chuckles at her response. Ekta says,' Will you be our son's godmother?' as she glances at Rohit for confirmation. Rohit simply nods in agreement smiling.

Ekta looks at Mahi, who loses the smile and replace it with a surprised look.

Chapter 8 Forgiveness or Relief from the Pain

'Will you be our son's godmother?' asks Ekta to Mahi. Ekta looks at Mahi who looks back at her with a surprised look. 'Please don't say no. I am not asking you this because you are married to Dev. Or this jerk is the Godfather to my son,' says Ekta pointing towards Dev. She continues,' You know it better. I never had a girlfriend. You are the first girlfriend I want to keep for life. And after today, I wouldn't trust our son's life with anyone but you. Of course, other than him,' glancing at Dev on the last sentence.

Mahi becomes overwhelmed at Ekta's insistence and looks at the baby to say,' You mom just used you by placing you in my hands.'

'Was I successful?' asks Ekta softly.

Mahi looks at her and narrows her eyes and nods as she smiles at her.

Ekta breaks into a loud cheer. Everyone laughs at her reaction.

Mahi and Dev stand outside the hospital entrance after they were thrown out by their friends. So that the new parents can have some privacy. Both stood there quietly as they waited for Shankar to get Dev his car.

The car arrives as Shankar gets down to give the keys to Dev. Dev asks Mahi for Ekta's car keys. She fishes them from her jeans pocket and hands him the keys. Dev passes the same to Shankar telling him to take Ekta's car to pick Rohit's mother from the airport and later in the evening Ekta's mother too. He instructs him to stay near the hospital as whenever Rohit needs him for anything else.

After giving Shankar all the necessary instructions, he moves to the driver's side door. He sees Mahi not moving towards the passenger side door.

'Mahi! Aren't you gonna sit?' asks Dev softly.

'No. I am gonna take the cab,' replies Mahi keeping a straight face.

'Don't be silly. I am not going to eat you,' says Dev frowning at her response of taking the cab.

Mahi glares back at his snapping.

'Sorry,' says Dev seeing her pissed off.

'Are you going home?' asks Mahi after looking around in an attempt to look for a valid excuse. So that she doesn't have to sit next to Dev.

'Yes'

'I am not. I have to be back at the office,' Mahi says hoping that she can find an excuse. To end the discussion.

'It's Sunday,' says Dev immediately realising Mahi is just looking for any excuse not to be alone with him.

Mahi closes her eyes in failure. Seeing her struggle so much to avoid him, Dev loses all hope and says,' Please. I'll drop you, office or home. I promise I won't say anything to you. Not a word.' He continues after a small pause,' I won't even breathe if you want.'

Mahi looks at him on his last sentence. What shook her from the inside was that reading from his eyes, he meant it. Without further torturing him, she opens the passenger side door and sits in. Dev lets out a deep sigh after Mahi sits in the car. He closes his eyes in exhaustion and puts his hand on them as he moves it through his hair before he opens the door and sits in.

As promised, Dev didn't say a word on their whole way. Mahi could not shake herself off from his last sentence. It struck her hard. She couldn't put the finger on what bothered her more. Dev's strained face from her tantrums or his willingness to comply with anything for her comfort. As far as not breathing. Mahi unconsciously sank in her seat as she looks out of the car, but flashing only Dev's face with his most sincere eyes. They were unfeigned enough to render Mahi questioned her anger towards him. Is it worth his life? She thinks to herself sending a chill down her spine. She suddenly becomes concerned for Dev. She feels an urge to look at him. To steal a glance at him, she looks at the clock on the dashboard. He glances at her as she turns her head back towards the window.

Dev senses her anxiousness. He was sure something was bothering her. Then it suddenly struck him that it's him. His remorse sinks him deep. Since that night Dev wishes every day that he could somehow take those words back or turn back time to take that hurt from her. Nothing ever bothered him this much but her being hurt. In these past days, the guilt of hurting her has eaten him more than anything. Maybe more than the hurt Yashika has caused him. Mahi has become his centre more than Yashika ever was for him. For him, not a single day goes by that doesn't involve a fragment of her in his thoughts.

After reaching home, both quietly resign to their respective rooms. With their own bothering thoughts, both just lie down on their beds with wide-open eyes. Thinking about each other, eventually, both drift into sleep.

Mahi wakes up after an hour and sees the setting sun. She freshens up and picks up some files from the table as she finds her way to back gardens. Not to lose herself in thinking about Dev anymore, she attempts to focus on her work. She seemed almost successful at doing so but realises Dev's presence behind her. She becomes still keeping her eyes on the opened file in her laps.

Dev bends down and places the small piece of paper on the table in front of Mahi as he says,' I can't accept this.'

Mahi raises her eyes to look at the cheque she wrote to Dev in front of her.

Dev doesn't wait for her to respond as he says,' I am aware that I have done something unspeakable and unforgivable. And every day I find myself looking for ways to apologise to you. Believe me.' He takes a pause and continues,' I am sorry but, I just can't accept this from you.'

Mahi doesn't move or turn her head on his words. But, she stays still. She intently listens to each of his words. She listens to his voice, drained out of energy. She feels his sincerity in his voice and in his words, even without looking directly at him.

'I cannot justify what I did...what I said. It should never be. I won't be giving you any reason for it because it won't be fair to you. So I am okay as long as you want to hate me but, know this. I didn't mean a single word. I regret it every day and I always will,' says Dev keeping his pain inside. Not getting any response from Mahi, Dev turns away to go.

Mahi hears him moving away and says,' You know that I don't need that cheque to give that amount to you.'

Dev turns back to her and sees her not moving from her place. She was speaking to him but without facing him. He says,' you don't know my bank account details.'

'I have the means.'

'I'll ask my accountant to return the amount back to you,' replies Dev.

'It doesn't work that way. You don't have my account details,' say Mahi looking straight ahead.

'And you think I don't have means to find that out,' replies Dev.

Mahi inhales sharply and straightens up. She closes the file in her hand and puts it on the table. She gets up picking up the cheque and walks up to Dev.

'You have to accept this,' says Mahi softly standing inches away from Dev.

'I can't. I...I just..,' Dev struggles to come up with words as he looks directly to Mahi. He thinks it was easy when she wasn't facing him like this.

Mahi sees him struggling and stops him by saying,' Listen to me. This cheque...is the only way I can keep my self-respect.'

She swallows her emotions and says,' You didn't just hurt me with your words but hurt my self-respect. And for a very long time, this is the only thing I have been living for.'

'I am terribly sorry. I didn't mean to. And I regret it from the moment those came out of my mouth,' says Dev with a little break in his voice.

'I know. I know,' says Mahi softly seeing him on the verge of breaking. She continues,' But, they are still there. You can't take them back.'

'I wish I could,' says Dev closing his eyes for a second.

'I know,' says Mahi almost in a whisper as she attempts to push back her emotions.

Dev sees her struggling with her emotions as she tries to keep them in check. It hurts him to see Mahi like that. He couldn't understand something when he sees Mahi right now. She is hurt by his words. But, she is still trying here to understand him. He couldn't fathom the kind of emotions Mahi keeps within her that she was still standing here in front of him, talking to him as politely as she could.

Mahi takes few seconds to gather herself and say,' Let's do this. If you accept this cheque, I'll take that as your apology.'

'You can't be serious,' says Dev little astonished at her suggestion.

'I am. This way, you get to apologise to me. And I get to keep my self-esteem,' replies Mahi with a beat of energy in her voice.

'And you will accept my apology?' asks Dev becoming little hopeful.

Mahi simply nods to his question as she says softly,' I will.'

'Why?' asks Dev involuntarily as he becomes curious behind the reason for Mahi to forgive him this easily.

Mahi sees the question in Dev's eyes. She couldn't come with an answer to Dev's question without disclosing her confused feelings. So she resorts to her diplomatic tactics.

'I am giving you a solution. You can't be choosy,' replies Mahi keeping a straight face.

'Yes. I get it,' replies Dev realising he cannot push Mahi to answer his curiosity without losing his chance to get her forgiveness. In anticipation, he continues,' So that means, we can go back to being friends again?'

Mahi couldn't help but notice a hint of hope in Dev's eyes. She has to be honest with him at this moment.

'No,' says Mahi crushing Dev's hope. She continues,' See. After what happened, it is already difficult for me to comprehend all of this. You weren't wrong when you said that I have forgotten the very reason why we got married in the first place. I did. We did. And I'll be stupid to repeat my mistake.'

'You didn't do anything wrong. I did,' says Dev realising how his one mistake has led Mahi to believe that she committed some grave mistake being friends with him.

'We both did. Let's accept that and move forward,' says Mahi softening her eyes on Dev. She continues,' I can't really say that we'll be friends like before. I don't know if we'll ever be. But, one thing I can say is that it will take some time for me to be normal again.'

Dev simply nods understanding Mahi's dilemma of forgiving him for hurting her self respect and still living with him in the same house. She had already given up a lot for Dev. Even her reason for doing so is something else. Dev knew he is in no position to ask Mahi for more.

A week goes by after Mahi and Dev reconciled cordially. They became cordial in each other's presence. No one was avoiding or ignoring the other. However, they kept the needed distance from each other to ensure they don't cross over into the friend zone.

It is Sunday. Dev and Rohit were sitting in front lawns. They were discussing the upcoming project and few legal variables in the project. Suddenly they hear a commotion at the main gate. After a few seconds, two men enter the premises dragging the watchman with them. They had roughed up the watchman. One who was holding the watchman from his collar had a small knife in his other hand. Another man with a medium built and rather more gruesome looks were walking in front of them. They looked more like hired goons. Dev and Rohit get up in shock as they see what was happening. Dev and Rohit attempt to move towards them to get Bahadur from their grip. However, the man in front takes out a Glock from behind and points at Rohit and Dev stopping them in their tracks.

'Dekh Bhai, apne ko lafda nahi chahiye. Bahut shaanti aur araam se samjhane aaya hu. Samajha. Highway wali Zameen pe kaam nahi chalega (Listen brother, I don't want any conflict. I have come here to make you understand very calmly. No work would be done on Highway property); says the man waving the gun in front of Dev.

'Kyun? Kiske kehne pe? (Why? On whose command?)' asks Dev keeping his anger in check by tightening his jaws.

'Abhi kaha na lafda nahi chahiye. Kaiko pange le raha hai baap (I just said. I don't want any conflict. Why are you messing around?)' replies the same man, getting little irritated.

Mahi was sitting in the living room when she hears the disturbance outside and walks out to see what is causing it. She witnesses the scenario outside and walks towards them.

'Kya ho raha hai yahan? (What's going on here?)' asks Mahi stepping on the lawns.

Dev turns his head towards the voice and becomes worried instantly as he loudly says, Mahi, get back inside.'

Mahi ignores Dev's direct order and keeps walking. The man also turns his head towards Mahi and says, Nahi nahi. Aane do madam ko. Aaiye Madam (No no. Let the madam come. Please join us madam); says waving the gun to tell Mahi to move towards Dev.

As Mahi reaches them, Dev holds her hand and lightly pushes her behind himself. He does that to shield Mahi away from harm's way. Mahi hides completely behind Dev's shoulder.

The goon, standing in front finds it amusing, seeing Dev protectively shielding Mahi. He says, Jaan se jyada pyaari lagti hai Missus. Isliye aakhri baar bata raha hu. Highway wali Zameen pe se boriya bistar baandh lo apna (Seems like she is important more than life. That's why I am telling you for the last time. Pack up your bags from the Highway Property).'

Mahi looks up to Dev facing his back as he keeps a protective hand around her, pulling her closer. Then she looks at the goon and sighs heavily, as she could not take this nonsense anymore. She says,' Safety on hai (Safety is on).'

Dev turns his head towards Mahi in confusion. So does Rohit. The man with the gun becomes puzzled and asks,' Kya? (What?)'

Mahi softly puts her hand on Dev's arms and whispers,' Trust me. Don't interfere.' She comes out of Dev's protective shield in front of the man with a gun. She stands centimetres away from the barrel. Dev becomes overly worried and says,' Mahi,' reaching for her hand.

She nods at him assuring she is okay and sending a silent signal to let her handle this.

'Madam sunlo apne Pati ki. Khilona nahi hai yeh (Madam, listen to your husband. It's not a toy),' says the man waving the Glock in the face of Mahi.

'Malum hai. Yahi batane ki koshish kar rahi hu. Safety on hai (I know. That's what I am trying to tell you. Safety is on),' says Mahi standing fearlessly in front of the gun.

'Kya? Kya safety. Kya bole...(What! What safety? What you keep saying....),' says the man in utter confusion. Before he could complete his sentence, he feels his hand twist with sharp pain and in next second an excruciating pain in his groin. He falls down on the ground holding his legs near to his chest to control the unbearable pain. As he opens his eyes to see what happened, he sees Mahi standing couple of feet away holding the same gun he had earlier.

CHAPTER 9 NEW REVELATION

The man standing behind holding Bahadur with a knife doesn't believe what happened. Before he could grasp the scene before him, Mahi asks him to leave the watchman and take out all of his knives or any other weapon he might be carrying on the ground. Then she tells Bahadur to pick all of that to put it away from them.

Man on the ground is still groaning loudly in pain. Dev and Rohit were in absolute shock as they saw Mahi swiftly taking the situation in her hands. It looked like they were witnessing some scene out of a movie.

Mahi kicks the man on the ground lightly and says,' Arre O, bahut ho gaya natak. Chal khada ho (Hey! Enough with your drama. Get up now),' waving the gun with one hand and putting another in her trouser's pocket.

The man stands up with much difficulty next to his sidekick.

'Haan toh Main kuch keh rahi thi. Safety (Yes. So I was saying something. Safety),' says Mahi. She continues,' Ise kehte hai safety (This is known as safety),' showing them a small switch on the Glock. 'Agar ye ON hai toh ye chalti nahi hai (If it's ON, then it doesn't work).' She immediately takes out her other hand and loads the gun sliding the top of the barrel back and forth and pulls the trigger pointing in their faces.

A small shriek comes out of their mouth. A second later, the goons open their eyes realising no sound of a gunshot came out as she pulled the trigger.

'Aur agar iss tarah ise OFF karde toh (And if it is turned OFF like this),' continues Mahi, giving the demonstration on how it works. She clicks the small switch on the side of the gun and pulls the trigger again. This time the sound thundered the surrounding as she had the gun pointed on the ground next to the goons.

Everyone, present there jumps at the loud sound of the gun shooting, except Mahi. Dev sees Mahi as calm as still water. It seemed another routine for her.

'Aaya samajh? (Got it?)' asks Mahi to the terrified goons in front of her. She says,' Very good.' She makes them stand on their knees with their hands up in the air. Both of them do instantly in horror what Mahi instructs.

Two constables run in after hearing the gunshot. They stand in attention and salute Mahi immediately.

'Lagta hai Sarkar ne tum logo ko Panwaadi ko Suraksha dene ke liye mere Ghar ke bahar tenaat kiya hai (Looks like the government has stationed you outside my house to provide security to the betel shop),' says Mahi sarcastically at the constables. She controls her anger on their absence. Both constables apologise feeling terrified from Mahi as they standstill.

'Ab kya meri shakal dekhte dekhte khud Thaane phone lag jaega? (Now would just looking at my face, police station would be informed)' asks Mahi in a scolding tone, keeping her anger in check. One of the constables immediately takes out the walkie and speaks into it while walking towards the gate.

Mahi turns her head towards Dev and Rohit and asks them if they are okay. Both nods together still grasping the reality in front of them. Even though the situation was under Mahi's control, they couldn't bring themselves to sit.

Mahi sits on the armrest of the chair, dangling the gun in one hand between her legs. She looks at the goons in front of her and very casually asks,' Haan bhai, Baap ka naam bata (Yes. Tell me your father's name).'

The guy still grimacing in pain says,' Banwari Lal' And the other guys follow him saying,' Suresh Kumar.'

Mahi puts her hand on her forehead, sighing in dismissal. She says with a tinge of irritation,' Jo baap tum logo ko paida karke apna sar peet raha hoga uska naam nahi pucha. Jo tum jaise dharti ke bhoj ko yaha paal raha hai uska naam pucha hai (The one who would be beating his head on the wall after giving you birth, I didn't ask his name. The one who is feeding you bloody burdens on earth, I asked his name).'

Both goons exchange looks and say together,' Nahi aisa toh koi nahi hai (No, there is no one like that).' Mahi knew that they coordinated their answers. She gets up to intimidate them a little. Both shudders and speaks up,' Hiralal.'

'Hiralal Chowari?' asks Mahi. Then both nod in unison. She closes her eyes and scoffs loudly. She keeps the smile on her face and says,' Phone laga. Bula yaha. Kehna Mata ji ne yaad kiya hai (Call him. Call him here. Tell him that the respected mother is asking for him).'

They do as she instructs. Waiting a few more minutes, a police Jeep enters the premises. An officer with four constables gets down and runs towards Mahi. The police officer stops a few feet away from Mahi, along with constables behind him as they salute her together. Mahi nods her head slightly in acknowledgement and says,' Patil do minute ruko, inn logo ke baap ko bulaya hai haajri dene (Patil, wait for 2 minutes. I have called their father to give attendence).'

'Ji Ma'am,' replies the man in uniform.

Within a minute, a middle-aged, healthy man enters the premises. He walks pacing fast, as he recognises Mahi from the gate. As soon as he arrives, he starts beating up the kneeled goons with all his might, cursing them simultaneously. Mahi silently watches the drama in front of her. When man exhausts himself by superficially beating his own men, he gestures his hand in half salute, greeting Mahi.

'Madam naye launde hai. Samajh nahi hai inko kahan muh maarna chahiye kahan nahi (Madam, they are new boys. They don't have the understanding where they should be wandering),' says the man panting.

'Kitna time hua Yerawada se nikle? (How long has it been since you got released from Yerawada?' asks Mahi to Hiralal.

'Aapki meharbaani se paanch mahine pehle (With your mercy, five months ago),' replies man smiling.

'Andar gaya bhi toh meri meharbaani se tha (You went in there with my mercy only),' says Mahi smirking at him.

'Aap chahte toh lamba jaa sakta tha. Par aapne bheja sirf 3 mahine ke liye. Bas aise hi aapka aashirwaad bana rahe (If you wanted, I could have gone for long. I just want your blessings keep bestowing upon me),' replies Hiralal.

'Hmm... Nirbhar karta hai tere agle jawaab pe. Kiske kehne pe bheja tha inhe? (Hmmm...depends on your next answer. Who ordered you to send them?)' asks Mahi seated on the armrest of the chair.

'Bataya na madam. Bachhe hai. Galti ho gayi (I told you Madam. They are kids. They made the mistake); replies the man becoming little hesitant.

Mahi gets up as she walks up to Hiralal. She stands in front of him and says,' Tere ye bacche, mere Ghar mein ghus kar, mere Husband ko bandook dikha ke kisi highway wali Zameen ko leke dhamkane aaye the. Galti se toh nahi aaye the yahan. Toh ab Tu khud batega ya tere lambe intezaam ki tyaari karu? (Your kids, entered in my house. They pointed the gun in my husband's face and threatened him for some Highway land. They didn't come here by mistake. Now, will you tell me or should I prepare for your longer arrangement?)'

Dev and Rohit silently watch how Mahi works up the scene.

Hiralal weighs his options before answering Mahi,' Sunrise Hotel wale. Shreeram Rawal.'

Mahi turns back her head towards Dev and Rohit,' Just answer in yes or no. Do you know anyone by that name?'

Both nods in reply to Mahi's question.

Mahi gets back to Hiralal. She says,' Tere liye naya kaam. Woh Husband hai mere. Devrath Jamwal (A new work for you. That's my hsuband, Devrath Jamwal); pointing her head towards Dev. She continues,' Aage se ab koi bhi kaam inke khilaaf tere paas aata hai ya tumare dhandhe mein aur koi ye kaam leta hai. Sabse pehle mujhe malum chalna chahiye. Aur tere aadmi ye dhyaan rakhenge ke inhe kuch na ho (From now on, if you receive any job against him or anyone else in this business of yours take up the job against him. I want to be the first to know. And your men will keep in mind that nothing should happen to him).'

'Madam, naam kharab ho jaega mera market mein. Aapko apne pet pe laat maar ke naam bhi bata diya. Nipat lo Aap. Mereko nahi padna aapki family ke lafde mein (Madam, my name will be ruined in the market. I just told you the name by kicking on my stomach. Manage yourself. I don't want to get involve in your family matter),' says Hiralal tensing up on Mahi's suggestion.

Mahi backs up and takes small strides back and forth in front of the man. She speaks a little loudly,' Patil. Maine kuch aisi baat kari kya jo samajh na aaye? (Patil. Did I just say something which was not understandable?)'

'Nahi Ma'am. Bazaar kaand ke baad toh aisa kabhi mumkin hi nahi ho sakta. Aap jo na kaho woh baat bhi samajh aa jati hai (No, Ma'am. After the Bazaar incident, it's impossible. What you don't say, even that is understandable),' replies the officer standing as he smirks a little while glancing at Hiralal.

Hiralal and his men's faces become terrified at the mention of the word ' Bazaar'. Dev and Rohit clearly notice the tension among them.

'Kitne time hua Bazaar ko? (How long has it been since Bazaar?)' asks Mahi taking her seat on the armrest again as she renders terror in them.

'Yahi kuch 10 mahina ya ek saal (Some 10 months or a year),' replies Patil participating in Mahi's play.

'Kaafi time ho gaya. Bhool gaye honge log. Naya tareeka dhoond-na padega samajhane ke liye (It's been long. People might have forgotten it. New method have to be searched to make them understand),' says Mahi slowly while looking at Hiralal and his men.

'Koi dhikat nahi Madam. Aap jaisa bologe waisa ho jaega (No issues Madam. It will be done as you say),' says Hiralal immediately foreseeing the consequences if he stays adamant any longer.

'Badiya! Chalo sabha sameto. Inn logo ko daalo ek raat ke liye andar (Great! Now wrap this assembly up. Put them behind bars for a night),' says Mahi to Patil pointing towards the kneeled men.

Hiralal looks at her confusingly. To which she replies,' Meri bhi reputation hai yaar. Ghar mein khada hai mere. Pati ko bandook dikhaya. Ek raat ke liye toh jaega (Even I have a reputation. Standing in my house. Pointed gun to my husband. They'll have to go in for a night).'

Hiralal nods understanding, as he turns to leave. Mahi stops him. She hands him the gun as she dissembles it in multiple pieces effortlessly. Hiralal gathers them and exits the premises. Constables handcuff the men and take them to the jeep.

Mahi stops Patil for a second and waits until Hiralal leaves and his men are out of hearing range. She picks up the shell casing from the ground. As she hands it to Patil, she says,' Yeh military-grade Glock ki shell casing hai. India mein sirf Special armed forces ke paas hoti hai (This a military-grade Glock's shell casing. Only special armed forces in India have these). Call the ordinance department and find out whether there is any discrepancy in their inventory. If yes, then find out how Hiralal has managed to get his hands on it. I'll let the ACP know about this.'

'Yes, Ma'am,' replies the officer.

'Also assign two constables to my husband and two on Rohit's family for 24×7 security,' says Mahi.

'No. I don't need that,' says Dev from behind.

Mahi ignores him and tells the officer,' Do as I say. You may leave now.'

The officer takes a step back to salute Mahi and leaves the premises in the jeep.

Mahi turns to Dev and Rohit. Rohit says,' You seem to know a lot about guns.'

'It's a hobby,' Mahi replies without giving much thought. Seeing their little shocked faces, she clears,' I am a licensed shooter. States.'

Rohit simply impressed nods at new information about Mahi. On the other hand, Dev doesn't seem very pleased with it. He draws the conversation back to his objection on having two constables tailing him. He says,' I don't need 24×7 surveillance. I can handle myself.'

'They are for security. Do not argue with me on this,' replies Mahi authoritatively.

Dev doesn't say anything to that unwillingly. He just sighs heavily showing his discontent. Mahi ignores his reaction and says,' Who is this Shreeram Rawal? Why doesn't he want you to work on highway land?'

Rohit replies to her,' He is the owner of Sunrise Group of hotels. He likes to call himself Dev's business rival,' smirking at last sentence. He doesn't lose the opportunity to tell Mahi everything. He continues,' He was also a competitive bidder in the lease tender for land on New Highway Road, next to that drive-through outlet. The land was supposed to be leased based on the business plan. He wanted to build a water park. We presented a different one. We got the lease.'

'Was it a Kids Entertainment Centre Plan?' asks Mahi.

'Yes,' says Rohit surprised as he never mentioned the plan. He immediately asks,' How do you know?'

'I was the one to sign off the lease,' answers Mahi. She continues,' So I am assuming threats and such ruckus didn't start today.'

'Its been going on for the past few months. We have been engaging the local police to deal with the matter. But, no resolution from their end so far. Before today, everything was limited to the construction site. This is the first time they went personal,' finishes Rohit explaining everything to Mahi with necessary details.

'Don't worry. I'll handle it. Today was the last time,' says Mahi assuring them.

Dev didn't feel right to involve Mahi into all of this. So he injects,' No! Just leave it to us. We'll work it out.'

Mahi looks at Dev indifferently and says,' It's a development project, leased off under my orders. So, it's under my jurisdiction to get involved in this. Not granting you any favour but, just doing my job.'

Dev sighs giving up on arguing with her. He simply says keeping his voice little stern,' So you better do it without putting yourself under any harm. I don't want you to be a hero like today.'

Mahi sees genuine concern tagged along with anger in Dev's eyes. She notes the apprehension in his voice. While ignoring his temper, she says,' I had it under control.'

'Still, it was dangerous,' replies Dev softly.

Mahi doesn't know how to respond to that. So she distracts herself from Dev's protective gaze. She looks at Rohit and says,' Can you come to my office tomorrow with all the related documents of the land. I know someone who can get this thing resolved. Legally and procedurally.' She glances at Dev as she quickly adds,' Without getting myself involved directly.'

Dev becomes relaxed and pleased at the same time as he notices Mahi heeding to his concern.

Mahi leaves garden on the pretext of making a call. However, before she leaves, she made the constables stationed outside to stay with Rohit to provide security to his family. Dev also tags along with Rohit to his house.

The whole way to his house, Rohit kept praising Mahi for what happened today. On the other hand, Dev didn't seem very pleased. Though, he was proud of the way Rohit kept commending Mahi. Even when they reached home, Rohit told Ekta everything in detail about the incident. Ekta kept listening to everything with a multitude of expression on her face from shock to surprise and awestruck. While Ekta listened to everything Rohit has to tell, she couldn't help but notice Dev lost somewhere else seated on the dining table.

Rohit gets a call and excuses himself to attend that. Ekta quickly leaves to check on the baby sleeping with his grandmother. After five minutes or so she comes back and continues the conversation with Dev taking the chair opposite him.

'How amazing is it that your wife can kick people's asses without any male assistance,' asks Ekta breaking the Dev's zoned out mode.

Dev grimaces a little as he nods saying,' Amazing and yet concerning.'

Before Ekta could question him, Rohit joins them speaking about the 'Bazaar' incident. He says,' Do you remember almost a year ago, I mentioned something about a female police officer, beating up the 3 gang members in the middle of the market. Behind the railway station?'

'Yeah, I remember something like that. You overheard some whispers in court. It got you so excited that you even exaggerated to the point that those men were hospitalised for days,' says Ekta chuckling at the end.

'Three weeks,' replies Rohit confidently. He continues,' I just confirmed the story from a friend in police. It was Mahi. The female officer who single-handedly beat up those men with a metal pipe. The men had multiple fractures which had them hospitalised for three weeks. Moreover, she paid their hospital bills.'

'Mahi is not a police officer. It can't be her,' says Dev raising a legit logic.

'I said the same thing. But it was Mahi. She was in a police jeep with a constable. And when people witnessed it, they simply knew that a female officer in civilian clothes with a handkerchief tied on her face beat up those men. It happened when those men were harassing the little girls in the market. When she tried to stop them, they started harassing her. She didn't take any and gave them back instantly,' says Rohit. He continues,' Nobody dared to file a report against her. Even locals appreciated her guts as they were victims too. Nobody knows Mahi's name and neither of the locals gave any description of her when journalists got the whiff of it. Till date police use that incident to get local gang members in line. It happened in the middle of the market, that's why it got the nomenclature as Bazaar Kaand.'

'I don't have words. I am just amazed,' says Ekta overwhelmed after listening to the story.

'I just think you got off way too easy. Do not dare to piss Mahi off again. You might not get lucky the second time,' says Rohit teasing Dev.

Dev doesn't respond to it as he was already somewhere far away in his thoughts.

Ekta notices his thoughtful and concerned expressions. She asks,' Why do you look so worried rather than impressed by all of that? We are talking about your wife here?'

'I don't know. It didn't seem like it was the first time Mahi has to deal something like that,' says Dev still looking far away.

'Clearly. Mahi is in this job for years. Now the question is, why does it matter to you,' asks Ekta, trying to figure out Dev's trouble.

'This is the first time for me, as well. To see Mahi like this. Not caring about herself and putting herself in dangerous situations without giving second thoughts. I don't remember her like this,' says Dev letting out the genuinely worried expression while talking about Mahi.

'How do you remember her then,' asks Ekta without breaking the flow of Dev's thoughts.

Dev lets out a smile while remembering the image just flashed in front of him. He says,' Small, Innocent with curious, big eyes. It was for the first time I met her. She was just nine years old when she came with her family to our house. I still remember. She was wearing a green T-shirt paired with denim skirts and white sneakers. She used to love those white sneakers. Till date she does.' Dev chuckles at the end.

Ekta and Rohit exchange looks becoming amused at Dev's quite detailed description of young Mahi.

Dev notice his friends exchanging looks and asks,' What?'

'That's quite a detail you remember from some 20 or more years ago,' says Ekta pointing out the strangeness of this conversation.

Even Dev realises this and mentally shakes off the trail and says,' It's nothing. I just have a good memory.'

'Hold on a second. Is Mahi that girl?' asks Ekta suddenly realising something.

'No! She is not,' says Dev immediately denying anything Ekta is going to imply.

'She is. OH MY GOD!!!,' says Ekta smiling and putting her hands on her mouth in sudden realisation.

Rohit becomes utterly confused and asks,' What! What is she not? And what is she? Tell me something.'

Ekta grins widely looking at Dev and says,' Dev married his first crush.'

'What! Really? So Mahi is that girl? The fourth standard girl you had your first crush on,' says Rohit in total shock.

Dev puts his hands on his face feeling embarrassed and regret-ting letting his sacred secret out in front of his best friends.

Chapter 10 First Crush or Something Else

'Dude! You married your first crush!' says Rohit laughing out loud.

'Yeah! Mahi was my first crush. So what!' says Dev becoming little irritated at their friends' reaction.

Rohit tries to control the laugh seeing that. Ekta doesn't try to calm this topic down. She draws her curious mode back,' Tell me this. Why you never pursued her? Or you did. And you never told us.'

'I did not,' replies Dev keeping a straight face.

'Why not?' asks Ekta becoming little disappointed at him.

'She was a nine-year-old kid. And I was a teenager. Don't you find that weird enough? And you wanted me to pursue her,' says Dev stating the facts straights to them.

'Ok! But, she eventually grew up. Aren't your families really close? You must have met her infinite times. You guys must have grown up together,' says Ekta.

'I grew up with you guys. In boarding school,' says Dev stating another fact.

'Like you never went back home in holidays,' says Ekta with a straight face.

'Yes. While Mahi used to go to her Naani's place in Gujarat for every summer break. I rarely saw her growing up. That's why she is more close to my parents and my sisters,' says Dev.

'What about after boarding school?' asks Ekta still hoping.

'Don't you remember graduation or post-graduation? I rarely used to go back home,' says Dev rhetorically hoping for Ekta to stop her inquiry.

'So you never happen to see her again. Not even once before your wedding?' asks Ekta losing all hope by now.

Dev rolls his eyes on Ekta's question and suddenly remembers. He says,' Except one time.'

Ekta brightens up and asks,' When?'

'Nivi Di's wedding. I still remember. She was next to Nivi Di all the time. Whole evening she was running errands with mom or Anu,' says Dev remembering every detail of that day. He continues,' She looked beautiful that day. She was wearing the traditional of teal blue and orange combination.' Dev doesn't realise how pleased he looked as he was speaking about that day. Rohit and Ekta notice that.

Something struck Ekta. So she runs to her room without saying anything. She returns with her laptop. She sits back in her chair in front of Dev. She opens the laptop in front of her on the dining table. Rohit and Dev just look at her in confusion. Both men couldn't bring themselves to ask Ekta what she is up to seeing her all serious. Rohit sitting next to her bends his head slightly to see. He smiles, realising Ekta's intention with it. Dev becomes although more confused seeing Rohit smiling.

He eventually asks in frustration,' What are you doing?'

Ekta slides through the screen in front of her in search of a specific item. She stops and glints with satisfaction. She looks up at Dev and says,' Wasn't it around you started dating Yashika. Didn't you take her to the wedding with you?'

'Yep! It was the first family event I took her to,' says Dev as he becomes serious yet again, losing all pleased expressions on the mention of Yashika.

'What was she wearing? Even the colour will do,' asks Ekta keeping a straight face.

'What?'

'She was your girlfriend. It was her first time attending your family function. You were just a year into your relationship. I am just asking you what your girlfriend was wearing. Or what colour was she wearing when she attended your family function for the very first time with you,' says Ekta emphasising slowly on every word.

Dev gets an idea where this conversation might be going. He narrows his eyes at Ekta. To which Ekta says,' Answer the question! Walk free. Simple.'

Dev sighs perceiving that Ekta won't be giving up unless he answers.

'It was yellow. Mustard may be. It has to be either of that,' says Dev looking away from Ekta bringing his voice down to under-confident.

'Yellow or mustard?' asks Ekta teasing her friend.

'Yellow,' says Dev firmly remembering that it was Yashika's favourite colour. It should be it, he thinks to himself.

Ekta smirks at Dev's answer. She turns the laptop towards him as she waits to read his reaction. Dev sees a bunch of people on screen from the wedding. Ekta had opened Dev's sister's social media page and fished out the pictures, from the wedding, 5 years ago. He sees Yashika standing next to him, not in the colour he just said. He closes his eyes when he realises he was wrong about the colour. She was in bright pink lehenga with a backless blouse.

'I bet nobody could forget what she was wearing. She is looking way too hot in that backless blouse and pink lehenga. She is the only one in a different attire in a traditional wedding though,' says Ekta pointing out to Dev how wrong he was.

'Fine! It can happen to anyone. What are you trying to imply?,' says Dev little irritated at Ekta not saying things clearly.

Ekta leans in and says,' Just drawing your attention to some-thing.' She clicks next on the laptop. Another picture of the Bride and groom appears on the screen. In that picture, there is a girl who catches Dev's eyes instantly. She is tall and lean, wearing traditional teal blue and orange colour. Dev takes the support of the chair. He doesn't say anything while he looks at Mahi from five years ago. She exactly is how he remembers her. And suddenly realises what Ekta is trying to point out.

'Don't you think it's little strange when you don't remember the colour of your girlfriend's dress, whom you claimed to be in love with for next five years,' says Ekta looking at Dev. She continues,' I just want you to think why! Why do you remember what Mahi was wearing 20 years ago when you first met her? Why you remember what she was wearing five years ago when you were in a relationship with another girl?'

She takes a small pause and continues keeping her tone gentle,' Why you agreed to marry Mahi when you really had the choice not to? Why do you feel strangely comfortable around her which you never felt with your ex? Why were you so mean to her that night? Why can't you stop worrying about her after what happened to-day? Try finding out the answers for these. Hopefully, you might become little less clueless.'

Dev listens to Ekta silently, then he simply slams the laptop screen to shut as he says,' I have had enough of my share of craziness for today.' He gets up from the chair and leaves the house without biding byes.

Ekta shakes her head amusingly. Rohit looks at his wife in wonder. He asks her,' What's on your mind?'

'Two things. Either Dev is lying to himself and denying it. Or he still doesn't realise it,' replies Ekta thoughtfully.

'Realise what?'

'The fact that Mahi has been more than a friend to him. Even way before Yashika came into his life,' says Ekta smiling.

'If you are right,' says Rohit pointing out his concern. He corrects his words immediately realising Ekta's stern look,' Which you always are.' He continues,' What about Mahi? Do you think she feels the same about him?'

'Oh, I am sure that she is not too far from all of this. She'll catch up soon,' replies Ekta confidently.

Next day Dev accompanies Rohit to Mahi's office. They reached an old government building with a board outside, Pune Metropolitan Region Development Authority. Since Mahi had already put Rohit in her guest list, they didn't have to go through the usual formalities of getting an entry into a government building. The building from outside looked like it needed some renovation. But, as they entered, it was nothing like an old government office. Anyone could misunderstand it for a corporate office. Mahi's office was on the east wing of the building. As they reached her office, the man who they guessed to be her assistant, greets them. He takes them to her office. Before they could enter, the assistant opens the door to her office and says,' Ma'am your 10:30 is here.'

He gets approval and let them enter the office. It was an enormous room with a sofa set followed by a big wooden desk and

Mahi standing behind it. She was standing half leaned on the table. While she is speaking to a middle-aged man in front of her with an unpleasant expression on her face.

Dev notices Mahi in a different mode. She had her hair tied roughly in a bun, leaving few of short strands. She was wearing her squared framed specs and had a lot of files on her desk. Her desk was the size of a dining table for eight. She looked fragile and yet sturdy behind that chaos. She looks up to see Dev accompanying Rohit to her office. She loses her focus as she didn't expect Dev to be with Rohit. She suddenly felt an urge to look at herself in a mirror. She straightens up, greeting them and gestures them to take a seat on sofas.

She asks them,' Give me 5 minutes to wrap this up.' The men on sofas simply nod in agreement. She continues pointing to her secretary still standing on the door,' Subhash Ji get me those New Highway Land development project files. Aur chai ya coffee bhijwaiye (and send some tea or coffee). Also, call Arjun, ask him what is the delay?'

'Yes Ma'am,' replies the secretary and leaves the room.

She turns her attention to the man standing in front of her across the table. She closes the file in front of her. She hands it to the man as she sternly says,' Quereshi Ji apne staff ko boliye mujhe Grant ke papers kal shaam tak mil jane chahiye. Mujhe dusri baar bolne ki aadat nahi hai (Qureshi ji, tell your staff that I should receive the Grant papers by tomorrow evening. I don't have a habit of saying it twice).'

'Ji Ma'am,' says the man taking the file from Mahi. As he turns to leave, Mahi stops him handing a package taken out from her side.

She says,' Bacho ki Eidi (Kids' Eid gifts).'

'Arre Ma'am iski koi zarurat nahi thi (Ma'am there was no need for this),' says the man.

'Aapke liye nahi hai. Bacho ke liye hai (They are not for you. They are for kids),' says Mahi smiling while looking for something on her table.

The man simply says his thanks feeling grateful and leaves the room.

Mahi gets what she was looking for. She takes out the phone between the files and starts dialling a number. Before she could hit call, a man opens the door and knocks on it.

'Morning Ma'am,' says the tall man saluting in police uniform. It was different from any other police officer's uniform, though. Because the badge on his shoulders said IPS with three stars over it.

Mahi raises her eyebrows and says,' You are late. And you can stop with saluting. Also didn't I tell you not to call me Ma'am?'

'Simply following the protocol,' says the man. He continues to say,' Ma'am,' teasingly with a wink.

Dev and Rohit notice the friendliness between the two. Dev couldn't help but note how young and good looking the man is.

Mahi shakes her head, rolling her eyes and continues to introduce him to the rest,' This is ACP Arjun Singh. Arjun, meet Devrath Jamwal and his friend and legal advisor Rohit Dixit.'

'Finally, we are meeting. Even though its a work-related meeting. Otherwise, if left to Mahi, we would have never met,' says Arjun shaking hands with Dev, as he takes a friendly jab at Mahi. Dev guesses him to be close to Mahi since he addressed Mahi with her nickname.

Dev responds awkwardly, not knowing what he meant by that. Arjun gets him and says,' From the looks of it, she never told you about me.'

Dev looks at Mahi for some hints in case he does not have to out her some secret. Mahi blinks softly and says,' Arjun is my friend from college.'

'Just a friend?' asks Arjun looking at Mahi, teasing her again.

'A close friend, a really close friend,' replies Mahi, sighing heavily, looking at Arjun. She smiles at the end of it.

'Really,' says Arjun hitting her arm softly, teasing her. Mahi rolls her eyes at her friend's poking.

Dev and Rohit exchange looks witnessing Mahi and Arjun's friendly interaction with each other. Mahi realising the audience, she brings back the attention to the real purpose of the meeting. They settle down and start discussing the issue at hand. They take into account everything they have in their hands and how could they resolve this matter peacefully. After an hour of discussion, Arjun suggests visiting the site. So that he could reprimand the local authority as well.

Dev feels little uneasy when Mahi chose to ride with Arjun while leaving for the site visit. He definitely wasn't pleased with Mahi's closeness with the young and handsome ACP. However, he consoles himself by reminding himself that he is no one to feel that way. Anyways how much does he know about her life?

After the site visit, a few things become certain. Arjun gets the local police station in-charge actively respond to the issue. By the time they were finished, the sun was ready to set. They all were standing next to their mode of vehicles before saying their goodbyes.

'Don't worry I'll get this thing under control, without involving Mahi in this. She told me about your concern,' says Arjun looking at Dev.

Mahi glares at Arjun as her friend oust her like a routine in front of Dev. To her dismay, Dev catches Mahi giving an eye to Arjun.

'I never said that,' immediately Mahi says trying to get rid of any attention from Dev.

Arjun looks at Mahi in confusion and sees her glaring. He also immediately says,' No. she never said that.'

Mahi sighs out, giving up at Arjun's not so subtle save. Arjun changes the subject before he could get in trouble with his friend anymore.

'Yaar Shruti is very upset with you. You haven't been in touch with her after you got married,' says Arjun to Mahi intently. He continues,' so is Krish.'

'I am really sorry. I miss both too. It's just that I always thought of visiting. But then our timings have been very off,' says Mahi genuinely feeling sorry.

'I am leaving for home directly, you wanna come with me,' asks Arjun to Mahi.

'I don't mind,' replies Mahi.

'Why don't you join us? Both of you' asks Arjun immediately realising that Dev is Mahi's husband. And someday he has to invite him to his house formally.

Dev looks at Mahi for confirmation since a lot has happened between them. And he didn't want to impose on her. She nods lightly agreeing to it. Dev relaxes a little since Mahi won't be leaving with Arjun all alone. Then he says,' Sure. Why not.'

'Let me give a call to my wife and inform her that we'll be having guests over,' says Arjun taking out his cell phone and speed dialling his wife.

Listening to word wife, Dev becomes glad inwardly instantly knowing that the man is married.

'I should leave then, Ekta would kill me if I don't go back home. You guys enjoy,' says Rohit.

'Arre I'll call Ekta and ask her to join us at his place. Anyways she was telling me this earlier. That she could use any excuse to leave the house,' says Mahi taking her phone out.

As soon as Mahi gets down from the Gypsy, a small kid runs to her, shouting out her name. Mahi bends down and picks up the kid in her arms joyfully. The kid hugs her cutely becoming extremely happy seeing Mahi.

'I missed you Mahi aunty,' says the kid keeping his small arms around Mahi's neck.

'Ohh! I missed you too Krishu,' replies Mahi in a cute baby voice.

Dev smiles, looking at Mahi's interaction with a kid. Soon a young woman in kurta and salwar comes out.

'Didn't I use to tell you, Never say never,' says the woman walking towards Mahi.

'Shruti,' Mahi squeals after putting Krish down and opening her arms to get a hug.

'Welcome to the club, baby,' says Shruti embracing her best friend in a hug. She continues saying,' Mrs Jamwal.'

She breaks the hug and looks at Dev standing behind Mahi on her house's porch. She says,' Is that right? Mr Jamwal.'

'Yes, Devrath. Hi, you may call me Dev,' says taking Shruti's hand and shaking it in greeting.

Mahi introduces Rohit to Shruti and tells her about Ekta, who'll be here any minute. Shruti escorts everyone inside their house. Reaching inside, a man stands up seated in the living room in formals.

'Rastogi ji, kal aapko bhijwa dungi audit report (Rastogi ji, I send the audit report tomorrow),' says Shruti to the man.

The man nods and greets Dev as soon as he sees Dev in the coming crowd. Dev doesn't recognise the man as he nods in reply. He immediately leaves becoming little awkward at Dev's presence.

Shruti realises that Dev didn't recognise him. So she clears his confusing by saying,' He was one of the officers at your fake raid, the next day of your wedding.' She smiles, looking at Mahi at the last word.

'Fake raid?' asks Dev getting more confused.

'He doesn't know? You didn't tell him?' says Shruti looking at Mahi. Mahi simply shakes her head as she says,' Never got the chance.'

Dev and Rohit still puzzled at what is happening. Shruti takes the initiative to clear their confusion.

'Uhmmm a few months ago you had an income tax raid at your company. It really wasn't the raid. It was just a smokescreen to distract the fish we were aiming for,' says Shruti, apologetically.

'We were?' asks Dev trying to get some answers.

'Shruti is an IRS officer, working for the Income Tax Department,' says Mahi to Dev's question.

'Ohkay. You said it was a smokescreen?' asks Dev.

'We had been working for months to get someone out of his cave. We even had an insider. But, when we got to know that he might have got whiff of our scheme. We needed him to believe that it wasn't him that we were targeting. So we just needed two more days to get him legally. And your records were clean to raise suspicion. That's why the unexpected raid. It was just for show,' says Shruti making a face.

'And you knew about this?' asks Dev looking at Mahi.

'Only after it happened. However, I did meet a couple of officers at the wedding. I thought they were your guests,' says Mahi.

'They were at the wedding too!' says Dev scoffing loudly.

'Few officers from the team were sent to the wedding. So that things look legit. Though none of them knew that the raid was a farce. Only the higher-ups, including the lead officer and the auditor, knew about it. I was the auditor,' says Shruti.

Dev listens quietly becoming not so surprised because he found the chaos around the raid superficial and suspicious. If the timing was different, he would have found out about it by his own means.

'Now at least I know why that man was giving me weird looks,' says Dev jokingly, bringing in a lighter mood. Everyone joins in laughing, leaving the intensity behind.

Eventually, Ekta joins them. Mahi becomes internally curious to introduce Shruti to Ekta. She remembered how she felt when she met Ekta for the first time. She didn't feel any different than interacting with her best friend, Shruti. Then only she imagined how things would turn out if or when both of them would meet. Mahi wasn't wrong. Shruti and Ekta clicked the way, either of them gelled with her.

After enjoying the fun-filled gathering, people were ready to resign to their respective homes. As soon as they get up to say their byes, a man knocks on the front door. He was the same man, the colleague of Shruti who sat in the living room earlier. Rastogi Ji asks for Shruti, to have a word with her urgently. Shruti engages with him, standing on the door for a minute or so. Everyone else just notices the intense expressions on their faces while watching it from far.

After conversing with the man, Shruti walks up to Dev and says,' He wants to talk to you. Urgently.'

Dev and everyone else becomes puzzled. He asks Shruti,' Me? But why? If it's about that raid, then tell him no hard feelings.'

'I did say that. But it's not. Its something else and wouldn't say it. Unless to you,' says Shruti frowning a little. She continues,' He is a good man and looks troubled. Just have a word with him,' while glancing at the man at the door.

Dev just nods and walks up to the man.

Chapter 11 Stirring New Tensions

Rastogi Ji asks Dev to talk in private, without an audience. Dev obliges his request as they move to the porch. Everyone inside takes their seats to contemplate what just happened and what really is going on.

Shruti guesses,' He is an honest person. Maybe he personally wanted to apologise to Dev.'

Everyone nodded silently in agreement. After few minutes Dev walks in dazed, unaware that everyone inside was waiting for him. He suddenly realises the attention towards him as they waited for him to kill their curiosity. He simply smiles and says,' He was just feeling guilty about the raid. That's all.' All of them sighs off hearing this, except Mahi and Ekta.

Mahi notices that Dev's smile didn't reach his eyes. She could clearly see that it was not about the raid. He just lied to everyone, Mahi could tell. So does Ekta. Both quickly exchange a knowing look and keep it to themselves. Ekta decides to interrogate Dev later, maybe tomorrow. However, Mahi contemplates whether she should ask him or not. He clearly looks perturbed, but Mahi promised herself not to pry in his life anymore.

Without further delay, everyone resigns to their respective homes, concluding the night cordially.

Dev doesn't say a word on his way to home. Mahi realises that Dev has been lost in some thoughts. Without taking notice of the fact that Mahi is seated next to him. His eyes seemed disappointed and sad. Mahi becomes curious and concerned at the same time. She tries hard not to ask him if he is alright. They reach home. Dev straight away leaves for his room, even without saying goodnight to Mahi, out of curtsy. Mahi realises that throughout the way and even when they reached home, not once, Dev looked at her. Mahi had got used to Dev's glances at her. But right now, she suddenly felt strange that Dev didn't even throw a glance in her direction. She takes her thoughts to her room to sleep it off.

In the middle of the night, she wakes up becoming thirsty. Seeing her jug empty, she picks it up and leaves for the kitchen to fill it up. She sees the kitchen's small lights on. While entering, she sees Dev standing next to the stove. He was half seated, leaning backwards, taking the support of the slab behind. Mahi sees a small pan with milk on the stove about to spill out, next to him. He was standing next to it, though out of his sight. He looked spaced out as he failed to notice Mahi's entry and the milk on the stove. She runs towards the stove and turns it off before it spills over. Dev becomes attentive with the movement around him. He sees Mahi standing in front of him after she turned off the stove.

'Where are you lost?' asks Mahi looking at Dev as she keeps the jug in her hand on the slab.

'Sorry! I just wanted to have some coffee,' says Dev with a low tone not even sparing a look at Mahi.

Mahi fails to keep her concern to herself and speaks up,' What's wrong? You don't seem yourself.'

'All is good. It's just another sleepless night,' says Dev forcing a smile on his face.

Mahi nods thoughtfully at first as she simply says,' Ok.' She turns to pick up the jug and moves towards the RO to fill it up. As she fills it up, she glances back at Dev, who hasn't left his position. He was still staring at the floor, becoming adrift again. As Mahi was about to leave the kitchen, she changes her mind. She stands in front of Dev, placing the filled jug on the slab this time.

Now she speaks more firmly,' Talk to me! Tell me. Why are you so lost?'

Dev tiredly looks up at her. He smiles at her and says,' As what you are asking me that question?'

Mahi looks away for a second. So that she could come up with a better intimidating answer to make Dev talk his mind to her. She replies less confidently,' As your housemate.'

Dev chuckles wryly and says,' I think you need to be more than that for me to share my mind with you.'

Mahi doesn't know what to say next. Because she was the one who decided to maintain this distance between them. She created this space between them. She was the one who said that she needed time to be normal again with Dev.

Seeing Mahi searching to come up with the right words. Dev stops her struggle and tries to sound more convincing,' Listen. I am fine. Absolutely. Its nothing. Nothing that should affect you.'

'It is definitely affecting me. Otherwise, why would I still be standing here,' says Mahi without giving a beat.

She felt like she confessed something to Dev when she said this. Mahi sees Dev looking at her with his usual soft eyes. Before he could find words to her strange confession, she continues,' You lied when you said it was about the raid, back at Shruti's place. Her colleague didn't talk to you about that raid. Right?'

'How can you tell I lied?' asks Dev at Mahi's certainty.

'We have been living in the same house for more than half a year. I can tell by now,' says Mahi keeping a straight face.

Dev looks at her for a moment. Then he gives in shaking his head, answering earlier her question. His eyes become densely sad as he tries to articulate his pain. Mahi sees that. Dev looks away in an attempt to control his emotions while remembering the conversation he had with the man earlier that night.

Mahi observes his expression becoming sad, disappointed and his consistent failed attempts to keep it in. For Dev, the whole scene flashed in front of him. The flashes from the wedding and then the words of that man from tonight.

'It was about the raid and the wedding,' says Dev looking straight distantly. He continues,' Specifically right before Yashika decided to leave me.'

Mahi becomes confused and asks,' What he could have to say about the wedding?'

'That Yashika got to know about the raid suppose to happen the next day. That the raid supposedly could make me bankrupt. That was the reason for her to leave me,' says Dev still looking at floor distantly.

'She couldn't know about the raid. That's not possible. They didn't even tell me. Few of them were my batchmates. There is no way they told Yashika about it,' says Mahi trying to make sense of things.

'Yashika always has her ways. She could make people say things that they don't even want to say. Apparently, that's what happened with that man. She overheard their conversation about the bankruptcy and the raid. Then she cornered him to tell her all about it. Making him swear on his family.' He chuckles dryly and continues,' As far as emotionally blackmailing him. She asked him what he would have done if he got to know that his daughter is about to marry the man who might become bankrupt the next day.'

That day flashes before Mahi. Specifically, when she went to Yashika's room in search of Saavi Maa. She clearly remembers that day, when Saavi Maa was literally begging Yashika not to leave Dev like that. Mahi recalls how she witnessed everything standing on the door. Yashika handed Saavi Maa the letter by saying that she has to think about herself first. Mahi couldn't understand what was happening in front of her eyes. She never saw her Saavi Maa broken the way she was that day. When Yashika was walking past Mahi on the door, she held Yashika by her arm to stop her.

'This is not right,' said Mahi to Yashika.

'You wouldn't understand when you could take steps in your life knowing how your future would be,' said Yashika jerking off Mahi's hold and leaving.

That time Mahi didn't understand what Yashika meant by that. But listening to Dev right now, she can simply join the dots in front of her.

'I loved that woman unconditionally for six years. I thought she loved me back. I thought she loved me for who I was, not for what I am. I guess, I was wrong,' says Dev joining all dots in front of him. He continues taking in another deep breath. He attempts to control his emotions,' I should have understood it when she sent me her wedding card.'

'She sent me her wedding card that night,' says Dev looking up at Mahi. He continues,' The night when I punished you with my anger, meant for her.'

Mahi simply looks at Dev, broken, feeling his emotions.

'You know what, I wouldn't have married her if I had got to know about my supposed bankruptcy or the raid. But, why does it hurt when she decided to do the same,' says Dev gathering his voice again.

'Am I that bad? Huh! I am not even worth more than my wealth. Even in six years, we spent together, not even once she could love me for who I was,' says Dev with a breaking voice. He continues in the same voice,' Didn't she see for once.....'

Mahi looks at Dev breaking down as he couldn't complete his sentence and hangs her head down in hurt. She understands him right now. What he is feeling right now, she felt those same emotions years ago. Those emotions broke her down, so much so that it almost took her life. Mahi couldn't stand long, seeing him blaming himself for what Yashika did to him. She couldn't see Dev like that. She feels an urge to console him, not to let him break down like this. So without giving any second thoughts, she gives in to that urge. She takes a step closer to him. She puts her left hand softly on his arm as she places her right on his cheeks, to pull his face up. She cups his face, pulling it up to make him look at her.

'You are not bad. Neither you are wrong. It's just you chose wrong. You chose wrong because Yashika didn't know your real worth. You are way more than your money. It's her misfortune that she couldn't see you for who you are,' says Mahi, slowly and softly, emphasising on each word. Her hand remains on his face, moving her thumb on his cheek in a repetitive motion. She continues,' You are the most beautiful person I have ever met, inside and outside. You are rarest of rare.'

Dev chuckles at her last sentence, barely holding his emotions. She smiles at his chuckle as she says,' So stop blaming yourself for her wrongs. You didn't deserve her. Cause you didn't lose her. It's her loss.'

Dev listens to Mahi quietly and feels tears blurring his eyes. Mahi sees him losing control of his emotions. She throws her arms around him and embraces him instinctively. He was almost at the same height as Mahi standing in front of him. Since Dev was already leaning behind on the kitchen slab. Thus, it was easy for Mahi to wrap her arms around his neck, drawing herself in a hug with him. Dev wraps his arms around her, pulling her in. He breaks into a soft sob as he buries his face in her hair, in her neck. Mahi feels his warm breath on her neck while he sniffles softly. She hugs him tightly as she rubs her one hand on his back, simultaneously lightly patting him.

Feeling Mahi in his arms, Dev slowly calms down. Her soft pats on his back, drain out all his sadness slowly and quietly. Both stay there without losing the grip on each other, breathing in sync for more than a few minutes.

Mahi realises Dev stopped sobbing when she feels him breathing normally. She breaks the hug to take a look at his face. She wanted to ensure if he is feeling better than before. As she faces him inches away from his, she reflexively soothes him and sets his dishevelled look by running her fingers through his hair. Dev just looks at her. He notices how comfortably she is touching his face and his hair. And he liked her touch. He doesn't blink, but, sees a woman in front of her, caring for him, unconditionally. Mahi catches his gaze on her. Dev doesn't look away from her eyes. Something stirs within both as they look at each other intently. He still has his hands around her from her waist. And Mahi has her hands on his shoulders. Dev tucks a loose strand of hair on her forehead behind her ear. As his fingers brush through her forehead and tip of her ear, it sends soft pleasure jolts through her body. Seeing Mahi not flinching on his touch, Dev curiously places his palm on her right cheek, cupping her face. When he holds her face, she leans into his touch, closing her eyes. She enjoys his touch. She gently opens her eyes with a look of wanting more. Dev traces the side of her face with his wandering thumb, sliding his hand down on her neck. Her face looks small in his hand. Her soft skin underneath his hand entices him. With every movement, Dev sees Mahi giving in to his touch. His thumb wanders close to her lower lips, so his eyes. He closes in reducing the inches distance between their faces to a couple of centimetres. Now both could feel each other's breath on their faces. Dev rests his forehead on her forehead, closing his eyes, feeling her in. So does Mahi, clutching his T-shirt underneath her hand.

A loud sound from outside makes them jump. It was a sound of someone unlocking a door.

Mahi and Dev look at each other in confusion. As if, the sound yanked them back to reality or pulled them out of a trance. Mahi realises how close she is standing to Dev, she immediately pulls back. Dev also straightens up blinking rapidly. Both become awkward realising what just happened or what could have happened if they didn't hear that sound. Before they could say anything to each other, Salma enters the kitchen.

'Arre aap dono subah 4 baje kitchen mein kya kar rahe ho? (What are you two doing at 4 o'clock in the morning, in the kitchen?)' Salma asks the couple standing awkwardly a couple of feet away from each other.

Both look at each other guiltily and looks away immediately. Both say together,' Kuch nahi (Nothing!).'

Both glance at each other again. Mahi quickly picks up the jug from the side slab saying,' Paani lene aayi thi. Le liya. Ab sone jaa rahi hu (I came to get water. Got it. Now going back to sleep).' She turns around abruptly and leaves the kitchen.

'Main coffee peene aaya tha. Coffee mili nahi toh ab sone jaa raha hu (I came to drink coffee. Didn't find coffee so now going back to sleep),' says Dev awkwardly and leaves the kitchen.

Salma becomes confused at their behaviour. But, she doesn't heed much attention to them, returning to her routine.

Both might have left saying they are going back to sleep at four in the morning. However, none was able to get a wink of sleep thinking about what just happened. Both were feeling a little shocked but more pleased. Both couldn't help but smile shyly to themselves at what happened down in the kitchen.

Next day Ekta impounds Dev with her usual self. She asks him about his yesterday's lie. He straightens out the facts that he got to know from Shruti's colleague. Ekta doesn't seem surprised. But, she was astonished at Dev's way of taking all of this very calmly. She doesn't hesitate in asking him why he seems calmer than last night when he looked pretty much lost. Dev simply replies that he had a talk with Mahi about the same, without letting out the details of the kitchen incident. Ekta at first rejoices at the mention of Mahi and at her consoling skills. But, then she becomes suspicious when Dev slips out a smile rather more pleased than consoled.

Since Ekta was already on some agenda today, she didn't indulge in asking Dev about the reason behind his smile.

'It looks like you are having a good day,' Ekta begins saying. She continues softly,' How about dinner today? The four of us, and Kabir.'

Dev loses his train of thoughts and narrows his eyes on Kabir's name. He simply asks,' What are you planning?'

'I am not planning anything. I am just attempting to get back the gang. The kind of friends we used to be. Right before that bitch ruined everything,' says Ekta without losing her ground.

Dev sighs at Ekta's response. To which Ekta replies,' I don't understand. Since the reason for your friction is not part of neither of your lives, why can't you guys try to be friends again.'

Dev gives a thought to Ekta's logic. It's true. Dev and Kabir lost on their friendship when Yashika started dating Dev, shortly after breaking up with Kabir. They never even tried to resolve the matter maturely by talking to each other.

'Is he willing to?' asks Dev to Ekta.

'Yes, he is,' says Ekta instantly. She becomes pleased at Dev's agreement to try.

CHAPTER 12 HER CHOICE OR ANOTHER TRIANGLE

Last night was very much like a sweet taste of exotic fruit, which was still fresh for Dev and Mahi's taste buds. Both felt immensely strained at the thought of them being in an enclosed area again, yet they are eager to see each other. Tension builds up when Mahi sees Dev's name in the notification on her mobile screen. She quickly drops the file in her hand and grabs the phone, leaving the staff in her office puzzled. Mahi's lips curves at one end in a smile while she opens the message from Dev. She feels the audience and quickly switches back to her earlier form of calm and poised self.

Dev felt the excitement as he stroked back and forth in his office. He was confused, whether he should call Mahi or leave a text. The dilemma was making him more nervous. But, somehow, he takes the courage and informs Mahi about the dinner at Ekta and Rohit's place through a text. Yet, he felt thrilled because this way, he'll get to spend more time with Mahi.

Mahi and Dev arrive at their place together but separately.

'I could have picked you up,' says Dev as soon as he gets down from his car, seeing Mahi getting down from hers.

'Yes, only if it had to be from my office,' replies Mahi, keeping herself as calm as she could. It seems like something switched in her. She is feeling nervous in Dev's presence. It was definitely something new, she noticed. Even when she tries hard to keep her pose, her actions gives her away. This time, it was her loose shirt. It gets stuck in the car's door when she closed it too fast. Without wasting any time, she quickly opens the door and frees herself. Though in that haste, a button from the end breaks off. Simultaneously her Chinese hairpin drops as she jerked a little while getting that shirt out. It makes a clinking sound on the concrete, leaving her long thick locks free. Dev could see her nervousness.

'Fuck!' Mahi exclaims reflexively in frustration. She quickly tries to adjust the shirt as she tucks the ends in the jeans. She gets herself to pick the pin, but she finds Dev standing in front of her with it in his hand. He takes a step closer. Mahi becomes motionless.

Dev softly sets some free strands from her face behind her ear.

'Leave them open,' he says, as he slides her longer locks over her shoulder. He continues,' I'll keep it safe,' smiling as he waives the pin to her and slides it down his trousers' pocket.

Mahi gulps sharply, looking at him and nods like a little kid. Dev smiles, seeing her nod and gestures towards the entrance, saying,' After you.'

Mahi moves towards the door. Dev exhales heavily behind her. He was holding in all his nervousness while what came over him to act with such confidence. Even he was perplexed at his actions.

A few minutes later, everyone is gathered in the living room. Ekta, along with Mahi and Kabir, is cooing loudly in front of her baby boy. They are sitting on the sofa in the middle of the room. On the other side, Rohit is giving company to Dev, who stands behind the small bar in the corner, showing off his bartending skills. Kabir sees a chance to speak with Dev, and he gets up to go to the bar.

As he is about to leave his seat next to Ekta, she leans in to whisper, ' Just a reminder. I have a strict non-violence policy in my house.'

Kabir takes a second and replies with a serious face,' Since when?'

'Since I gave birth to him,' responds Ekta to his sarcasm.

'Ah! I'll try my best,' says Kabir teasing Ekta with a wink, as he leaves before Ekta could say anything.

Seeing Kabir moving towards the bar, Rohit takes a cue and leave the two boys with their matter.

'Whiskey with soda?' asks Dev as Kabir takes a seat in front of him.

Kabir gives a knowing smile and nods. Dev pours him the drink and slides to his side of the counter. Before an awkward silence takes over, Kabir starts speaking.

'So Ekta was talking about some no violence policy in this house,' says Kabir.

Dev scoffs and says,' Since when?'

'I said exactly the same,' replies Kabir. He turns his seat slightly and looks at Ekta when he continues,' She is the one who is most violent among us.'

Dev looks at Ekta and the baby,' Not anymore, I guess.'

'Damn! She is a mother,' says Kabir smiling.

'We have grown up,' says Dev thoughtfully.

'Hmm. Can grown-ups start a club?' asks Kabir, still looking at Ekta and the rest.

Dev looks at him in confusion,' What club?'

Kabir turns back to Dev and says,' We can start a club. After all, we two are the victims of the same person. Even though you are still rich.'

'Seriously,' Dev changing his expression to blank on Kabir's joke.

'Fine, dude. I'll start it by myself,' replies Kabir rolling his eyes, when he didn't get the desired response.

'How did you.......Ekta!' begins Dev to ask but answers it before completing the question.

'Yeap. My only legit source of gossip,' says Kabir smiling.

Dev simply smiles.

'Jokes apart. I get it. I know what you must be going through. Because honestly, I went through the same,' says Kabir with seriousness.

'And what that would be,' asks Dev being all defensive.

Kabir looks at Dev's scepticism and smiles before he answers,' I'll tell you what I went through when she left me for you. And you can tell me if you relate to it. Even remotely.'

'I am not interested,' says Dev keeping a straight face.

Kabir ignores Dev and starts off saying,' 'I questioned my worth. Worth in terms of material things, she used to love. Then I begin to find flaws in myself. It made me lose my self-confidence. For a long time, I blamed myself for everything that went wrong. Eventually, I pulled myself from all of that drowning. All by myself. That's when I started writing my first novel.'

Kabir takes a pause to see Dev looking thoughtfully, with a strained expression. Dev felt relatable and sorry at the same time. Because of one person, he lost his friend.

Seeing Dev in his own thoughts, Kabir continues,' Now I think of it, I wish someone had pulled me out of all that despair. Someone who could simply say that I am worth more than any material thing.'

Dev looks at Mahi sitting across the room. She was playing with the baby on her lap. Dev smiles, seeing her smile. He says,' I agree.'

Kabir sees Dev pleased while he looks at something or someone. When he follows his gaze, he finds Mahi at the end of it. He looks back at Dev with a concern of his own. Kabir sets his sight on Mahi as well. He becomes thoughtful and says,' You are lucky she was next to you when you needed her.'

Kabir continues as he keeps looking at her,' Mahi is different. I can tell. I wish I had met her before.' Dev turns his head to see Kabir when he continues,' I hope it's not too late.'

'What do you mean?' asks Dev keeping his anger in control.

'C'mon! I know the reality of your marriage. It's temporary. Right?' says Kabir confidently.

'That's none of your business,' replies Dev without giving out his strained emotions.

'I agree. But you shouldn't mind if I make it mine after your temporary arrangement is over,' says Kabir intently.

Dev realises Kabir is not joking around. Kabir continues,' Don't you think she has a right to choose. After all, she has the right to hope for someone she could be with, to spend the rest of her life. We all have that right. Just because she is married to you for the sake of some arrangement, that doesn't mean she should forego her desires and dreams. She should at least have that chance to choose her life partner.'

Dev looks at her thoughtfully and realises that somewhere Kabir is right. He can't snatch Mahi's right to choose herself a life partner just because she is married to him. It struck him that he can't impose himself over Mahi, even though she is married to him. Mahi has her own life, and she will continue to have it after their arrangement comes to an end, after these 2 years are over. Dev comprehends, he can't manipulate Mahi to stay next to him for the rest of their lives.

Later that week, Mahi receives Kabir's call, asking out on lunch. Mahi couldn't respond immediately with a no but, she made an excuse to check her schedule and get back to him. Mahi became confused at Kabir's sudden invitation for lunch. She reminds herself not to read too much into this. Anyways seeing things from dinner that night at Ekta's, she was sure that Dev and Kabir somewhat have mended their friendship. They were surprisingly cordial with each other. Ekta and Mahi noticed that when they exchanged knowing looks. Mahi didn't mind going on lunch with Kabir as they had become good friends and Mahi liked talking to him about books. Still, Mahi felt as if she should ask Dev before she should confirm anything with Kabir.

Later that same day, Mahi arrives home from the office. As she enters the house, she sees Dev seated in the living room. He seemed busy viewing some files. As soon as their eyes meet, both smile heartily at each other.

'Hi,' says Dev, still smiling sweetly at Mahi.

'Hi,' replies Mahi smiling involuntarily seeing Dev's handsome face. She continues,' Busy?'

'Not for you,' replies Dev reflexively. He mentally slaps himself for letting his tongue loose. He immediately asks,' Tell me. You have something on your mind?'

'Actually yes,' replies Mahi. She continues,' I just thought you should know. Just because I don't want you to misunderstand anything or things should become weird with us.'

'Okay. What is it?' asks Dev becoming intended towards Mahi.

'Kabir asked me out for lunch tomorrow,' says Mahi as she notices Dev's expression changing to unreadable at Kabir's mention.

She continues,' He wanted me to review his new book. That's why he asked me to meet him for lunch.'

'Great! So that's what you wanted to tell me?' asks Dev trying not to give away any expressions.

'You don't mind?' asks Mahi becoming a little disappointed at Dev's reaction.

'Why would I mind? Because he is someone I used to hate. No. I am no one to mind your business,' says Dev keeping his discontent within him.

'So it's okay since you don't hate him anymore,' says Mahi sarcastically.

'That's not what I meant,' replies Dev.

'That's okay. I just thought you should know,' says Mahi keeping a straight face. Dev nods in reply as he tries to engross himself in the file in front of him. Mahi becomes a little impatient at Dev's response and continues,' I won't go if you'll tell me not to.'

Dev looks up at her intently. He recalls Kabir's words when he said that Mahi has every right to choose. Dev reminds himself that he has no right to stop Mahi. He replies,' It's your choice. I would never tell you what to do.'

Mahi felt as if her emotions just took deep dive. She literally handed Dev her feelings, and it felt like he sweetly wrapped it up and gave it back to her. Mahi felt disappointed and confused. She doesn't know why she is feeling so disappointed. It is like she was expecting some kind of discomfort from Dev. But, he seemed calm and unaffected.

'You are right. I should better go and do what I am supposed to do,' says Mahi as she takes an escape to her room. She didn't want to feel more embarrassed in front of Dev.

When Mahi left, Dev hangs his hand in disapproval of his emotions. He controlled himself to let out any discontent he felt when

Mahi told him about Kabir. He almost gave in when Mahi asked him to tell her not to go. But he felt that would not be fair to Mahi.

Being Saturday, Dev got himself out for a swim. After a few laps and a shower afterwards, he enters the living room from the back doors, intending to eat something. At that moment, something stopped him in his tracks. It was Mahi, who was descending from the stairs in a floral grey and sage green off-shoulder jumpsuit. Her hair was still wet from the wash. Dev notices the length of her hair, how it has grown till her waist. Dev sees she isn't wearing any makeup. However, she is wearing a liner to define her already beautiful eyes and a mauve shade of lipstick on her plush lips. Damn! She looks beautiful. Dev thinks to himself.

'Salma,' calls out Mahi while picking up the box of her glares and a sling from the table. Salma comes out of the kitchen immediately to attend to her calling. Mahi continues, ignoring Dev standing just a few feet apart,' Aaj main lunch aur dinner ghar pe nahi karungi. Toh mere liye mat banana (I won't be having Lunch or dinner at home. So don't make any for me).'

'Weren't you going out for just lunch?' asks Dev without taking a breath.

Mahi looks at him with a straight face and continues,' yeah, but then I thought since we are having late lunch, our discussion might extend till dinner. And anyway, it's Saturday, and I am in a mood for some drinks too.'

Dev almost scoffs in disapproval. But he keeps his troubled hikes to himself. He simply says,' Alright.'

'I wasn't asking you,' says Mahi instantly, without realising she is poking him. She was expecting a different response but gets disappointed again.

'I wasn't approving,' replies Dev.

'Great.'

'Good then.'

Mahi turns around and leaves the house. As she exits the door, Dev says,' Mera bhi khana mat karna (Don't make food for me as well).'

'Aap bhi bahar khaoge Bhaiya? (Even you'll eat out?)' asks Salma.

'Nahi. Hotel jaa raha hu. Wahi kuch kha lunga (No. I am going to hotel. I'll eat something there),' replies Dev, still looking at the door.

'Aaj toh Shaniwaar hai (It's Saturday today),' says Salma in confusion.

Dev simply gives her a pissed off look. To which Salma nods quietly and leaves for the kitchen.

Dev grunts in frustration and takes the stairs to his room.

Kabir and Mahi meet up for lunch at a cafe. Mahi gets impressed with its ambience as it was a little funky and had books of all types. Soon Mahi realises that all collection of books were a part of its interior.

'I never knew this place existed,' exclaims Mahi as she takes the seat opposite Kabir.

'I know. It's the few of the places I love in this city,' replies Kabir becomes extremely delighted at Mahi's reaction.

'Okay. I am sorry. I cannot stay longer. I have to meet a friend in the evening,' says Mahi. She already planned her evening with Shruti. She did so that she didn't have to stay for long. She knew that the longer she stayed with Kabir, Dev would never like it. Even when she lied, just to tick Dev off, she subconsciously didn't want to piss him off.

'What! Why? I was hoping we would extend it till dinner,' says Kabir becoming a little disappointed.

'Sorry, can't do anything,' replies Mahi, smiling apologetically.

'I was really hoping to spend some more time with you,' says Kabir.

Mahi laughs awkwardly. She says,' why?'

'Well, since you asked, I should be honest with you. Right?' replies Kabir smiling nervously.

Mahi notices his nervousness and immediately finds herself praying internally for not to happen, whatever she is thinking might happen next.

'Well, you know that I know the reality of your relationship with Dev,' says Kabir slowly.

'Yes. How does that matter to you?' asks Mahi becoming serious and intrigued about where this is going.

'It surely does. I also got to know that after two years, you'll go back to your own lives. So when you do, I just want to be part of that life of yours,' says Kabir very confidently yet consciously.

Mahi doesn't know how to respond to that. She ends up saying,' I don't understand,' with a confused expression.

' I like you,' says Kabir without a beat. He continues before Mahi could say anything,' I am not asking you to go out with me right away. I am aware of your obligation towards Dev. So I am ready to wait for you. There is no rush. I'll be here.'

Mahi becomes quiet for a few seconds. Kabir looks at her in anticipation. Mahi takes a deep breath and says,' I am sorry, Kabir. I don't know how else to say this. But I think you misunderstood me. If you feel I somehow sent out the signals, then I am sorry. I never intended to do that.'

'If you are saying no because I am friends with Dev. Then let me tell you that there is nothing to worry about it. We have talked about it. And it's not a problem,' says Kabir immediately so that Mahi's reason to back out is not this.

'What do you mean by "we"?' asks Mahi, instantly listening to Kabir mentioning Dev.

'Dev and I. We discussed this. Very maturely. I told him that you have every right to have a life of yours and choose a partner with whom you want to spend the rest of your life. And he agreed,' replies Kabir quickly and sincerely to her question.

Mahi becomes still. She felt betrayed by listening to this new information. It would sound exaggerated that she didn't felt such a pain before. She felt it like a little less than a stab. She is feeling the anger brimming within along with hurt.

Kabir sees Mahi becoming silent and lost in her thoughts. He notices her disappointed expression. He becomes concerned and asks,' Mahi! Are you alright?'

Mahi looks at him and says,' I am fine.' She takes a few breaths and continues with a stern expression,' Kabir, first of all. I am not interested in you the same way you are. Second thing. You, or anyone else, has no fucking business to discuss me. My future, my choice or my rights. No one. I don't care who thinks or who agrees whether I should have the options or not. Or rights on how to live my life.'

She says everything without taking a pause and slowly emphasising every single word. After she finishes, she gets up and says,' I think we are done here for today.'

As she turns around to leave, Kabir says,' It's Dev. Isn't it?'

This stops Mahi in her tracks. He continues with a loud scoff, 'Of course. You are living under one roof for almost a year. How can you not!'

Mahi turns around to face him. She simply says,' I am not obligated to tell you anything.'

Kabir nods becoming disheartened. Mahi looks at him with a pitiful look. She says,' Bye, Kabir.' With this, she leaves the cafe.

On the other hand, Dev paces in his hotel suite. Dev does this a few times. Whenever he needs a change of place, or he wants to distract himself from something, he gets all his work to this room in his hotel. He buries himself here at work. But today, he feels restless more than he usually should. He couldn't concentrate on work, even when he got here for a change. He intermittently made calls to the house. Just to check whether Mahi came back. Every time he received an answer in no.

It is past 9 o clock at night. He just made another call at the landline. The answer was the same. He becomes anxious with every passing minute and every other call he made to the house. He becomes engrossed in strange thoughts of how good Mahi looked when she left the house this afternoon. They must be enjoying their time together, Dev thinks to himself.

A loud and haste knock on the door pulls Dev out of his train of thoughts. He sighs and walks up to open the door. He becomes astonished at what he finds when he finally opens the door. He sees Shruti, Mahi and Ekta, in the same order from his left to right.

'Oh! That's my husband,' Mahi exclaims in a little loud and cheery voice.

CHAPTER 13 HIS PROMISE

'Oh! That's my husband!' exclaims Mahi in an excited voice, seeing Dev open the door. Dev sees the 3 women on his door. He couldn't help but notice the happy yet drunk expressions on Mahi's face and a little pissed off on the rest of the two ladies. She is drunk clearly.

'Aww! You guys are so nice and responsible. You got me to my husband,' says Mahi squeezing Ekta and Shruti in a side hug. Then she takes a step towards Dev and puts her hand on his chest for support. She continues seeing Dev up close,' Oh! you are tall!' And she wraps her hands around him in a hug as she rests her head on his chest, nuzzling close to his neck, closing her eyes. Dev reflexively holds her, wrapping an arm around her. He looks at Ekta and Shruti questioningly.

Ekta turns her head towards Shruti for an answer. To which she replies,' She drank 3 bottles of wine. All by herself.'

'What!' says Dev in surprise.

Mahi opens her eyes and looks up to Dev, keeping her head on his chest. Dev looks down to meet her eyes.

'Hi,' says Mahi smiling sweetly to Dev.

Dev smiles at her innocent face and replies in a gentle voice,' Hi there.'

Dev sees Mahi changing her sweet expression to a concerned one. He asks,' What's wrong?'

'I need to pee,' says Mahi straightening up.

'Here, I'll show you to the bathroom,' replies Dev, not taking off his protective hand around her.

'I can go by myself. Just show me the way,' says Mahi in a little confident and yet slurred voice.

'You sure?' asks Dev, simultaneously looking at the ladies for help.

'We'll come with you,' asks Ekta, understanding Dev's looks.

'No!' says Mahi, turning around to reply to Ekta. Then she speaks to Dev,' Yes, I am sure. I am not a baby.' With this, she turns around, walks off unstably towards the bathroom.

Dev comes back to the door and asks,' What happened? I have never seen her like this.'

'Neither have I. For as long as I have known Mahi, she never gets drunk. She drinks but never drunk. We were supposed to meet up for dinner today. However, she called me up early, after lunch or so. That too here,' says Shruti.

'Here? You guys were here?' asks Dev in disbelief. And he was thinking where she might be this whole time. He also becomes little pleased listening to Shruti about her dinner plans with Mahi.

'Yes. Since 4 o'clock or something,' replies Shruti. She continues,' I don't know what's wrong. But, she seemed a little upset. She didn't tell me even when I asked her, I don't know how many times.'

'It's alright. It's someone else's headache now,' says Ekta putting an assuring hand on Shruti's arm.

Shruti exhales, relaxing a little as she says,' I called up Ekta for help when it was becoming a task to get her home. She came down immediately and told me you were here only. So the rest you know,' says Shruti quickly.

'That's good,' replies Dev, actually feeling glad that she brought Mahi to him.

'Also, please don't tell Arjun that I let her get drunk. He'll be really pissed,' says Shruti to Dev.

'Yeah! Even I would have been the same. Only if you hadn't brought her to me,' replies Dev becoming a little serious as he means it.

Shruti lets out a nervous laugh. Then she says,' We should take your leave now.'

'Yes. Why don't you go ahead? I'll join you in a bit,' says Ekta to Shruti.

Shruti agrees and leaves first. As soon as she leaves, Ekta turns towards Dev and says in a very stern tone,' It's you! When I asked her about you, she cursed you under her breath. You did something to upset her. I don't know what. FIX IT!'

Ekta doesn't wait for Dev to respond and leaves him in confusion. He closes the door after Ekta leaves.

'Nooooo...'

Dev hears Mahi voice from the bathroom. He runs towards the door but stops himself from opening it. He asks Mahi if she is alright. Mahi responds back with the same voice of saying,' No,' with a more upsetting tone.

'Mahi. Please tell me you are okay,' asks Dev becoming more worried.

'Oh! No. No. No,' Dev hears Mahi going on and on in the bathroom.

'I don't care if you are decent or not. I am coming in,' says Dev as he feels the frustration and opens the door.

When he enters the bathroom, he sees Mahi fully clothed but twisting and turning around half bend. She is looking for something on the bathroom floor.

Dev sighs out in relief and asks,' What is it? What are you looking for?'

'I can't find it. I was just adjusting the bolt,' replies Mahi without looking at Dev with a whiny voice.

'Huh?'

'My earring,' says Mahi getting annoyed. She straightens up and says,' See! I still have the bolt,' showing a small piece of metal in her hand to Dev.

'Okay. Let's just leave it for now. I'll get someone to look for it in the morning,' says Dev in an attempt to get her out of the bathroom.

'No! They are my favourite earrings,' replies Mahi sitting down on her feet and looking for them.

'C'mon. I'll get you the new one, the exact same. I promise,' says in another attempt to dissuade Mahi.

'No! I bought them. They are my favourite. Why would you get them for me?' asks Mahi in a most innocent voice.

Dev gives up looking at her and says,' Let's look for them together.'

After a few minutes of searching down on the floor, Dev gets up and sees the earring on the basin slab. He scoffs softly. He picks it up and says,' Found it!'

Mahi sees the earring in Dev's hand. She gasps in shock at first and then gushes cutely. She takes the earring from him, saying,' Here you are!'

For Dev, drunk Mahi is adorable. He chuckles at her reaction. He sees her trying to put on the earring but gets amused seeing her failed because she is too drunk to do it.

Dev gently takes the earring from her hand, moves closer to put it for her. And Mahi lets him. He finishes putting it on, saying,' Done.'

Mahi turns herself towards the mirror and says, smiling,' Thanks.'

'Your Welcome!'

Mahi looks at herself in the mirror and grins widely. Dev quietly looks at her charmingly at her actions. She giggles and says,' Wow! I look so drunk.'

Dev chuckles softly and says,' You are drunk.'

Mahi turns her gaze, losing the smile towards Dev in the mirror at first and then to him standing next to her. She says,' I don't want to talk to you.'

Dev sees her smile fading and asks,' Why?'

Dev sees Mahi becoming upset. She sighs loudly in response and walks out of the bathroom, taking the support of things on the way out. Dev quietly follows her out. Mahi takes off her heels, reaching the room. She sees a half-filled glass of wine on a side table of the couch. She walks up to the table barefoot, picks up the glass and gulps down the wine. When she picks up the bottle next to it, Dev quickly walks up to her and gently takes the bottle from her.

'I think it is enough for today,' says Dev while taking the bottle from her.

Mahi jerks off her hand from his grasp and walks away to the balcony door. She unlocks it.

Dev asks her,' Where do you think you are going?'

'Balcony se kudne,' replies Mahi with a pissed off expression as she opens the door and moves out. Dev quickly sets the bottle on the table. He follows her behind. But when he sees her going straight towards the railing, he almost runs to her. Before she could reach the end, he grabs her, wrapping a protective arm around her waist from behind. He slightly picks her up, holding her like that and places her away from the railing.

She laughs off and says,' I am not gonna jump. I was just kidding. I need some air.'

Dev puts her down and faces her while he says,' Couldn't take the risk.'

'Don't worry. You are not getting rid of me that easily,' replies Mahi, becoming serious again. She takes the support of the high glass railing and looks out.

'Who wants to get rid of you!' Dev states softly, standing next to her and not leaving her from his sight.

Mahi sneers at Dev's reply. Then she says,' You are obliviously so good at pretending.'

'Excuse me!' exclaims Dev at Mahi's allegation.

Mahi looks at Dev sternly and then looks away, sighing in exasperation. Dev realises that she might be drunk but, she is pissed too, for some reason. However, he doesn't understand why. So he asks her softly,' Hey! Why would you say that? Why do you think I want to get rid of you?'

'Don't you! Of course, you do,' replies Mahi turning towards Dev. She continues as she takes a step closer to him,' If, not get rid of me. But you sure are pushing me away.'

Dev becomes more confused at her claims. What made her think like that? That's all Dev could think of at this moment. He simply replies,' What! No! Why would I want to do that?'

'Maybe you want to do some charity. Maybe you want to give me some options. Maybe you want to give me a CHOICE,' replies Mahi in a little slurred speech, but gritting her teeth at last word.

'Mahi,' Dev says softly, realising what she might mean.

'No!' replies Mahi strongly. She continues,' You want to give me my right to choose. You are just giving me options to choose from. Or just Kabir. Right?' sarcastically.

Dev simply shakes his head without saying anything. As he was about to explain himself, Mahi speaks up,' Or wait. You wanted to give me an option of Kabir because you just want to compensate him for what you did to him years ago.' Mahi becomes immensely sad as she said this. Dev could clearly see that. He immediately says,' No. You are misunderstanding the whole thing. That's not what I want.'

'Really? Then tell me why would you not stop me when I asked you to,' says Mahi in a soft voice. Her eyes well up as she continues in a breaking voice,' Is that much you don't want to see me in your life. So much so that you would willing offer me up to someone else.'

Tears roll down Mahi's cheek as she looks at Dev with a question in her eyes. It breaks Dev to see Mahi hurt. He reflexively raises his hands and wipes off her tears, saying,' No. That's not true.'

Mahi pushes Dev's hands, saying,' I don't know what's true. And I don't want to know anymore.' She puts her hands on her eyes and sniffs once, then runs her hand from her face to her hair. She says,' Anyways, I am too drunk to remember any of this. So it doesn't matter.' She takes another sniff and says,' I want to go home."

She leaves Dev on the balcony and walks away to the room. Dev sighs heavily, becoming disheartened when he sees Mahi walking off.

When Mahi enters the room in her unstable drunken walk, she hits her foot with the table's edge.

'Ow! Ow! Oww!' Mahi winces loudly with pain.

Dev quickly enters the room and picks Mahi up from behind while she prances on the single leg, holding the other in her hand.

Dev places Mahi on the Sofa behind. Then he gets the ice pack from the small fridge in the corner of the room. While Mahi groans with pain sitting on the sofa. Dev sits next to her. He takes her legs across his laps and places the ice pack on her foot. As the ice pack hits the spot, Mahi holds onto Dev and clutches his t-shirt from his shoulder with one hand. And her other hand grabs his collar from the front. She closes her eyes as she whimpers in pain. Dev removes the ice pack and starts massaging the foot so that she doesn't feel colder.

After a few minutes, when the pain subsides, Mahi feels the warmth of Dev's hand on her foot. She had her head rested on Dev's shoulders while Dev massaged her foot. She leans back a little, removing her head from his shoulder. She looks at Dev, who is still caring for her foot, now more softly without looking in her direction. Mahi notices Dev's soft wavy hair from his side. She feels an urge to touch them. So she does. She runs her hand in them, making Dev turn to her. She doesn't flinch when she meets Dev's eyes. Dev's face is just a couple of inches away from her own. Dev sees her smiling softly through her eyes. She raises her other hand and runs her fingers in his hair over his forehead. Dev closes his eyes for a second to feel her touch. His musky perfume hits her nostril, which leads her to smile softly. She continues her exploration over his face with her both hands now. She begins with his forehead, tracing the smoothness of brows, then drawing her fingertips over his defined nose. Finally, her fingers reach his lips. All this while, Dev becomes still and afraid to move. In case he might disturb Mahi in her pursuit. Her touch was definitely arousing him. It is becoming really difficult for him to keep his eyes open on her touch. He didn't want to lose the chance to read Mahi's expression. Mahi trails longer over his lips with her fingers, lost in a trance. Her lips part as she says softly,' I always wanted to...'

She doesn't complete her sentence as she leans in, closing her eyes and places her lips over Dev. Dev doesn't move at first. Then he feels her warm lips over his. Mahi parts her lips a little more to get better at Dev's lower lip. As she does so, Dev feels the tip of her tongue on his lips and finally gives in, closing his eyes in response. He could taste the wine from her lips. When he was ready to respond to Mahi's move equally, she breaks from him. Dev opens his eyes in confusion and sees Mahi smiling as she opens her eyes softly. She says,' Sweet.'

She leans in, closing her eyes and, so does Dev thinking she'll continue what she started. However, Dev feels a soft thud over his chest. When he opens his eyes, he sees Mahi dropped on her chest, closer to his neck. He could feel her uniform breathing on the neck. Dev sighs out amusingly as he says,' You can't pass out after kissing me like that.'

Dev chuckles softly at his situation with some pity for himself laced with it. He gently picks Mahi and cradles her in his arms as he stands up from the sofa. He walks to the bed and places Mahi softly on it. He tucks her in without disturbing her. As he finally sets the pillow below her head, he looks at her lovingly, bending over her.

'You made your choice quite clear today. I am never letting you go. I promise,' Dev whispers, smiling. He places a soft and lingering kiss on sleeping Mahi's forehead in a promise to keep her next to him for the rest of his life.

It is the morning. Mahi stretches herself and opens her eyes. A strong jolt of pain seize her head and make her groan. She sits up, holding her head and eyes closed, still moaning softly with pain.

'Good morning!' says Dev seated on the sofa across Mahi. He is dressed in a casual green polo t-shirt with khakis. He looks like a model, who's not a single hair is out of place. His voice startles Mahi. She sees Dev across the room and winces again with a headache.

Chapter 14 'It was a Mistake'

'There is a glass of water and an Asprin for your headache. Take it. What you are feeling is called a hangover,' says Dev keeping a straight face. Mahi turns her head to see what Dev just told her. However, she sees another glass.

'The other glass is lemon juice for your dehydration. From what I heard, you had 3 bottles of wine. All, by yourself. You need that lemon juice. Believe me,' says Dev seeing Mahi's confused looks.

Mahi couldn't take the pain anymore. So, she does what she is being told. After she gulps down half a glass of sweet and salty lime juice, she looks at Dev with a lot of questions in her head.

'Where are we?' asks Mahi in a low voice.

'You don't remember?' asks Dev in counter.

Mahi tries to remember but, nothing comes to her except a few flashes of the bathroom. She shakes her head after trying to remember. She asks slowly,' What happened?'

'I was hoping you could tell me that,' replies Dev looking intently at her. He sees Mahi becoming more perplexed at his comment. She struggles to remember. But, nothing comes to her.

'We are at my hotel. This is my room,' says Dev.

'How did I end up here?' Mahi asks with hesitation in her voice.

'Shruti and Ekta dropped you here while you were too drunk to remember anything,' replies Dev keeping his expressions blank.

Mahi remembers coming to his hotel and calling up Shruti. She suddenly remembers the reason she came down here. She looks at Dev and immediately looks away. She doesn't ask anymore, afraid she might not want to listen to it.

Dev sees Mahi struggling and stealing eyes from him. He says,' Anyways, here is some change of clothes for you from home. Why don't you get fresh? We'll leave in half an hour,' says Dev picking up his phone from his side and looking at his wristwatch. He continues while getting up from the couch,' There is everything in the bathroom you might need.'

Mahi gets down from the bed and sits back when she feels the soreness on her toe. The scene of hitting her toe last night flashes in front of her. She quietly stands up and starts walking towards the bathroom. Dev sees her every movement with the side of his eyes as he pretends to be busy on the phone. He didn't expect Mahi to remember anything. Yet, he hoped she could remember the part right before she passed out.

Twenty minutes later, Mahi comes out after taking a quick shower. Dev looks at her coming out wearing a pair of denim with a white v necked T-shirt. Her hair half open and half clipped from the side. She wore a slip-on instead of heels. Dev recalls when he called up Salma in the morning to send Mahi's clothes. He specifically asked for a slip-on instead of her favourite converse. He knew her toe must be sore from last night so, shoes won't be comfortable for her.

He looks at her for a couple seconds more and then says,' Chalein? (Shall we?)'

Mahi picks up her stuff in a bag and nods softly to Dev's question.

Dev walks to the door as Mahi quietly follows him. Dev turns around right before he was about to open the door. Mahi halts a foot apart seeing Dev looking at her.

'Are you feeling hungry?' asks Dev without letting out any expressions.

Mahi is unable to read him, shakes her head, saying,' No.' However, the sound from her stomach betrays her the very next moment. She places her hand on the stomach and hangs her head in embarrassment. Dev also looks down amusingly at the sound and lets out a smirk.

'Let me ask again. Are you hungry?' says Dev with a controlled smile on his face.

Mahi frowns as she nods. Dev couldn't help but smile at her surrender. He opens the door and leads the way.

When they enter the lift, Mahi's stomach growls again. Mahi sinks in embarrassment. Dev simply smiles and presses the button for the top floor. Mahi notices that and asks,' Why are we going up? Aren't we leaving yet?'

'We will. After addressing your growling tummy,' replies Dev gesturing towards her stomach. Mahi rolls her eyes at Dev's teasing.

Both arrive on the top floor of the hotel. It is where the hotel's fine dining, cafe and extravagant bar is located. Since it was a little early in the morning, the place was less crowded. The staff greets Dev and Mahi when they move to the dining area of the Restaurant. The manager himself shows them their seats and makes them seated across each, a little secluded, away from the crowd. Soon a tall and healthy man in a clean white uniform approaches them. He greets Dev warmly.

'Morning, Mr Jamwal,' says the man smiling. He turns to Mahi, he continues,' Welcome, Mrs Jamwal.'

Mahi greets back the man and notices the pin on his shoulder in the shape of a Chef's hat.

'I am sorry for calling you this early, Chef,' says Dev.

'No. Absolutely not. I have to be here when I heard you are not coming alone,' replies the man, smiling politely. He continues,' Tell me. What you want to have?'

'I am okay with anything. You may ask Mahi,' says Dev gesturing towards her.

'Same goes for me. I am good with anything,' says Mahi quickly.

'Then let me get you something special and refreshing,' says the man, smiling.

'One thing. Ma'am is allergic to shrimps and doesn't like mush-rooms. Though she loves eating spicy,' Dev points out, smiling as he glances to Mahi.

'Noted,' says the Chef and leaves the area.

Mahi looks surprised at what just happened. She sees Dev with shock and surprise. Dev notice her gaze and asks,' What?'

'How do you know about my allergies and mushrooms?' asks Mahi becoming genuinely intrigued.

Dev smiles mysteriously at her question first, then says,' I notice. More than you think.'

Mahi blinks a few times as she becomes flushed at his response. Soon their moment ends when a young man approaches Dev in a very informal greeting.

'Hey, Mr Owner. What's up?' says the man in a foreign accent, shaking Dev's hand. Dev gets up and greets him.

'Hey, Max! I am good buddy,' replies Dev.

Max looks like a hippie with all piercings and tattoos. He is a foreigner. With his European accent, Mahi guessed French. As soon as he notices Mahi, he goes,' Hey, you are the wine lady.'

Mahi becomes a little confused. Dev intervenes and introduces them, 'Max, this is my wife. Mahi.' He continues,' Mahi. Meet Max, the bar manager here and a very talented bartender. And he is french.'

'Hi!' Mahi greets him. Mahi didn't recall him. So he says,' I think you don't remember me. I am the one who served you those 3 bottles of wine last night.'

Mahi doesn't remember him but the mention of wine bottles sends a recall message. She chuckles embarrassingly.

'You must be going through some heavy hangovers right now. Let me get you my amazing hangover mocktail,' says Max and leaves them.

He soon returns with the drinks. He sets a drink for Dev and a different looking drink in front of Mahi. He insists Mahi try it. Mahi does involuntarily. Surprisingly she likes it. Dev becomes pleased at Mahi's relaxed expressions. Soon their breakfast arrives with lots of seafood and some fusion dishes which, she didn't care to know. She digs in heartily as she was famished. Dev looks pleased as Mahi eats without saying much but only giving out smiles full of content.

After they are done with breakfast, they leave the hotel in Dev's car. When they arrive, Mahi seemed lost in some thoughts. She was trying to remember what happened last night. It made her anxious, not knowing the hours of her life she spent in a drunken state. Seeing Dev calm, she suspected something definitely happened last night. Something which Dev isn't telling her willingly. As they arrive and Dev notice Mahi lost somewhere, he pulls her out of her thoughts by saying, they are home.

Mahi nods in response and tries to unbuckle her seat belt. It gets stuck as she tries to unbuckle it. Dev sees that and helps her. In the process of getting her seat belt off, he leans in closer. His musky perfume hits Mahi's nose. Mahi likes how he smells every time she gets to sniff him. His fragrance is about to get her smile, but something flashes in front of her. She recalls last night when she felt the same perfume when she pulled him close to her. And then that happened. Mahi becomes still as she remembers the moment right before she passed out. At the same time, Dev unbuckles the belt and frees Mahi. Without saying anything, Mahi quickly grabs her belongings and runs to her room. Dev becomes confused at her sudden rush.

It took a few days for Mahi to feel normal again in Dev's presence. Otherwise, every time she saw Dev, she would remember that night, specifically that part of the night when she kissed him. Even when she manages to push that thought from her head while Dev is around, she still ends up gazing at him and then at his lips. She has to mentally jerk herself out every time she does it. She just hopes that Dev never gets to know that she remembers it and how she has begun to feel about it.

Slowly and gradually, they end up spending more time with each other. Now that's what both like to do voluntarily. Its been almost two weeks since they started to spend their evenings together. Sometimes discussing something very irrelevant part of daily routine or sometimes just enjoying the tea or coffee on the Verandah. They even started to enjoy each other's company in silence.

One such evening, Dev gets the two mugs from the kitchen and takes them to the backdoor. He moves outside to the Verandah as he sees Mahi standing facing the garden. She is enjoying the sudden change in weather as dark clouds take over the skies. Dev hands her one of the mug.

'Here. Your jasmine tea,' says Dev handing her the mug.

'Thanks,' replies Mahi as she takes the tea from him. She is still wearing her short cotton Kurti, paired up with jeans. She had just come from the office when she found Dev in his casual tees and track pants. He was making coffee for himself in the kitchen. She had politely asked him if he could make some tea for her too. Dev gladly obliged her request.

'Wow! The weather took a sudden turn today. Looks like its gonna rain,' says Dev, taking the support of the pillar next to him as he takes a sip of coffee.

"Its gonna pour like anything,' says Mahi, grinning with the idea of raining heavily.

Dev notices the excitement in her voice. He smiles, seeing her look at the clouds eagerly.

'So are you ready to host the event of the year,' asks Mahi teasingly.

'What?' asks Mahi, not knowing what he meant.

'Anukriti's Engagement. It's next week. In our house,' says Dev. Mahi nods in response. Dev continues,' You must have got all the details from your Saavi Maa. She even called me up yesterday to notify her arrival in 5 days,' says Dev rolling his eyes.

'Oh! So she'll be here on Friday then. Great,' replies Mahi, getting the new information.

Dev notices the hint of surprise at Mahi's face. He instantly asks away,' Didn't you know? She didn't tell you about her arrival. Her most favourite daughter. How's that possible?'

'I guess I am not her favourite anymore,' replies Mahi smiling and trying to keep the sadness within.

Dev sees something off about the last comment. It felt like she wasn't joking about it. He asks her,' Why didn't she call you?'

Mahi looks at Dev with a blank expression at first. Then she takes a pause and says,' She isn't speaking to me.'

'Since when?'

'Since the wedding,' says Mahi letting a fake smile with it and while she looks outside. She notices the shock and confusion on Dev's face. She continues,' It's alright. She is just upset with me.'

'What could she be so upset about that she hasn't spoken to you for almost a year,' asks Dev becoming really concerned.

'For my decision to marry you and ultimately going for it,' says Mahi.

'What! Isn't she the one who forced you,' says Dev becoming more confused.

'No. I have told you this earlier, it was my decision. I was the one who prompted the idea. It was all me,' says Mahi.

Dev quietly looks at Mahi, becoming sadder as she looks at the sky thoughtfully. She says,' Saavi Maa and my Dad were the two people who were hell-bent against my step. They tried every possible way to deter me.' Mahi takes a pause and then continues with a scoff,' Saavi Maa even made me swear on her. Even when it meant that it could destroy her family. Destroy you,' looking at Dev at last two words.

She becomes quiet for a second or two and then says,' These are two people in my life who mean the most. And now they don't even like to talk to me because I am the reason they are upset.'

'Your Dad too,' asks Dev softly.

'Hmm,' says Mahi nodding and pasting a smile on her face.

Dev looks at her, thinking how much is she carrying with her. She never let out her anguish, except today, that too with a smile. All this time, Dev never realised how much she must be going through. He was engulfed with his own sorrow that he never thought what Mahi has given up in her life to be here, next to him. She has never failed to stand tough whenever Dev needed her. Even the wedding. How he could be engrossed in his own pity that he never saw her hurting.

The clouds thunder as it starts pouring heavily. After a minute or so, while Dev enjoys watching Mahi, who was enjoying the rain, something struck Dev. He sets his mug on the side and walks down in the garden. Mahi is in absolute shock laugh off seeing Dev.

'Mausam ki pehli baarish, bheege nahi toh fir kya kiya (Season's first rain, if didn't get drenched then what did you do),' says Dev, dramatically getting all soaked in the rain.

Mahi just laughs and says,' Oh god! So filmy!'

'C'mon on! Join me,' says Dev standing in the garden facing Mahi on the Verandah.

'Oh! No. Thank you. I am super fine here,' says Mahi as she sits down on the stairs.

'Ah! What a bore. You are missing the fun,' says Dev trying to insist one more time.

'No. No. I am enjoying the show. Kindly continue. I am guessing you are gonna dance next,' says Mahi teasingly.

'Nope. I do that only on special occasions and only for a full house audience. I am an expensive artist, you see,' replies Dev sarcastically.

'Too bad I can't afford you,' says Mahi grinning.

'Yeah. Too bad,' says Dev as he walks to the side of the garden, where flowering plants were planted. He continues,' Since I am an artist. Did you know that I am a good painter?' He picks the mud from the bed of the plants.

Mahi sees that, raising an eyebrow, saying,' No. You won't.'

'You wanna see it? I can give you a live demonstration,' says Dev as he walks towards the Verandah.

Mahi slowly gets up and says,' I dare you not to.' Dev stops in his tracks at a distance. Mahi sees that her challenge worked. But in the next moment, she feels the wet mud on herself. She looks down at her clothes and then looks at Dev, who stood quietly waiting for her reaction.

'By any chance, if you thought. That by doing this, you'll get me' says Mahi looking at the eager Dev. She continues, 'then it worked.'

Dev smiles and loses it instantly when he sees Mahi bending down. She picks the mud from where the stairs of Verandah ends and the garden starts. She straightens up and says, 'Oh! You are dead. You see, I like my clothes.'

Within a minute, the backyard turns into a war zone of mud throwing competition. Dev taking advantage of his height and size, he makes Mahi immobile. He paints her face with the garden dirt. Mahi also gets back at him as she shots the full hand of mud straight on his face. She does it a few more times. The last one lands on Dev's face but, it hits his eyes too.

Mahi instantly, becoming worried, runs to him as he winces when the dirt stings his eyes.

'Show me. Don't move,' says Mahi pulling his face down to her height. He bends a little as she holds him still, keeping her one hand on his neck and trying to clean his eyes with the other. Since it was pouring hard, almost everything got washed off.

While she tries to clean the last of dirt around his eyes, she says, 'Aur khelo. Kisne kaha tha ye karne ko (Want to play more. Who said to do this).'

'You have hit me in the face,' says Dev in an attempt to defend himself.

'Who started it,' says Mahi countering his defence.

'It was fun,' says Dev grinning as wide as he could.

Mahi looks at his handsome face smiling widely and smiles back equally, agreeing with what he meant by the idea of fun. He got her out of her comfort zone and tried to distract her from her nostalgia. She gives out a loud chuckle at the end when she sees his whole self with some of the piece of grass stuck in his hair.

'What?' asks Dev smiling as he becomes intrigued at what made Mahi laugh like that beautifuly.

'Look at yourself. There are pieces of the garden on my artwork,' says Mahi as she picks the pieces from his hair.

'And you thought I would leave my piece without such decorative stuff,' says Dev smirking as he pulls a piece from Mahi's hair, right above her forehead.

Mahi scoff saying,' Still mine looks much better and handsome,' taking out the last of the grass from his hair.

'Really! Well, if you could see mine,' says Dev, still taking out the ones from her hair on her crown. He slides his hand under her hair around the neck, brushing his fingers on her neck,' you would think...'

Mahi suddenly feels his touch. She becomes aware of nearness and his touch on her. Dev also realises the closeness and Mahi becoming still and attentive to his touch. He softly continues, pulling out another piece,' That how something could be so beautiful.'

Mahi looks up at him, looking at her with wanting eyes. The attraction burns within them as something stir warm, which keeps them from looking away from each other. Rain pours with the same intensity. Dev gives in to his feelings when he slides his hand under her ear and pulls her to himself as he bends down, crashing his lips on her. He holds Mahi in a kiss as he takes hold of her face with his hand and pulls her in, holding her waist with the other. Mahi immediately replies to his inquiry through his lips by parting her own, closing her eyes. Dev softly works through her lower lips as he tastes it with his tongues as he slides his other hand too on her waist. He pulls her in, sliding one hand on her back and holding her waist closer to him with the other. Mahi replies with equal vigour, wrapping her hands around his neck as she runs her hand in his hair to get better of him. Both now move their lips in sync, responding to each other's thirst and desires. Underneath the choreographed performance of their lips, their tongues do the magic when they come in contact with each other.

Mahi suddenly realises what is actually happening. She reflexively pushes Dev away, becoming little horrified thinking of something. Dev becomes a little surprised at the jolt as he balances himself from the push. He sees Mahi panting with an expression of shock and a terrified look in her eyes.

'Mahi! What's wrong?' asks Dev, panting himself, with confusion. They both were enjoying the most beautiful moment in their lives seconds ago. Suddenly something changed. He tries to find out what is it. He was sure that he was not alone in that spark. Mahi responded to him as well.

Mahi is still in shock, thinking about how to face this. She gives in to her terror and says,' We shouldn't have,' still breathing heavily. She gulps sharply and then says,' It was a mistake.'

'What!'

CHAPTER 15 'I Love Her'

'It was a mistake,' says Mahi letting out an intensely stressed and disturbed look.

'What!' exclaims Dev at her response. He continues,' What are you trying to say?'

'Yes. It is a mistake,' says Mahi, not looking Dev in the eyes as she is still lost in her horror. She further breathes,' We shouldn't have done...' and before she could complete that sentence, she takes off running towards the house.

Dev gets stunned at the turns of the event. He stands still, gathering himself from what just happened. He sees Mahi leaving the garden and running to the house. He as well doesn't stay and follows her calling her out to stop to get some answers. Mahi doesn't stop and runs straight upstairs to her room, drenched wet, dripping water on the floor. So does Dev. However, when she reaches her room, she locks it from inside. Dev fails to get hold of her in time. Dev calls her out from the door.

'Mahi! Open the door. Please. Talk to me,' says Dev knocking on the door.

Mahi becomes still when she locks the door, drawing blank in mind. She doesn't say anything when she listens to Dev on the other side of her door.

Not getting any response from Mahi, Dev takes a failed calming breath and then continues softly,' Mahi. You are making me worried.' He says,' Please. Talk to me. Just...say something.'

Mahi listens to his soft voice on the door. Her eyes fill up as she rests her forehead on the door, closing her eyes in despair.

'Mahi,' says Dev, moving closer to the door.

Mahi gathers her voice as she replies in a low voice,' I don't want to talk. Please leave me alone...for some time,' holding in her tears.

'Okay. Okay. I can do that,' says Dev becoming a little relieved yet not completely satisfied with her response. He puts his forehead on her door for a few seconds before he decides to leave.

When Mahi listens closely, the receding footsteps of Dev, she let lose control over her emotions and cries her heart out. She feels helpless at that moment. There was no doubt about what happened in the garden was the most beautiful moment of her life so far. But, she knew in that instant that it was nothing less than an alluring dream for her. A moment, she could only dream and experience once but cannot have for life. Somehow she is convinced that this moment of happiness cannot be part of her life unless Dev gets to know that chapter of her life. However, she believes that it is a far fetched idea even in some alternative universe, she decides to tell him. In this universe, it ain't happening for sure. She cannot, in the right state of her mind, recite that chapter again to someone. Not even to someone like Dev, for whom she feels so strongly.

Dev, on the other hand, sinks in the chair placed in the corner of his room. His thoughts go back and forth about what happened downstairs in the garden. He tries to figure, where he went wrong for Mahi to react in such a manner. He did notice her terrified looks but, he couldn't place them at the appropriate place. What happened in the garden with both of them was the most natural outcome. Dev wouldn't have initiated it if he wasn't sure about Mahi's feeling. He did see consent in her eyes before pulling her in a kiss. And he was sure, after that night. A person usually tends to shows his/her true feeling when they are drunk. And Mahi drank in the first place because she got affected by Dev's actions. And Dev was well versed with it. He could simply join the dots when Mahi showed up drunk at her door. Then how everything could go south in a moment. Dev jogs his head the whole night on repeat to get at the least one different piece, which could explain Mahi's reaction.

Dev looks for Mahi, the first thing in the morning the next day. However, he doesn't find her in her room or in the house. From house help, he gets to know that she left for work early. Dev tries hard not to read anything from it and thinks that she'll eventually get home. Then he'll talk to her. However, he fails to do so as he returns a little late. She had already locked herself up in her room, pretending to sleep early. He tries the same the next day. However, he finds her room locked as she hasn't left yet. He tries to knock on her door but doesn't get any response. He becomes restless but, he gets called off to the office urgently. He was already getting a little busy at the office to arrange his younger sister's engagement. Again he fails to meet Mahi. This repeats the next day too. This time, his self-esteem doesn't allow him to knock on her door because he already read this very rightly that Mahi is avoiding him. But he stayed downstairs to wait for her to come out of her hiding so that she could give him some answers that he deserves. However, he gives up as his priorities at the hotel takes over.

For four straight days, Mahi tried her best to avoid Dev. She didn't have in her to face him as she couldn't muster enough courage to lie to his face. And if she didn't lie, then she is definitely not telling him the truth either. So the only option she was left with was to avoid him till she can. Anyways in 2 days, the house would be swarmed with the whole family and some relatives as they would be coming here to attend Anukriti's engagement. Then maybe she could breathe a little.

For the past 4 days, to avoid Dev, Mahi used to stay in her room until she used to see Dev's car driving out. Today as well she waits for his car to leave the premises. When she sees the car driving off, she sighs off softly as she gets ready for the office as well. She comes down and readies herself to leave the house as well.

'So you are alive,' the voice behind her startles her and stops her in her track. She doesn't turn around. She recognises the only voice she likes to hear as she clenches her hand in a fist. Finally, Dev cracked her pattern. With a trick of his own, Dev got her out of her room while he is here.

'For how long have you been planning to avoid me? Huh?' asks Dev walking towards her. He watches her back and notices that she isn't turning around.

Mahi doesn't reply to Dev, staying still, closing her eyes, feeling his gaze boring a hole in her back.

'Wow! Now you don't even want to see my face,' says Dev sighing off as he feels dejected.

Mahi couldn't humiliate him anymore. So she slowly turns around to face him.

'I should really thank you for this kindness,' says Dev sarcastically.

Mahi still doesn't say anything as she doesn't look at him stealing her eyes. Dev becomes frustrated at her silence.

'What! Are you still not gonna say anything. Are we not gonna talk about it. Or are you that cool "kiss and not care" type of a person?' says Dev with annoyance in his tone.

Mahi looks at him as she feels a little offended at his last comment. Dev finally gets to see her eyes and immediately regrets saying that.

'Sorry!' says Dev genuinely. He takes another breath and says,' Mahi,' holding her softly from her arms. He continues,' Please talk to me. Tell me what's wrong. I can't take this silence anymore. Is it something I did? I thought a lot. But I couldn't understand what went wrong. Because what happened was not wrong at all. You know that. Then why did you...what happened?'

Mahi listens to Dev as he softly asks her, almost begging her to clear the tension in his head. He says,' Because I know for sure, you were as much as part of that kiss as I was. You felt the same. We have been feeling this for each other for some time now. You know this right.'

Mahi gulps down her emotions. She wears a poker face, she says,' Dev. It was a mistake. You got it all wrong. I am sorry. But I don't feel that way for you.'

Dev does not believe what he is listening. So he tries to reason her,' You kissed me back.'

'Yes. I did. In the spur of a moment. It didn't mean anything,' says Mahi pushing down hard her emotions as she keeps a straight face.

Dev doesn't understand what she meant by that. He loses calm with her. He says,' Mahi, are you trying to tell me off just because I am in love with you?'

Mahi becomes still for a second when Dev tells her that he loves her. She doesn't let her self internalise that information as she sees Dev on the edge of losing the endurance. She instantly gets back to her stiff self and says,' I am just telling you this. That kiss was a mistake. I don't feel that way about you. And nothing can happen between us.'

Dev takes a step back in disbelief at what he just heard. He felt like Mahi very cruelly crushed his feelings just to get back at him for some reason. He felt the anger coming to the surface. He looks at Mahi for a couple of seconds. Then he turns around, hitting the big vase placed at the side table in the living room. The vase shatters in pieces. It leaves Mahi startled at Dev's anger. Then she notices the blood dripping from Dev's hand, who stood showing his back to Mahi.

Mahi quickly reaches his hand to see if he got hurt badly.

Dev sees Mahi becoming worried as she takes his bloody hand in her own. Dev, getting the best out of his temper, jerks his hand off Mahi's grip. To which she looks at him in concern.

'No need to pretend that you care,' says Dev tightening his jaws in anger.

'What the hell is going on?' says the woman, loudly standing on the entrance, in an authoritative tone. She looks older, not very old. But older than middle-aged women. She is wearing a maroon silk saree and had a suitcase next to her.

Dev looks at her and scoffs at her timing. He says,' Why don't you ask that question to your favourite one here!' He walks off towards the exit, but he stops right before the door and turns to say,' By the way. Welcome home, Mom,' with a tinge of sarcasm in his tone. With that, Dev leaves the house.

Savitri doesn't care about the way her own son greeted her. But, at this moment, her sole focus is on the girl standing across the room. As soon as Dev left, Mahi sees her Saavi Maa. She gives up control over her suppressed emotions as she drops down on the floor and burst into tears sitting there. Savitri almost runs to her and holds her in the arms as she tries to console her. Mahi doesn't say anything but cries heavily in her Saavi Maa's arms. Savitri becomes concerned for Mahi, seeing her like that. She forgets that she hasn't spoken to her in a long time. She pats her affectionately as she cries her heart out without a break for the next several minutes. Savitri feels regret for not keeping in touch with her, realising what she might be going through here all alone.

When Mahi quiets down a bit into soft sobs, Savitri asks her why she broke down like that. Also, why her son behaved in such an un-acceptable manner. Mahi doesn't let out her reason as she simply dismisses it by saying that she just missed her Saavi Maa. Savitri understood Mahi's intentions of not sharing the real reason. She also doesn't press on it.

By the end of the day, Savitri settles herself in Mahi's room and transfer part of Mahi's belongings to Dev's room. Knowing that by tomorrow, the rest of the family would reach here. She tries to keep the arrangement between Dev and Mahi under wraps. It was already too much for her to know about it. She didn't want anyone else to pass any judgements on them and make them uncomfortable. As they were already going through something serious, that she still had to figure it out. She calls up Dev's office to inform him about the changes she is making to keep their private life private. He doesn't heed any concern as he lets her do whatever his mother feels she should do. Savitri asks multiple times Mahi before making these changes as she was aware that nothing is normal between Dev and Mahi. And Savitri never wants to put Mahi in a difficult spot. Mahi doesn't oppose her and simply agrees, though becoming tensed in her head, thinking how to face Dev. She didn't give it a thought earlier that this might happen. She thought she'll be a little relieved when guests would be here. However, the opposite is happening where she has to share a room for the next few days with one person she thought she'll be avoiding these days. She felt the karma is being a bloody bitch to her right now.

Dev comes home and goes straight to his room. He opens the door to his room and goes to the bathroom without noticing someone else in the room. Mahi also doesn't realise Dev's arrival in the room as she was lost in her own thoughts, standing in a walk-in wardrobe. Dev comes out of the bathroom after taking a quick shower. His hair still wet, he looks for towels in the cabinet next to the bathroom's door. He doesn't find them, so he walks towards the wardrobe. He slides open the door and finds Mahi getting startled. She looks pale as Dev notice that she isn't wearing any kajal under her eyes. Her eyes looked heavily puffed like she had been crying a lot. Mahi jumps at his presence, turning around to face him, just a few feet apart. Dev sees her clothes behind her in the portion which was anyways empty. He looks at her as her gaze darting from his pissed off face to his bandaged hand. As she opens her mouth to speak, Dev walks towards her, making her quiet and nervous in the spot. He comes close and bends to pick up the towels next to her. Placing the towel on his head, he turns around and leaves the wardrobe wiping his head. Mahi exhales sharply as he had been holding her breath for a while. She follows him out into the room.

'I can't sleep with Saavi Maa tonight,' says Mahi with a small voice she gathered.

Dev turns around with a blank expression.

'Nivi Di's flight lands at 2 am. Saavi Maa said that there is no need to advertise our...arrangement to everyone,' says Mahi hurriedly, to his questioning eyes.

Dev looks away scornfully and says,' I don't care. Do whatever you wanna do.' He drops the towel in the basket next to the dressing and walks towards the door picking up his phone from the side table.

He stops right before the door. He says,' You can sleep on the bed. I'll sleep on the couch.'

'No need to,' says Mahi instantly to instructions regarding the sleeping arrangement.

'Don't argue with me on this,' says Dev becoming a little annoyed at her refusal.

'I am not arguing. There is no need to be dramatic. It's a huge bed. I'll sleep on one side. You sleep on the other. Nobody has to be uncomfortable,' speaks Mahi from a place of logic. She sees Dev's surprised look and continues,' Unless you are?'

Dev looks away and pretends not to care as he says,' Whatever. Sleep, however, you like.'

He leaves the room without continuing the conversation further.

Mahi sighs off again, not relaxing even for a bit. Though, she becomes a little relieved as she noticed Dev's rudeness towards her. This means he has believed her lies. Mahi assures herself that she can tolerate his anger as long as he doesn't question her feelings towards him.

Dev tries not to recall whatever happened today and think much about it. He sits in his study, downstairs, working on a few pending things. The study is the large room, under the main staircase of the house. It had a set of brown leathered sofas, matching with wooden bookcases instead of walls. At the end of it, a vintage oak wooden table is placed. Behind that, Dev sits in his comfortable brown leather chair.

Savitri knocks on the door of his study before asking his permission to enter. Dev, out of curtsy, asked her if her trip was okay.

Dev is in no mood for small talks with his mother. So he pretends to be busy with work in front of her.

Savitri gets up from the sofa to leave him with his work. However, she works up her mind and asks him,' Is something wrong between you and Mahi?'

Mahi's name from his mother's mouth catches his attention. He simply replies,' It's none of your business.'

Savitri doesn't give up. She walks back in and says with a tinge of warning in her tone,' I will make it mine if Mahi gets affected. Whatever it is. You need to stop. Stop punishing her for whatever reason you think I ever did to you.'

Dev, taken aback at his mother's insinuation, says,' Is that what she said to you? That I am punishing her.'

'She didn't say anything,' says Savitri answering him truthfully. She continues,' After you left like that, she just cried. I don't know for how long. The last time I saw her like that was...It was a long time ago.' She says this with concern in her voice. She changes her tone and continues,' And I promised myself that I wouldn't sit still if it happens again. So whatever you are doing to her. You need to end that. Even though you are my son, I wouldn't let you hurt her in any manner. Take this as my warning.'

Savitri places her caution and turns around to leave the room.

'I love her,' says Dev in an exhausted voice, looking down. It was enough for Savitri to stop in her tracks as she turns around in shock. Dev looks up to his mother's surprised face and says,' I am in love with her.' She notices the genuineness and pain in his voice. Also, it was the first time her son meant those words. He had told her these words for someone else once, before this. That time, it was mere words he used to compel her to give her permission for him to marry that girl. This time, he looks different when he said it.

'And that's what I said to her. Before I left in the morning. Before you arrived,' says Dev. He walks around the table to stand in front of it. He runs his hand in his hair in frustration as he takes the support from the table behind him. He continues,' I have never felt like this before for anyone.' Dev sighs before he says further,' But, she doesn't feel the same. She said that nothing can happen between us.'

'No! She does,' says Savitri, immediately refuting Mahi's words to him. She couldn't understand her emotional burst out earlier. Now she knows the story behind it, she is finally able to figure out the real reason. Savitri sees Dev struggling with his emotions as he talks about Mahi.

Dev becomes hopeful at his mother's words as he asks,' Did she tell you that?'

'No. I know Mahi too well to know how exactly she feels,' says Savitri smiling unapologetically.

'I don't know! Why would she lie to me? Why would she push me away? Why she'll torture herself and me?' says Dev in an exasperated and exhausted voice.

'I think I know why she would do that,' says Savitri becoming sorrowful thinking about it.

'Why?'

'Would you take my advice?' says Savitri drawing attention back to her son. She continues,' Patience! That's what you need with her. You really need to be patient with her. Just know this. She is not pushing you but protecting herself.'

Dev doesn't understand what his mother meant. Savitri takes a deep breath as she says,' She went through something you and I cannot even fathom. It was a long time ago. It was traumatic enough to still affect her.'

Dev becomes thoughtful at her mother's words. He immediately asks,' Did something happened to her when she was still in school.'

'How did you know? Did she tell you that?'' asks Savitri becoming astounding at this information.

Dev shakes his head, denying it. He says, 'I guessed.'

'What do you know?' asks Savitri, trying to find out how much his son knows about Mahi's past.

'Nothing. Just this. Mahi suddenly becomes nervous whenever that time from her life gets mentioned. Or someone from that part appears in front of her,' says Dev thoughtfully.

'Who appeared in front of her?' asks Savitri getting worried for Mahi.

'It was months ago. There was a woman from her school. It was very brief. But it kind of shook her,' says Dev. He sees his mother's expression changing from concerned to somewhat relieved. He asks her,' What happened to her?' He could tell that his mother knows what happened.

'That's not my story to tell,' replies Savitri with a sad smile. She continues,' But, I can tell you this. Whatever it was, it happened years ago. And it took her years to recover from that. Somewhere she is still recovering. Sometimes she feels that she can never heal the scars from it. It changed her. That trauma still affects her.'

Savitri very calmly, emphasising each word, says next,' So please! Be very careful and gentle with her.'

Dev nods lightly, assuring his mother.

Savitri smiles and turns around to leave. As she reaches the door, she turns to her son and says,' I am happy that you found her. Found each other. I bless you two with the whole of my heart. Something tells me, going forward, everything will be just good.'

Chapter 16 "I'll Wait"

S avitri leaves the study. Dev thinks deeply about the conversation with his mother. After finishing up his work in the study, he walks up to his room.

When Dev enters the room, he notices the lights in his room were dim. Only a small lamp lit next to the other side of the bed. He sees Mahi asleep, curled up on the side. Since she had already tired her eyes from all that crying, it didn't take her long to doze off. Dev walks up to her side. He looks at her sleeping. He sits down on his feet next to where her head is. He stays there for the next couple of minutes, gazing at her sleeping face quietly, with folded hands on his knees. While he intently looks at her breathing softly, he resolves not to give up on her so easily. He thinks back about the morning interaction with her. He did notice something off about her eyes and facial expressions when she denied having any feeling for him in the morning. But now, after listening to his mother. He becomes resolute to stay next to her and to believe her eyes more than her words until she accepts her feelings truthfully.

With the tip of his fingers, Dev caresses her forehead lovingly. He gets up and switches off the lamp. He then opens the blanket at her feet and drapes it gently over her.

The next day, the house starts bustling with all type of noise. A kid is running around in the living room with a lot of energy to stream off.

'He was in a 12-hour flight. Right?' says Mahi seeing the kid, amusingly. She is wearing a yellow cotton salwar kurta as she sits in one of the chairs in the living room.

'Oh! Yes, where he slept like a rock. I am the only one who is recovering from jet lag,' says Nivriti in an exhausted voice. She is having tea in her hand as she is seated on the sofa next to Mahi, wearing printed white kurta and salwar. Nivriti is Savitri's first and eldest daughter. She seemed wide awake yet exhausted from a long flight from Norway.

'Let him be. Don't disturb my favourite grandson,' says Savitri catching the running Veer. She pampers him as she picks him up playfully.

'He is your only grandson,' says Dev giving his mother the reality check, seated across the room on the dining table having his late breakfast.

'Yeah! Only till someone gives us another good news,' says Nivriti with a teasing smile at Mahi. Mahi raises an eyebrow at her poking.

Dev picking up the hint of what his sister means, replies,' Why? Are you expecting again?'

Nivriti throws a small cushion in Dev's direction as she says,' I was talking about you two, idiot.'

Mahi chuckles softly, seeing the playful teasing of the siblings in front of her. Savitri changes the topic by asking,' Where is the star of the event? Doesn't she know that it's her engagement tomorrow?'

Everyone chuckles at Savitri's accusation for her youngest daughter, Anukriti.

'She should be here anytime. Her flight landed an hour ago,' says Mahi informing everyone about her friend slash sister-in-law's arrival.

'Looks like I am gonna live another hundred years,' says the lean, average height girl at the entrance, wearing a denim jacket with a pair of black jeans. In the next moment, she screams,' Nivi Di!!' And then, she runs towards her sister and wraps her in a hug affectionately. She greets her mother next and then hugs Mahi with the same excited affection calling out her name.

'Bhabhi bol (Address her sister-in-law),' says Nivriti hitting playfully on Anukriti's arm.

'No. We are friends first,' says Mahi wrapping an arm around her waist.

'Yeah? Right, buddy,' says Anu, putting her hand on Mahi's shoulder and high-fiving her.

Nivriti gives up, knowing how both always have been. Since the time they were kids. Anu then goes to her brother and hugs him, greeting him. She says,' Bhai, I hope she is not troubling you much,' teasingly.

Dev looks at Mahi and says,' Well! You don't say it.'

Nivriti and Anu exchange an amusing look.

'Oh! My God! Dev!' shouts another woman with an accent in an excited voice. Everyone turns to the new voice at the entrance. Mahi notices that the woman is not Indian but a blonde with a skinny stature. She runs to the Dev and hugs him very sweetly. Dev hugs her back awkwardly with a surprising look pasted on his face.

She breaks the hug, still holding him from his arms. In her British accent, she says,' How long has it been?'

Dev still is in surprise. He awkwardly looks at Mahi. Something makes him glance in Mahi's direction. He ends up saying,' Kate. How have you been?'

'I am good. It's so nice to see you after these many years,' says Kate with an excited voice and still holding onto Dev.

'I happen to meet Kate at the airport. She is touring Pune this week. She doesn't mind staying for the engagement,' says Anu standing next to Dev as she looks at him with a guilty expression. He shots her disapproving look. So Anu quietly goes and stands next to Mahi and her sister.

As Dev and Kate still exchange their pleasantries, Nivi quietly asks Anu about Kate. To which Anu replies,' She was Bhai's fling in London. I met her when I was there during that exchange programme in college.'

Nivi realises that Mahi heard Anu as she quickly signals Anu not to say anymore. Mahi listens to Anu and looks at Kate with more observing eyes. She sees that the woman is white, blonde and even good looking with an amazing ass. Dev realises that everyone is waiting for him to introduce Kate to them.

Dev politely breaks Kate's hold on him as the first person he introduces to her is Mahi as his wife. Kate gets surprised that Dev got married. She first congrats him and then greets Mahi by pulling her in a friendly hug. Mahi greets her back politely. After introductions, everyone settles in the living room. Soon Dev's extended family members also arrive, turning the house into complete stead festivities.

In all of this, when Kate and Dev catch up on their respective lives, Mahi couldn't help but find herself looking in their direction now and then. Dev notices Mahi's eyes at them. She gets a little irritated at their closeness. Savitri seeing Mahi's uneasiness distracts her by asking her to prepare few things. A ritual is to be done for Anu so, Mahi does so. She leaves the living room and goes to the kitchen.

'She is just a friend,' says Dev leaning against the door frame, hands in pockets. Mahi stops what she was doing and turns around to face Dev with a straight face. Dev becomes uncomfortable with her darting stare. He moves, standing in one place and says, giving in to her glare,' A friend who I went out with for few weeks. That's it.'

'Ah huh!' says Mahi nodding in response to Dev's acceptance. She turns around to resume her work. Dev lets out a chuckle at Mahi being bossy with him. But he liked the way Mahi got jealous.

Savitri enters the kitchen about to say something to Mahi but stops seeing Dev also present there. Then she sceptically looks at Dev and then decides to tell Mahi.

'I didn't get a chance to tell you earlier. Shree called in the morning,' says Savitri addressing Mahi.

Mahi turns around to look at Savitri and then at Dev. Her expression changes to sadness at the mention of her mother. She doesn't look surprised as she says,' I know. I already got the call.'

Dev sees the sad smile coming around Mahi's face and his mother responding with a pitiful smile. He gets confused. So he asks,' What is it?'

To which Mahi says, with a straight face,' My parents won't be coming for the engagement.'

Dev notices the disappointment in Mahi's voice as she maintains her poise of being unaffected. Here Dev notices, Mahi is in the constant practice of suppressing her true feelings. That is why that day, he couldn't figure out the difference between what she said and what her eyes meant.

Dev's train of thoughts ceases when Nivriti and an Aunt enter the kitchen in a jolly mood. They together start preparing few ingredients for some ritual they need to perform for Anukriti before tomorrow's engagement. Dev gets the call from the hotel and leaves the kitchen. Soon Kate also joins them, becoming intrigued about the Indian rituals and customs.

While getting out of the kitchen with a couple of bowls of turmeric, Heena and Vermilion mixes, Kate asks Mahi to let her help them by carrying one of them. Mahi reluctantly hands the bowl of liquid Vermilion to Kate. Not to Mahi's surprise, it slips from Kate's hand and crashes on the floor, turning everyone's head to the sound of a crash. Feeling instantly sorry for dropping the dish, Kate bends down to get the pieces of glass from the floor. Seeing that she might cut herself, Mahi immediately stops her from touching any of it. Mahi successfully stops her. In doing so, the back of her hand comes in contact with the sharp end of the broken glass. She winces without making any noise as she feels the cut at the back of her hand. Salma runs to her with a piece of cloth in her hand. She sees Mahi getting injured. As she is about to bring everyone's attention to it, Mahi shushes her with her eyes. She takes the cloth from her hand as starts wiping liquid along with broken pieces of glass. To her relief, nobody noticed it, as everyone asked Mahi and Kate if they are not hurt. Dev was about to join them but stops listening that thankfully no one got hurt. Mahi goes back to the kitchen and washes off her hand with blood and vermilion over the sink.

It is late afternoon as Mahi goes to the room upstairs to take a quick nap. As she enters the room, she sees Dev asleep on the bed. She knew Dev came up earlier to change. However, she thought he might have gone as he was supposed to leave for the hotel in the afternoon. She takes off her slippers so that it doesn't make the unnecessary noise and disturb his nap. She walks up to him barefoot. She looks at him sleeping as her gaze travels his face and then stops at his bandaged hand over his chest. She looks back at his sleeping face as she sits on her feet. She raises her hand to touch his hair and his face but, she stops. She gets up, sighing off. Then she softly touches his bandaged hand and turns to leave. As she turns around, she winces with pain turning back to Dev, seeing him awake, holding her injured hand. Dev sits up, loosening grip over her hand where she is hurt but not letting it go.

'I knew it,' says Dev, now holding her hand from her wrist, seeing the back of her hand with an open wound. Mahi tries to get her hand from his grip but, he doesn't nudge.

He stands up, holding her hand and then looks at her, saying,' Come with me.' He takes her to the bathroom.

'I am fine. It's just a small cut. It will heal on its own,' says Mahi, still insisting and trying to get loose from Dev's grip.

Dev takes her to the bathroom. He makes her sit on a small seat next to the window. It is a foot away from the bathtub on one side and a wooden cabinet to the other end of it. He says as he makes her sit with a firm,' Just shut up and stay still! Just for 5 minutes.'

Then he moves to the cabinet, opening it, getting a first aid box from it. He sets the box next to Mahi as he opens it, sitting on his feet in front of her. Mahi doesn't say a word after Dev asks her to stay quiet and still. She sees Dev's movements silently.

Dev feels Mahi's eyes on him as he nurses her wound. He disinfects the wound first as he says without looking up at Mahi,' I don't know why you are like this.'

'Like what?' asks Mahi, not removing her gaze from Dev.

'Like you don't feel anything. But you do,' says Dev, still tending to her cut on the hand. He continues,' Do you realise that you have this habit. Of keeping in every emotion suppressed that you think will make you weak.'

Dev doesn't wait for her response and continues, looking up in her eyes,' But you also don't realise that you have the most expressive eyes.' As soon as she meets Dev's eyes, she looks away, trying to avoid his gaze.

'Looking away just proves my point,' says Dev, still looking at her. He then takes a deep breath and gets back to bandaging the cut. He says,' There is something you should know.'

Mahi looks back at him with soft eyes as he focuses on her hand. He says softly,' I am sticking to what I said earlier. And there is nothing that will change it, even your denial. Not even your stubbornness can change the way I feel about you. Because for the first time in my life, I have felt something like this. And I am never letting it go.'

'I don't know, what is your reason to dismiss your feelings. I can only hope someday you'll resolve them and come to me. Because however long it might take, I'll wait. I am not going anywhere,' says Dev while he finishes wrapping the bandage. He continues,' I know for sure that I'll rather live while I wait for you than believing your lies that you don't feel the same way about me.'

Mahi now tries hard not to give even a glimpse at her own con-flicted feelings in front of Dev. She quietly listens to Dev's words with constrained expressions. She fights within not to give in to her sentiments, to confess in front of Dev. Dev finishes bandaging Mahi's hand. He closes the first aid box as he gets up, picking up the box and puts it back in the cabinet.

Dev comes back to Mahi, sitting in front of her on his feet. He puts his hand over hers as he says,' I don't know what is it that is stopping you. Whatever is holding you back to love me back, to rely on me, to trust me. Whatever it is, I just. I hope you'll just let me in. Just for once. And I promise you wouldn't regret it.' He looks down at her hand as he takes it in both hands now. He raises her hand close to his mouth. He keeps it there for a few seconds, closing his eyes. Mahi looks at Dev, feeling his warm breath and lips on her hand. She sees a man holding in just for her sake. It disturbs her witnessing the same man struggling. She hates herself as of right now for letting him suffer, who just opened his whole heart in front of her. Mahi reflexively raises her other hand to caress Dev's hair. But, she retreats when she sees Dev open his eyes as he looks straight into hers. He sees her tense face, struggling hard to keep up her poker. He puts down her hand and stands up. Mahi doesn't let go of his gaze as he places his palm on her cheek. He then bends down, planting a soft kiss on her forehead, which makes her close her eyes in response. Dev leaves after assuring his trust and determination with a kiss on the forehead.

As soon as Dev leaves Mahi in the bathroom, she starts breathing rapidly, thinking about every word he said to her moments ago. Then she fails to keep her stress in and breaks in soft weepings as tears start running over the face. Dev quietly watches Mahi crying as he sneaks a peek at her, standing out on the door. He doesn't like that Mahi starts crying but, he becomes certain about one thing. His words made an impact on her. His mother was right earlier about her suppressed feelings. He also becomes concerned for Mahi as he doesn't know why is it painful for Mahi. He stays on the door for few more seconds before he decides to leave for the hotel.

Later in the evening, he receives a request from her younger sister to take the family out for dinner. To which Dev gladly obliges.

When Dev comes back to a quiet house, nobody seemed to notice his return as everyone was busy getting ready for dinner. He also takes the stairs to his room. He opens the door and hears Mahi calling out for his younger sister. He sees Mahi walking out of the walk-in wardrobe. Her hair tied in a rough bun, wearing an untied off-white blouse from behind, as she walks to the mirror, tying a knot of the underskirt on her waist.

'Anu, close it and tie these know,' says Mahi as she walks towards the mirror in the corner of the room, without looking in Dev's direction. She doesn't realise that it's Dev instead of Anu on the door. Dev becomes a little surprised seeing Mahi half-dressed, with a completely open back, walking around in his room. He doesn't move at first.

Mahi picks the kajal stick from the table in front and finishes putting it on. She expected Anu to tie the knots. However, she realises that Anu has not responded to her. So she turns around and becomes shocked to find Dev. In that stunned state, she quickly picks the cherry red saree from the settee next to her and holds it close to her torso in an attempt to cover herself.

'I-I thought. I thought it was Anu,' says Mahi, stammering.

CHAPTER 17 REPULSIVE ENCOUNTER

Dev doesn't say anything but keeps looking at her with intended eyes. He throws the blazer in his hand on the chair next as he starts walking towards Mahi. Becoming nervous, Mahi doesn't move. Dev halts in front of Mahi and then slowly takes a step closer without leaving her gaze. To that, Mahi nervously steps back. But loses the balance coming in contact with the settee behind. Dev reflexively puts his hand around to stop her from falling. While doing so, he places his hand on her naked back. As Mahi feels his hand on her, she tries to move back again but fails as Dev doesn't let her. Instead, he uses the same hand to pull her in closer. Now Mahi could smell his perfume. Dev slowly slides his hands at the side of her chest as he takes the ends of the blouse behind and closes it by placing one end in a hook of the other. Mahi tries a calming breath as the closeness with Dev always makes her dizzy and weak in her knees.

After buttoning Mahi's blouse, Dev leans back so that he could see her flushed face. He also feels a rush of blood in his brain as he stands this close to Mahi. Yet, he doesn't let her go. He notices Mahi is not resisting his touch. So next, he slowly turns her around, holding her from her shoulder to face the mirror behind.

Both look at each other quietly through the mirror for a couple of seconds. Then, Dev breaks the gaze looking down on Mahi's still half-exposed back where a couple of laces hangs untied. He slowly starts tying them, making his fingers brush her skin on every opportunity it gets. Mahi, still holding onto the saree in front of her, feels every touch as a hot object touching the cold surface, slowly melting her. When Dev finish tying up the loose laces, he rests his hand on Mahi's shoulder and looks at her through the mirror in front. Mahi returns his gaze with the same soft and steady looks. Dev gives in to his urge as he leans down closer and places a kiss on her nape. As he does that, he looks up to see Mahi closing her eyes at his kiss. He doesn't stop there. He lingers there and slowly starts planting soft kisses on her neck. Mahi also leans back, closing her eyes, as she tilts her head to the other side to give better access of her neck to Dev. As he begins the soft caressing of her neck with his mouth, his hands slide down on her exposed stomach. He pulls her pelvis closer to him, removing any space between them. Without breaking his series of soft kisses, he turns Mahi around to face him.

Both almost panting, open their eyes to watch each other flush. Dev takes out the small clutch from her hair, letting her long locks fall free. He runs his fingers in her hair close to the back of her neck. She closes her eyes involuntarily, feeling his fingers in her hair. Dev watches her enjoying his touch. He continues as he leans down to her neck, planting soft open mouth kisses, tasting her again from there. Dev's tongue on her neck sends another pleasure jolt in Mahi, heightening the tension she had been feeling down there, between her thighs. In those sensations, she doesn't know, when the saree in her hand got dropped on their feet as her hands are on Dev's chest, clutching on tightly to his shirt.

Dev breaks the assault on her neck as he sees Mahi, still not opening her eyes. He cups her face with a hand and keeping the other on her lower back. He rests his forehead on hers for a couple of seconds to catch his breath. Mahi opens her eyes to look in the happy eyes of Dev, full of desires. Both now breathe in sync, holding themselves in that position. Dev leans back without breaking the gaze as he slides his hand from her cheek to hold her chin up. He leans in close to her lips, to which Mahi also closes her eyes.

'Bro, are you rea-SORRY,' says Anu turning around apologetically as she sees her brother and friend in an intimate position.

Mahi's eyes become wide, hearing her friend slash sister-in-law's voice. She immediately pulls away from Dev's hold. Dev sighs off, getting annoyed at the worst timing of his own sister. After that day, today, he got Mahi lost in his touch as they were about to have their second-most romantic moment.

'Bhai! Privacy basics. Lock the door!' says Anu teasingly, turning back slightly.

'Anu! Etiquettes basics. Knock the door!' replies Dev in the same tone, laced with annoyance.

Anu lets out a loud chuckle. She says, turning around to avoid facing the already embarrassed couple,' Anyways, I came to inform you that we all are almost ready. So we were thinking of leaving in 20 minutes or so.'

She continues with a teasing smile,' You've got 20 minutes. So you may continue.' She leaves before Dev could reprimand her for the untimely interference and Mahi's explanation. Dev looks at Mahi, who also happens to looks up at Dev. Feeling flushed, she quickly picks the saree from their feet and tries to walk away. Dev holds her from her arm, stopping her escape.

'She said that we have 20 minutes. We might wanna continue,' asks Dev with excitement in his voice and eyes.

Mahi widens her eyes, becoming astonished at Dev's suggestion. She slaps Dev's stomach with the back of her hand as she gets herself from his grip.

'Keep dreaming,' says Mahi, before leaving Dev high and dry in the room as she goes to the wardrobe to drape the saree. Dev looks at her smiling while she walks off and closes the wardrobe door behind her.

When Dev comes out of the bathroom, all freshened up, he finds the room empty. He quickly gets dressed and goes down.

Mahi feels a little annoyed as she waits for Dev downstairs in the living room, all dressed, all alone. Her clever friend somehow arranged the car system that left Mahi with Dev. First, they didn't stop teasing her as Anu couldn't keep her mouth shut about what she witnessed up in her room. Then they left her here to wait for Dev. Mahi feels the more she tries to avoid Dev, the more the universe plans against her. She sighs and raises her head to look up. She sees Dev coming down the stairs. He is wearing a pastel green shirt paired with a brown tweed jacket, along with his favourite stressed jeans. She couldn't help but let out a pleased expression as she looks at him, walking handsomely towards her. She thinks to herself, this tall, beautiful man claims to love her. The sound of it sends a tickling sensation in the bottom of her stomach. Dev also looks at Mahi with absorbing eyes as she stood elegantly in the middle of the living room. She looked as beautiful as she was without a saree, moments ago, in his arms. The image sends sweet tickles to his manhood. Dev notices the soft and pleasing look on Mahi's face as he sees how glued her eyes are on him. He quietly goes straight to her as she stands there fixed in a trance.

'Are you checking me out?" says Dev teasingly as he makes it sound like he is being harassed.

'What! No!' replies Mahi sprinting out of her daze. She continues, within a second,' Why would I check you out?'

'Why not! When your one look can stop my heart, why it can't do the same to you,' says Dev, softly tilting his head and placing a hand above his chest.

Mahi gulps down sharply as she struggles to give an appropriate and non-revealing answer to Dev's query. Dev simply smiles, seeing Mahi's eyes shaking in the guilt of his accusations.

'Chalien?' asks Dev softly, pulling Mahi out of her confused state.

'Huh?'

'You can think of an answer on our way to the hotel,' says Dev teasingly.

Mahi sighs off. Both leave the house in Dev's car. When they reach the hotel, Dev makes Mahi get down at the entrance. He leaves to park the car himself as he didn't find the valet in front. When she got down, he told her to go ahead with the rest of the family as he needed to reprimand the valet service people himself. Mahi simply nodded to his instructions. She enters the building. She sees the rest of the family in the lobby waiting for them. As soon as they see her, they all start teasing her again. Savitri scolds them gently as she asks Mahi about Dev. To which Mahi tells everyone to go ahead and leave for the restaurant on the rooftop. She says she and Dev will join them soon. All agree and leave for the elevators.

Mahi stays in the lobby as she sees the family members getting on the elevator.

'Mahi Solanki!' says the voice behind Mahi. 'Is that you?' continues the same voice. Mahi turns around only to get shocked and horrified to see the source of that voice.

'It is you,' says the man, same height as Mahi's, with a smug on his face. If Mahi ever hated any human being, then today, that very person happens to be standing in front of her. She thought 12 years ago would be the last time she had ever had to see this face. But, clearly, the universe is not letting her get her own way.

Mahi stands there as she tries hard to maintain a straight face. She tries to hide the feeling of extreme discomfort and shock.

'You do remember me,' says the man with a leer. Mahi goes numb for a second. The man in front of her makes her remember the ugliest phase of her life.

Mahi looks away, trying to control herself as she tries not to let him see her getting affected.

'Of course. You should. Doesn't every girl remembers their first,' says the man in a low voice, taking a step closer to her. He grins widely with overconfidence and a sneer.

Mahi feels disgusted to see this man's face. To Mahi, it is no surprise, he is the same self-obsessed and ill-mannered being he used to be. She controls her rage as she grips the clutch in her hand tightly. She feels a little dizzy as she struggles to stay strong in front of him. To her relief, she feels a familiar hand around her as she turns her head to look up to her handsome saviour.

'Hey! What are you still doing here? I thought you would have gone up,' says Dev softly, putting an assuring yet protective arm around her. He continues smiling, looking down at her pretty face,' Were you waiting for me?'

Mahi simply looks up at him at first. She suddenly feels a rush of relief with Dev's arm around her. She could feel her confidence coming back. Mahi lets out a faint smile as she softly nods.

The man gets irritated as Dev comes in swiftly and breaks his flow. He then gets upset seeing his closeness with Mahi and a little uncomfortable at Mahi's response of how calm she looked in his arms. He interrupts the moment between Dev and Mahi as he says,' Hi! Druv Sharma.'

Dev feels a little lost seeing Mahi's smile. But, he gets pulled out when this man introduces himself to Dev. Dev straightens up as he turns his head to look back at him. He takes Druv's hand in a cordial handshake, saying,' Devrath Jamwal. Do you know my wife?'

Druv gets surprised at the word wife as he chuckles internally. He replies,' Yes. Quite well.'

Dev turns his head towards Mahi as he sees her expression changing from calm to terrified.

'The same school,' continues Druv with a smug on his face as he tries to provoke a response from Mahi.

Dev notices Mahi's discomfort. So he softly moves the hand, holding her from around. He firms the grip softly enough to let Mahi know that he is here. Right next to her. Mahi feels Dev hold, again realising that she can't get weak. Not right now. She gathers her strength back.

'Same school, but not important enough to remember,' says Mahi, confidently looking him straight in the eyes.

Druv sees Mahi not breaking under pressure. Before he could poke her more, she speaks up, turning her whole self towards Dev,' We are late already.'

She puts a hand on Dev's chest softly as she continues,' We shouldn't make them wait.' Without giving Druv a chance to say anything else, Mahi takes Dev's hand in her hand and walks off.

They leave Druv at the lobby as Mahi doesn't let go of Dev's hand while walking to the elevator. Dev knew she held it only for optics, yet he doesn't feel used. As the elevator doors get closed, Dev notice Mahi lost in some thoughts with a frown on her face. She was so lost that she is still holding onto Dev hand, that too tightly. Whatever is going on in her head, Dev notices her grip getting stronger with every passing second. Dev sees the tensed expression on Mahi's face. He saw the same look when he saw her down in the lobby, right before he decided to intervene. He felt something got stirred within Mahi after the encounter with yet another one from her school. However, this encounter doesn't feel right to him. The elevator dings as the door open to the top floor. Mahi gets startled at the sound and realises her hold on Dev's hand. She pulls her hand from his hold and gives herself a mental throttle to get going.

Both get down and starts walking towards the entrance of the restaurant. Mahi tries to keep calm. But, as they were about to reach the doors, she starts feeling stifled. She stops and looks at Dev briefly, to which Dev returns her gaze with a question if she is okay. Then Mahi says,' Go ahead. I need some air.'

'Are you alright?' asks Dev worriedly as he sees Mahi's face leaving its colour.

'Yeah Yeah! I am fine. Just some fresh air,' says Mahi taking a step back as she turns around and almost runs for the doors leading to the open terrace.

She pushes the doors open for the terrace and runs towards the end of it. As she stands there trying to catch her breath, she finds it difficult to breathe. In turn, she holds her chest in striking pain she feels.

No! I thought I was recovered for good. Why now? She thinks to herself. An image vividly flashes in front of her eyes, of herself in a pool of blood.

'Fuck!' she exclaims loudly as her eyes widen, getting horrified by it.

Not helping, she thinks to herself, still holding to her chest, trying to breathe.

'Hey! Are you alright?' says Dev standing behind her, watching her struggling to breathe.

Mahi, with a frown on her face, turns to face Dev. She didn't expect him to follow her. She doesn't say anything at first. She just tries to calm herself by breathing heavily and fast-paced now.

Dev sees her holding her chest in pain. 'Let's get you to the doctor,' says Dev holding her from shoulders with a worried expression now.

'No! No!' says Mahi.

CHAPTER 18 CONCERNED, MORE THAN CURIOUS

Mahi, with a frown on her face, turns to face Dev. She doesn't say anything, just tries to calm herself by breathing heavily and fast-paced now.

Dev sees her holding her chest in pain. 'Let's get you to the doctor,' says Dev holding her from shoulders with a worried expression now.

'No! No!' says Mahi taking a step back from his hold, still taking unsteady breaths. She response to Dev's surprised look,' No need for a doctor-I'll-I'll be fine-5 minutes.'

Dev looks at her questioningly, not convinced with her answer. She again says with staggered and fast-paced breathing,' I am going through a panic attack. I have done this before. I can get it under control. It's just I didn't have these in years. I need 5 minutes. No doctor.'

Dev sees her getting rid of her heels as she struggles. He watches her wrapping her arms around herself tightly.

'How can I help?' says Dev softly, offering himself so that he could help her to calm down.

Mahi looks at him in surprise yet with a frown on her forehead. She hesitates as she looks longer at Dev.

'Say it!' says Dev reading her doubt on her face.

'Hold me! Tightly,' says Mahi giving in to Dev's offer to help. Because she had been trying to get herself calmed down. And she is nowhere to be successful. She is desperate to do anything right now to get this damn panic attack in control. She can worry about the rest later.

Dev gets shocked at her instructions. He hesitates as he thinks that if he heard her correctly.

Mahi looks at his face full of query and surprise says,' My pressure is high. A tight hug helps...to get it lower.'

'Ohkay!' says Dev, immediately taking a step closer to Mahi and wrapping his arms around her in a hug. Mahi closes her eyes, turning her head sideways so that she doesn't bury her nose in Dev's shoulder.

'Tight enough?' asks Dev holding her firmly close to him.

'A little more,' says Mahi instructing him. Dev does so.

Both stand there quietly for the next few seconds, yet no change in Mahi's condition. Dev could feel her shaking under his hold as she still feels breathless. Mahi scolds herself mentally, not to drag her mind to the past. But her mind betrays her as she still fails to stop her trembles with this uneven breathing.

'Distract me,' says Mahi.

'Huh?'

'Talk to me or tell me something so that I don't think about what I am thinking right now. Distract me with something or anything,' says Mahi in between her breathes.

'Okay!' says Dev as he thinks about something for a second, holding her tightly. He continues,' Your ears are right above my heart. Listen to it.'

'What!'

'Listen to my heartbeat and try to sync your breathing with it,' says Dev gently.

'It's beating really fast,' says Mahi listening to it.

'Yes! It is,' says Dev closing his eyes, feeling a little embarrassed. He then quickly continues,' Do this. On every 4 beats, take a deep breath in and hold it for 2 and then, let it go.'

Mahi tries doing what Dev told her. As she does it few times, she feels her breathing getting steady. She keeps doing it, keeping her eyes closed as her head rests on Dev's chest.

A few minutes pass by as both stand on the hotel's terrace, holding each other. Mahi's eyes still closed as she breathes calmly, listening to Dev's heart. She had her hands wrapped around Dev as he holds her softly now. Dev looks far ahead quietly as his chin lightly rests upon Mahi's head. He keeps moving his thumb, on Mahi's back, in a repeating motion. He notices that her shaking has stopped, and she is breathing normally for a while now.

Their comfortable hold on each other gets interrupted. Dev's phone vibrates in his back pocket of his jeans. Mahi opens her eyes and realises for how long they have been here. Like this. She unwraps her arms around Dev as she tries to straighten up. Dev takes his phone out as he still keeps an arm around Mahi, not letting her get out of his hold yet. Mahi doesn't protest and stays in Dev's arms as she puts her hand on his chest softly to maintain a distance between their faces.

Dev picks up the call and speaks into the phone,' Yeah! We are on our way!' He hangs up the call and puts the phone back in his pocket.

He looks down at Mahi's face with concern as he asks,' Feeling better?' Mahi simply nods, looking up. At the exact moment, he sets her loose strands around her forehead. He then rests his palm cupping her face in it. He rubs his thumb on her cheek as he asks her again,' You sure?'

Mahi looks at his concerned eyes as her heart skips a beat for a second there. She nods, placing her hand on the back of his hand, which is holding her face, as she says,' Yes. I feel much better. Thanks.' Dev smiles and feels more relaxed to see the colour returning to her face. He takes the same hand of hers in his own as he says,' Let's go then.'

Dev walks past Mahi and picks up her heels. He places them in front of her, kneeling down. As he puts the footwear on her, he says,' Everyone's waiting for us. I told them something urgent came up in the office so, I took you with me.'

Mahi lets out a smile as Dev tells her about the excuse he made for the family. Dev stands up and takes Mahi's hand in his as he says,' Chalein?'

Mahi simply nods.

Both enter the restaurant holding hands. When Mahi notice everyone's eyes on them, she pulls his hand from Dev's grip. As they approach the table, nobody present tried to tease them as Anu, one cousin, was away for the buffet. Dev quietly pulls the chair for Mahi adjacent to his mother's. Mahi takes the seat as Dev sits next to her.

'What do you wanna have?' Dev asks Mahi softly.

'Anything,' replies Mahi with a little tired voice.

'Okay, I am in a mood to eat something heavy. Should I order the same for you?' asks Dev without pestering her more to decide what to eat. He just wants her to eat as he looks at her drained face.

She hesitates a little, listening to the word 'heavy.' So she says,' You place it for yourself. I'll have few bites from yours only.'

'You need to eat,' replies Dev with a command in his voice.

Mahi pouts a little, listening to Dev's assertion. Dev almost gave in, looking at her pouting cutely but, he doesn't change the expression.

Mahi sighs softly, she says,' Okay. Order for yourself so that I can eat from yours and from the buffet.'

Dev nods, agreeing to her suggestion. Mahi smiles faintly, getting up to join the girls around the buffet.

Savitri notices the sweet interaction between the two. A smile slips to her lips. Then Savitri exchange looks with her husband, sitting across the table reminiscing about their days. Mr Maan Jamwal also notices the wife's pleasing looks and returns it with a smile.

After Mahi leaves the table, Dev finds an opportunity to ease his curiosity about what happened to Mahi today. And other than her, only one person he is sure of could give him some answers. He slides to Mahi's empty chair, closer to his mother.

'Can I ask you something?' says Dev leaning in closer to Savitri.

Savitri nods at his son's question.

'Do you know anyone named Druv from Mahi's school?' asks Dev in a low voice.

Savitri's eyes widen at the mention of the name as her expressions change from nothing to a frown. She asks,' Druv Sharma? Why? What happened?'

Dev knew that the man he met earlier has definitely had to do something to Mahi's concealed past. His mother's worried face just proves that.

'Nothing much. We happened to bump into each other. Earlier, in the lobby. Don't worry. Mahi handled it quite well. It's just...,' Dev takes a short pause before telling his mother what happened after. He continues,' When we came up, she...she had a panic attack. That's why we were late.'

'She didn't have one in years. I have to check on her,' says Savitri getting up from her chair and leaving to see Mahi.

Dev sighs off before he could ask more. He sees his mother grabbing Mahi away from his sisters. She speaks to her as Mahi glances at Dev. Then, she tells his mother something with a calm expression on her face. Dev could read the lips saying that she is fine now.

When everyone was almost done with the dinner as all were busy with their respective desserts.

'Here,' says Anu coming to Mahi, handing her a bowl of ice cream.

'Thanks. Only you could know this is my favourite flavour,' says Mahi taking a spoonful in her mouth.

'Belgium Chocolate is your favourite? Wow, I never knew this,' says Anu stating a fact to Mahi's surprise. She takes a seat opposite Mahi. She continues with a smirk,' By the way, Bhai told me to give you this.'

Mahi gets surprised at first then tries to ignore that detail. Anu continues,' Belgium chocolate was over. Bhai got them to open the new box just for you. From the looks of it, the kitchen guys were already planning to wrap it up.'

Mahi turns her head in Dev's direction. He was standing far, speaking to the manager. He looks back at Mahi in the next second as if he could feel Mahi's eyes on him. Mahi mouth the words 'thank you.' Dev nods, smiling as he gets pleased, reading Mahi's lips.

When everyone gets ready to leave the hotel, all wait in the lobby for the car. Mahi looks around to make sure if an unwanted person doesn't show up again. Dev notices her getting tensed as she looks around the lobby. He thinks of something and takes his father on the sides. He asks him about something and then smiles, thanking him. His father pats him on the shoulder, encouraging Dev proudly.

Everyone leaves the same way as they came. Mahi, while seated next to driving Dev. She becomes tense as she expects that now might be the time when Dev might ask her about today. Mahi glances at Dev a few times, waiting for him to speak. But, nothing. Dev notices Mahi getting a little anxious.

'How about a coffee before we go back?' asks Dev.

Mahi was about to respond otherwise because she doesn't drink coffee. But, she simply says yes as she realises that Dev might want to ask her while they'll sit somewhere quiet.

Dev continues on the highway for few more kilometres before he takes a sharp turn to the rough road with small street lights and dense trees on both sides. Driving for a minute or two on the unpaved road, they take another turn to the left. After a couple of seconds into the turn, Mahi notices soft lights coming ahead. A big iron opened gate comes. It looks like a private estate. As they enter, Dev drives around a small fountain in the middle and park the car next to a couple of already parked cars.

As they get down the car, Mahi asks,' Where are we?'

'You'll see,' says Dev with a smile and eagerness to watch Mahi's reaction.

Through a hedged entrance, they enter a big open garden. It had a few antique-looking tables and chairs spread across it. On one side of the space, there is a natural flowing small stream. On the other side was a small white house. It looked old and yet preserved beautifully. The garden was lit with a lot of small lamps placed all over the place. The place is aptly bright in the open night sky.

Mahi takes in the view, and Dev takes in her reaction of looking at the place. Dev interjects,' Dad used to take Mom here on their dates.'

'Really?' asks Mahi becoming surprised and intrigued with what Dev said.

'Mmm mm. Both used to come here so often that Dad became quite good friends with the estate owner,' says Dev while he guides her to one of the unoccupied tables.

They take the seat opposite each other when an older looking man with a turban on his head and a smile approaches them. Dev recognising the man gets up and greets him.

'Welcome, Betaji,' says the man greeting Dev in a hug. Dev greets back. The man continues,' Aaj kaise yahan? (How come you are here today?)'

'Uncle, inse miliye (Uncle, meet her),' says Dev turning the man towards Mahi. Mahi gets up, saying,' Hello Uncle.'

'Oye ye kon sundar bacha hain? (Who is this beautiful child?) Hello ji,' replies the man smiling sweetly at Mahi.

'Mahi. My wife!' says Dev looking lovingly at Mahi.

'Oye hoye. Welcome! Welcome Ji,' says the man getting excited.

'Mahi. Meet Gurmeet Uncle. Owner of this place and Dad's friend,' says Dev.

'Bacha aapko dekh ke aaj dil khush ho gaya. Inke baap aaya karte the apni hone wali wife ke saath. Aaj beta aaya hai apni wife ke saath (Kiddo, my heart is happy seeing you today. His father used to come here with his would be wife. Today his son is here with his wife),' says the man laughing out loudly.

Dev and Mahi both laugh at Gurmeet Uncle's little joke.

'Acha, I won't disturb you guys anymore. Tell me. Kya bhijwau? (What should I send?)' asks Gurmeet Uncle.

'Coffee for me and Jasmine tea for Mahi,' replies Dev. Mahi looks at Dev in amazement at how attentive and detailed he is towards her. Mahi gets happy and feels a pinch of sadness at the same time.

'Right away,' says Gurmeet Uncle snapping his fingers as he leaves them.

Soon a young boy comes with their order and leaves after placing their respective beverages in front of them. As they take few sips, Dev continues telling the stories of his parents. Mahi quietly listens and enjoys them. But, at the back of her mind, she waits for Dev to ask her. He should be asking her the question for which he took an effort to bring her here. Just like that, time passes but, Dev doesn't ask her anything.

Mahi eventually becomes impatient. So she asks Dev,' Why are you not asking me?'

'What I am supposed to ask?' counters Dev to Mahi's sudden interject.

Mahi takes a deep breath as she says,' For the reason, you brought me here.'

Dev smiles at Mahi's suggestions. He brings his serious face back as he asks,' And what exactly that would be?'

Mahi becomes confused as she is unable to read him. She takes a pause and says in a small voice,' About what happened today at the hotel. Aren't you curious?'

Dev smiles politely at her question. He says,' Do you want me to be honest with you?'

Mahi nods lightly.

Dev says,' I was curious. I am not anymore.'

Mahi doesn't understand what he means by that. Seeing Mahi's confused looks, Dev says,' Now you can ask me why.'

'Why?'

Dev looks a little longer at Mahi before replying. He says,' Because I don't like to see you hurt.'

He continues after taking a short pause,' When I saw you today on the terrace. You were in pain. Literally! Yes, at first I wanted to know what could be the reason for your condition like that. Then, while holding you in my arms, feeling your trembles and how hard you were struggling to breathe. It struck me if just thinking about it be so tormenting for you, how worst it could be if you had to speak about it. Then only I decided. I don't want to know about what happened today. I realised my curiosity was way smaller than my concern for you.'

Mahi listens to Dev's confession silently. She thinks to herself, how much space and how many more chances he gives to her. He doesn't question her or just to find the answer to his curiosity. He doesn't want her to tell him the most dreaded past of hers. Thinking about it, Mahi wells up as she tries not to give in to her overwhelming emotions.

Seeing Mahi's eyes getting moist, Dev gets worried as he asks,' Hey! I am sorry. I didn't mean to remind you of it.'

Mahi shakes her head, looking away as she wipes the moisture from the side of her eyes. She gulps down her emotions when she says,' No. That's not it.'

'To be honest, I got you here so that you could forget all about today. And just relax,' says Dev softly, keeping his tone gentle.

Mahi returns his gaze as she says,' Thank you.'

'For what?'

'For everything,' says Mahi smiling.

Dev simply returns her smile with a smile, involuntarily.

Both spend some time there quietly, taking in the fresh night air around them. When they get home, thankfully, everyone was in their respective rooms. Taking their beauty sleeps before the big day tomorrow.

It is the middle of the night. Dev wakes up from the noise he unable to discern. He hears soft sobs with sniffles. He opens his eyes, struggling to keep them open. It's still dark outside. He turns his head to his left, where Mahi is supposed to be sleeping. However, he sees Mahi seated, still on the bed. Dev sits up to see what's wrong. He sees it is her sobs which woke him. She is sitting, holding up her left-hand wrist tightly with her right hand. She is crying softly.

'Mahi! What's wrong?' asks Dev in a hoarse voice.

'I can't stop it. It keeps bleeding,' says Mahi while crying softly and holding her wrist.

Chapter 19 A Nightmare or a Glimpse into Her Past

It is the middle of the night. Dev wakes up from the noise he unable to discern. He hears soft sobs with sniffles. He opens his eyes, struggling to keep them open. It's still dark outside. He turns his head to his left, where Mahi is supposed to be sleeping. However, he sees Mahi seated, still on the bed. Dev sits up to see what's wrong. He sees it is her sobs which woke him. She is sitting, holding up her left-hand wrist tightly with her right hand. She is crying softly.

'Mahi! What's wrong?' asks Dev in a hoarse voice.

'I can't stop it. It keeps bleeding,' says Mahi while crying softly and holding her wrist.

Dev gets worried. He takes her hand to look what she means that she is bleeding. He couldn't see clearly. So he quickly bends back to turns on the sidelights. He sees her hand. He doesn't see any blood but, he sees Mahi still holding her wrist tightly.

'Let me see,' says Dev softly, asking her to remove her hand. She does. He doesn't see any blood but an old scar. He gets confused. Mahi wraps her hand again on her wrist as she says, whimpering,'

I didn't have a choice. I didn't know what to do. I don't want to die. Please help me stop this.'

Dev looks at her, crying for real. He suddenly realises that she seems awake but, she isn't. She is sleepwalking. Or Sleeptalking.

'Mahi. Look here. It's not real,' says Dev wiping her tears from her face, trying to wake her up.

She doesn't respond to him. So he holds her from her arms and gives her a firm jerk to wake her up. Mahi wakes up from the jolt, becoming confused. Her eyes are wide open in bewilderment.

'What happened?' asks Mahi seeing Dev next to her. She sees outside. It is dark as she sees the clock on the wall to confirm.

'Nothing. You were just having a nightmare,' says Dev trying to calm her.

She feels her face wet, and so her eyes. She asks,' Was I crying?'

'Yeah! I guess,' says Dev.

'Was I talking as well?' asks Mahi looking at Dev becoming tensed.

Dev recalls what exactly happened moments ago. He says,' Just mumbling. Couldn't understand.' He makes her lie back and tucks her in, asking her to try sleeping again.

He switches off the sidelights and lies down, turning towards Mahi. He sees Mahi still wide awake with concern on her face.

'Can't sleep?' asks Dev seeing her wide awake.

She turns her head in his direction with worried eyes. She shakes her head in a no.

Dev opens his left arm as he reaches for her arm with his right hand. He says,' Come here.'

Mahi slides closer to Dev, placing her head on his arm, closer to his shoulder. She puts her hand on his chest as Dev lies on his back and closing Mahi in his arms in a cuddle. Mahi, now resting her head on his chest closer to his neck. Dev feels her stress while holding her close to him. He starts moving his left hand in soft rubs on her back to soothe her as he places his right hand on her left arm.

'Don't worry. It was just a bad dream,' says Dev as he places a soft kiss on top of her head. Mahi relaxes in his arms as she closes her eyes. Listening to Dev's heart beneath her ears, she drifts to sleep, hugging him.

Dev feels her heavy and steady breathing as he realises that she is finally sleeping. On the other hand, Dev couldn't sleep for some time. He thinks about the events, happened today. First, meeting that man in the hotel lobby, then a sudden panic attack on the terrace and now this. He thinks, was this really just a nightmare or fragment of reality. He doesn't want to think much about it but, everything he witnessed so far seems to point him in some unknown direction. Dev looks down at her hand on his chest. He softly picks it up and turns it slightly to see the scar on her wrist. He caresses it as he thinks back to the story Mahi told her how she got it. Then his mind runs the flashes of Mahi moments ago, talking in her sleep. He places her hand back on his chest, softly rubbing the back of it. He then caresses her head softly as he plants a kiss on her forehead, holding her. He presses her gently to him. He eventually, still holding her protectively in his arms, falls asleep.

The alarm goes off, waking Mahi up. Reflexively she turns half and slides it off. She turns back to her earlier comfortable position. She feels a warm breath on her face. Last night flashes in front of her eyes, making her open her eyes. She sees Dev's face.

Dev is fast asleep an inch away from hers. She looks down at his arm around her. And feels another of his arm under her head. She pulls her hand close to her mouth, becoming still for a second. Then she sees the quiet face of Dev. He looks amazingly calm as he breathes uniformly. Mahi recalls the last night on the hotel terrace and then his words in that cafe. Mahi feels an urge to touch his face. She feels like she got an opportunity to admire his feature this close without him realising. She lets out a smile as she traces his profile with her fingers, close enough to almost touching him. She stops her tracing on his lips, trailing there longer. She touches his lower lip softly. Then, she slowly pulls back the hand to her chest. She moves her head up, closing in, planting a soft kiss on his nose. She smiles, seeing him still asleep.

She tries to get up from his hold slowly without waking him up. As she slowly half gets up, sliding away from him, she feels the arm coming alive. She gets pulled back in Dev's arms.

"It's very early. Sleep some more," says Dev gruffly while keeping his eyes closed.

Mahi becomes still in his arms. Dev feels her becoming stiff. He opens his eyes as he says, 'I am not ready to say good morning yet.'

'How long have you been awake?' asks Mahi in a faint voice.

'Since your alarm went off,' says Dev closing his eyes back as he tightens his arms around Mahi, pulling her closer. Their foreheads, now touching each other. The whole night, he was subconsciously aware of Mahi next to him. However, she slept peacefully in his arms without making any movements or any bad dreams. When her alarm went off, waking her up, Dev also wakes up with her moving in his arms. Yet, he keeps pretending to sleep as he was anyways too lazy to open his eyes. He then feels her becoming still as he waits for her to make some movement. Then he faintly feels her fingers on his face and a soft touch on his lips. He continues to pretend to sleep as he lets her do something desirable for once. It gets difficult for him to stay like that when he felt her warm lips on his nose.

He sees her getting nervous as she realises that he was awake this whole time. He leans back a little as he says,' How did you sleep? Any bad dreams after that?'

Mahi shakes her head slowly, stealing her eyes from him.

'Good,' replies Dev, leaning in again, closing his eyes, placing his forehead close to hers.

Mahi starts moving, trying to leave from his hold, saying,' I have to go.'

Dev doesn't loosen his grip as he asks,' Where? It's too early to go anywhere.'

'Today is Anu's engagement. There is a lot to be done,' says Mahi, still protesting against his hold.

'The event doesn't start before 8 in the evening. And there are a lot of other people to manage things without you being there. Why don't we sleep for some more? We'll join the rest on breakfast,' says Dev.

'We can't,' says Mahi, to which Dev open his eyes, looking straight in Mahi with questions. She immediately continues, answering them,' I can't. I promised Bua to take her to temple early in the morning.'

Dev closes his eyes again, saying,' Nobody is awake this early. You can just relax.'

'I can't,' says Mahi, trying to leave his hold.

Dev frowns as he says,' It'll keep getting tighter unless you stop moving.'

Mahi stops, becoming still, giving up. Dev smiles, still keeping his eyes closed. He pulls her closer as he shifts her head on his shoulder, her nose closer to his neck. Dev rests his jaws on her forehead. Mahi stays quiet, breathing in his closeness. She thinks to herself, how can someone smell pleasant, even in the morning. Dev feels her getting relaxed under her hold. He thinks to himself, this feels nice, her in my arms. He silently makes a wish that he gets to spend every morning with her like this.

Mahi's feels comfortable lying in his arms. Suddenly a thought crosses her mind. She can't let this happen for long. She has to set a boundary between her and Dev. Dev feels her getting tensed up again. He starts caressing her arms with his thumb in a repetitive motion. Both stay like that for the next couple of minutes. Until a knock on the door ends their comfortable embrace. Both hear Anu shouting on their door, calling Mahi urgently. Mahi looks at Dev silently, waiting for his response. Dev sighs heavily, loosening his hold over Mahi. She amusingly looks at Dev's frustrated look as he can't protest against her younger sister's tantrums. She loses the smile, thinking about what she just decided to do. She quickly gets up before he changes his mind.

Later that morning, Dev catches Mahi in the garage looking for something in stored boxes of hers. He stands quietly with hands folded against his chest as he watches Mahi getting worked up searching for something. She picks one of the boxes and turns to place it down but drops it when she gets startled seeing Dev standing there.

'What are you doing here?' asks Mahi with a tinge of annoyance in her voice.

Dev smiles amusingly at her habit of being jumpy whenever she sees him. He sees her sitting down on her feet as she puts the books on the floor back in the box. Dev quickly walks up to her, sitting down across her helping her put the books back in the box.

He says,' I was looking at you,' with a flirtation laced in his tone.

Mahi ignores him. Dev notices her getting tensed as she doesn't respond to him. She continues to focus on knocked over stuff in front of her. He holds her hand,' Hey! What's wrong?'

Mahi pulls her hand back with a jerk saying,' No! Nothing's wrong! It doesn't have to be something wrong every time for you to sweep in to ask me what's wrong.'

'Fine. Don't have to be rude about it. I was just concerned. You look tensed,' says Dev trying to understand her mood.

'You don't have to be concerned about me every time. It's not your job. And, I am not some damsel in need who would be glad every fucking time you interfere in my damn business,' says Mahi standing up. She gets more upset with Dev's presence.

Dev scoffs in disbelief, looking at her, snapping at him as he stands up too. He says,' You think I am interfering in your life?'

'Then what you are doing here right now?' asking Dev rhetorically.

'Wow! You are really trying hard to push me away this time,' says Dev sarcastically.

Mahi sighs off in frustration as she says,' I am not pushing you away. I am simply saying thank you for your help so far. I don't need it any more. So just move on. You don't have to wait for me. I am not gonna change my mind.'

'Clear enough,' says Dev with a smirk on his face.

Mahi feels exasperated at his reaction as she runs her fingers in her hair, grunting and moving back and forth. Dev notices her getting all furious.

'Anything else?' asks Dev putting his hands in track pant's pocket.

'Yes, please. Don't stand here on top of my head waiting for my command. Do whatever pleases you. Find someone else to entertain you,' says Mahi fuming and trying to be as rude as she can.

'Good to know that you think that I am around you only for entertainment purpose,' says Dev with a straight, attempting to see her limits.

'Aren't you?' says Mahi with a scoff. She continues, with the same tone,' In the past 48 hours, I have encountered enough drama to entertain you. But, unfortunately for you, I am not left with any more.'

'Don't count this one out,' says Dev as a passing comment.

'Yes! I am probably being dramatic right now. Why? Not entertaining enough!' replies Mahi with not pretending to fume this time.

She continues,' Why don't you try with Kate? Maybe she has better entertaining drama for you than me.'

'So we are playing Push and Pull now?' says Dev with an unfounded calm voice, irritating enough for Mahi. He continues,' Great! That's what you wanna do? Let's play this properly then.'

'What do you mean?' asks Mahi with an irritated tone.

'I'll tell you what I meant,' says Dev as he takes a step closer. He says,' Well, I have been interested in the Pull part of the game. But, as of now, you are insisting on the Push part of the game. Desperately.' He continues to take another step and stand exactly in front of Mahi, only a couple of feet away. He leans down close to her height as he says,' So let's give it a try to your part. You want me to try again with Kate. And it's perfectly okay with you since you are not jealous of her.'

'I am not jealous of anyone,' says Mahi, keeping her teeth clenched.

'And you don't mind if I cheat on you as well,' says Dev, keeping his voice as steady as possible to incite Mahi.

Mahi takes a small calming breath. She continues in a low voice,' We are married on paper. Nothing is going on between us. And noth-'

'Nothing will ever happen,' Dev completes her sentence with a smirk. He says,' Heard it before.'

He leans back, straightening up as he continues,' So it is decided then. I'll try my best with Kate before she leaves the city. And it will have nothing to do with you.'

Mahi tightens her jaws, controlling her anger as she says,' Thank god for that.'

Dev smiles slyly at Mahi's replies as he could clearly see her anger almost surfacing. Mahi feels the heat as she sees Dev smiling confidently. She feels as if Dev is possessed by his evil twin, who has arisen only to trigger Mahi. Dev inclines closer to Mahi's ear as he softly says,' Anyways, I am sure Kate will be much less stiff than you. Oh, wait. I already know so.'

He straightens up as he steps back, turning around, leaves Mahi standing alone in the garage. Mahi stays in the same place fuming with anger and disappointment at the same time. She is breathing fast as she becomes furious with passing seconds thinking about what just happened. She kicks the box hard when she fails to contain her rage.

She takes the support of the boxes stacked behind as she hangs her head in exhaustion from getting angry. She thinks to herself, that's what I wanted. To draw the line. I better start getting used to this.

In that afternoon, Mahi stood beside the sofa where Savitri, Bua and one more extended relative are seated. Below them on the carpet sat the young cousins of Dev, along with Nivi and Anu. They all were arguing on how to decorate the plates which will be carrying the rings. A silver plate, along with laces, some fancy items spread across the centre table. In all this chaos, Mahi's attention was focussed somewhere else. On the pair of humans who stood across the room. Away from the chaos, enjoying among themselves. Nivi asks for Mahi'a suggestion in between the very high pitched conversation among the cousins and ladies on the sofa. When she doesn't get a response, she turns her head behind to see Mahi, burning holes somewhere far with her eyes. When Nivi follows her gaze, she sees Dev and Kate engaged in some serious discussion across the room as if they are planning something. In between those discussions, Nivi could see Dev being friendly with her as she laughs out loud at Dev's silly jokes. Nobody else notices Mahi's irritated expression. Nivi signals Anu towards the ongoing situation. Both slyly gets up and stands next to Mahi. Discussion on decorating plate continues even when both the sisters get up, leaving the place. Mahi feels the sisters standing next to her but, she doesn't give up on her glare.

'Tell me something? Does every man who studies abroad had a foreigner fling,' asks Mahi with an annoyed tone.

'Sam never had one. None I know of,' says Nivi chuckling a little and then losing the smile when Anu gives her a glare.

'Amit had one. He told me while we dated. But, it's okay. He is marrying me,' interjects Anu, emphasising the last statement.

Mahi sighs without looking at them as she says,' Does his fling also have an amazing ass like hers?' She said this, looking at Kate.

Both the sisters look at each other first, and then both lean back a little to look at Mahi from behind. Nivi places a slap on Mahi's arm.

'Oww Oww!' exclaims Mahi a little loudly, simultaneously twice as she gets one from Anu too.

'Do you have any idea how envious we have been growing up with you?' says Nivi in a low voice.

'What! Why? What did I do?'

'Because you are born with an amazing ass. Hers is nothing in front of yours,' replies Anu getting agitated.

'So amazing that even your kurta can't hide that,' says Nivi hitting her again at the same spot.

Mahi frowns, rubbing her arms. She says,' Okay! You are making me conscious now.'

'Well, you asked for it,' says Anu.

'And anyway, Dev is not like any other men. I am not saying this because he is my brother. I am saying this because he looks at you differently,' interjects Nivi thoughtfully.

'Right! Differently,' scoffs Mahi sarcastically.

'He never looked at Yashika like that,' says Nivi drawing Mahi's attention.

'Because he loved her,' says Mahi, again countering Nivi, whatever she is trying to point.

'Because he never did,' replies Nivi. She takes a pause as she continues,' Men has a look when they are in love. One can tell when they look at their partners or whomsoever they love. I never saw that look on Dev, even though he almost married her. But, I see that when he looks at you. Trust me. I am not just saying this because you are married now.'

Mahi sighs off, thinking that she is already aware of it. But, her concern is that she can't do anything about it.

'And this is not the first time I have seen this. Concerning you,' continues Nivi in a low voice, looking away.

Before Mahi could ask, Anu prompts,' What do you mean? You are seeing Bhai here for the first time after they got married.'

'It was at my wedding,' says Nivi in a voice as low as possible.

'What?'

'My wedding. It was the happiest day of my life but, one thing about it disturbed me a lot,' says Nivi, opening up to Mahi and Anu. She continues,' Apart from the fact that Dev got his girlfriend in the most outrageous attire at my wedding. It didn't matter to me as much as the way he kept looking at you. Even when he was with his girlfriend. Then'

'After that, I kind of hoped that he'd soon approach you and get over Yashika. But, one fine day, I hear that my brother has decided to marry her. I thought maybe I saw it wrong. But in these past 2 days, I knew it. I was never wrong,' says Nivi with a pleasing voice. She continues,' So stop worrying about any foreigner fling or her not so amazing ass. You are all he sees.'

Mahi turns her head in Dev's direction after listening to Nivi. She sees Dev looking at her. When he meets her eyes, he stays there for a couple of seconds and then looks away.

'Didi ye kahan rakhna hain? (Where should I keep this?)' asks Karim standing behind them, breaking the three's ladies conversation. When they turn around, they see Karim carrying a heavy box half-opened. Mahi opens it to see what is in it. She sees lots of small candles and some decorative stuff in them.

'Ye kis liye hain? (Whom this is for?)' asks Anu standing next to it, eying the stuff.

'It's mine,' says Dev as he closes the box and takes it from Karim as he leaves with it.

Ladies are left with confusion as Dev disappears with the box. Without giving any explanation to them. They look at each other puzzled and shrug their shoulders. They return to the chaos in the living regarding the plates for rings.

After lunch, everyone has already left for the venue with their belongings. No one else was in the house. While Mahi is about to leave the place to pick Anu from the salon. When she opens the door, the guard appears on the stairs with buckets of flowers behind him. He says some delivery guy left them in the name of Dev. There are a lot of red roses and white carnations. She thinks maybe the decoration guys mistakenly delivered them to the house address. Within the next second, Dev appears next to her, asking the guard to take them into the house.

'Are these for decoration? Why have they delivered here?' asks Mahi, thinking that the flowers must be for the engagement function.

'You must be getting late. Be on your way,' replies Dev ignoring her query. Before she could counter, he leaves to get inside.

CHAPTER 20 A PARTIAL CONFESSION, YET ENOUGH?

Mahi sighs off and leaves.

Later that evening, before the event, everyone gets ready in the rooms at the venue. Mahi's mind every now and then wanders off to morning's event in the garage and then in the afternoon, followed by the time when delivery of flowers took place. She looks around the room where all the ladies are busy getting ready for the engagement function. Mahi is already all set, wearing a light rose-gold zari work blue and green shaded saree with a rose gold brocade blouse. Everyone praised her choice of saree and how beautiful she looked wearing such simple and elegant attire. As she helps the rest, getting ready, she runs a quick eye around the room, looking for Kate. Mahi was sure till afternoon she saw Kate at the house. After that, she lost track of her whereabouts. She goes to Anu and asks her if she has seen Kate. Anu replies that Kate might get late for the function as something important came up. Mahi feels uncomfortable with her answer. So without thinking much, Mahi leaves the room and walks quickly towards the venue. She reaches the fully decorated banquet hall with an open garden at the end of it. She looks for one person she hopes will be there.

And there he is. Dev. He stands wearing black traditional light embroidery work Jodhpurs, with the top button opened casually. He looks handsome even when he wore his professional mask of being the boss. Mahi stands there for few seconds, looking at him from far, sighing off. He is instructing the people around for last-minute checks on all the arrangement.

'Excuse me, Ma'am,' says the man standing behind Mahi, breaking her focus on her husband. Mahi turns around to address him.

'Sorry to disturb you. Actually, I was supposed to deliver this ring to Mr Devrath. I can't find-oh there he is,' says the man, without completing his sentence as he walks off seeing Dev.

She sees a man approaching Dev. She notices Dev's expression turning into tense seeing the man. Man hands him the small box as he briefly says something and leaves the place. Mahi notices Dev thinking of something as he starts walking towards her. As soon as he notices Mahi standing at the entrance, he slows down his pace of walking. He sees Mahi with a look, Mahi is unable to read. As he notices her eyes darting from his eyes to the box in his hand, Dev quickly puts it in his trouser pant's pocket. Mahi thinks to herself what ring the man was talking about. As for the Engagement rings, she had them with her in her bag upstairs in her room. Then what ring, the man handed to Dev?

Dev doesn't say anything to Mahi as he tries to walk past her. Mahi stops him by saying,' Where are you going? Guests will be here soon?'

Dev stops as he says without looking at Mahi,' I have something to deal with. I'll be back soon.' He leaves before Mahi could stop him with any further reasoning.

Mahi stands there as Dev leaves the venue, taking the exit. She stands for a couple of seconds, getting perplexed. Then she looks around the empty decorated banquet hall. She notices that the flowers that got delivered in the afternoon were not part of the decoration. Then her mind runs back to the box of candles that Karim brought in earlier in the day. She stops her mind from thinking anymore as she widens her eyes, trying to control her wild imagination.

Now, Mahi doesn't think. She acts as per her emotions. She quickly walks through the exit, moving to the parking. She spots Shankar standing at the corner next to the guard's cabin. Shankar sees Mahi walking towards him as he quickly runs towards her asking where he needs to take her.

She shakes her head as she says, putting her hand open in front of him,' Gaadi ki chaabi (Car keys).'

He gets confused and insists,' Main le chalta hoon Ma'am. Chaliye. (I'll take you Ma'am. Let's go)'

She controls her anger as she almost raises her voice,' Chaabi! (Keys!)

Shankar doesn't dare to say anything anymore as he hands her the car keys quietly and quickly.

Mahi walks to the car, getting in as she drives it off. She drives straight to the house, knowing it would be empty at this time.

She reaches the main gate. As the guard pulls the gate open, she sees Dev's car on the porch. She drives the car inside and pulls in behind the Dev's car. She gets down from the car and shuts the door. She notices the main door wide open. She walks up to the door, noticing the living room without any lights. But, she sees the back door to Verandah opened and soft fluttering light coming from there. She slowly walks towards the light, saying a silent prayer, hoping not to see what she imagined before coming here. She smells an aroma of roses as she nears the back door. When she reaches the door, she sees candles lit, drawing up a path out to Verandah. It is filled with roses and white carnations decorated along the borders. She walks out in the Verandah when it turns left towards the extended portion of Verandah. She sees Kate dressed in an Indian Ethnic attire on her knees with a small box opened in her hand.

'What the Fuck!' exclaims Mahi seeing her.

Kate stands up, getting tensed and shocked as she says,' Mahi! Darling, what are you doing here?'

'It's my question. What are you doing here?' asks Mahi getting furious, seeing her all dressed as her imagination has already gone wild.

'Mahi! Why are you here?' asks Dev standing down in the garden, getting all confused with her presence.

Mahi turns around to him, losing her cool,' What the fuck is going on here?'

Dev walks up the stairs of Verdandah as they all hear the car door at the front.

'Oh no! He is here. Hide. Quickly,' asks Kate to Dev and Mahi, almost kind of begging them to disappear at this moment for now.

'Who is here? What's going on?' asks Mahi getting almost irritated with Kate.

Both shush her together, telling her to lower her voice.

'Not now. Please Hide,' begs Kate this time.

Dev takes Mahi's hand as he says,' Come with me.' He takes her by hand as they both move towards the hedges. They enter the pool area. Dev takes her with him as they hide behind the hedgerow, which divides the pool and the garden.

'What are we doing here?' asks Mahi, getting aggravated more with Dev as he almost drags her here. As if he is about to scold her for showing up here and disturbing his plans.

'Can't you be quiet for a few seconds?' says Dev, with annoyance. He continues as he asks her to look through hedges, 'Look for yourself.'

She turns her head with a frown on her face and tries to look through hedges. She could see the Verandah and Kate at the end of it. Kate looks nervous as Mahi notice someone coming through the doors. At first, Mahi sees a silhouette and then sees a man walking towards Kate as she kneels down, holding the small box opened in front of her.

'Kate wanted to propose to her boyfriend. She asked me for help. I came here to drop the box of the ring. That idiot was supposed to deliver to Kate. But, he delivered it to me. I was about to leave back when you showed up,' whispers Dev softly, explaining to Mahi what actually is happening here. Mahi becomes shocked at listening to it at first.

'What are you doing here?' asks Dev, still whispering as they both stood half bent, hiding behind the hedges.

Mahi avoids looking at him as she takes steps back, straightening up. She slowly walks towards the other end. Dev follows her quietly. She doesn't answer Dev as she still grasps the situation, why exactly she came down and expecting what. She keeps on walking as she takes the small passage through the laundry area of the house. It is a small space between the house and the boundary walls of the premises. It leads to the front of the house.

When they come out in the front, Dev notices Mahi not responding and not looking at him as she keeps walking straight towards the second main gate. He calls out her name, stopping her in her tracks. She turns around to face Dev, a couple of metres apart. Dev notices the stress on Mahi's face.

'What exactly are you doing here?' asks Dev, getting confused at Mahi's expressions. He sees Mahi not standing still but taking small steps back and forth, becoming nervous or maybe stressing about something. He suddenly asks her,' Did you follow me?'

Mahi looks up at him, with a pang of guilt readable in her eyes. She looks away immediately, getting tensed, running her fingers in her hair in a frustrated manner. She sighs heavily and then starts pacing back and forth in small steps, getting all panicky.

'Mahi!' Dev calls out with a question in his tone. She looks at him with shaky eyes. Her expression overly tensed, like she is going through something but unable to work through it. He notices the worry in her eyes as he sees her now panting almost. He says,' Say it. What is it?'

'I don't know what to do. What- what am I supposed to do now?' says Mahi, immediately replying to Dev's insistence. Dev quietly listens to her fumbling through her emotions. She continues,' What I am gonna do? How-how am I supposed to move from here? Where am I- How should I go? I-I can't. I can't decide.'

'Decide what?' asks Dev softly, trying to read through her apprehension.

Mahi sorrowfully looks at Dev. She takes a deep breath in as she says,' Us... You and I.' She shakes her head softly as she continues,' I mean. I don't know how to deal with this. It is decided that we can't be together. I can't bear to imagine you with someone else. Clearly, I couldn't control myself to be rash enough to follow you here, thinking god knows what. I thought it would be okay if I'll push you away. It will be okay not to let you know how I feel. Anyways, this arrangement between us will end in a year. You'll move on with your life here. I'll take up the transfer to some other city, and I'll manage my feelings. But I never thought that moving on in terms of being with someone else. It enrages me thinking about it so, I cannot do this. And I am unable to manage this feeling. How am I suppose to deal with this? I have never felt like this before.

I am losing my control over it. We can't be together, and I can't see you with someone else. My head is in chaos right now. I don't know what to do.' Dev could see the pain on her face when she rants about her dilemma. In doing so, she doesn't realise what she has actually confessed in front of him. She takes a scanty pause to breathe and continues, looking at Dev,' What I am gonna do?'

After Dev listens to her rant silently, he thinks about Mahi following her, doubting him. But that's not what caught his attention. His mind gets stuck at one statement of Mahi that they can't be together as if Mahi decided it for both of them. Like in some form of fact. It felt like it is determined for them not to be together. He takes a brief pause when he says,' Why can't we be together?'

Mahi looks at him with pain emerging in her eyes as she says in a low voice, trying to control her emotions,' We can't.'

'Why?' asks Dev again, with little more emphasis. He sees Mahi's eyes tearing up as she tries hard to gulps down her emotions. Mahi sniffles, trying to control her feelings, almost at the edge of pouring out. She could see the pain in Dev's eyes even at a distance he stood from her.

She couldn't take it anymore. She breaks into soft sobs as she speaks,' I am scared.' She continues as tears run down her face,' I am shit scared. To lose myself. Again. In you. In this. I'm...I am terrified to lose you before even you could be mine. I am scared that if I give in to my feelings...I am afraid you would not see me the way you see me now. You would not feel the same the way you do now.' She says all of this with a broken voice as she still tries to control her tears.

Dev's heart sinks, watching Mahi breaking down, opening up about her fears. He breathes in and asks her softly, standing still away from her,' Why would I see you differently?'

Mahi gathers her brows together in the centre of her forehead as she feels the stress of Dev's question. In between her sniffles, she looks away in an attempt to gather enough courage to come clean in front of Dev. She looks at Dev, gulping her emotions sharply but still unable to stop the flowing tears. She says, shaking her head,' You don't know everything about me. You don't know about my past. Nobody does. If we were to be together, I have to tell you about it. But, I am not sure if you'll ever want to be with me after knowing that.' Mahi puts her hand on her eyes, unable to stop whimpering as she completes saying her worst fear out loud.

Dev looks at her as he sighs off. He is unable to see her breaking down. So he quickly moves closer to her. He kind of already guessed the reason for Mahi's constant effort to push him away from herself. He became sure in the morning that her past has to do something for her to force herself into something she doesn't want. Dev pulls her hand down from her face as he wipes her tears from her face. Mahi doesn't resist his touch as she tries to control her weeping.

As Dev gently wipes the tears off her face, he says,' There is nothing that could change how I feel about you.' He holds her face, placing his hands under her ears, as he caresses her cheeks with his thumbs. He continues, in a soft voice, looking down at her,' No past, however scary that is, can change the way I look at you. Ever. You've got no idea how much I love you.'

Mahi closes her eyes, trying to control the flooding emotions after listening to Dev. She builds up the small resistance within herself as she opens her eyes, looking directly at him. She asks,' Even if I have tried to kill someone?'

Dev looks surprised at her question. He then reads through her terrified eyes and yet another attempt to push him away. So he doesn't loosen his hold and answers her honestly to her question,'

Even if you have killed someone. I don't care.' He takes a pause and continues changing his tone,' If you are worried that, that someone might get hold of you because of that, then don't worry. Rohit is a good lawyer. For real. I'll protect you. And if you think you have killer tendencies, and I might be at risk of it. Then, there is no better way to die from your hands,' says teasingly.

'I am not kidding,' says Mahi looking seriously at Dev.

He says, getting all straight faced' Neither am I.' He takes another pause as he throws his head back for short, gathering his thoughts, still holding onto Mahi. He leans in back closer to her face as he looks at her first and then rests his forehead over hers, closing his eyes. He breathes in her perfume as he says, keeping his eyes closed,' Our past is something which happened but stays in the past.' He opens his eyes, resting his forehead over hers, continues,' What we have is our present, which we can grab. And our future, which we can plan together. Both of these has nothing to do with our past. So why worry about it now.'

'But, it changed me. What I am today partially because of what happened to me in the past. I am not the same person I used to be. How can I allow myself to punish you with it?' replies Mahi softly.

Dev opens his eyes, straightening up. He looks at Mahi's worried expressions as he says,' I agree. Sometimes, some life experiences change us. It can change our perspective, our behaviour towards few things. But, even then, it fails to change our inherent character. It doesn't change our nature, the real us. I didn't fall in love with the person you are today. I fell in love with the person you've always been. Even when you were just 9. You can't change that. It's just like how you can't change the fact that you can't imagine me with anyone else. And how much you love white sneakers just like you used to when you were just a kid.'

Mahi looks at him as he closes his eyes again, keeping his forehead over hers. She holds him from his elbows, she softly says,' But you need to know about it. I can't keep you in the dark. I have to tell you. You should know.'

Dev opens his eyes as he takes off his forehead over hers. He slides his hands from her face to her arms as he holds her gently. He says,' Fine. I'll listen to it. Only when you feel like you want to tell me. Not because you have to or you need to.' Mahi opens her mouth to protest but, Dev doesn't let her say anything as he says,' Please. Agree with me on this. Hmm?'

Mahi stays quiet, looking at Dev, trying to understand him. She silently thanks the universe for his presence in her life. But at the same time, she gets worried about how is she ever gonna tell him everything about her life. How is she going to convince him to listen to everything she has to say. She must explain to him. Even though she doesn't have the heart to do it. She sighs off, putting breaks on her tiring thoughts. She hangs her head down in exhaustion as she leans in, placing it on Dev's chest. Dev keeps holding her from her arms, softly rubbing his thumbs, caressing her.

'Why do I feel so relieved when I am closer to you,' says Mahi keeping her head down.

Dev lets out a pleased smile at Mahi's admission as he says,' Because you can be an idiot sometimes to realise something this simple. But, you can't fool your soul that how much you love me.'

Mahi sighs out heavily as she moves closer, ending the space between them. She straightens her head, burying her nose in between Dev's shoulder and his face as she wraps her hands around him. Dev also simultaneously wraps his hands around her, filling her in his arms, hugging her softly. She takes a pause as she feels calm sweeping over her.

'I am not stiff,' says Mahi in a low voice, complaining as she keeps her nose buried in his neck.

Dev lets out a small smile as he says,' I know. I just said that to make you furious. I didn't mean it.' He takes a brief pause, then says,' You are too cute when you are angry.'

'But you are right about one thing. I am an idiot. How can I fool myself when I failed to fool you,' says Mahi, keeping her face buried in Dev's neck.

Dev leans his head back as he pulls Mahi away from him so that he could see her face. Mahi looks up at his face, still holding onto him. He says,' So you are finally accepting that you love me?'

Chapter 21 A Cheesy Romance with a Disappearing Act

'So you are finally accepting that?' asks Dev.

Mahi looks at him softly as she takes a long pause breathing in a few times, taking in his expressions. Dev waits for her response patiently, looking in her eyes, trying to read her through them. He hopes for her not to dismiss everything that just happened and simply give in, not resisting her feelings for him. Mahi reads through his hopeful expressions as she says,' Do you still doubt it?'

Dev breaks into a soft chuckle at Mahi's acceptance. Seeing him smile, Mahi couldn't help but smile. Looking at her smile, Dev couldn't hold it and leans down to capture her lips with his. Mahi closes her eyes as Dev draws her in a soft and yet passionate kiss. Both respond to each other's yearnings through their lips at first and then giving passage to each other's mouth. They express their long-awaited feelings as they kiss each other even without breaking away to breathe. They move their lips in sync as they devour each other. They keep kissing in a dimly lit front of their house, expressing the rush of emotions through it.

They get drawn back to the real world when Dev's phone rings in his coat's pocket. Dev groans while ignoring the ringing, keeping himself busy on Mahi's lips. Mahi tries to politely break away from him but fails. So she barely says through the kiss,' Take it. Someone must be looking for us.'

Dev groans again as he finally breaks away from her lips to take the call. He picks it up in frustration as he keeps his one hand around Mahi, keeping her close. Mahi, too, holds onto him as she keeps an arm around him and her other hand on his chest. Dev picks up the call and speaks into it,' Yes. We are on our way.'

He ends the call as he puts the phone back in his pocket. Mahi notices the disappointment on his face.

'We have to go back,' states Mahi, knowing the call must be about. They completely forget about the world around them when they are lost in each other.

Dev nods as he softly sighs off rests his forehead on hers.

'I don't wanna leave yet. I just got you,' says Dev.

'That's not true. You had me for a while.'

'Yes. You know what I mean,' Dev says, softly tightening his hold around her.

'I know. Neither do I. But, we have to.'

'How about we skip this one?'

'We can. Only if you are prepared to receive cursing from Anu. For the rest of our lives.'

Dev straightens up his head and then says,' No. I don't think I am.'

'Thought so.'

Dev leans down to her. He softly rubs the tip of his nose to hers as he says,' just for few more seconds.'

Mahi nods, closing her eyes. Both stay quiet, leaning on each other and breathing in the other-self.

'Chalein?' asks Mahi, after minutes of quiet, as she gives a nudge to Dev. He leans back, smiling as he notices Mahi stealing his dialogue.

'Why? Only you could say this?' asks Mahi, acting innocent.

Dev simply keeps smiling as he says,' Nope. It just...you did notice what I was doing.'

'I notice every little thing you do. Be it you teasing me at every small chance you get or every time your eyes takes rounds of the crowd to find me.'

'You sure don't miss a thing,' says Dev adoring Mahi in his arms.

'Never. If it's you,' says Mahi tiptoeing, rubbing the tip of her nose to his. He smiles at her sweet little gestures and then leans in, placing a soft kiss on her lips before he says,' We can leave now.'

Mahi notices something shocking and amusing at the same time when both get in. She exclaims,' Oh God!' She didn't see it earlier as it was dark outside. But thanks to the light in a car, she got to know.

Dev turns his head,' What?' as she takes a tissue from the box on the dashboard. She holds it out and starts cleaning Dev's lips.

She chuckles softly,' My lipstick.' As she removes the remains of her plum red lipstick from his lips and around, Dev says,' Does the colour not look good on me?'

'Well, it looks more like you've been assaulted.'

Mahi smiles, feeling a little shy with Dev's expressions and finding the situation funny.

'Indeed I was,' says Dev teasingly.

Mahi scoffs at his accusation and says,' I thought it was consensual.'

'Yes. It was,' says Dev smiling with an expression of satisfaction.

Mahi shakes her head, smiling, turning in her seat as she pulls down the mirror from the sun visor. She says,' I'll have to redo it.' She starts cleaning the smudged eye shadow around the eyes.

While they both drive back to the venue, Dev doesn't let go of Mahi's hand. He keeps the one hand intertwined with Mahi's in her laps and the other on the steering wheel.

Dev's phone connected to the car goes off on the screen in front. It reads Nivi Di. Dev picks up the call.

'Kahan hain tu? Aur Mahi ko dekha kya? Uska phone aur bag bhi yahi hain. Kahan gayab ho dono? (Where are you? And have you seen Mahi? Her phone and bag is here. Where are you guys hiding?)' asks Nivi becoming a little agitated at the end.

Dev glances at Mahi before he answers,' Haan. She is with me. She forgot something back at home. So we came back to get that.'

'Okay. Just be here soon. Guests have started arriving,' says Nivi, sounding a bit relieved.

'Yeah. Almost there,' says Dev. Nivi hangs up the call after getting the answers from her brother.

'I forgot something at home!' exclaims Mahi at Dev's lie.

Dev smiles as he throws a quick glance at Mahi while driving the car. He says,' Didn't you?'

'Did I? Like what?' asks Mahi, countering him.

He says with a teasingly innocence in his voice,' Me.'

Mahi lets out a small laugh at Dev's cheesy and yet, funny comeback. Dev feels happy simply listening to Mahi laughing. He takes their intertwined hands closer to his mouth. He lingers his lips on the back of Mahi's hand as he says,' God, I missed that sound.'

They reach the venue, Mahi takes the side stairs to go up to their rooms to redo her face. When she sees Dev following her, she stops and asks him,' Where do you think you are going?'

'Umm... washroom,' says Dev with a surprising look on his face.

'There are plenty of washrooms down at the banquet,' replies Mahi, pointing out the obvious.

'Yeah. And to reach there, I'll have to cross Dad's chatty friends. And I can never do the necessary in time if I stop to greet them,' replies Dev.

'Alright,' says Mahi giving up as she turns around and unlocks the door of the room. She walks up to the mirror as Dev rushes to the bathroom.

Mahi goes to the dressing table with a mirror. She stands in horror as she sees her smudged liner from all that crying. But, she couldn't help but smile shyly when her eyes stop at the faded colour of lipstick on her lips. She quickly cleans up her face and begins redoing her eyes. As soon she is done with her eyes, she takes out the lipstick to put it on. She feels Dev's hands snaking around her waist and pulling her in his arms. He snuggles his face in her hair around her neck. Mahi feels her heart quickened as she feels Dev behind in such an embrace. She feels his breath on her neck. She gathers her voice and says softly,' Dev. We don't want to be late.'

She feels him nodding with a humming but still holding onto her. She looks up in the mirror to see his face. She notices his head resting on her shoulder, closer to her neck and his eyes thoughtful far ahead. She closes the lipstick in hand and places her hands on his forearms which engulfs her from the waist.

She caresses his hands softly as she asks,' What is it?'

Her question breaks his train of thoughts. He looks at her through the mirror in front. He just fails every time to focus whenever he sees her face. So he just smiles as he straightens up and places his mouth on the side of her head, right above her ears.

He asks her without moving his mouth,' Promise me something?'

She simply nods. Dev hesitates at first and then says,' Don't ever leave me.'

Mahi turns around to face him. He is unable to read Mahi's expressions as soon as he voiced his worst fear. It makes him more nervous as he continues,' I don't mean to tie you to me. It's just- even if someday you decide to leave me, then do it after letting me know about it. Don't just disappear. At least tell me whenever you feel like doing it. In-person.'

Mahi listens through Dev's nervous and sincere rumbling. She just ends up smiling.

'What? You think I am such a fool,' says Dev becoming a little disheartened.

'No! I don't think you are a fool,' says Mahi with defence in her voice.

'You are smiling,'

'I am smiling because it's funny.'

'Right. Because I am sounding like an idiot,' says Dev looking away as he feels embarrassed by the passing moment.

'No!' Mahi exclaims with a frown as she holds onto his arms. She sighs heavily. She continues softly and slowly,' It's not because of you. It is funny because you've got no clue how much I love you.' This grabs Dev's attention back to her. She never explicitly said it before. And here, she said it. The words send little flutters down to Dev's stomach. Still, he controls his expression, not letting out any. She continues,' I cannot think of any legit or logical reason now or in future to leave you. Unless you cheat on me or you decide to go back to your ex.'

Dev feels content, smiles as he says,' you can let go of the exceptions too, cause that ain't happening. Ever.'

Mahi smiles, nodding, but immediately loses the smile when she says,' But I am not so sure about you.'

Dev looks at her questioningly.

'You might not be too sure about being with me...when you'll get to know about my not so glorious past,' says Mahi with a sad smile on her face.

Dev pulls her closer as he holds her face with both hands now,' Hey! I might be repeating myself. But I'll keep doing it till you believe me absolutely. I love you. For who you are, not for what you are. And there is nothing that could change the way you mean to me.'

Mahi wells up, listening to him. She blinks a few times to stop getting emotional all over again. So she hits Dev lightly as she exclaims,' Stop it. I don't wanna do my eyes again.'

She turns to grab the tissue so that she really doesn't have to redo her eye makeup. Dev chuckles as he puts his hands in his breeches pockets and stands there gawking Mahi, complete her final touch.

Both arrive at the banquet, where it starts to fill with familiar faces of guests. When Nivi sees them, she starts bombarding them with questions and bashing them for behaving irresponsibly. Dev tries to defend them but, Mahi stops him with a small gesture without Nivi's notice. Savitri is nearby speaking to the priest, who is about to conduct the engagement ceremony for Anu and Amit. She turns to witness the scene and notice something different about Mahi and Dev. She gives out a knowing smile and walks up to them, interrupting Nivi. She asks Dev and Mahi to go and sit next to the priest as he wants the recently married couple in the family to perform some ritual. Both quietly oblige and leave to do so.

After they leave, Savitri whispers to Nivi standing next to her,' Do you notice something?'

Nivi getting confused and concerned, asks,' What?'

Savitri points at Mahi and Dev, settled down cross-legged next to the priest,' Them.'

'What about them?'

'Don't you see something different? Being next to each other.'

Now when Savitri pointed out, Nivi did realise what exactly her mother meant. She sees Dev and Mahi not acting awkward around each other. Both seem like teenagers, smiling stupidly, as they catch glancing at each other. Nivi chuckles as she says,' Finally.'

'Yes. Finally,' replies Savitri with a heavier sigh. She continues,' I just wish nobody jinx them.'

The engagement ceremony goes through gleefully with friends and family gathered around. Throughout the function, Dev kept looking in Mahi's direction as both stealing glances from each other. After attending, the lot of close and distant relatives, Mahi finally gets time to relax when she stands next to Rohit and Ekta. She plays a little while with baby Aryan until Nivi takes him along with Veer to get the kids together under one responsible eye of grand elders. After the kids were taken away, Mahi and Ekta break into a random conversation where they rope in Rohit. The chat was mostly Ekta complaining about her tiring days as a new mother with a toddler to consume all her energy. As they were standing on the corners of the banquet, it was difficult for Dev to spot them at first. Then he soon recognises the sound of Ekta talking continuously and Mahi chuckling softly next to her. Ah! Her voice is music to his ears.

Dev cuts in Ekta as he joins them and stands next to Mahi, placing a hand casually on her back. He softly looks at Mahi with a smile and says,' Hi!'

To which Mahi smiles and replies,' Hi!'

Rohit and Ekta notice the interaction between the two. Ekta being impatient, cuts in, saying,' Hi there!'

'Hi, Ekta. Rohit,' says Dev straightening up, losing the stupid smile. He immediately continues,' Did you guys had your dinner?'

'Yeah. We did.'

'Thanks for asking,' replies Ekta sarcastically.

'Sorry, yaar. Couldn't attend you guys properly.'

Rohit instantly interjects,' It's alright. We are not guests. We are family.'

Like this, Dev successfully diverts the topic of conversation from them, even before it could begin.

Soon after, Dev's Dad calls out his name, looking for him. Dev sees his dad with his old school teacher to his dislike.

'Damn, he is standing with Rana Sir. I don't want to talk to him about how bad I was in Social science in 5th std,' says Dev trying to hide behind Mahi and the rest.

Mahi chuckles and says,' Go! He won't stop calling out your name unless you go.'

He sighs off and straightens up. He looks at Mahi and says,' Don't leave without me. Wait for me. We'll go home together.' As he says this, he very casually plants a kiss on the side of her head, on her hair. Ekta and Rohit exchange surprised look as they witness this. Before they could say anything, Dev looks at Rohit and takes him by the arm, saying,' You are coming with me. I am not gonna suffer alone.'

Rohit and Dev leave the ladies behind, with Ekta looking accusingly at Mahi with questions all over her face. Mahi loses her smile as soon as she realises how much PDA just Dev gave to Ekta.

'Interested to Explain? Because I would love to hear it,' asks Ekta with her devilish smile.

'What?' replies Mahi trying to keep her face straight and act innocent.

'Really! We are going to play that game now,' says Ekta rolling her eyes.

'I don't know what you are talking about,' says Mahi, now acting out completely indifferent.

'C'mon! You guys confessed that how madly you are in love with each other,' exclaims Ekta exasperatedly. To which Mahi opens her mouth in shock with widened eyes. She quickly blinks a few times, gathering her shocked self from how much Ekta already knew. She sheepishly says,' Maybe.'

'Oh My God! I want details,' says Ekta a little loudly with excitement.

Mahi laughs at her reaction and says,' No details.'

'Please tell me.'

'Calm your tits, woman. It's not that exciting.'

'Please! So far, it was exciting enough. I don't expect less,' says Ekta with a teasing wink.

After Mahi tells almost everything to Ekta, she breaks into a mini celebration shrieking quietly. Both get busy talking among themselves, not realising that many guests have left as the function has reached an end.

Mahi looks for Dev as it would be easy to spot him when there are just a few people left, wrapping up. But she fails to find him. She couldn't spot him as she becomes sure that he is not here at the banquet. As Rohit comes with sleeping baby Aryan and joins them, asking Ekta, 'we should leave too.'

Mahi asks him if he has seen Dev. Rohit says that he saw Dev leave the venue some half an hour ago without saying anything. He further adds that some phone call came, and it seemed urgent.

'I thought he must have informed you by now,' says Rohit seeing Mahi becoming tensed.

Before Mahi could say anything, Rohit's phone starts ringing in his pocket. He gently hands the sleeping baby to Ekta and fishes out the phone. Seeing the caller ID, Rohit reads it loudly,' It's Dev.'

He immediately picks it up and speaks,' Where are you, bro?'

He quietly listens to the call and instantly looks at Mahi with stress forming around his brows and then immediately shifts his gaze to Ekta while listening to Dev. He then quickly replies,' I am on my way.' And then ends the call. He avoids looking at Mahi at first. He speaks to his wife with a deep voice,' Drop Aryan home and reach Dev's house. Wait for me there.' He continues as he turns to Mahi,' Mahi. Leave with everyone for home.'

'Why? What's wrong? What did he say?' asks Mahi.

'Just leave with everyone else for now. I am sure Dev will call you soon. In case anyone asks about him, tell them something urgent came up at the hotel,' says Rohit as he is about to leave too.

Mahi stops him saying,' Is it really the hotel?'

Rohit hesitates and then softly says, trying to assure her,' Just.. .go for now.'

Rohit leaves Ekta and Mahi puzzled. Both do as they are told. But, Rohit's mysterious expression bothers Mahi. What was so urgent and confidential? Dev didn't care to give her the call or even drop a message. Her thoughts were going through the worst versions. But nothing seems to make sense. On the way home, Mahi tries calling up Dev. But to her dismay, it went to his voicemail. When everyone reached home, Savitri was the first to ask about Dev's whereabouts. She definitely noticed her son's absence for almost more than an hour. Mahi replies with the same answer, the one Rohit told her to say. Savitri doesn't believe her words. So she presses again, and this time, Mahi says what she knows. She doesn't know anything for sure. Soon Ekta also arrives at the house. Seeing Ekta here this late, Savitri guesses that something is definitely going on, which Dev didn't want anyone to find out yet. Thus, the anticipation of where Dev and Rohit might be kept everyone in the house stayed up in the living room. Maan tries to get in touch with Dev but fails to get through the call. Mahi wears a calm mask for everyone's sake as inside of her, a blizzard was taking rounds. Ekta's phone rings. It's Rohit. She picks the call and listens to what Rohit has to say.

'Police Station!' Ekta exclaims at first, and then she quietly listens.

Everyone looks at her intently but, her eyes dart to Mahi with a tensed look as she listens to her husband. She immediately looks away as if hiding any suspicion. She ends the call and tells everyone,' They are on their way. They'll be here in half an hour so.'

'What was about the Police station?' asks Nivi immediately.

Ekta avoids Mahi's gaze as she hesitates at first and then says,' Didn't say much. Dev asked everyone to wait for him. They are on their way. He said he'll explain in person.'

The whole family somewhat relaxes a bit since Dev would be home soon. Mahi seemed to feel the opposite. To distract herself, she excuses from the living room on the pretext to make some coffee and tea for whoever needs it.

Ekta accompanies her to the kitchen. When they reach the kitchen, Mahi abruptly turns around and faces Ekta.

'What's going on?' asks Mahi to Ekta.

Ekta doesn't say anything as she looks at Mahi, realising what she might be gaining at.

'You looked at me the exact same way Rohit did when he was on the call with Dev. So don't you dare tell me to wait for Dev and let him tell me when I can clearly tell that there is something you guys are hiding from me. Purposely,' says Mahi in a single breath feeling agitated now.

Ekta opens her mouth slightly. But tightens her lips with a frown as she fails to form the right words to says but shakes her head, becoming stressed, to come up with something more assuring.

'For God sakes! You are quiet Ekta!' exclaims Mahi with an edge of fury. She continues with a little louder and affirmative voice,' There is definitely something's up. Before I begin to lose my mind, I am begging you to speak up.'

Ekta sighs off and decides to tell her before Mahi's minds do the worst situation rounds.

'Yashika. It's Yashika,' says Ekta finally with a small voice contrary to her nature.

'What!'

CHAPTER 22 THE EX FACTOR

'It's Yashika,' says Ekta. She continues in a small voice, unlike her usual,' Yashika is with them. They are coming home with her.'

Mahi blinks a few times at first, then closing her eyes, she tries to gather her focus at the name of her husband's ex. An ex whom he almost married. If she hadn't left him, there was no way today Mahi and Dev would have become so close, in love. The name would not have bothered her if their relationship was merely contractual like before. But, now things are different. She never thought that she would end up falling for Dev. Now the fact is that Dev is bringing home the same woman who left him on his wedding day, whom he loved for 6 long years yet, she chose to leave him. It's not been even a year since Dev and Mahi got married and not even more than a couple of months that Dev might have fallen for Mahi. How can she compete for the six years of a relationship with a couple months of love, companionship? Or maybe months of infatuation? Was it just an infatuation? Not for her. May be for him? Mahi's head starts aching as she tries to contemplate everything or whatever might happen to her. How is she going to comfort herself?

Mahi steps back, losing herself in all the chaos going on in her head. Ekta notices her getting tensed. She speaks up,' Don't jump on any conclusions. Okay! Just...' She takes a deep breath and continues,' Trust yourself. Trust him.'

Mahi shoves down her feelings and gathers herself together. She pulls a small voice,' I am fine.'

She makes herself busy making some tea and coffee. Her quietness makes Ekta immensely nervous and worried. She silently prays for Dev not to disappoint them, especially Mahi.

Both move out of the kitchen, helping get everyone the teas and coffees in the living room.

Soon after, they hear the car outside. Mahi stands still as she listens to the car door opening and closing. Ekta comes and stands next to her as she puts an assuring hand on Mahi's arm. Mahi takes a deep breath and turns her head to Ekta,' Don't worry. I am not trying to jump on any conclusions.' She takes another deep breath to steady herself,' I am just preparing myself for the worst.'

Everyone watches in shock, except Ekta and Mahi when Dev enters the house with Yashika. Rohit enters right behind them. Yashika looked unrecognisable at first as she wasn't in her best looks. She had Dev's coat around her shoulder, her hair dishevelled a bit. She was small in stature next to Dev's tall frame as she wasn't wearing any heels. Mahi just noticed that she wasn't even wearing any footwear. As they walked in closer, now everyone could see the bruised face of Yashika. Everyone can notice the fresh wound on the side of her forehead, along with blue and red bruises and heavy redness on her cheeks. Her eyes were swollen too, maybe from excessive crying. Everyone now become curious as they saw the state Yashika is in, along with the shock. Dev has been stealing a glance at Mahi's face when she looks at Yashika with detailed observation. He immediately looks away when Mahi catches him looking at her. Mahi feels uneasy when Dev avoid her gaze. She loses more hope than before.

Yashika staggers as she loses her footing and ability to stand stably. She takes the help of Dev's arm to stand straight. Dev and Rohit help her stand straight. Savitri, Mahi, Ekta and Nivi come forward to help as well. When they approach Yashika, Dev and Rohit instantly give way for them to help her. Mahi and Nivi hold shaken Yashika and take her to the guest room. Dev asks for some water as he and Rohit settle down in the living room. Mahi and Nivi come back from the guest room after helping Yashika. Mahi can't get off her mind what she saw when she and Nivi helped Yashika to change into fresh pair of clothes. She looked shaken, terrified. She had bruises all over her body. Fresh and old. They helped her clean up as Yashika looked more lost but aware.

When Mahi and Nivi arrive back in the living room, they see Dev and Rohit settled and everyone else seated, waiting for them to answer their silent questions. When Dev sees Mahi in the living room, he begins to tell what happened. He tells everyone that he just received a phone call from the police station saying some female friend has given them the number.

'At first, I thought it must be some kind of a prank but, then nobody other than close friends and family had my phone number. So I left for the police station. Without telling anyone,' says Dev as he looks up to Mahi. She was standing behind the sofa across from him. He continues looking back at everyone,' I didn't want anyone to worry so...when I reached then only I got to know that it was her.'

'What happened to her?' asks Maan, thinking about Yashika's state.

'She ran from her abusive husband. The police officer said that she filed a report against him. She came running to the police station. When police went to pick him up, he was gone,' replies Dev.

'Why did you bring her here?' asks Nivi, now getting seriously concerned with the situation.

Dev looks at Mahi first and then answers,' I asked if she wants me to drop her to any of her friends. She doesn't have any in the city. I told her that I can arrange for her to stay at the hotel. But, she was too shaken and out to leave alone. Then I called Rohit. I didn't feel right to leave her like that.'

'You did the right thing,' says Mahi. Everyone looks at her in surprise. Her face projected the calmness that can fool all except Dev. He could read her eyes like a neat book. He could tell that she meant what she said. But, there were a whole lot of questions in them for him.

Savitri asks Mahi,' Are you sure you don't mind this?'

'She just got assaulted by her husband. And she doesn't know anyone else in the city. As a woman...and a human, I think we could do at least this much,' replies Mahi with a steady voice.

'I have already informed her parents. They'll be here tomorrow,' adds Dev, drawing attention from Mahi. Everyone takes in the situation silently.

All the elders eventually retire for the night. Rest go to the guest room to check up on Yashika, except Mahi. She goes to her room to gather back her nerves as she changes out of the saree into a night suit with a long shrug on her arms.

In the guest room, everyone including, Ekta, Nivi, Anu, Rohit and Dev, are gathered around the bed, where Yashika is seated with the support of the bedpost. Dev was on the chair next to Yashika while the rest were standing or sitting around the bed.

Yashika looks better with first aid taken care of her injuries. She smiles at the rest, saying thank you. She ends her gaze at Dev with a smile and more gracious thanks. Dev simply replies,' It's alright.'

He informs her about her parents coming the next day. She puts her hand on his hand, which was resting on his laps,' What would have I done if you hadn't come for me.'

Ekta, Nivi and Anu raise their eyebrows together at her gesture. Dev becomes a little uncomfortable as he pulls back his hand from her touch,' I would have done the same for anyone.'

Mahi, standing at the door, witness the whole scene. She knocks at the door before entering with a glass of warm milk on a small tray. Yashika loses her smile when she sees Mahi at the door. On the contrary, Dev suddenly feels the rush of relief seeing her. Mahi walks up to the side of the bed, walking past seated Dev. She places the tray on the side table,' Have it warm. It will help you sleep and in healing your injuries.'

Mahi walks back and stands at the end of the bed. Yashika notices Dev's eyes not leaving Mahi from the time she entered the room. A faint frown forms on her head, seeing Dev watching Mahi.

Mahi turns to Dev,' Dev. Why don't you go and change? We all are here.'

Dev gets up, nodding gladly. He walks past Mahi but pauses as he holds her hand loose on her side and leaves after pressing it briefly. Mahi glances at Dev but doesn't respond back. Yashika notices the intimate interaction between the two. She becomes a little worried, thinking if Dev has really moved on from her.

After Dev leaves, Rohit and Ekta also leave. After sitting silently for few more minutes with Yashika, rest also leave the room, asking her to rest and take care.

Dev nervously waits for Mahi in the room after changing into a fresh pair of t-shirt and tracks. Almost an hour passes by, there is no sign of Mahi. Dev becomes restless. As he goes down, the house was dead silent as everyone has probably been asleep. It is the middle of the night. He checks the guest room from outside and sees the lights are out. It means Mahi and everyone has already left it. He looks around thinking, where she must have gone this late. He goes to the front lawns to look for her. Then he stops by the kitchen and finds it empty. Then he moves towards the back doors, which leads to Verandah. When he sees through the glass door, he sees Mahi seated on one of the chairs, facing the gardens. He quietly slides open the door and moves out. Just then, Yashika gets out of her room and sees Dev walking towards the back door. She smiles and follows him to the door. She stops losing the smile when she sees Dev walking towards the seated Mahi.

Dev stands quietly next to Mahi. He notices her lost in her thoughts that she didn't even feel him coming. She is seated with her legs up on the chair with her knees close to her chest, hugging them.

'Hey,' Dev speaks softly, breaking Mahi's focus.

Mahi looks up to him,' Hey!'

Dev takes the chair next and moves it closer and facing her before sitting on it. Mahi looks back at the garden, thinking far ahead.

Dev doesn't remove his gaze from her.

'I was waiting for you in the room.' Dev breaks the silence between them.

'I needed some time to myself. To internalise everything,' replies Mahi without looking at Dev.

Dev looks down briefly and then speaks,' I know it must be difficult for you. You must hate me for not calling you and telling you first. I am sorry. But, I wanted to do it in person.'

Mahi turns her head towards him,' I think I understand. I get it.'

'What?' asks Dev, not getting what she exactly understands.

'You and her,' Mahi gulping down her feelings. She continues looking away at the garden,' I understand. Six years is a long time. You have a lot of history. You can't get away that easily. I get it.' She turns her head towards Dev,' Maybe we weren't meant to be.'

'Wait! Mahi, you are not-'

'I just said it as a joke. I didn't know it will come back to me in such a way and bite me,' says Mahi chuckling dryly.

'What joke?' asks Dev with utter confusion looming over his head.

Mahi looks at him with moist eyes,' The exceptions. Unless you cheat on me, or you'll go back to your ex.'

Dev burst out in a small laugh loudly and shuts up immediately, looking at Mahi,' Oh God! What have you been thinking!'

Mahi frowns at Dev's reaction. Dev leans in, dragging her chair to turn it towards him and pulls it closer, reducing the distance between them. He takes her both hands in his,' Do you remember what I'd said after you made that joke?'

Mahi nods her head, still frowning in confusion,' That I can let go of those exceptions because it ain't happening.'

'Ever. I said ever. And I meant it.'

Both silently look at each other for few seconds, reading each other.

'You didn't believe me,' Dev breaks the silence.

Mahi simply looks on, giving off a puzzled and disbelief gaze. Dev tugs at her hands as he pulls her,' Come here!'

He pulls her to get up from the chair and makes her sit on his laps, with her legs to one side. As she sits, he puts her hand around his shoulders and keeps another in his, closer to his chest.

'What made you think I was going back to her?' asks Dev as he tucks a loose strand of her hair behind her ear.

'You didn't call me. You didn't even pick up my call. I was worried sick. Didn't see you for hours,' says Mahi, complaining.

'I didn't want you to worry. Police station and all,' Dev says, thinking about that moment.

Mahi rolls her eyes,' Police station doesn't worry me. Did you forget what I do for a living?'.

Dev smiles as he shakes his head. 'Sorry. I'll keep that in mind from next time.'

'Will there be a next time?'

'In case,' Dev corrects himself.

Mahi sighs and then continues,' Then Ekta told me about her before you guys came home.' Dev closes his eyes in disbelief. She defends Ekta,' I forced her to.'

'Still, she wasn't supposed to.'

'It wasn't her fault.'

'I know,' replies Dev, softly accepting.

'You avoided looking at me. When you guys came home,' says Mahi pointing out the further reason, her doubt almost turned into reality for her briefly.

'I got scared...I knew I must have hurt you somehow by not telling you. It didn't pan out the way I thought. I thought I'll drop her at the hotel and then come to you and tell you everything. But then...' he takes in a deep breath. 'It just... I didn't want to tell you through a call.'

Dev sighs off,' I am sorry.'

Mahi looks at him, feeling like an idiot to even doubt him. She scolds herself for running wild with her thoughts. How can she not trust this beautiful man in front of her? He loves her, beyond her imagination, and thinks deeply about not hurting her? How could she not love him back with the same earnestness? She does.

She now knows for sure. She leans in, closing her eyes, resting her forehead on his.

Dev closes his eyes too as he wraps his hands around her. Mahi keeping her eyes closed, she breathes,' I am sorry for doubting you.'

She pulls her head away from his to look at his face. She runs her fingers in his hair, admiring him in dimly lit Verandah. Keeping them partly in his hair at the back of his head as her thumbs trace his jawline,' I didn't realise until today that how scary the thought of losing you can be.'

Dev lets out a smile after listening to her,' I am right here. I am gonna cling to you for the rest of your life.'

Both breaks into a soft chuckle leaning into each other. Dev places one hand under her ear, caressing her cheek. He pulls her closer to his lips when the sound of the sliding door makes them aware of someone. Both instantly turn towards the sound as Mahi gets up assuming, someone from the family found them fooling around. However, she finds Yashika standing there.

Mahi sighs off, relaxing that it was no one from the family. Dev gets off the chair, with a frown forming around his forehead.

'Sorry. I didn't mean to disturb you,' Yashika speaks up, clearly acting innocent. She has been standing behind the door from the time Dev came to Mahi. Through half-shut glass doors, she even faintly witnessed the rest.

Dev and Mahi exchange looks. Yashika continues,' Actually, I was unable to fall asleep. I was feeling restless. So I came out for fresh air.'

'Did you drink the milk I gave you?' asks Mahi intently.

'No. I don't take the dairy after 6 in the evening,' replies Yashika, being a snob.

Mahi press her lips to control the smile,' You should have. Old remedies help in healing and in a lot of other things.' Mahi felt amused at her behaviour. Even after going through this much, her arrogance has not faltered a bit. She is the same Mahi remembers her from a year ago. When they formally first met before the wedding preparations.

Dev reads Mahi's expressions, getting amused. He interjects before things get awkward between his ex-girlfriend and his wife,' It's late enough. We won't get between your fresh air. Good night and rest well.' Dev takes Mahi's hand to leave for their room.

Yashika speaks,' Uh Dev. I was hoping we could talk for a moment.'

Dev and Mahi stop in their tracks and look at each other. Dev speaks up,' It's late. Can we do this tomorrow?'

'Tomorrow, I don't know if I'll get the chance,' Yashika reads the hesitancy on Dev's face. 'Please,' she adds.

'Alright. What you want to talk about?'

'Can we talk in private,' Yashika glances at Mahi uncomfortably.

Dev reads Yashika looking at Mahi,' Mahi is my wife. It's private enough. You can talk comfortably in front of her.'

Yashika gets a little irritated,' Please! I at least deserve this considering the years we have known each other.'

'Considering how you ended those years, you don't even deserve standing in front of me,' replies Dev curtly.

Mahi feels that the conversation is getting way too heated. She jumps in,' It's okay.' She turns to Dev,' I am fine. I really don't mind.' She touches his arms lovingly,' I'll be up in the room.'

Dev simply nods after listening to her. Mahi turns to Yashika, giving her a look that she really doesn't care about whatever she has rolled up in her sleeves. Mahi leaves as she brushes her hands against Dev while walking back into the house.

Yashika clearly isn't liking the way Dev responds to Mahi's touch. To her, it was like he is suddenly the obedient and relaxed person around Mahi. When Mahi leaves, she takes few steps towards Dev, 'I am sorry. I know I don't even deserve to stand here in front of you.'

'What did you want to talk about?' Dev asks with a straight face.

'Us.'

Dev looks at her, puzzled. She continues, 'I know I have made the biggest mistake of my life. I know. Now, I realise this. But I thought you would understand the reason. Why I did what I did. I hope you got the letter I left you. Did you?'

'Oh yeah. I did,' says Dev curtly.

Yashika tries to understand his tone but fails. 'No, you did not.'

'I got your letter Yashika. What is your point?' asks Dev rolling his eyes.

'No, you did not. If you did, you wouldn't be behaving like this. Talking to me so rudely,' Yashika now sure that he didn't get her letter.

'I gave it to your mother. She must have changed it. You know she can do that.'

Dev clenches his jaws together, trying to hold it in. He speaks,

'Dear Dev. I am sorry I am doing this to you. I had no choice. I am forced to do this. I cannot take the instructions, taunts and hate for the rest of my life. I love you but, I cannot be with you at the expense of my self-respect. I am really sorry. I hope you will understand. Love Yashika.'

Dev puts his hands in the pockets of his tracks as he finishes reciting the letter word by word.

Yashika becomes confused as Dev recites the exact words she left for him before leaving him. She fails to understand his current attitude towards her. For as long as she has known Dev, the words in that letter were definitely not supposed to impact him this way. She made sure the blame of her leaving can never come on her, but his mother. She made sure in these years to separate Dev from his mother's influence. But what she is witnessing right now is the contrary of that. He is indifferent towards her and not at all polite with her. She thought she could get back with him after realising what a mistake she made believing the news of him getting bankrupt. But she pushed her plans when she heard him getting married anyways to someone else. Meanwhile, she also found someone who could take care of her needs. Though, she chose wrong as to how that has left her all wounded, physically and mentally.

Seeing Yashika speechless for few seconds, Dev says,' What? Did I miss anything? This is what you wrote.'

Yashika still doesn't speak, contemplating the following words from her mouth.

'Yashika. It's alright. You can come clean about the real reason for leaving me,' says Dev.

'Real reason?' says Yashika thinking that there is no way he would know.

'C'mon. You got to know about the raid. And my supposed bank-ruptcy,' says Dev sarcastically.

Yashika gets shocked at Dev's words. She loses her grip on the conversation. She doesn't know where to take it. 'Wha-what bankruptcy?' as she stutters.

Dev scoffs dryly, watching her still acting innocent. 'It is fine. You can stop pretending. It doesn't matter now.'

'I don't know what you are talking about. I didn't know anything about the raid or the bankruptcy,' Yashika claims shamelessly.

'I don't really care if it was the letter or the bankruptcy news. I have moved on. So should you,' says Dev, sincerely.

'You think I left you because of the bankruptcy. That's why you have moved on,' exclaims Yashika.

'No. Because I have realised I have been in love with someone else this whole time,' replies Dev smiling.

'Her? You can't be,' says Yashika in total disbelief.

'I know it's not easy to believe this. Trust me. It took me to years to realise this,' tells Dev.

'Years?' asks Yashika, getting puzzled.

Dev takes a brief pause as he elaborates,' I am sorry, but I don't think I have ever been honest with you about my feelings. Not even with myself. Not until Mahi came along. It was her who made me realise what real love is all about. What we had for those six years was not love. And that's why I don't blame you for leaving me like that. In fact, I am glad you did. If you didn't, then we would have been living a really miserable life together. How can I be in love with you when Mahi had already taken that place in my heart. Yes. I have been in love with her, even way before we met. It just in these past few months I was able to realise this.'

Yashika now somewhere understands the way he has been be-having. For however long, she denies it. But she can't ignore the way Dev's eyes speaks more than his words. She could clearly see that she has lost all her chances to get back with him. It just struck her that she had lost it years ago.

'Way before me. Of course. I should have accepted it then only,' says Yashika thoughtfully. She continues,' Honestly, you are the real reason I disliked her from the moment I met her.' Yashika gives up on Dev and shares her opinion honestly,' Because you didn't stop looking at her in your sister's wedding, where you took me to meet your folks for the first time. I ignored it, thinking that she must be your old crush. But it was my mistake to ignore it. Now I know that I lost you then only.'

After cordially concluding the conversation with Yashika, Dev comes back to his room. He finds Mahi in bed, sleeping sideways.

The small bedside lights were still on. She must have fallen asleep waiting for him, Dev thinks to himself. He quietly turns off the lights, leaving the dim lights under the bed. He takes the blanket under her feet and gently drapes it over her. He pauses for a few seconds, hovering over her, admiring her features in a dimly lit room. A smile takes over his lips as he sits on the footrest of the bed. He sits there for the next few minutes, gazing at sleeping Mahi. He takes her hand in his own. He looks at her, shifting in her sleep then, her eyes open, fluttering. She finds Dev sitting down next to the bed.

'Hey! Why are you sitting there?' asks in a sleepy voice.

'Just watching you sleeping,' says Dev with a smile.

She shifts backwards, tapping lightly on the bed, gesturing him to come to bed. Dev does so. He gets into bed next to Mahi as she holds her head up for him to put his arm under it. He lies on his back, taking Mahi in arms, placing her head on his shoulder, closer to his chest. He softly strokes the back of her arms as he feels her breathing on his neck.

'Aren't you going to ask me? What we talked about?' asks Dev, smelling the fragrance of jasmine conditioner from her hair.

'I will. When I am wide awake,' says Mahi as she pats Dev's chest once and then stroking it gently.

'Okay,' replies Dev smiling. He tries to control an urge at her cuteness but fails. He simultaneously caresses her face as he pulls it up to face him. He leans down sideways to take her lips in his own. He deepens the kiss, playing softly with the tip of his tongue on her lips. Mahi responds fervently. After few seconds, he completes the kiss by breaking away, tasting her from his own lips.

Mahi asks,' What was that for?'

'I was just finishing what we were supposed to start downstairs. Before we got interrupted,' replies Dev calmly.

Mahi smiles, becoming shy as she sneaks her nose in the crook of his neck, hugging him tightly. Both fall asleep soon after, holding onto each other in a cuddle.

CHAPTER 23 A STORY OF A GIRL

The following morning, Mahi wakes up to soft touches on her cheek, followed by lingering kisses. She opens her eyes and finds Dev lying next to her. He was watching her sweetly as he keeps his head propped up with the support of his hand angled at the elbow.

'Good Morning!' says Dev as his knuckles caress Mahi's face.

Mahi pulls up the cover till her eyes and says shyly,' Good Morning.'

Dev leans in to place a soft kiss on her forehead. He stays close as he slowly pulls down the cover from her face. He then places long kisses on her eyes, followed by on the apple of her cheeks. Mahi feels every kiss with closed eyes. Finally, he reaches her lips. He begins with soft, brief touches on her lips with his own. He lingers longer on her lips and then takes hold of her lips entirely by making the kiss deeper. She responds equally and fervently to his movement. Her hand slides into his hair, pulling him towards her. He continues to taste her as his one hand, which was under his head earlier, finds refuge in her hair. And other hand drums at her belly at first and then slyly moves up to her rise. The same hand moves down to sneak inside her t-shirt. Mahi gasps in between the kiss as she feels Dev's hand doing all sorts of mischief underneath her t-shirt. As both explore each other with their mouth, their tongues performing a duet of their own, Dev pulls her closer. He moves his hand slowly towards her belly as he grazes her jawline and taking in her neck through his lips. When his hand slips past her belly down into her pyjamas, Mahi gasps heavily, gripping Dev's hand from his wrist. Dev breaks away to look at her sudden reaction.

'Do you want me to stop?' asks Dev, panting. Mahi heaves a few times, looking at Dev in surprise and feeling the excitement at the same time. Dev could see the edge of excitement and nervousness in her eyes. He now says more calmly, 'I'll stop. Just say it.'

Mahi shakes her head smiling as she loses the hold on his wrist and now placing them on the side of Dev's face. She pulls him to kiss her and continues to do so. Dev takes in her consent, and while kissing her with more vigour, his hand slips past her pelvis. His fingers find her womanhood as they start with a polite greeting. The heat welcomes him as he feels Mahi radiating under his touch. He begins with soft caressing down there. Slowly he gains movement when he slides inside her through her moist opening. Mahi, enjoying his touch, moves her hips in the rhythm of Dev's hands. She keeps letting out small yet deep moans from her mouth. The sound from her encourages Dev to continue stroking her pleasure points as his manhood feels the same.

Both stop in their tracks when they hear a loud knock on the door. Mahi's eyes open wide, and Dev breaks the kiss, halting every movement and becoming absolutely still.

'Bua is leaving for the airport in 15 mins,' shouts Anu from outside the door.

Dev rolls his eyes, resuming his movements down as well as on her neck.

Mahi shouts back,' Coming. In 5 minutes.'

'Yeah right,' murmurs Dev, chuckling as he goes back to her neck.

'Dev.'

'Hmm.'

'Stop!! We have to go,' says Mahi panting as she tries to suppress another moan from her lips.

'You only said 5 minutes. I promise I'll be quick,' says Dev, still kissing her and working up his hand with more frequency.

Mahi gathers herself to focus. She holds Dev off from his shoulder, making him looks at her and stopping him. She says, heaving,' You don't want our first time to be a quickie. Do you?'

Dev rolls his eyes and drops his head in the crook of her neck, groaning loudly in frustration.

Soon both arrive downstairs in time to bid goodbye to Bua and the rest of the guests. Soon after, Yashika's parents also arrive at the house to pick their daughter. Considering the history between the two, they didn't stay long. They thanked Dev for all his help, despite Yashika's actions.

Now, the only family is left in the house. Nivi has her flight back to Norway for the next day in the evening. Whereas, Anu and Dev's parents decided to stay for a couple of days, as Dev needed Maan to be here for some hotel business. And Maan insisted for Savitri to stay with him. Anu, on the other hand, has some free days. Before she has to be back at her job. So she decided to spend the week with her childhood friend, now her sister-in-law, Mahi.

Everyone settles in the living room after having breakfast. Anu shakes out an old album from the garage to pass the time. She settles down with it next to Mahi on the rug. Nivi sits right behind them on the sofa, next to Savitri. While, Dev sits across Mahi, pretending to be busy on the phone while he is just there to gawk at her. Maan is already out in the garden, with some calls.

Mahi and Anu turn the album pages with pictures of these three siblings from when one of them was just taking steps. The photos were from the time before Mahi, with her family, shifted to the same city as Savitri. Mahi sees Dev's pictures when he was just a year old. Savitri had him clinging to him on her side. She teases Dev showing that from across the centre table. Dev simply gets amused seeing her happier just going through some old pictures of him. Mahi notices in most of the snaps Dev had Savitri next to him, where some way or the other, he doesn't let go of her.

'Was he always such a clinger?' says Mahi teasingly.

'Oh! You have no idea,' exclaims Nivi from behind. She continues,' I have seen him growing up. He used to be around Mom all the time. Whenever they used to be in the same room, you can find one in the pretext of the other.'

'Oh, I remember he used to get jealous of me when I was small, and Mom used to pamper me as the youngest. He never had that privilege,' says Anu chuckling, remembering the time.

'Even until he was a grown man. You know he is the exact definition of Mumma's boy,' says Nivi.

'Was. Not anymore,' replies Dev curtly.

'Yeah, right! As if she is not your mother anymore,' replies Nivi with a taunt in her tone.

'I wish that was true,' Dev voices without looking in their direction.

'Dev!'

'Dev!'

Mahi and Nivi exclaim together at his rudeness as Savitri is right there listening to everything with a tinge of sadness in her eyes.

Dev looks up at the rising tone of his sister and wife. Then his eyes dart from those two to his mother sitting next to them.

'You can stop being an ass, at least for once,' Nivi becoming furious with his brother's behaviour towards their mother.

'Well, someone has to be one. Or there won't be anyone to raise the voice against the obsessively controlled order. How boring it would be otherwise,' says Dev being more mean with his words.

'Since when have you start thinking like that,' asks Nivi, now genuinely concerned.

'Since I got to know what kind of a person my mother is,' replies Dev sternly. He gets up,' I have a conference call to attend. Excuse me if I don't indulge you with this conversation any further.' He leaves the living room with a bad mood behind and takes the door to his study, shutting it after him.

Mahi becomes a little shocked to see the way Dev behaved with Savitri. And in all of this, she also noticed Savitri not saying a single word to reprimand him or defend herself.

'How long exactly are you planning to let this happen?' asks Nivi directing the question towards her mother. ' Why don't you say something to him?'

Savitri doesn't say anything at first, and then she looks at Nivi,' Leave him be.'

'Yeah! Like that has ever helped!' replies Nivi with a touch of sarcasm at the end. 'What happened? Since when is he like this? And why do you not say anything?'

Savitri doesn't say anything trying to hide her sadness. She simply avoids it. 'Your Dad has been on the phone for a very long time. I'll check on him.' With this, she gets up and leaves the living area.

Mahi witness everything quietly. She feels Savitri's silence, Nivi's frustration and Dev's hate. She understands the first two but, she fails to grasp the last. It wasn't something new that happened in terms of Dev's dislike towards his mother. In these past few months, she very much got the taste of his hatred. But now she can't ignore it anymore.

After an hour or so, Mahi takes a cup of coffee to Dev in his study. When she enters after knocking on the door, she finds Dev busy with a video conference. Dev gestures her to wait.

'Guys. Let's take a 10 mins coffee break,' Dev speaks into the screen in front of him. Mahi puts the cup of coffee on the end of his study table and steps back to recline, taking the support of the sofa behind. She half stands, placing her hip on the edge of the sofa.

Dev shuts the laptop screen down, getting up from his chair. 'Hi!' he says with a smile.

'Hi!' replies Mahi smiling back involuntarily, looking at his handsome face. He walks around the table towards Mahi. She gets nervous and excited as he comes around and pulls her in, wrapping his arms around her.

'Coffee. I made it. Just how you like it,' Mahi speaks, trying to keep her nerves steady. She feels terribly jittery with Dev's touch. Every single time.

'Ah Hmm,' Dev loses himself in her as he pushes her loose strands of hair over her shoulders. Mahi feels his fingers brushing against her skin, sending mini jolts of warmth in the pit of her stomach. She speaks up, trying to divert her focus from his touch to the coffee,' Why don't you try it.'

He eyes her neck, remembering the morning they had in their room. 'Alright!' he nods and then bends his head down, planting a soft kiss on her collar bone.

Mahi closes her eyes, making a little gasping sound. He pulls back to see her face as he feels a little satisfied with her expression.

She opens her eyes, feeling embarrassed,' I meant the coffee.' She places her hands on his chest as he still holds her.

'Umm... I don't know about the coffee but, you taste just perfect,' replies Dev with a deep voice. He tilts his head and leans in to place another lingering kiss right below her ear.

'You are yet to taste me. Properly,' says Mahi, surprising Dev and herself at her response. She feels the heat in her cheeks.

Dev chuckles at her boldness. 'Then why are we waiting. Let's get done with it. Right here.'

'Sure. 10 minutes so much better than 5 minutes,' says Mahi pointing out the obvious and feeling proud of herself for finding her wit back.

Dev smiles, nodding and getting amused at her reply. He leans in as he kisses her softly, this time on her lips. And then continues to do so while moving to her neck.

'Dev. Can I ask you something?' Mahi says softly between his distracting touch.

'Hmm mm. About what?' Dev still going at her neck.

Mahi hesitates as she becomes quiet and not responding to Dev's question. Dev breaks away to look at her, becoming curious about what made her silent. Still holding her in his arms, Dev notices a concerned look on her face. 'What is it? What you want to ask?'

'About you,' says Mahi. Then looks down once and up again,' And Saavi Maa.' She sees Dev's face losing all expressions, and an unfamiliar mood takes over. He looks away, controlling his displeasure at the mention.

'Can we not talk about it?' Dev speaks up.

'Why not?'

'Because I don't want to talk about it right now,' Dev snaps back.

'Then when do you want to?' asks Mahi genuinely.

Dev becomes uncomfortable with Mahi's questions. He straightens up, backing away from Mahi. He walks away towards his chair, saying,' I have to get back with the call. It's an important one.'

Mahi looks at him in disbelief as he avoids the topic and her. He sits in his chair, opening his laptop. He doesn't look at Mahi, still standing with questions on her face. He keeps his gaze at the screen without acknowledging Mahi's presence. Mahi feels a little insulted at his behaviour. She scoffs to herself, 'Alright then. I shouldn't disturb you anymore.' She turns on her heels and leaves the room. Dev sighs off, feeling disappointed at himself.

When Salma knocks on the door with his lunch, Dev feels disappointed for not finding Mahi. He thought he might make up for his behaviour when she'd come back with lunch. However, he feels worse for not seeing her face. The rest of the day goes by, as Mahi doesn't appear again in his study. Even when he made himself busy through the dinner as well.

On the other hand, after indirectly getting kicked out by Dev, Mahi tries to find some answers from Savitri. But, in return, she just gets one response from her.

'Promise me. You won't try anything at the expense of your relationship,' says Savitri, with seriousness in her voice. She continues, 'It's been long since I have seen you and him this happy. Don't test it on my account.'

Mahi tries to protest but, Savitri stops her. Mahi doesn't say anything further but becomes more determined to find the solution. She just can't let the two important people in her life at odds with each other.

After dinner, everyone retires to their rooms, except Dev, who hasn't stepped out of his study since morning. Neither Mahi has seen him since she left the study, after that. Mahi sits lost with her thoughts along with a book on the balcony after dinner. She sits facing the pool, which she could still see the edge of it, even seated. She sits sideways on the long seat, with her legs stretched in front and a book in her laps. The balcony has separate living room style furniture and lights enough to spend the evening in the peace and quiet of nature.

'Sorry,' a deep familiar voice pulls Mahi back to the real world. She snaps her head towards the voice and finds Dev standing, leaning against the room's door with his hands folded over his chest.

'For what?' asks Mahi with a straight face. God, I missed him. She thinks.

He straightens up as he takes slow steps towards her,' For being a jerk today.'

'For which one?' asks Mahi bluntly.

Dev sits on the edge of the table placed in front of Mahi. 'The one where I was, with you. In the study.'

'What about the other one? Before me. In the living room,' asks Mahi.

Dev looks at her without saying anything.

'No?' asks Mahi. Dev shakes his head once. 'Alright! Apologies for the study room accepted.' With this, she returns to reading the book in her hand. At least, pretending to read.

Dev looks at her, puzzled. ' That's it?'

'Yeah! What else? Should there be more?' Mahi looks up once and then goes back to her book.

Dev feels something off. So he takes the book from her hand and places it aside. 'What?' asks Mahi, now puzzled. Dev gets up, picking up her stretched legs and sitting down next to her as he puts down her legs over his laps.

'You are not gonna ask me?' asks Dev again.

'What should I ask you?' counters Mahi, knowing what he means.

Dev understands her, pushing him to speak up but, he doesn't say, just stares. 'Your mother?' says Mahi.

'Your Saavi Maa,' Dev replies, nodding.

'Do you wanna tell me?' asks Mahi this time.

Dev pauses briefly, then says,' Maybe.'

'You hesitated. So I should still take that as a no,' replies Mahi.

'I didn't say that.'

'You didn't say yes as well.'

Dev feels conflicted about whether to share his feeling with Mahi or not. Or is it too soon to burden her with his troubles. Mahi notices the stress on Dev's face.

'It's okay. You don't have to,' says Mahi taking his hand in her own.

Both stay quiet for few seconds as Mahi runs her free hand through his overgrown soft wavy hair, pushing away his stress. He feels her touch doing the magic for him.

'Do you wanna listen to a story?' asks Mahi smiling after few seconds of silence between them. Dev smiles at her perkiness. ' The one you have been reading?' Dev gestures towards the book on the table.

'Maybe. Maybe not,' says Mahi mysteriously.

Dev unconsciously runs his free hand along with her open locks. He rests the same hand on the side of her back as his thumb does repeating movement. 'Go ahead!'

'Okay,' Dev notice Mahi gulp a couple of times before starting. He finds it adorable as she prepares for something she has been reading. Dev watches her intently and attentively as she begins.

'It's about a girl in her teens. Late teens. Maybe 16 or close to 17. She was a type of girl, who was sincere, innocent, a school topper, popular too but not that smart. But she used to experience every new thing with zeal. She does the same with her first crush. First love. That's what she thought it was. Like I said, not very smart even with her feelings. He was a boy at the same school. A senior.

She felt lucky to experience such love at such young age. They soon became a popular couple of the school.'

'Have you been reading those young adult novels these days,' Dev teasingly interrupts.

Mahi scowls back adorably,' Patience, Sir!'

'Sorry. Keep going,' smiling apologetically.

Mahi narrows her eyes at Dev and then pauses briefly to continue. 'So where was I? Yes. A girl falls for a boy. They soon became really close in terms of dating and going out. The girl was head over heels for him. She gave him everything, from her time, affection, heart... to even her virginity. It happened at his house, where they used to spend most of their evenings. The girl was happy. At least that what she thought until she went back to school the next day. She felt something different at first. Everyone was eyeing her. Looking at her differently. Girls were whispering in corners and used to freeze whenever they spot her. Boys were giving her creepy smiles. She couldn't understand. Then, one of her friends drags her to the washroom and takes out the phone and plays something on it. A video of a couple having sex. However, she notices that the woman's face is blurred in the video and couldn't see the man's face. She freezes in her tracks, realising that the blurred face is hers.'

Dev notices Mahi's expressions becoming grim as she recites the story looking far away. He observes the way she becomes thoughtful before continuing.

'Eventually, she gathers herself and confronts the boy. The so-called boyfriend. She furiously burst out on him about how can he make a video of their private moments and that too without her consent. The boy was shameless. He didn't feel remorse, rather comes clean about his sinister intentions. When the girl realised how wrong she was about him, she tells him to take him to the authorities if he didn't delete her video. In response to that, the boy threatens her to release the video without blurring her face. The boy was smart to read the terrified expressions on her face. So he goes on asking her for sexual favours... in return if she doesn't want to get popular as a teenage porn star.' Mahi takes a brief pause as she takes a deep breath,' Not just for him but for his bunch of friends too. And he gives her time of few days to think about it. How thoughtful of him.' She says the last sentence bitterly.

Dev frowns as the story takes an ugly turn. He still listens intently.

'The girl loses her shit. She feels humiliated and exposed. She could not grasp at first what was happening. She thought of sharing this with her parents. When she faced her parents, she couldn't gather enough courage to tell them. Seeing their hopeful and trusting faces, she decides to do otherwise. She couldn't do that to them. Her parents raised her with such love and care. How can she make them ashamed because of her? She could never do that to them. She thinks of every possible way to get out of the situation. To find a solution for it.'

'And the school was becoming an unfriendly place for her. She couldn't focus on anything. She couldn't get out of the situation. She just had 2 choices in front of her. Either she tells her parents and crush their all hopes and expectations or swallow her self respect, dignity and do what the boy wants from her. And she knew that if she chooses the latter, it won't be just one time. She'll never be able to get out of it. But she couldn't lose her self-esteem.'

Mahi sighs off heavily as she continues,' She was lost. So lost that she wasn't in her right mind.'

'It so happened that one day, right before the day, she has to give her answer to that boy. Because he was not losing any chance to blackmail and make her life hell as it was already. She was at home... all alone. She just grabs her Dad's favourite wine bottle and starts to uncork it. While doing so, she loses the grip and breaks it.'

Mahi takes a pause as her breathing becomes short. Dev feels her shaking. Mahi's gaze goes to her hands in her laps, where she was unconsciously rubbing the scar on her wrist. Dev gasps silently, realising that the girl in the story is not fictional. But Mahi herself. He looks at her in shock as she continues, not looking at him. 'The next thing she remembers that she had a piece of broken glass in her one hand...and.... a bleeding wrist of the other hand.' Mahi starts panting now as she still holds her wrist tightly, thinking about that scene.

Chapter 24 The Talk

Dev holds Mahi by her arms and gives her a soft jerk to pull her back to reality. Back to him. 'Hey!'

Mahi looks up with her eyes welled up and red. She looks at Dev as she says,' I didn't mean to do it. When I started feeling dizzy, it struck me that I don't want to die.' Tears start rolling over cheeks.

'I know,' Dev replies softly, believing her. He immediately fills her in his arms, embracing her. She wraps her hands around Dev's neck as he pulls her closer. She breaks down in soft sobs on his shoulder, holding him tightly and letting him soothe her. She speaks through her sobs, still holding onto him and letting him embrace her.

'I am not suicidal.' She speaks up after a while, after controlling her weeping.

She breaks away from Dev to see him in the face. She feels the need to look at him while she says this. 'I am not suicidal. I don't cut myself in the next opportunity when something goes wrong in my life.'

Dev nods as he wipes the tears from her face,' I believe you.'

She takes a deep breath before she continues,' My panic atta cks... are not caused by thinking what he did to me. I get them because I am still unable to accept the fact that I almost lost my life because of one weak moment.' Dev looks at her as she unfolds herself in front of him, still holding her.

'I get scared... I am scared. Of Myself. I am scared of that version of myself, who almost took the life I am living,' says Mahi with a break in her voice as she hangs her head down in exhaustion and in shame. Dev holds her face up. She keeps her eyes closed, feeling self-conscious and not so confident.

'Open your eyes,' Dev softly asks as he rubs his thumb over her jaws. 'Look at me.' Mahi opens them and looks at him with still moist eyes.

Dev smiles and, then he asks,' What do you see?'

Mahi gulps once and speaks up,' You.'

'And?' Dev prompts.

'Still here.' Mahi speaks with little hesitancy, feeling not so sure or confident.

Dev smiles proudly this time. 'Exactly! I am still here. Right next to you. Not leaving you. And never will.' He briefly pauses before he continues,' And you can stop being scared of yourself or your past. Since I am not going anywhere. And will love you for the rest of my life. All of your versions.' He places an assuring kiss on her forehead. He stays there and then slides down, resting his forehead over hers. Both hold like this for few more seconds before Dev plants a soft kiss on her lips, wiping her remaining tears.

A few minutes later, Dev is leaned back on the same bench with his legs stretched on the table in front. He sits there half lying on his back with Mahi in his arms. She had her face resting in the crook of his neck, eyes closed as her legs are still sprawled over Dev and her hand with a scar in Dev's hand, over his chest. The hand which had Mahi wrapped around close to him was caressing her back in a slow and repeating motion.

Mahi opens her eyes as she shifts her head back a little to see Dev, watching the starry sky above, lost in some thoughts.

'Where are you lost so deeply? Having second thoughts?' asks Mahi, burying her face again in his neck.

Dev doesn't reply immediately. But when he does, he speaks with his utmost sincerity and emotions. 'I am so grateful that I can feel you breathing like this, next to me. I am thanking the universe. I just can't imagine my life without you in it. If anything were to happen to you...' He pauses for a couple seconds before he continues,' I would have been so lost.'

Mahi smiles at his sweet confession. She feels grateful for Dev being in her life. For staying next to her, even after knowing her dreaded past.

She speaks up,' If you really want to thank someone, then you should thank your mother. If Saavi Maa didn't turn up at the house just to check on me. And if she hadn't rushed my unconscious self to the hospital in time. Then, I really wouldn't be here. Not only this. She really helped me to get out of that mess too and start afresh.'

'What do you mean?' asks Dev, now becoming more curious.

'The Druv issue didn't just end with me being in the hospital. When I woke up in the hospital. I found Saavi Maa next to my bed. She went out on me about how irresponsibly I acted in the absence of my parents. And whatnot. I was just glad to be alive, so I burst out crying and confessing everything that had been going on with me. Do you know what she said?' Mahi ends with bright eyes.

'What?'

'First, she held me and then she said, "I promise you that no man would ever dare to hurt you. Ever. And I will take care of this."'

reciting the exact words that she still remembers from 13 years ago.

'And she really did. She had convinced my parents to send me away to a new school, a new place to start afresh. She even got someone to erase any sign of that video in public as well as him. When I went back home from the hospital, I tried searching for the video on the internet or any social media. I couldn't find it. It was as if it never existed,' continue Mahi.

'You don't know for sure. Vikram Uncle is quite capable of doing that as well,' counters Dev, stating the logic.

'My parents didn't know,' says Mahi in a low voice. 'They still don't. Nobody does. Except for Saavi Maa and my psychiatrist... And you. They know the same story as everyone else... They can never know,' says Mahi becoming sad at the end of it.

Dev tries to reason it,' You do realise that our mothers are besties. They share everything. How can you be so sure that my mom never let Shree aunty know about such crucial detail of her daughter.'

'You know my mom. Right? She is transparent like glass. She can't keep a secret. I could tell,' replies Mahi, half smiling.

Dev becomes thoughtful after listening to Mahi as small frown forms over his forehead.

'You don't want to give her credit,' says Mahi reading Dev's troubled expressions.

'Oh, I give her enough credit. Believe me. Because I know this. Whatever she did good for you, she got that back, paid in full by manipulating you into marrying her own son.'

'No! she didn't,' says Mahi rolling her eyes.

'How can you be so sure?' asks Dev, looking down at her.

'Because it was my idea. I came up with the idea of getting you married to someone else in the first place. And let not the media get the whiff of it. I was simply managing the crisis. And it was all me when I suggested myself to be that someone else,' says Mahi in a swift breath. 'It's true that I did it for Saavi Maa. This way I could giver her back some for saving my life.'

'Then you don't know my mother well. She is quite talented enough to put ideas in your head and words in your mouth,' replies Dev with another counter.

'Right! And then it was all part of her plan to not talk to me for a year to make me believe that it was not her doing, but mine,' replies Mahi with sarcasm.

Dev simply shrugs at her sarcastic comment.

Mahi shakes her head in disbelief as she sits up. She decides to tell Dev something that she has never got the chance to.

'Do you remember the letter Yashika left for you?' asks Mahi.

'Yes! What about it?

'Do you remember anything different about it?'

'Like what?'

'Like a tear on top of it?'

'Yeah! So?'

'Where do you think that came from?'

'My mother must have thought of destroying it. When she almost did, someone must have seen it,' replies Dev with a logic behind it.

'Again. It was me. And nobody walked in to stop me. But, your mother took it from me, stopping me. I was there when Yashika handed that letter to your mom and left. When I read it, I just decided to tear it into pieces. Because I knew what it could do to your relationship with her,' replies Mahi thinking about that night.

'You wouldn't lie to me just to save your Saavi Maa. Would you?' asks Dev, now sitting up, getting all puzzled at Mahi's assertion.

'You can tell when I am lying and when I am not,' replies Mahi looking straight into his eyes.

A frown forms on his head as he stresses at this new information.

Mahi continues, '"My son deserves these last words of the woman he loves. Even if it destroys him and my relationship with him." Those were her exact words.'

Dev becomes uncomfortable listening to Mahi because he knows that she isn't lying to him. And it is difficult for him to believe that his mother could do anything selfless like that. For some years now, he believes that there is always a subtext or other underlying agenda behind his mother's words or activities. Mahi notices Dev's thoughtful and yet concerning expressions.

'Why is it so difficult for you to believe that your mom could do something like this?' Mahi asks him genuinely.

He looks at her, thinking to come up with something that doesn't sound too mean and hateful towards his mother.

Mahi reads Dev's expressions of contemplating his following words. She asks something different this time,' Why are you so reluctant to share your feelings with me about your mother?'

Dev hesitates to answer that first and then finally decides to say,' She means a lot to you. I don't want to mar your feelings towards her with mine.'

'You mean a lot to me too.'

Dev smiles,' You mean a lot.'

'Then talk to me,' Mahi speaks up softly, insisting as she slips her hand in his.

'I don't want to tarnish your love for her.'

'Try me,' replies Mahi raising a brow, challenging him.

Dev chuckles softly at her confidence. He simply nods.

'I have grown up listening to how close you and Saavi used to be. Everyone around I know never stopped talking about the bond you guys used to share,' Mahi says with an intended look. She continues,' What changed that? Since when you started doubting her intentions?'

Dev looks ahead, becoming thoughtful. He then looks down at Mahi's fingers, intertwined in his. He speaks, keeping his gaze on their hands. ' I was always aware of the bond we used to share. But, I never realised that in the pretext of that bond, she was trying to control my life.'

'How did you realise that?' asks Mahi after listening to him intently.

He turns his head to see her face. 'You sure you wanna listen to this. Because this involves Yashika.'

Mahi smiles mysteriously at Dev. She simply nods. 'I still want to.'

Dev looks away, smiling and then losing the smile as he recalls a specific memory.

'When I ignored her advice about not to get serious with Yashika, after meeting her for the first time. She kind of threatened Yashika that she wouldn't let her stay next to me.'

'That doesn't sound like her!' says Mahi getting surprised.

'Neither to me at first.'

'She didn't say it in front of you?'

Dev shakes his head,' She said that to Yashika when she went to meet her again alone. She decided to win my mother's heart after I casually slipped my mother's opinion about her.'

Mahi becomes thoughtfully,' So you got to know that from Yashika.'

'I know what you are thinking. I shouldn't have believed Yashika blindly. And I didn't. So I went to confront her. My mother. And she didn't deny it,' Dev counters, anticipating Mahi's response.

'How did you confront her? I mean, what exactly did you ask her?' prompts Mahi, thinking something.

'I don't remember exactly, what I said, but I remember very clearly that she never denied it. She never pleaded that she was not guilty.'

'Unless she really wasn't.'

'You are saying that because you love her.'

'Don't you?' asks Mahi, silencing Dev in his tracks. 'I mean, I understand the disappointment but, that doesn't mean you don't love her.'

Dev ignores her claims. 'That wasn't the only time she did that. She made it really difficult for Yashika from then onwards.'

'Well. That's what future mothers-in-law is supposed to do,' dismissing Dev's another accusation.

'By trying to insult her indirectly on every next occasion and hurting her self respect by sending unnecessary gifts to her family. I get that now she might deserve all of that. But, not then.' Dev tries to make his point.

Mahi doesn't say anything for the next few seconds as she couldn't move forward from one thought.

'I get it. Saavi Maa underestimated your choice.'

'Yeah. My mother tried taking things into her hands when I didn't comply with her advice,' says Dev looking ahead.

Mahi stays quiet for few more seconds before she shifts closer to him, still holding his hand in hers. She draws his attention towards her. She rests her chin on his shoulder. 'Can I ask you a little favour?'

Dev turns his head to face her, 'You are not gonna ask me to go talk to her once. About this. Confront her again?'

'You won't?' says Mahi with a frown on her forehead.

'Damn it, Mahi! You can't be asking me that,' says Dev chuckling dryly and feeling a little irritated.

'I thought maybe the second time is the charm. This time you should go with a definite question. For instance, ask your mom if she actually said all those things to Yashika. Did she really threatened her?' says Mahi becoming a little defensive.

'Even If I do. Even if we make up by some miracle. How does it matter to you?' asks Dev, becoming pensive.

'You seriously not asking me that question?' Mahi feels a little hurt by Dev's curt question.

'I am,' replies Dev with a genuine curiosity in his eyes.

Mahi wryly chuckles as she looks down at first and then looks up to face him. 'Two most important people in my life don't see eye to eye. One is the love of my life, and another is the one who gave me another chance at life. Because of that, I was able to give a chance to love for the second time.'

Dev immediately regrets asking her that as he sees sorrow in her eyes as she speaks with a stifle in the end. She takes a deep breath to not let her emotions take over. ' I don't want to pressure you to do something you don't want to. It's just...lately, it has become easy to share everything with you. So forget it, I ever asked you to do that.' Mahi says, smiling with sincerity, which even Dev notice.

Dev smiles in return. 'So I am the love of your life,' Dev says teasingly, changing the mood.

Mahi closes her eyes in embarrassment as she turns her head away. Dev chuckles loudly at her reaction. 'Oh, come on. You can't turn away from the love of your life.'

Mahi scoffs at his teasing. 'Oh, God! I wish I never said that.'

'Why!' Dev exclaims as he wraps his one arm around her, pulling her close. He makes her face him as he places his other hand under her ear, pulling it closer. He then continues in a deep and low voice,' Cause I would absolutely love it when the love of my life would tell me that I am the love of her life.'

'God! You are cheesy!' exclaims Mahi feeling his breath and becoming excited with his touch.

Dev doesn't let lose his grip on Mahi. He leans in, capturing her lips with his, catching her in surprise. She gives in, closing her eyes and finding her hands in his hair in the next second.

The following morning, Mahi wakes up to an empty bed. When she looks at the clock to check if she has overslept. She relaxes, seeing that it's still early for Dev to wake up. She leaves the bed. After she gets fresh, she leaves the room to look for Dev. First, she looks in the study in case he got pulled into another international conference call. But, she doesn't find him there. So she looks for him in the whole house. She even goes out in front to check if he left for somewhere, but she finds his car parked outside. She pulls out her phone to call him, then it struck her that she hasn't checked the pool and the backyard. When she reaches the back door, she stops in shock before opening it. Through the glass door, she could see Dev seated with Savitri in the middle of the garden. They seem to be talking. She pauses in her tracks.

She jumps when Maan and Nivi come and stand next to her in shock, seeing the same scene.

'I am hallucinating now!' exclaims Nivi.

'Me too,' says Maan without removing their gaze from the scene in the garden.

'If we are hallucinating the same thing, then we are definitely suffering from the same illness,' Mahi adds.

Anu comes down in half sleepy mode with an empty jug of water.

'What's going on?' All three jump when they hear Anu standing behind them, puzzled.

Mahi pulls her by her arm and makes her watch outside quietly.

'I think I am still sleeping,' says Anu with an open mouth in shock.

Four of them stand there quietly, waiting to let the scene before them sink.

Dev couldn't sleep properly after the talk they had last night. His thoughts kept him quite busy while Mahi slept peacefully, next to him, in his arms. He kept thinking if only he could let go of his ego for once for Mahi's sake and try talking to his mother. He couldn't deny the fact that Savitri's advice of being patient with Mahi has made this happen. If he hadn't come clean to her about his feelings about Mahi, then he probably wouldn't have reached an understanding about Mahi. And he has to be thankful to her for saving Mahi.

Mahi's question definitely prompts him to think about the trajectory of his relationship with his mother. He does love her. After all, she is his mother. He has to try it once, not for himself but for Mahi.

He clearly remembers Savitri's routine. She likes to take her first tea in the early hours of the morning alone when nobody is awake. So first thing Dev did was to find her. Savitri was seated in the garden with her cup of tea when it was still a little dark outside.

'Good Morning,' says Dev as he comes and stands feet apart from where Savitri is seated.

Savitri, becoming shocked at first and then immediately composing herself to speak up. ' Good Morning!'

'Can I talk to you for a minute?'

'Sure.' replies Savitri, still reeling from the shock of his son standing here, speaking to her.

Dev takes a seat on the chair across from her. He suddenly feels a rush of nervousness and a little awkwardness.

After fighting the uneasiness, Dev speaks,' I'll come directly to it. I have something to ask you. Can I?'

Savitri, still feeling the shock of his own son coming of his own to talk to her, just nods awkwardly.

'At that time. When Yashika came to you, without me. Did you really threatened her to leave me?' asks Dev, becoming intensely curious about her mother's response.

Savitri looks at him and shakes her head, 'No.'

'Why didn't you say that when I asked you then? Years ago,' Dev asks, becoming a little frustrated.

'You never asked me that question. Until today,' replies Savitri with a calm and satisfied voice. Finally, her son is asking her the right questions.

'What! You never denied it when I came to you,' tells Dev, trying to find a logic behind his mother's statement.

'When you came to confront me, you had already believed that I was the culprit. You never gave me the benefit of the doubt. If you remember the day clearly, you came to the house furiously. Not to talk to me but to bombard me with warnings and challenges. You never asked me if I ever said that. You came to express your anger, not to confront me or to find out if I did say that to your then-girlfriend,' replies Savitri justifying her stand.

'You should have told me then,' replies Dev, immediately regretting the memory of that day.

'If I had denied it, I would have made it worst. You had already believed Yashika, and you were not ready to listen to me. I would have only tried you to understand me in vain,' says Savitri.

'What happened exactly?' asks Dev, finally trying to find the actual answers.

'She came to meet me. I understood her eagerness to meet me again, without you as you would have told her about my opinion. When she met me, at first, she asked for the reason. Why I don't like her. So, I told her honestly that she is not the type of person my son would be happy, in the long run.'

Savitri continues, smiling and recalling the event that struck the bond with her son. 'She somehow took my audacity to be direct as a challenge. And put forth a challenge that she'll make sure that my son would become her husband first and then maybe my son, if she let him be,' says Savitri recalling her exact words.

Dev simply scoffs in disbelief at this new revelation. He somehow is not surprised. He realises he never knew the woman whom he claimed to be in love for six years. And he almost married her.

Savitri sees Dev's sly smile. 'I am sorry. I never meant for her to leave you. And I swear, I did everything for her not to leave that day. I was surprised at her reason for leaving but, I still never meant to be the reason for your hurt.'

Dev looks at Savitri with apologetic eyes. He sees the sincerity in his mother's eyes. He suddenly feels remorse taking him over as he let his mother believe that she is somehow the reason for his unhappiness. He misunderstood her. He feels terrible for punishing her and himself for no reason at all.

Dev shakes his head as he continues,' You were not the reason she left.'

'But, the letter,' replies Savitri becoming perplexed.

'She just wanted me to find someone else for the blame, but her. She somehow got the whiff about the raid next day and a rumour that I might become bankrupt with that raid.' Dev states the truth, which he recently got to know.

Savitri becomes shocked and then thoughtful, understanding the actual reason for her sudden departure.

'All along, you were right about her. She was not with me for love. Her interests were much bigger than mine,' says Dev smiling.

'I am sorry,' says Savitri feeling for his son's betrayal.

'I am sorry for putting you through all of this. For nothing,' says Dev as he gets up and sits next to her, holding her hand. He genuinely missed holding his mother's hands. They still had the same warmth.

Savitri gulps down the tears as she holds his son's hand after so long. Her child is back to her after losing his way home. After few seconds of silence, Savitri speaks up,' But, I am grateful too.'

'Because of Mahi?' asks Dev.

'Because of Mahi,' nods Savitri. ' I am happy truly to see you two together. It makes me so relieved that you found each other.'

Dev smiles at his mother's pure confession. 'Then, I should thank you. For keeping her alive and saving her years ago.'

'She told you?' asks Savitri with bewilderment.

Dev nods softly. 'She did.'

Savitri smiles back with a most content. 'Finally, she found someone to trust again. How is she?' asks Savitri instantly, realising it must have been difficult for her to recite the most dreaded part of her life to someone.

'She is fine. It was difficult for her to tell but, she slept quite peacefully after that,' replies Dev assuring his mother. Savitri sighs off, relaxing.

'I have something important to say now,' says Savitri with a grave expression. Dev just nods and wait for her to continues.

'Hurt her, and I'll forget that you are my son,' says Savitri with a friendly and yet warning smile.

Dev chuckles at her mother's seriousness and then nods with a serious face. 'I would never, intentionally. She means the world to me.'

'Good. I am pretty sure Mahi feels the same,' replies Savitri smiling gleefully.

Dev smiles back at his mother. 'Hey, mom,'

Savitri replies, listening to him call her 'mom' again. 'Yes, my boy.'

'Can I get a hug?' asks Dev sheepishly.

Savitri just breaks into tears as she stands up, opening her arms, 'You never have to ask.'

Dev stands up and embraces his mother in a tight hug. 'I really missed clinging to you like this.'

'Me too.'

'Did we missed the invite to this family reunion?' asks Anu, teasingly. Dev and Savitri turn to see Anu, Nivi, Maan and Mahi standing few feet away in the garden.

Dev and Savitri chuckle loudly. 'No. You weren't invited. Because this isn't the family reunion but just a mother-son reunion,' says Dev keeping an arm around his mother's shoulder.

Anu gasps dramatically,' Haw! What about the daughters?'

'Ah! not to worry. The daughters have their father,' injects Maan, joining joviality. As he says this, he opens his arms to embrace Nivi and Anu, who cutely run to their father. Maan gestures to Mahi to join them.

Everyone breaks into a burst of laughter at the silliness being played.

'Savitri Ji, don't forget your husband after reuniting with son,' Maan speaks up teasingly.

'Never. I can never dare to forget my better half,' replies Savitri as she walks to Maan. Nivi, Mahi and Anu swiftly step back as Maan takes his wife in a sweet embrace.

Mahi turns to see Dev, who was adoring his parents. He shifts his gaze from them to Mahi, standing next to them. He simply gestures by raising an arm for her to take it. Mahi smiles shyly as she quietly walks up to him, taking his hand as he wraps an arm around her. Both exchange a knowing look and gaze back at their parents with a wide smile.

'I guess we are the only ones with our better halves not present, Anu,' says Nivi, teasingly. She notices Mahi and Dev following the suit of their parents.

'It's alright, Di. We have each other,' replies Anu, pulling Nivi in a hug.

All burst out in another laughter. The morning becomes lively with the sound of happy sounds.

'Now, it would be just perfect if we could all just be teleported to some holiday trip,' says Anu, dreamingly.

Chapter 25 The Kidnapping

'Yeah, we didn't have those in years,' says Nivi, pointing out the obvious. She recalls, before she got married and went to Norway, the Jamwals were known to go for a family vacation every year.

'We can always go on one now,' Dev speaks up as he looks at his father. Maan and Dev exchange the knowing look. 'Phuket?'

Dev nods,' Anyways, I was planning to go there. I had to check a few things at the hotel and opening for that new resort. I would love to have you take a look at it.'

'But, when?' asks Savitri.

'I can get us the flight tickets for today. Late evening. We'll land in the morning.' says Dev.

'I have a flight today in the evening for Norway,' speaks up Nivi complaining.

'Cancel it. I'll book you and Veer another flight from there,' Dev with an instant solution.

'Aur mera Pati?' asks Nivi, not feeling like leaving her husband and go on a vacation without him.

'Sameer Jiju can join us there directly,' replies Dev. Nivi smiles, getting satisfied.

Dev continues before Anu raises her eager query,' And you may ask Amit too. But, I am booking you two separate rooms.'

'Fine,' replies Anu, getting flustered at her brother's comment.

'Can you get off for another week?' Dev asks Mahi.

'A week! It's too long. I can't. Let's keep it for 3-4 days. 4 days max,' jumps in Anu, getting all worried.

'I wasn't asking you, idiot. The trip will be for 3-4 days. I wanted Mahi and me to extend it for a week. It's our anniversary next week. And we haven't been on any holiday since we got married,' says Dev turning his gaze back at Mahi.

'Right! The anniversary!' exclaims Anu.

'Can you spare me another week?' asks Dev, looking at Mahi.

'I don't know. I'll have to see. Might have to make some calls,' says Mahi, thoughtfully.

'Then make them now. I want you for myself this week,' says Dev with a charming smile.

Nivi clears her throat, reminding the lovebirds about the audience. 'We'll have her for the initial four days,' Nivi adds teasingly.

'Partially, then she is all mine,' replies Dev with a wink. Mahi slaps his arm, becoming flustered at his shamelessness.

Mahi leaves to make some calls as Dev makes one to his secretary to book the tickets for his family members. He asks his secretary to wait before booking for his and Mahi's.

After some time, when everyone scatters around planning the trip, Dev looks for Mahi to confirm her week off. He finds her in his mother's room. It was her room before she shifted to his room. Now their room. She still had few work-related files in here. Dev enters the room. He sees her rake through one of the cabinets next to the window with a phone on her ear. She speaks in her usual tone as she barks few orders on the call. He sits on the edge of the bed quietly, watching her getting irritated at her staff while she looks for some documents. When she finally finds it, she read out the specific content. She returns to her normal voice as she listens to the person speaking.

She notices Dev sitting on the bed and watching her. He tilts his head when he catches her eyes. She tilts her head as well, smiling, still on the call, speaking few words in between. She walks towards him to stand between his legs.

'Check the new office building budget file,' Mahi speaks into the phone as she runs her fingers through Dev's hair while looking at him adoringly. Dev closes his eyes as her fingers work the dizzying charm. She continues to stroke his hair few more times as she speaks into the phone.

'I'll drop by in the afternoon to check the rest,' says Mahi as she hangs up the call. She throws the cell on the bed to get her both hands stroking Dev's hair.

'I had us booked in the next flight. The 10:30 one. So we'll reach an hour late than the rest,' says Dev as he makes Mahi sit on his laps so that he could have a better and closer look at her.

'Why not with the rest?' Mahi exclaims softly.

Dev smiles mischievously,' I told everyone that there were no more seats in that flight.'

Mahi raises a brow at his confession.

'I'll have you to myself for just a few hours before you get consumed in this family vacation,' Dev continues.

'Okay,' replies Mahi gazing at Dev lovingly. She leans in and places a soft kiss on his lips.

'What was that for?' asks Dev smiling.

'Because I can,' replies Mahi proudly.

'Then why just one?'

'Because I can,' replies teasing him back.

He breaks into a light chuckle.

'Thank you,' says Mahi with seriousness.

'For what?'

'For talking to her. Making up with her,' says Mahi as she caresses his skin along the collar of his t-shirt.

'Well, would you feel bad if I say you are not the only reason I did it?' asks Dev with hesitancy in his voice.

Mahi looks at him with surprise. 'What was the other reason?'

'Something that you said last night got stuck with me. However long I am disappointed with her, it doesn't mean I don't love her,' says Dev pointing out the other reason.

'So I thought logically, I can't drag this childish behaviour for long. I do love my mother. And while I spend time staying mad at her, I am not only hurting her but, I am hurting myself as well. I'll have to face it someday and let go of this. Then why not give it a try when it also means a lot to you.'

Mahi looks at Dev lovingly as she says,' You know what. You did it for yourself. I had nothing to do with this.'

'No. That's not what I meant,' says Dev, thinking Mahi has taken an offence.

'Hey, I am not mad. In fact, I am more than happy you did it for yourself. Because if you did, which obviously you did. You did it willingly without any external influence.' Mahi smiles proudly at him. Dev falls in love with her all over again.

Dev looks on adoringly,' Thank you.'

Mahi looks on questioningly.' For what?'

'For finding the courage to share the most difficult part of your life with me. As much as I am grateful to you for that, I am proud of you too.' He continues,' I think, if you hadn't gathered up the strength to share your past with me, I don't think I'd ever come to you to share my feelings about mom.'

Mahi simply shrugs at Dev's confession.

'You already knew,' states Dev, smiling and reading Mahi's proud glint in her eyes.

Mahi envelops her arms around Dev's neck as she draws in, closing her eyes, to lean her forehead over his as her nose brush against his in soft motions. 'I am just happy. You and Saavi Maa sorted your differences. She is speaking to me again. And I have got you. I feel like everything will be okay now.'

Dev speaks up, thinking about something as he strokes her back. 'I was thinking since we are going on a family vacation. I can call up Vikram Uncle and Shree Aunty to join us.'

'No. Don't,' Mahi speaks up immediately, pulling her head back straight.

'Why not? At least let's give it a try.'

'My mother will agree but, there is no way my father will. The man hasn't spoken to me for a year. His only daughter. His stubbornness has no bounds. That's the very reason he is still reputed among his army peers even after his retirement. So don't waste your energy there,' says Mahi.

'I think it's my fault too. I am a bad son-in-law. I should have called him at least once after the wedding. I thought of doing it so many times but never build up the courage to do it. He was more of a friend than a mentor to me,' Dev says, feeling more remorse. He continues,' If it wasn't for him, I would have never build up the balls to join my father's business and that too of expanding it. He was the reason for my confidence building.'

'I know,' says Mahi softly. 'It's no one's fault. Let's give it the time. I have realised in these last few days that time does all the magic.'

Dev looks at Mahi as she speaks so deeply about the situation and relation with her father.

'Shouldn't I be the one to say these things? To console you. Since we are speaking about your Dad,' says Dev smiling apologetically.

Mahi sighs off, smiling as she rests her forehead over his. 'Yes. You should do it.'

'Yeah. But, I do it differently,' says Dev as he touches her arm around his neck and then runs his fingers softly along her back and passing through her hips, onto her thighs. Mahi feels ticklish as she feels him teasing her over.

'Sure, it is different. And effective,' says Mahi, feeling the thrill with Dev's touch.

A knock on the door makes them startle as Mahi stands up. Both see Savitri looking away, pressing the smile on the door.

'Anu is looking for Mahi. She wants to go shopping before we leave for the trip tonight,' says Savitri.

'Right. Even I have to check few things at the office. So I should get going,' replies Mahi, feeling totally embarrassed. She quickly picks her phone from bed and leaves the room, stealing her eyes.

'These doors. They do close and, if necessary, they lock too,' Savitri kidding her son.

'They do? Strange! I never knew this,' replies Dev, playing along with his mother.

Savitri shakes her head, smiling at his son's unabashed response,' Bloody Shameless!'

It is evening. Savitri tries calling the girls as they'll have to leave in two hours if they have to catch their flight on time. Mahi's numbers seem unreachable whereas, Nivi and Anu are not answering her call. As she keeps trying to get worried by the minute, she hears the car entering through the main gate. Savitri becomes determined to give them a good scolding.

Before she could say anything, Anu runs inside, panting and crying uncontrollably. Savitri sees her younger in such a state, as Anu runs and hugs her.

'What's wrong? What happened? Where are Mahi and Nivi?' asks Savitri, now becoming more tensed.

'Mahi. Ma-Mahi. Mom Mahi,' Anu speaks in between her whimpering.

While Savitri tries to get Anu speaking, Maan and Dev also join them, hearing the commotion from the study.

'Anukriti Jamwal. Get hold of yourself and speak up,' Savitri loudly scolds as Anu tests her patience.

Anu fails to calm herself, but she speaks up,' Someone-took Mahi from the Mall.'

'What!'

'What!'

'What the fuck is wrong with you? Anu, I am warning you if this is some kind of a sick joke-'

'I am not lying,' Anu cuts his brother's warning. She continues,' We were supposed to meet Mahi in the parking. She said she is waiting for us, next to our car. When Nivi di and I got there, she wasn't there. So Nivi di tried her cell. We found her phone ringing and lying under the car next to us. We became intensely spooked. At first, we thought, maybe she is playing some kind of a joke on us. So we search the whole parking floor. We couldn't find her. So we went to the security office and told them about this. They pulled up the CCTV footage from around the time we got Mahi's call.'

Anu starts sobbing again as she rambles through the incident. 'The footage showed Mahi, waiting for us, next to our car. But...,' she breaks down again.

'But what?' asks Dev becoming impatient.

'Two men grabbed her from behind and dragged her against her will, covering her mouth. She tried to fight back. But, they were twice the size of her. I am sorry. I didn't know what to do,' Anu starts crying again. As Dev hugs her as he says,' It's okay. Where is Nivi di?'

'She is still at the mall with the security team, trying to find some clue to trace those men through CCTV footage,' replies Anu in between her sobs.

Savitri takes Anu from Dev and leads her to sit. Dev becomes silent for a second as Maan stands next to him, taking out his cell.

'I am calling the commissioner,' says Maan as he dials the number. He notices Dev zoning out, becoming still. He pulls him out by calling out his name with more firmness.

Dev pulls himself up back to reality, which he wished was not real. 'I'll go there. Get Nivi Di.'

With this, Dev makes his way out. On his way, he calls up Arjun and lets him know about the situation. Arjun tells Dev to meet him directly at the Mall.

After some time, Dev, Nivi and Arjun, along with some police officers, stand in the security room of the Mall. They are going through the CCTV footage. They see Mahi standing alone in the parking as she gets off the call. Within the next second, two men almost twice her size approach her. She kicks one man hard in the groin while the other narrowly escapes her hit. He overpowers her by pulling her hair from behind and locking her hands behind as the other one gets up. He takes out something looking handkerchief from his pocket and places it on Mahi's mouth. In the next second, they drag Mahi's impaled body in a Black Scorpio and drive off.

'I have put the car on the lookout as soon as I got your call,' says Arjun. He continues,' It's been 3 hours already. If it is just a kidnapping, then they'll make the ransom call soon.'

'What do you mean by 'If'? Is there another possibility?' asks Dev, getting perplexed at Arjun's use of words.

Arjun takes a pause as he carefully continues,' Mahi had a reputation. There are a whole lot of people who don't like Mahi very much.'

'Has. You said had,' Dev prompts curtly. ' She is very much still alive. I know this. Many also know that she is Devrath Jamwal's wife. So it should be kidnapping. We'll get the ransom call soon.'

Dev outrightly chooses to ignore any other possibility. Because he believes this doesn't get over this soon and that easily.

Arjun realises his mistake and immediately apologies. 'No, you are right. We cannot rule out the kidnapping.'

Just then, Arjun receives the information about spotting a suspicious Black Scorpio just on the highway. Dev insists to tag along with him. Arjun hesitates at first. But then, he agrees, thinking it's better to keep Dev next to him. This way, he can keep him close when the ransom call comes.

Back at home, Savitri paces around worriedly and praying silently for Mahi's well being as Maan engages himself in making several calls, making financial arrangements. He prepares beforehand when ransom call comes as there should be no delay in saving Mahi. Soon Savitri receives Shree's call. She becomes concerned before picking it up. She looks for Maan for some support. Maan tells her not to let out anything about Mahi as they'll worry. But when Savitri listens to her best friend's voice, she breaks down, spilling everything.

It's been more than 5 hours since Mahi went missing. And there has been no ransom call. As time advances, Arjun becomes intensely worried. So does Dev, but he keeps telling himself that nothing has happened to Mahi. He tags along with Arjun as he makes several rounds running every possible lead.

The striking pain in the head makes Mahi becomes conscious. She tries raising her hand to her head but fails. She feels her hands tied as she finds herself seated on some old wooden chair. As she opens her eyes, she finds herself in the dark. She smells molasses. When her eyes get adjusted to the darkness, she could see around better. She remembers two men approaching her in the parking of the Mall as she tries to fight them back. But, after that, all blank. She hears the loud but unclear voices outside the enclosed room she is in. She then realises she is in some sugar factory as she sees the refinery next to her with a lot of sugarcane waste next to it.

Just then, three men open the main metal door of the factory and walk inside. She could notice that the two men on the sides wore some old yet strikingly cheap shirts, whereas the third man was in formals. The man in formals is tall and somewhat good looking. He looked sophisticated. He notices Mahi awake and looking at him with a focus.

'Hello Mrs Jamwal!' says the man in formals. The two men, along with the man in formals, stop at a distance. While the man pulls an empty chair next to Mahi right in front of her. He makes himself sit on it.

Mahi tries to control her anger as she first tries to get hold of the situation calmly. She gets one thing that she is here because of this man. She hasn't seen him before so becomes now curious what this man possibly wants from her.

Seeing Mahi quiet with serious expressions, he laughs off wickedly. 'What! No greetings?'

Mahi just stares at him. 'Who are you? Why am I here?'

'You are direct. I like that,' replies the man with a smile. He continues,' You are quite beautiful as well. I just noticed.'

Mahi looks away disgustingly at his last comment.

'I don't get it. When Devrath Jamwal has such a beautiful wife, why the fuck he would become nosy with someone else's wife.' The man's expression changes into fury.

Mahi looks at him confusingly. She doesn't understand that who this man is and what relation does Dev has with him. She understood another thing. She is not here because someone had some grudge with her but, it has to do something with Dev.

Looking at Mahi's confused face, the man becomes irritated. 'Oh, c'mon. You would have felt the same. Didn't you! When he brought his ex-girlfriend and my wife home,' says with a gritted teeth.

'You are Yashika's abusive husband,' says Mahi more to herself than to him.

'Bingo!' shouts the man. 'Armaan Singhvi. Nice to meet you. Well, too bad we are meeting like this. I mean, we are so the victim of our respective spouses. Don't you feel?'

Mahi looks at him with blank expressions. 'You used to hit her.'

'That's fucking nobody's business. What happens with a husband and wife should be kept within the walls of their bedroom. Nobody should be nosy in other's business.'

'She ran away from you,' says Mahi, trying to poke a reaction from him.

'Well, that happened. Yashika could have run away in any direction. But that bitch chose to run away to her ex-lover,' says Armaan becoming furious again.

'And your husband took her home. How dare he?' says, standing up, getting upset. He paces around a couple of times, trying to control his fury, thinking about Yashika with Dev.

'I am sure you felt the betrayal too when he brought her home. Didn't it make you go crazy,' asks Armaan standing in front of Mahi. She notices the man is not in a stable state of mind.

'You know what! You should see a doctor. Probably a psychiatrist,' says Mahi taking a jab at him. This makes him lose it as he slaps Mahi with all his anger.

Mahi takes the hit as she feels the warm blood gushing out from the corner of her mouth.

'You made me do this.' says Armaan.

'Right,' Mahi says, nodding. 'Would you care to tell me what am I doing here?'

'It is simple. I am returning the favour your husband humbly bestowed upon me,' says Armaan smiling satisfactorily. 'He took my wife home for a night so, I just took his wife away for a night.'

'So you gonna keep me here for a night. Then what?' asks Mahi with confidence.

This makes Armaan think. 'We'll see then.'

With this, he turns around, places instructions to the hired pair of goons and leaves the premises. The men stay there for some time, then they call out someone. A younger and leaner looking man appears. They talk in some dialect which becomes difficult for Mahi to understand. But, she gets one thing that the men are not from here. Not at least from this city. Because if they were, they wouldn't make the mistake of kidnapping her. Both bulky looking men leave the room with Mahi and the leaner looking boy behind. The boy looked familiar to Mahi but, she couldn't place him. He simply steals eyes from Mahi and then makes himself busy on the side, lighting the stove and putting on the pot.

Mahi quietly observes their activities. She notices that the two men with dialects only came inside to have the dinner the boy prepared. Then they left to guard the factory from outside. Whenever they opened the metal door, Mahi could see the dark sky out. She tries to calm herself and looks around for something. She needs to find something. So that she can free herself from the bounds and make a run for it. Because, looking at the tensed faces of the two men, they are not planning to keep her alive with the dawn. So she just has few hours to make her escape. After a couple hours, when night becomes silent, the boy quietly comes to Mahi. He starts untying Mahi, so she becomes aware and nervous about what he means to do with her. As she is about to speak up, he gestures her to stay quiet.

He then whispers, 'Yaha se bahar nikalte aap seedha daudte chale jana. Thodi der baad highway aa jaega. Ye log subah hote hi aapke saath kya karenge mujhe nahi pata (Getting out from here, run straight. You,'ll find the highway after sometime. I don't know what they'll do with you as soon as it's morning).'

Mahi becomes confused at him. 'Meri help kyu kar rahe ho? (Why are you helping me?)'

'Madam shayad aapne mujhe pehchana nahi. Main aapke ghar aaya tha ek aur aadmi ke saath. Aapke pati ko dhamkane (Madam, maybe you haven't recognised me. I came to your house with some other man. To threaten your husband),' says the boy.

Now Mahi realises why he looked familiar. But still, Mahi couldn't understand why he would help her. 'Ye Hiralal ke log hai? Aur tum meri madad kyu kar rahe ho? (Are these Hiralal's men? And why are you helping me?)'

He shakes his head, 'Nahi ye Hiralal ke aadmi nahi hai. Naye hai shehar mein. Mere gaon se hai. Par inhe ye pata nahi ke aap kaun ho. Mujhe zabardasti kheech liya iss kaand mein. Aap bas police ko kuch mat batana. Iske baad mujhe ye dhandha hi nahi karna (No. They are not Hiralal's goon. They are new in the city. They are from my village. But, they don't know who you are. They dragged me into this. You just don't tell the police about me. After this I am leaving this line of work. I am done with this).'

Mahi simply nods as he takes out the last of the ropes around her legs. He gestures her towards the side door. And ask her to make a run quickly.

Mahi doesn't think twice as she dashes for it. When she gets out, it is still dark outside. She sees the field of sugarcane in front of her. She runs into them, following the instructions given to him by the boy and runs straight without making a stop. While running, she stumbles upon the rock and trips spraining her ankle. At the same time, she hears the commotion from the factory behind. Loud noises of men. She holds down the pain getting up and picking up her pace again. Soon she sees the busy night highway, a little elevated than the fields. She climbs up the road and looks for help. Stands on the drive, making a car screeching its break in front of her.

A woman and a man in semi-casual clothes get down, seeing Mahi in front of their car. As they approach her, they hear a loud thundering noise. It was clearly the sound of gun shooting. The sound came from the fields.

Mahi tenses up. She asks them, panting,' Please help me. Take me to the nearest police station.'

The couple exchanges the look and helps Mahi get in their sedan. As soon as they drive off, the woman in front asks Mahi,' Who were you running from?'

'My kidnappers,' replies Mahi. She continues,' If you don't mind can I use your phone to make a call.'

The woman hands her the cell phone,' Sure.'

Mahi draws a blank for a second as she stares at the keypad. She realises that she doesn't remember anyone's number except her father's. A sudden pang of pain pinches her. So she jerks her mind off that and dials 100. She tells the controller to connect her to ACP Arjun. As soon as she hears Arjun's voice, she sighs off. He asks her about the location. To which she replies that she'll make it to the next police station. She asks Arjun to immediately send his team to the factory where she was being held if they don't want to lose any lead on her kidnappers. With all the necessary details in the next few seconds, she hangs up the call. She thanks the couple as she hands them the cell back.

With little hesitancy, she asks the couple,' If you don't mind. Why help a stranger like me? People would be reluctant to help anyone in today's time. That too at such an hour. And on a highway.'

The couple exchanges the look with smiles at her questions. ' That exactly what any civilian would do,' says the man.

'And you are not civilians?' asks Mahi immediately.

'We are Indian Army, Ma'am,' says the woman with a polite smile. Now Mahi understood the attire. The polo t-shirt semi-casual look and fit figure underneath.

'Uh.. can I ask to see some ID,' says Mahi, still pondering over her scepticism. Both laugh loudly but hand her the ID.

Mahi sees the card with the familiar department. 'ICT. My father used to serve the same department,' says Mahi more to herself than to them as she hands back the card.

'Your father is in the army?' asks the man driving the car.

'Was. Retired a couple years ago,' replies Mahi.

'If I may ask his name. We might know him,' asks the woman.

'Brigadier Vikram Singh,' says Mahi. The couple in front exchange a shocked look.

The woman turns in her seat towards Mahi,' Brig Vikram Singh Solanki is your father! You are Vikram Sir's daughter.'

Mahi smiles back awkwardly as the woman looks at her with surprised expressions. She simply nods. 'You obviously know him well.'

'Who doesn't. Your father is quite a legend in this field. He is the one who gave the security system which the defence services use. Even the Indian government uses it.' The man driving says this with an excited voice.

Mahi simply nods, knowing the achievements of her father. But she instantly becomes sad thinking, how long has it been that she has seen her father.

'Let us drop you home. That's the least we can do for you,' says the woman sitting in the front.

Mahi simply smiles and says,' Thank you so much.'

Soon the sky starts changing its colour from black to dark blue. After half an hour of drive, the car pulls through the gates of the house. It moves on the driveway towards the house. Mahi sees everyone waiting for her out in front. She suddenly becomes stills when she sees the familiar figures among the crowd of people waiting for her. Her mother and father.

Chapter 26 The Return and The Reunion

Vikram sees his daughter's expressions even through the glass window. Along with everyone, Shree and Vikram approach the car as it pulls up on the driveway.

When Shree casually called Savitri in the evening to catch up on Anu's engagement and the rest, she didn't expect to hear the devasting news about her own daughter. Mahi is missing. She is probably being kidnapped, dropped Shree's heart. Thankfully Vikram was next to her when she heard Savitri breaking down on the call. Vikram got hold of his wife as he spoke to Savitri and Maan about the situation. It didn't take more than a couple of seconds for Vikram to decide to leave for Pune immediately.

And here they are after a one and half hour flight from Ahmedabad. When they reached the house, Maan updated Vikram and Shree about the police efforts, also Dev's whereabouts. Vikram also makes few calls to his contacts to increase the police effort to find his daughter faster. A couple hours later, they receive Dev's call telling them that Mahi's on her way home. He'll tell the details when they'll reach home.

Within half an hour of that call, a white sedan enters the premises. Everyone leaves their seats to approach the vehicle. Mahi gets down from the back door of the car. Shree almost runs to her and fills her in a hug. It's been a year, she has seen her daughter. Mahi too gives in to her mother's embrace as her mother breaks down when she sees Mahi dishevelled. Even while hugging her mother, Mahi keeps curious eyes in the direction of her father. Vikram stood right next to his wife. As soon as Shree breaks the hugs, Vikram welcomes his only daughter with a firm embrace. Mahi becomes emotional seeing her parents here, waiting for her. Eventually, Mahi notices everyone as the sky become lighter.

She could see Amit, Shruti, Ekta and Rohit as the addition to the crowd who were already home. But, she couldn't locate Dev in them.

Savitri notices Mahi's wandering eyes, 'Dev and Arjun are on their way. It will take them another half an hour to reach. They went a little far looking for you.'

Mahi nods lightly to an answer to her silent query. She immediately turns towards the couple and introduces them to her friends and family. The pain from her sprained leg makes her limp as she starts to walk towards the house. She finds her father next to her, holding her and helping her walk with a smile.

Soon after she settles on one of the sofas, the family physician arrives to check on Mahi. He cleans the wound on the corner of her mouth and takes care of her sprain by injecting some sedatives. The doctor asks her that she should relax a bit and let the sedatives do some healing. Mahi just agrees verbally, but she becomes restless as she waits for Dev. Meanwhile, she fills everyone with the details of what all happened and how she escaped.

Mahi is seated on the sofa next to her mother, holding her hand as everyone else stood or sat surrounding her. Even the doctor stood silently on sides waiting for sedatives to kick in so that he could relax a little. Within the next twenty minutes or so, the sound of a car entering the gates reaches Mahi's ears. Soon after that, Dev enters half running, followed by Arjun behind him.

The moment Mahi sees Dev's face, faint smile forms around her mouth that Vikram quietly observes. Vikram also notices Dev stopping briefly at a distance to see Mahi seated and losing his tensed expressions as he takes urgent strides towards Mahi. He takes her in his arms, sitting down next to her, without giving any heeds to the audience he might garner. At this moment, his only concern is the woman in his arms. The one he can feel breathing in his embrace.

'You are alright?' asks Dev, not breaking the embrace.

Mahi nods, smiling and wrapping her arms around him. 'Yes.'

Dev sighs off, closing his eyes as he tightens his arms around her. Everyone just watches the duo silently and lets them have their moment.

Within the next seconds, Mahi also gives in to the sedatives and loses her consciousness in Dev's arms. Dev feels her hands dropping on the sides. He, immediately along with others, becomes alarmed as he cradles Mahi's head in his hands. He calls for the doctor standing away from the crowd.

'It is alright. Mahi is just resting. I gave her the sedatives,' says the doctor.

Dev places Mahi's head on his shoulder as he protectively wraps an arm around her. He tenses up as he caresses her face as it rests on his shoulder, closer to his neck.

'Looks like she just allowed the medication in her system to take over her,' says the doctor thoughtfully.

Dev looks at him confusingly. 'I injected the sedative around 20 minutes ago. Usually, it takes just a couple of minutes for them to work. But, she was holding them back,' answers the doctor to Dev's confusions.

'She was waiting for you,' says Savitri standing, watching Dev's concerned face. 'Take her up and let her rest in her bed.'

Dev nods as he gently picks Mahi in his arms and moves towards the stairs for their room. Shree, along with Savitri, also follows them.

Maan tells everyone to get some rest, while Vikram thanks the couple who helped Mahi get back to her family. He quickly catches up with them and soon sees them off. Then he leaves for Mahi's room to see her.

When Vikram enters the room, he sees Savitri seated at the end of the bed close to Mahi's feet. Mahi is resting in the middle of the bed as Shree is on her one side. Vikram notices Dev seated on the other side, holding Mahi's hand in his. Vikram joins them silently.

'Dev. We all are here. Why don't you go and freshen up a little,' Savitri speaks up.

Dev looks up at his mother for a second. And then he realises that Shree and Vikram are also here. He just realises the presence of Mahi's parents. Shree speaks up,' It's okay. I am right here.' She tells Dev to go ahead, assuring him not to leave Mahi's side while he is away.

Dev simply nods, smiling. He then looks down at sleeping Mahi. He caresses her hair once and places a soft lingering kiss on her forehead before he gets up. Shree and Savitri just smile contently at Dev's small gestures towards Mahi.

Meanwhile, Vikram also silently takes notice of Dev's movement concerning his daughter. He could clearly see the difference between the two from the last time he saw them. The time when they just got married for optics. They looked more like some strangers than two people getting married. Vikram remembers that too clearly. He vehemently opposed Mahi's decision to sacrifice herself for the sake of her Saavi Maa. He knew how much she loved Savitri. But, her decision to marry her son was something Vikram could not come to terms with. He felt as if his only daughter has no expectation from her life in terms of love or a loving life partner. He could never understand her stubbornness to go ahead with her decision. So he did what any father would have done, being upset with his only child sacrificing her chances of happiness. Stubbornness was in the DNA. That's why he never made an attempt to talk to her for a year, protesting her step. However, he didn't care about his protest when he heard his only child's life might be in danger. As much as he regrets not speaking to Mahi for this past year, he also somewhat discovers something is changed. The very reason he was upset with his daughter might no longer exist. It wasn't like he didn't like Dev. He has known Dev since he was just a boy. With passing years, he became more like a friend of the same calibre. But, he also knew that Dev was heartbroken at the time of their wedding. And he possibly is not the one with whom Mahi would ever be happy.

After few minutes, Vikram finds Dev standing a little away with his hands folded in front as he gazes at Mahi thoughtfully. Vikram goes to him, breaking his focus from Mahi. Dev straightens up when Vikram approaches him. At first, he nods lightly, greeting Vikram as he unfolds his hands. Vikram being at the same height as Dev, goes and stands next to him facing Mahi.

'I am sorry. It's my fault,' Dev speaks up as both set their gaze on Mahi.

'It's nobody's fault,' replies Vikram.

'If I had been with her. This wouldn't have happened,' counters Dev.

'She is not a kid. She can clearly take care of herself,' states Vikram, pointing out how she managed to escape.

Dev takes a deep breath in as he turns towards Vikram,' I am sorry. I should have called you. Not just now. But earlier. A lot happened in this whole year. I thought of calling you up. But, failed to find the words for it.'

Vikram simply smiles as he pats Dev's shoulder once. ' It's alright. Even I was stubborn for keeping any contact.'

'Mahi misses you a lot. She didn't mean to hurt you. She did it with a good heart. Even though the reasons for our wedding were different. Now we have found the real reason for this marriage. I really hope you'd forgive her,' says Dev with a sincerity visible to Vikram.

Vikram doesn't say anything immediately. He pauses a little and then says,' Do you know the reason why I never supported her decision to marry you?'

Dev looks on questioningly. Vikram continues,' Not Because I did not approve you. But, I disapproved of her decision to destroy her chances of being happy. You were heartbroken at the time. The one you loved has just left you. How could have I expected this marriage to work? I wanted what any father would dream for his daughter. A life partner who would love her, cherish her, protect her with life. At that time, she was going for a loveless marriage. How could I have approved of that for my only child.'

Dev nods softly at Vikram's honest answer. 'I love her. With my life,' says Dev, coming clean with his intentions.

'I know that now. And I can tell Mahi is happy with you. So I don't have any reason to be upset with her anymore,' says Vikram smiling at Dev.

Dev smiles back, feeling comforted at Vikram's reply.

Soon Dev and Savitri leave the room as they ask Shree and Vikram to take some rest. Dev goes down to get the updates on Armaan from Arjun. He informs Dev about nabbing the kidnappers from the location Mahi provided. They'll soon get Armaan too. He also informs Dev that the department was able to keep this whole incident from the media to his relief. After Arjun leaves, Dev takes a quick nap on the sofa in the living room.

He kept taking quick and small trips to his room, just to take a quick peek at Mahi for every few minutes.

A couple of hours later, a bright day shines outside as the house starts bustling with people again. Dev takes another of his trips to his room. This time he stays at the open door longer. He sees Mahi sit up and her parents seated in front of her on the bed.

'How are you feeling now?' asks Vikram as he softly pats her head once.

Mahi, trying to control her overwhelming emotions, nods. 'Much better.'

'You gave us a scare. You know that?' says Shree holding onto her daughter's hand.

'Sorry,' replies Mahi in a small voice.

'No worries. As long as you are alright,' injects Vikram.

'I am sorry,' says Mahi in a breaking voice as tears start welling up. ' I am sorry for everything.'

Vikram embraces her as he soothes her silently for the next few seconds. After calming down a bit, Mahi breaks away to look at his father. 'You are not mad at me anymore. Right?'

'How can I be mad at you ever!' replies Vikram to Mahi's query.

'You were mad at me for marrying Dev,' says Mahi in between her soft sobs.

Vikram smiles at her daughter complaining. He tells her what he said to Dev hours ago. To which Mahi replies in exact same words as Dev replied in,' I love him. With my life.'

Vikram laughs loudly at the symmetry of their answers.

'I know. You guys are not really discrete,' replies Vikram teasingly. Mahi smiles, looking down.

He becomes serious as he takes Mahi's hand in his own. 'You know it's been years since I have seen you this happy.' Vikram turns Mahi's hand and traces the scar on her hand.

'The last time we saw you happy was before this,' says Vikram looking down at her scar. Vikram gulps down sharply as he looks up at Mahi,' We know it was no accident.'

Mahi gasps shockingly at this revelation. She looks at his mother, who nods with sorrow on her face as she darts her gaze back at her father with an expression of shock.

'We don't know why you took such an extreme step. What made you take such measures. We don't know. We never asked. And we'll never ask until you'll want to tell us. We just want you to know that whatever it is or it was, doesn't matter more than you and your happiness.' Vikram says with extreme difficulty as he tries to get hold of his emotions.

Mahi just let the tears blur her vision as she takes in her parents' unconditional love for her. Shree also let her emotions take over her as she rubs Mahi's arms, soothing her and herself as well.

'I hope Dev loves you unconditionally as we do,' says Vikram.

Mahi nods, crying,' He does.'

Vikram embraces Mahi again as she burst to cry. He wraps an arm around Shree too.

Dev watches everything leaning on the door frame without making himself visible to the reuniting family. He simply smiles, seeing Mahi smiling and crying at the same time.

Savitri quietly comes and joins Dev.

'Some good came out of this fiasco,' says Savitri to Dev. To which he simply nods, agreeing with her.

'Nothing scares me more than the thought of something happening to her. The mere thought of losing her made me forget how to breathe,' says Dev watching Mahi.

Savitri looks at his son as she says,' She is fine. She is right here.'

Dev nods as he looks at her mother, smiling. 'Thank you for bringing her into my life.'

'Even I had no idea that I would be the reason she would walk into your life like that,' replies Savitri smiling. She continues,' But then, she was your first crush. The thought was already floating in the universe.'

Dev looks at his mother in surprise,' You knew!'

'Of course, I knew. How can I forget when my 14-year-old son kept gawking at my best friend's 9-year-old daughter,' replies Savitri with a scoff.

Dev chuckles quietly, becoming embarrassed at the information.

'Whenever you used to come back home for holidays. You always had indirect questions about Mahi,' says Savitri with bright eyes recalling how Dev used to behave concerning Mahi.

'You are right. It's me. Definitely, I was the one who put out that thought. I am the reason Mahi is part of my life,' says Dev, ending his mother's teasing row.

Savitri breaks out giggling. She simply pats his arms as she enters the room. 'Haan Bhai. All sorted? Rested well?' Savitri asks, looking at Mahi.

Mahi responds, smiling. To which Savitri says,' Shree Vikram breakfast is served. I have put your luggage in the guest room. Freshen up, and please join us in the garden.'

Vikram and Shree get up, saying,' Sure.'

'I'll send someone with your breakfast,' says Savitri looking simultaneously at Dev and Mahi. Both simply nods to her.

When Savitri leaves with Shree and Vikram, she shuts the door of the room behind them.

Mahi looks at Dev standing a little away from the bed. She looks at him and softly speaks up,' Hi!'

Dev sways his head,' Not enough.'

Mahi sighs off and then looks up. She just holds out her arms open and stares cutely at Dev, gesturing to come and hug her. Dev gives in to her adorable tactics as he immediately walks towards her.

Dev fills Mahi in his arms as he sits close to her on the bed. Mahi too encircles her hands around his neck as he pulls her in a tight hug. He buries his mouth and nose in her hair, in the crook of her neck. He holds her tight as he feels her in his arms, feels her breathing. Dev closes his eyes as he firmly embraces her. Mahi feels a sudden rush of relief from all the tiredness. She feels her tensed nerves loosening in Dev's embrace. For the next couple of minutes, both stay tranquil, embracing each other, sighing heavily from time to time, feeling each other.

'You are the best drug to my exhaustion,' says Mahi, keeping her eyes closed and holding onto Dev.

'You scared me,' huffs Dev while keeping his face buried in her hair.

'I was scared too,' says Mahi in a small face.

Dev breaks the hug to face her. Mahi continues,' I was shit scared.'

'You are here now. Safe,' assures Dev as he places a palm on her cheek. To which she winces a little. Dev notices faint blueness on her cheek and a small wound on the corner of her mouth. Frown takes over Dev's expressions. He softly touches Mahi's face,' He did this?' It was more of an exclamation filled with anger than a question.

'I provoked it,' replies Mahi. Dev looks at her, not giving in to her effort to calm him down. 'I'll make sure he pays for this,' says Dev tightening his jaws, controlling his rage.

'He is not stable. Mentally. He was just upset and taking revenge that you brought Yashika home,' says Mahi trying to reason this.

'I don't care if Armaan Singhvi is mentally sick or not. He dared to put his hands on you,' says Dev, now fuming with fury.

'What did Arjun say? Did he call? Any updates?' asks Mahi trying to change the subject.

Dev nods as he fills Mahi on the situation where kidnappers are in custody, and the police are onto Armaan. He'll be arrested soon.

'Good,' replies Mahi after getting the update.

Dev cleans the remnant of smudged kajal from the corner of Mahi's eyes. While he does that, he speaks,' Vikram Uncle and Shree Aunty are here.'

Mahi eyes brighten up at the mention of her parents. She grins as she nods,' Yes.' Immediately next second, her eyes become moist thinking about the conversation she just had with her parents.

'Hey! What's wrong? Did something happen?' asks Dev cupping Mahi's face as his thumbs caress her cheek.

Mahi nods, gulping down the overwhelming emotions. 'They knew.'

'What?'

'About this,' Mahi darts her eyes towards her wrist down. She still finds it difficult to spell the incident. 'They don't know why. But they knew. All this time.'

'Did you tell them why?' Dev softly asks.

Mahi shakes her head. 'I can never. They can't know. Ever. I can't let them-' Mahi speaks up, almost panicking at the idea.

'It's okay. No issues,' Dev instantly calms her down.

Mahi looks down, taking deep breathes, closing her eyes. Dev pulls her close as he rests his forehead over hers. He quietly soothes her, keeping a hand under her ear, holding her face. Mahi places her hands on Dev's chest, holding onto his shirt as she shifts closer.

'All is good now. Isn't it?' Dev breathes out, holding onto her.

Mahi nods. She slowly tilts her head to meet Dev's lips. Dev captures her lips with his, kissing her gently and then deepening it with the realisation of her being safe and sound in his arms.

Both break the kiss, panting lightly and resting their eyes as they lean on each other through their foreheads.

'That's it. I don't want any more adventures in our lives,' says Dev caressing Mahi's cheeks with his thumbs.

'Except this,' replies Mahi widening her eyes, meaning to their intimacy.

Dev chuckles at her expression as he nods and then kisses her again. 'Except this. And a promise of a lot of this.'

Mahi grins with excitement capturing her eyes.

Anu enters, followed by Nivi, with Dev and Mahi's breakfast in hand. Ekta and Rohit also enter to ask about Mahi's well being. Soon after, Shruti, along with Arjun, join them. Arjun updates them about arresting Armaan and preparing a lengthy charge sheet to file against him. Mahi and Dev's room becomes the source of loud laughter in the house. While the seniors of the house enjoy their breakfast in the garden.

Two days later, the whole family lands at the Phuket International Airport. At reaching the hotel, the rest of the family departs to their reserved rooms through the elevator.

While Mahi waits in the lobby for Dev. He converses with the Manager of the hotel for a while, catching up on the updates.

'Sorry. I didn't know it will take this long,' Dev says as he walks up to Mahi. She stands up from her half seated pose on the armrest of the chair.

'That's alright,' replies Mahi smiling when Dev comes to her. 'You know I can go ahead. Just show me the way. You can come after you are done here.'

Dev mysteriously smiles as he pulls her closer, snaking an arm around her waist. 'I am done here. We can go now. Together.'

Mahi smiles at his playfulness. She simply nods. Dev leads Mahi outside where the greens of the hotel are.

'We are not going to our room?' asks Mahi as she becomes confused because the rest of the family left for the elevator for their rooms.

'We don't have our room here,' says Dev smiling as they step outside.

Chapter 27 The Vacation: The Last The First and Many More to Come

'We don't have our room here,' Dev replies as they step outside. Sun is already setting over the immense length of the beach. Mahi could only pause for a second to let in the beauty of nature in front of her.

'That's our ride,' says Dev pointing towards a small cart in front of them.

'Where exactly is our room?' asks Mahi becoming confused at Dev.

Dev points to the direction where the bunch of trees in density begins. They were at the stretch of the beach and along with the building of the hotel. The green has a narrow paved path for the small vehicles like the cart in front of them.

'You better not make me sleep in some tent,' says Mahi, shooting warning towards Dev. She is well versed with the Dev's favourite pass time of going camping.

Dev breaks into a small laugh as he says,' Don't worry. We won't be spending our first night here in some tent. But, we will in the coming days. You wouldn't mind that. Would you?' asks Dev becoming tensed suddenly.

Mahi breaks into a chuckle seeing Dev's worried face. 'I was kidding. No. I don't mind living in a tent. If it's with you. I don't even mind sleeping with you under the open sky,' Mahi ends with a teasing.

Dev leans in close to her ear as he whispers,' We'll see about that.'

Mahi punches him softly. Both get on the cart and drive along the curvy path into the little dense green. As they move along the narrow path, Mahi notices small cottages along the way into the forest, at some distance. Each hutting seems isolated but beautifully designed. They pass through some four such build-ups before some dense trees follow. The path twists and turns a few more times. But, it comes to an end. The end, which had a beautiful cottage, was a little bigger than what they have seen on the way. It had a small yard in front with a small gate. Dev pulls the cart in front of it. He then takes Mahi's hand to lead her through the gate. They walk a couple of steps before stepping on the stairs to the cottage. Dev clicks the key card on the knob and opens the door.

When they enter, Mahi gasps at the size of it. It was no less than a suite. It has its own living space and a small pantry on the left. On the opposite of it was a partitioned room, probably the bedroom. But, she becomes stunt when Dev goes past her and draws up the curtains to add to her amazement. The view of the beach through the wall size glass doors catch her eyes. When Dev slides the door open, a soft sea breeze sweeps across her face. Dev stands there quietly, taking in her every little reaction with a smile on his face. She glows with joy when she notices the accessibility of the beach from that door. It's like they have their private beach.

'It's beautiful,' Mahi breathes.

'Hold that. There is another thing you are yet to react to,' Dev takes Mahi by hand and leads her through the partition into their bedroom. The king-size bed with white floral sheets and beige covers. The room also had a beach view, continued from the living.

'The bed. Of course. It's beautiful too. It's huge,' says Mahi becoming a little awkward.

Dev chuckles loudly as he draws down the curtains, turning the room almost dark. It takes a couple of seconds for Mahi to adjust her eyes to the darkness as she becomes more nervous.

'I didn't mean the bed,' whispers Dev in Mahi's ears, to which she jumps. Just seconds ago, he was next to the door, and now he is behind her. 'I meant this.' He hands Mahi a small device, more like a remote with just two buttons on them.

'Press the top button,' speaks Dev into Mahi's ear. She feels ticklish, feeling Dev's lips on the curves of her ear. She presses the button. With a faint beep sound, the shutter over the ceiling starts moving. The room lights up with the setting sun. The middle of the roof transforms into a circular opening with a glass top. It has a view of the sky, right above the bed. The room brightens up completely when Dev pulls up the curtains again.

Mahi becomes silent, lost at words.

Dev silently looks on, waits for her to speak first. Mahi feels lost for words, doesn't know how to express this. She looks around and then sets her gaze on Dev, who was just watching her getting overjoyed.

'Does every cottage have this?' asks Mahi, finally finding her voice as she points to the glass roof.

'No,' Dev shakes his head once. He continues,' At first, I thought of putting up this in every Honeymoon suite/cottage. But then I wasn't too sure.' He pauses a little and then says,' I might give the go-ahead if you approve of it.'

'I approve it,' says Mahi smiling.

Dev smiles but becomes hesitant as he asks,' Did you really like it?'

Mahi nods her head as she takes steps towards Dev,' I love it.'

'More than me?' asks Dev with a raised brow.

Mahi reaches him as she coils her arms around his waist. She looks up,' Is that even possible?'

Dev also places his hands on her back as he smiles, shaking his head. 'No.'

Mahi tip-toes as she places a soft kiss on Dev's lips. She brushes her nose gently against Dev before setting her ankle down. 'But, honestly. It's beautiful. Everything in here is just so beautiful. Including you.'

Dev tilts his head with a smile on her last words. ' Wow! Nobody called me 'beautiful' before.'

Mahi chuckles loudly. 'You are beautiful.'

'Must be true if it's coming from you,' says Dev acting with serious expressions.

Mahi shrugs off the compliment. Both break into a small laugh.

'How long before we have to leave for dinner with the rest?' Mahi asks with hesitation.

Dev turns his wrist to get a look at the watch while holding Mahi. 'In about 3 hours.'

Mahi nods thoughtfully. Then she glances at Dev, and looking away, she speaks. 'We've got time. So what you wanna do?'

Dev catches Mahi's nervousness. So he replies, keeping a straight face,' I think we should rest a bit. It was a long flight.'

Dev picks up the disappointment from Mahi's face as she says,' Yeah. Right. Sure. I'll go and change first,' Mahi fumbles, trying to hide her disappointment as she tries to leave.

Dev breaks into a mischievous smile as he pulls her back in his arms. He holds her face and crashes his lips on hers. He explores her mouth as she gives in to his longing. It felt like they are just breaking their two-day long fast.

'God! I missed you. These past two days felt like forever,' as Dev pants in between the kisses.

'I missed you too,' Mahi breathes too as she slips her fingers in his hair. Since the incident, Dev and Mahi rarely got time alone as her parents, someone else was always around. Both looked helplessly at each other when Shree requested to sleep with Mahi. Since her mother has been away for too long and didn't get the time to spend with her only daughter, Dev didn't say anything. Mahi also remained quiet, knowing it would be really awkward if they said anything, protesting it.

Eventually, Dev made the plan to execute the vacation. He convinced Shree and Vikram to join them. However, right now is the first time in the last 2 days they are alone. Thus, both give in to their longing for each other. They crash on each other like it's been forever since they even touched each other.

Dev continues to devour her with soft, passionate kisses over her lips as he keeps playing at her lower lip for longer. Then he moves his hands under her shirt, pulling her closer. Mahi moans as she responds with the same intensity. They move in sync towards the bed. Softly landing on the mattress, Mahi with her back resting on bed and Dev doing the intermittent rounds from her lips to her neck. He gently massages the rise of her chest as she lets out small gasping moans in between their breathless kisses. He begins to undo her shirt's button. Mahi's head suddenly becomes aware of his movements. She freezes, thinking of something.

'Wait!' breathes Mahi.

'Wh-What! Why,' asks Dev becoming confused.

Mahi holds her unbutton shirt tightly. Dev becoming perplexed, asks,' Did I do something?'

'No! No!' Mahi strongly responds, becoming afraid she might have offended Dev. He looks on being confused. Mahi quickly continues,' It's not you. It's me. It's just-I need to use the washroom.'

She gets up quickly as she straightens up. She grabs her handbag and runs to the bathroom, leaving Dev totally confused.

Dev quietly waits for Mahi while lying flat on the bed. He hesitates to call for her or ask her if everything is alright. He simply assumes that she needed to use the washroom. Nothing more. So he chooses to wait for her patiently.

Meanwhile, in the washroom, Mahi stands still in front of the mirror. She shakes her head in disbelief at herself. Particularly at her choice of wearing a really uncoordinated pair of lingerie. She smiles as she feels embarrassed, thinking what Dev would have thought about her. She knows he probably wouldn't have minded it. Though she feels she could have done better than pairing two totally contrasting colours for her undergarments. She then looks at her handbag that has a lacey pair. The one that Ekta and Shruti forced her to purchase. It wasn't like she never had good lingerie or something with laces. She always had those pairs. But she never had those fancy ones. And standing here, she feels more excited and nervous at the same time to get in one of those.

She takes more than the usual time in the bathroom. It took her time to calm herself and encourage herself to go for it. When she finally steps out wearing the bathrobe, she feels more nervous but thrilled too. However, she ends up breaking into a chuckle when she sees Dev.

Mahi watches Dev being laid flat on the bed, dozed off in heavy sleep. While waiting for Mahi, he doesn't realise when he gave in to his exhaustion and dozed off. Mahi thinks about the past two days when she rarely saw Dev resting. He got busy with the police case and then arranging this whole vacation while handling the hotel at the same time. In addition to his worries for Mahi, he did all of that single-handedly. Mahi couldn't help but smile, watching him breathing heavily. She slowly gets on the bed without making many movements. She adores him for few more seconds before lying down next to him and giving in to her tiredness.

A call on the landline in the room wakes Dev up. He picks it up. He listens to it merely for two seconds and hangs up, saying thanks. Dev's movement and the call wake up Mahi too.

'Who is it?' asks Mahi in a hoarse voice as she stretches without opening her eyes.

'A wake-up call I had asked them to give before dinner,' replies Dev. As he too stretches, he reflexively places a soft kiss on Mahi's temple. When he is wide awake, he realises that how he ended up sleeping.

He looks at Mahi, turning sideways towards her,' Sorry! I don't know when I dozed off. You should have woken me up.'

Mahi smiles as she sees him with apologetic expressions. She leans close to him as she places a peck close to his lips,' It's okay. You were exhausted. So was I.'

Just then, Dev notices the bathrobe. He picks up that she is probably not wearing anything underneath.

He smiles slyly,' Why are you in a bathrobe?'

Mahi sits up quickly, trying to think of an answer less embarrassing. She fumbles,' I thought of taking a shower but, then seeing you sleep, I got lazy and slept like this.'

Dev too sits up, smiling. 'You do know that you are a bad liar. And I can tell when you are lying.'

Mahi closes her eyes tightly, placing her hands on her face in embarrassment. Dev chuckles loudly at her cute reaction.

He leans in closer as he fiddles with her robe's end,' It's okay. You didn't have to go to the bathroom to undress. I would have done that here.'

Mahi looks at him in surprise,' Oh My God!' She exclaims as she says,' I didn't go inside to get undressed. I am not naked underneath. I mean, I am. Partially. But, not entirely.'

Dev becomes confused as he asks,' Then why did you go inside? You are wearing something underneath this?' Now becoming intrigued.

Mahi sighs off heavily as she looks up briefly, giving up her embarrassment. 'I wasn't wearing the right kind of undergarments. So I went inside to change.'

Dev chuckles amusingly,' You went inside to change into lingerie. Why? They would have come off anyways.'

'I know. It's just that. It wasn't lacey and sexy enough,' says Mahi sheepishly, after gulping down her awkwardness.

Dev grins widely at her confession. He notices her getting flushed at coming out honest like this. 'You are more than sexy enough for me. No matter what you wear. Or not,' says Dev softly.

Mahi smiles, feeling a little shy.

'Now show me,' Dev says, immediately changing the tone to curious and excited.

'What! No!' says Mahi getting up from the bed.

'Why? Didn't you wear it for me,' Dev tries to reason her. 'I want to see,' now almost pleading.

Mahi shakes her head,' You lost your chance. You sleep you lose.' Mahi enjoys teasing him. She stands a little away from the bed. Dev, still sitting on the bed, frowns.

'C'mon. Once. Please,' now officially pleading.

Mahi smiles at his excitement and eagerness. She sighs off, preparing herself. 'Okay.' Dev's eyes brighten up at Mahi's affirmation. Seeing that, Mahi exclaims,' Just once.'

Dev simply nods like an obedient kid.

Mahi takes in a deep breath, closing her eyes. She unties the knot of the robe in front. She slowly opens it up.

Dev internally gasps as he gawks at Mahi in black laced lingerie. The laces were barely covering her private parts. Her curves over her lean figure were peaking out confidently. Dev just becomes silent as he loses himself in admiring Mahi in just two pieces of clothes that were barely covering her. Instead, they were igniting something sensual within Dev.

Mahi opens her eyes to see Dev's reaction. She watches him becoming silent as his eyes do multiple rounds over her whole self. She suddenly feels shy and excited as she watches Dev's eyes changing their intentions. She slowly closes the robe looking away, becoming shy, and breaking Dev's devouring focus. He leaves the bed and walks towards Mahi. She becomes still as she curiously waits for Dev to come closer.

Without leaving her gaze, Dev stands tall in front of Mahi as she looks up at him. She couldn't look away. He leans down to place a soft and yet awakening kiss on Mahi's lips. When he breaks away, he slowly opens the robe and slides it down over her shoulder. He tilts his head to plant a kiss under her ear. Mahi closes her eyes as he lingers longer while placing soft kisses along her bare shoulders. As he moves towards her neck, he takes off the robe and drops it on the floor. He moves up now, capturing her lips fully in his own. Mahi kisses him back as they both deepen their kiss while their tongues tease each other. Mahi envelops her hands around his neck when Dev picks her up, wrapping her legs around his hips. Without breaking their kiss, Dev moves towards the bed.

Bending down, he places Mahi on her back. He continues his deep kisses while softly grazing her lips between his teeth. And doing the same to her jawline. While Mahi finds his shirt's button and starts undoing it. She loses her patience to undo the button all the way down so, she pulls it out over his head and throws it away on the floor.

Now Dev moves his mouth on her neck as his kiss arouses Mahi. He gains the movement towards her rise. He unties the knots from the side of the laced cloth that was holding it up. He tastes her from the middle of her chest. He takes off the piece gently as he begins to play with her now exposed bust. The peak of her breast comes in contact with Dev's tongue. Mahi throws her head back, feeling the pleasure reaching her groin while she lets out a deep moan. He simultaneously pleasures her one breast with his mouth while his hand does the other one. When he feels her getting firm inside his mouth, the streak reaches his manhood. He feels the pain of it as it itches to get free. Then only he feels Mahi's hands going for the button of his jeans. She unbuttons his jeans as he goes back to her lips. He places a deep kiss once as he steps back to stand. Both don't let go of each other's gaze, panting heavily. As Dev unzips his jeans, he watches Mahi with just a piece of black lace between her thighs as she props us on her elbow, folding her leg. She watches Dev getting out of his jeans and standing just in his underpants. Just seeing the bulge sends another heightening stroke to her pleasure points. He bends down to kiss her knees. He slowly moves towards her thighs. When he places soft kisses on her inner thighs, Mahi struggles to control her sensations. While tracing her thighs from his mouth, he inches close to her womanhood. Dev slides down the last remaining piece of clothing over Mahi. Mahi, not able to contain her yearning, pulling Dev up to herself. She takes his lips in her own while pulling his hips closer to hers. She feels him all stiff down there. She wraps her legs around her hips, pulling him towards her. Dev responds to her movements equally.

Dev, not able to contain his own arousal, breaks away from Mahi to see her face. He looks for her consent before moving ahead. Mahi reading this much from his eyes, breathes, holding his face with her hands,' I want you.'

Dev nods, delighted. He drops his head again, kissing her while getting rid of the last piece of clothing over himself. He lets his manhood free. Both don't let go of each other's gaze when they come in contact. Dev thrusts in her as she gasps with an open mouth. Her moist and tightened opening accelerates pleasure around his hardened manhood every time he moves into her. The repeating movement of their meeting concentrates every pleasure points to a single igniting flame. Both synchronise their movements while expressing love for each other. Both work up to reach the climax. When she reaches her peak, her whole body shudders with the sweetened rapture. Instantly Dev too achieves his orgasm as he crashes on Mahi.

Dev lies down on his back next to Mahi while both catch their breath, smiling at each other.

'We are going to be late for dinner,' breathes Mahi, not willing to move an inch.

Dev rolls towards her. He engulfs her by placing a leg over her legs and an arm over her exposed bosoms. He shifts his head closer to her, resting his face in the curve of her neck. 'We probably won't make it.'

Mahi feels his heated breath. 'We have to,' Mahi says, stroking his arm and then his hair beyond his temple.

Dev hums, not agreeing,' Let's skip it.' He continues as he rouses kissing her neck,' Because I am not done with you.'

Mahi, closing her eyes, gives in to his touch. Both express their love through their bodies for few more times, forgetting about the dinner. They do it with little breaks. They don't just stay in bed but explore the room while they do it, including the shower. They eventually exhaust themselves to sleep.

The next day on one of the decided outings, Mahi and Dev avoid the subject of dinner. So does the rest. Afterwards, Mahi gets to know that nobody came down for dinner except their parents. Anu lets her on this information as Mahi amusingly realises that they are not the only ones who got busy with their respective spouses or soon to be.

Around noon, when the weather seemed pleasant, everyone gathered to go for some beach sports. Anu was excited to go for parasailing as the rest just got dragged to it. On one of the public beaches, Anu located the sport happening. Parents decided to stay and enjoy their catching up in the shacks behind with a cold beer.

Nivi and Mahi find themselves a good pair of beach chairs with a view of the beach. While Dev leaves to get something to drink for them. The beach was decently crowded with tourists. Mahi and Nivi found a place suitable where they could watch Anu and her excited self parasailing and see their parents behind in a shack at a distance from them. Nivi and Mahi busy themselves enjoying the view of Anu, struggling with Amit along with the sports instructor. Nivi keeps an eye on Sameer, who took Veer along for a closer look at the waters.

'Hi,' Mahi and Nivi turn their heads towards the voice coming from a man standing next to Mahi's beach chair.

'I couldn't help but notice you from a distance,' says the man in an accent. He was a foreigner. American from his accent. He looked young. He was bare chest but wearing beach shorts. He greets both Mahi and Nivi but, he directs the following words to Mahi.

'Can I buy you a drink maybe?' asks the man with confidence in his voice as he keeps the charm in check.

Mahi looks at Nivi in confusion, to which Nivi just shrugs, getting amused.

'Um...I don't mind as long as my husband doesn't mind as well,' replies Mahi keeping a polite smile on her face.

'C'mon! You could have done better than this. I would have believed a boyfriend but, the husband is a bit stretch,' replies the man, complaining for Mahi not being a sport.

Nivi breaks into a chuckle at his response. Mahi smiles as she says,' I am not lying. I am married.'

'Well, I don't see a ring,' he points out as he smiles, getting confident at his wits.

Mahi looks down at her empty fingers. 'That's because Indian weddings don't involve rings,' Mahi replies, outsmarting him.

'I have Indian friends back home. And I know very well that your weddings don't have rings. But, they do engagements. With rings,' replies the man, not willing to give up on getting her a drink. For him, it was just becoming interesting. He continues,' She's got one.' He points at Nivi sitting next to her.

Mahi looks down for a second as it hits her that Dev and she might be married today. But, they never got to experience all the ceremonies or any functions together. She didn't even get the proposal. She pulls herself out of that saddening train of thought.

'You are right. But, ours was an impromptu one. So we never got to do what normal people do when they get married,' Mahi speaks up with a tinge of disappointment. Nivi notices the change in her voice. So far, she was enjoying the part where Mahi gets flirted by a foreigner. But, this time, she decides to put the breaks.

'She isn't lying. She is married,' injects Nivi trying to end this conversation for Mahi's relief.

'And you are her friend who will say anything to support her,' replies the man in a friendly tone, feeling all confident again.

'I am her sister-in-law,' replies Nivi with a smile more convincing.

The smile from his face gets dropped. He now believes them. 'Really? I am sorry. It's just that you are such an eye-catcher that I couldn't help but approach.'

'That's okay,' replies Mahi keeping the smile.

With that, Dev reaches them with their drinks. When he sees the man standing next to Mahi, he simply greets him. To which Nivi injects,' Her husband. My brother.'

'Oh! Hi man,' says the man greeting Dev. Dev greets him back, getting confused.

'Man, you better put a ring on her soon. Look around. I bet I am not the only one who has not spared the glimpse of your girl here,' says the man. He instantly leaves without waiting for Dev's reply. He leaves Dev in a confused state. He looks at Mahi and then Nivi for some clarity. Nivi simply shrugs and says,' You wife just rejected his offer to buy her a drink.'

Dev looks at Mahi in surprise. To which Mahi just rolls her eyes, looking away. Nivi excuse herself as she gets distracted by her husband and son.

Dev takes a seat next to Mahi on the same beach chair. He takes her hand in his as he sits close to her.

'Was he just hitting on you?' asks Dev, still surprised, not shocked. As he is well aware of how attractive his wife is.

Mahi smiles, nodding her head as she looks straight, keeping her eyes on Nivi or Anu.

'What did you say?' asks Dev, now becoming curious.

'That I have a husband,' replies Mahi keeping a straight face.

'And?'

'He didn't believe me,' Mahi adds, scoffing as she recalls it.

'Why?' asks Dev, now becoming interested.

'Because he said I wasn't wearing any ring. It was so stupid. I told him that not every Indian married woman wears a ring to symbolise their marriage.' Mahi replies, rolling her eyes and dismissing the feeling along with it.

Dev looks at her for a couple of seconds quietly as he notices that she avoided looking at him. He realises that she is doing so that he doesn't see her real emotions behind her answer. He then looks down at their hands and their intertwined fingers.

Mahi realises Dev's silence as she turns her head towards him to find him staring at their hands.

'Hey!' speaks Mahi to make him look at her. ' I don't need some token of love to wear on my finger to show people that I am yours or you are mine. Because we know this.' She takes a brief pause before she continues. 'And this...is enough for me,' says Mahi as she rubs her cheek against his shoulder affectionately.

Dev nods once smiling. Mahi then rests her head against his shoulder as she looks ahead towards the sea. Both sit quietly for the next couple of minutes, enjoying each other's presence next to each other. Mahi successfully distracts herself by watching the fun Anu is having. While Dev sits quietly, looking at her hand in his own. He keeps playing with her fingers.

Mahi feels something cold slipping through her warm finger in Dev's hand.

'Dev!' she gasps as she looks at the platinum ring. It had two blue gemstones with white stone in the middle studded on it. It rests on her ring finger perfectly. She becomes stupified as she looks at Dev in utter amazement.

'Our story isn't normal. We didn't meet like others or fall in love like others. We didn't get to do what normal people do. They usually meet first, get to know each other and then fall in love. Then follows the confession, proposal and then the wedding,' says Dev while keeping his eyes on her hand in his. He looks up at her,' We never got the chance to do the usual.'

He shifts a little, leaning in closer to her. 'But, even though we didn't get the order right. I sure do want to check everything off the list.' Dev notices Mahi's expression turning from surprised to soft emotional. He continues,' And I want you to have this token of our love. I want everyone to know that you are mine. And if it is possible, I would shout every day to tell everyone that I am all yours.'

Mahi closes her eyes, keeping her state of emotion in check. She sighs off, leaning in as she rests her forehead over the bridge of his nose.

Dev chuckles off as he caresses her hair softly with his free hand. Mahi breathes in and out deeply, thinking about what has she done to deserve him.

Mahi breaks away to see his face to ask,' When did you...' as she fails to complete the sentence.

Dev prompts,' Bought this?' pointing at the ring. Mahi nods lightly. 'I had our mothers' help. I literally pestered them for these past few days.'

Mahi smiles at his confession.

Dev looks down at her fingers with a ring. He asks,' I was told you don't like diamonds. I was like, what woman doesn't like the bling. But then I thought it has to be you.' He grins widely. Mahi chuckles at his insertion. He continues,' They told me you like these blue and white stones.'

'Sapphires and moonstone,' says Mahi, admiring the ring on her finger.

Dev changes his expressions to frown as he says,' Now I have to think of something else with your surprise for tonight.' Mahi looks on in confusion. He continues smiling,' I had planned to give you this at midnight. It's our anniversary tomorrow.'

Mahi feels terrible for ruining Dev's surprise. 'I could have waited till midnight.'

Dev speaks up,' You might have. But I couldn't. It has to be like this. Maybe that's why I have been carrying it with me this whole time.'

Mahi couldn't hold it as she leans in to place a soft and yet deep kiss on Dev's lips. Dev looks around to see back at the shacks behind. He then looks at Mahi with a surprise,' Our parents are here.'

'I don't care,' Mahi replies with a smile. She continues,' Anyways, the beach is crowded. They didn't see us.'

Dev breaks out in a small laugh at Mahi's boldness. He relaxes on the beach chair as he takes up his earlier position, with his back relaxed, next to Mahi.

Mahi looks at him with excitement and arousal in her eyes. She asks him,' Do you wanna go for that?' She points at the sport happening in front of them, at a distance from them.

'I don't know. I can if you want to. Do you?' asks Dev, not realising Mahi's play yet.

Mahi shakes her head slowly. She leans closer, and she speaks up almost in a low and deep voice,' I want you to take me back to our room.'

'Why? Do you not feel well?' asks Dev becoming worried for her.

Mahi gives off a mysterious yet suggestive smile as she says,' I feel more than just fine. But I don't care if you'll use that as an excuse to get us out of here. Back to our room.'

Dev looks on, surprised at her suggestion and just realising her intentions. He gulps down quickly. 'Right away.'